Praise for

NEW TRICKS

"If you like urban fantasy, this one is a cut above the rest."
—*CA Reviews*

"A suspenseful tale that's supported by strong characters and a delightful infusion of magic and mystery."
—*Darque Reviews*

Praise for

DOG DAYS

"The supernatural lives, breathes, and slithers in a San Francisco where the dog days don't just get you down; they eat you alive." —Rob Thurman, national bestselling author of *Trick of the Light*

"A compelling magical mystery, filled with twists and some uncomfortable turns as it follows a likable new character through a mostly familiar San Francisco . . . I thoroughly enjoyed *Dog Days*. It's proof that there's still a heck of a lot of potential for variation in the urban fantasy genre, and it's a highly satisfying read . . . an excellent start to a promising new series." —*The Green Man Review*

"Appealing, fully founded characters . . . Levitt promises to be a novelist worth watching . . . Readers will enjoy the roller-coaster ride through dangers both magical and mundane. Anyone who likes solid storytelling will enjoy *Dog Days*. Here's looking forward to the next adventure."
—*SFRevu*

continued . . .

Ace Books by John Levitt

DOG DAYS
NEW TRICKS
UNLEASHED

UNLEASHED

JOHN LEVITT

ACE BOOKS, NEW YORK

THE BERKLEY PUBLISHING GROUP
Published by the Penguin Group
Penguin Group (USA) Inc.
375 Hudson Street, New York, New York 10014, USA
Penguin Group (Canada), 90 Eglinton Avenue East, Suite 700, Toronto, Ontario M4P 2Y3, Canada
(a division of Pearson Penguin Canada Inc.)
Penguin Books Ltd., 80 Strand, London WC2R 0RL, England
Penguin Group Ireland, 25 St. Stephen's Green, Dublin 2, Ireland (a division of Penguin Books Ltd.)
Penguin Group (Australia), 250 Camberwell Road, Camberwell, Victoria 3124, Australia
(a division of Pearson Australia Group Pty. Ltd.)
Penguin Books India Pvt. Ltd., 11 Community Centre, Panchsheel Park, New Delhi—110 017, India
Penguin Group (NZ), 67 Apollo Drive, Rosedale, North Shore 0632, New Zealand
(a division of Pearson New Zealand Ltd.)
Penguin Books (South Africa) (Pty.) Ltd., 24 Sturdee Avenue, Rosebank, Johannesburg 2196,
South Africa

Penguin Books Ltd., Registered Offices: 80 Strand, London WC2R 0RL, England

This is a work of fiction. Names, characters, places, and incidents either are the product of the author's imagination or are used fictitiously, and any resemblance to actual persons, living or dead, business establishments, events, or locales is entirely coincidental. The publisher does not have any control over and does not assume any responsibility for author or third-party websites or their content.

UNLEASHED

An Ace Book / published by arrangement with the author

PRINTING HISTORY
Ace mass-market edition / December 2009

Copyright © 2009 by John Levitt.
Cover art by Don Sipley.
Cover design by Annette Fiore DeFex.
Interior text design by Kristin del Rosario.

ISBN: 978-0-441-01798-0

ACE
Ace Books are published by The Berkley Publishing Group,
a division of Penguin Group (USA) Inc.,
375 Hudson Street, New York, New York 10014.
ACE and the "A" design are trademarks of Penguin Group (USA) Inc.

PRINTED IN THE UNITED STATES OF AMERICA

10 9 8 7 6 5 4 3 2 1

ACKNOWLEDGMENTS

I'd like to thank Don Sipley for all the wonderful covers he's done for the Dog Days series.

Also, thanks to my copy editor, Emma Stockton, and all the people at Ace Books—art department, production, promotion—everyone there who works so hard to make the books as good as they can be.

ONE

A FRESH BREEZE, CARRYING A SALTWATER TANG, pushed inland from across the ocean. The sky had just turned that purplish hue of dusk, and the top of the Golden Gate Bridge was just visible over the tops of the trees. A fine San Francisco evening, perfect for sightseers, dog walkers, and lovers. And hunters.

Somewhere in the undergrowth and tangled brush, the creature waited for us. Victor was over to my left, carrying the sawed-off shotgun. Not much of a weapon if you need to aim, but for close-up work it's unbeatable. Lou ranged ahead, light on his paws, using only his dog senses for once. His magical talents were useless in tracking this thing, but he still had those sharp ears and an even sharper sense of smell.

He moved his head from side to side, nose twitching, constantly testing the air. Victor watched intently, and when Lou finally stopped and focused on a particular patch of thick brush, he moved up behind him. He motioned for me to hang back—the last thing he wanted was for me to be anywhere near the line of fire. A sawed-off shotgun sprays pellets like a garden hose, and even if you're not directly in the line of fire, you can be struck anyway. And since each double-ought pellet is roughly the size of a .32 bullet, even one of them can kill you.

I didn't have a gun. My job was to take care of the magical side of things. The creature wasn't much affected by any use of magical talent, but situations can still arise where a clever spell might come in handy.

The patch of brush was edged by tall, leafy trees, a pocket of wildness on the edge of the urban landscape. Lou edged closer, but he looked puzzled, as if he'd picked up the scent, then lost it. Maybe the thing had slipped away once again. We'd been hunting it for months, off and on, without success. It was as smart as it was vicious.

Victor moved toward the underbrush, shotgun held easily at hip level, ready to swivel in any direction. He stopped well before he reached the tangle of bushes; shotgun or no, he wasn't pushing his way into an overgrown space where anything lying in wait would have every advantage.

I don't know if Victor heard something or if a sixth sense kicked in, but he suddenly glanced up and then dove sideways just as the thing dropped down from an overhead tree branch. It aimed for his shoulders, hoping to get its muzzle close to his throat. That would have been the end of that story. It missed, but even so it raked his arms on the way past and knocked the shotgun flying. It was up and at him again in an instant, a blur of claws and teeth and snarls.

Lou charged forward and tried for a back leg, but Victor and the creature were rolling on the ground, momentarily inseparable. I ran toward the shotgun and scooped it up. The shot pattern wouldn't spread if I could press the muzzle right into the creature. All I'd need was a moment's separation between the two.

It saw me coming with the shotgun and broke off the attack, darting into the cover of the bushes. Victor hauled himself up into a sitting position and gasped something I couldn't catch. He shook his head as I approached him, and reached out his hand.

"Mason. Give me the gun," he finally got out. "It may come back."

Clearly he thought he was better able to handle the threat, torn up as he was, than a healthy Mason would be. He might have been right.

"How bad is it?" I asked, squatting down and handing over the shotgun, wincing as I watched blood dripping onto the ground beside him.

"I've been better." He'd managed to protect his vital parts, but his right leg was a mess of blood and torn tissue. The fabric of his black jeans hung in shredded strips. "Hiding in the tree," he muttered, talking half to me, half to himself. "How could I have been so dumb? Rookie mistake. Look up; always look up."

It took him ten minutes to be convinced the creature wasn't returning. Lou sat next to him, keeping guard as well. Victor kept hold of the shotgun the whole time, but he was beginning to have trouble holding it. Blood loss was rapidly weakening him. Finally, he reluctantly handed it to me and tried to climb to his feet. His leg, not surprisingly, gave way and I had to catch him to keep him from falling over.

"Might be time to go home," he said.

"Yeah, sure. A good night's sleep is all you need."

"I'll survive."

"Sorry," I said. "We've got to make a quick stop first."

He looked at me suspiciously.

"Where?"

"It's a special place, one you may have heard of. It's called a hospital emergency room."

TWO

YOU MIGHT SUPPOSE THAT ALL ERS ARE MUCH
the same, but they're not. San Francisco General is like the
ones you see on TV—gunshot victims, knife wounds, heart
attack patients staggering in clutching their chests and gasp-
ing for air. Luckily, we were over at UCSF on Parnassus,
a kinder and gentler place.

Victor wasn't the kind and gentle sort, however. He
never is, but right now he was more pissed than usual
since the lower half of his left leg was shredded, almost to
the bone in places. His pants leg was now soaked through
with blood, which was the only reason he'd finally agreed
to an ER visit.

"Pit bull attack," I explained to the admitting nurse.

If only that had been true. Victor had been savaged by
something far worse, and it was my fault, at least in part.

"Did you notify Animal Control?" the admitting nurse
asked. He seemed genuinely concerned.

"Not yet," I said. "It ran off and I was too busy getting
my friend over here to even think about that."

After months spent hunting the creature off and on, this

time we had almost got it. We'd started taking an interest in tracking it when odd stories about mutilated pets had begun to surface in the newspapers. We were fairly sure we knew what was responsible for those attacks. But it didn't become a priority for us until it started attacking Ifrits whenever it could. And now, it had apparently started targeting people as well. That was when we had got serious about it.

But we hadn't been able to track it down. It was fast and it was smart. Being smart was a given, seeing as it was an Ifrit of sorts. Not a real Ifrit, like Lou, but the product of an incautious incantation by some very peculiar individuals. I had been instrumental in bringing them what they needed to accomplish it, and so I felt it was partly my responsibility. And Victor and I are also enforcers. Our job is to prevent problems like that from happening, not to help create them.

True Ifrits are small—seldom over ten pounds or so, although Lou, my Ifrit, was twelve and would have been twenty if I'd let him eat every time he felt like it. They are companions to practitioners—the lucky ones at least. Not everyone has one, although all practitioners wish they did. The reasons why Ifrits are relatively rare are still not clear, although we'd come up with some interesting theories lately.

Most Ifrits take the form of cats or other small animals; a few, like Lou, are small dogs. Lou looks just like a shrunken-down Doberman with uncropped ears and tail, black with a tan chest patch and muzzle and eyebrow markings. But he's not a dog, not really.

The creature we were hunting was more like forty pounds. That may not sound very impressive, but your average wolverine weighs no more than forty pounds, either, and they can tear through the roof of a mountain cabin and have been known to drive an adult bear away from a tasty carcass. And I had no doubt this thing could have taken a wolverine in a fight.

If it had been only an animal, even a smart one, there would have been no problem. Animals just want to be left alone; they don't plot revenge or possess agendas. But it was more than that, and psychotic as well. It killed just to kill, and it had an unquenchable hatred for true Ifrits.

An orderly helped Victor onto a gurney and rolled him into a side room. Sometimes it pays to be compact—Victor fit on the gurney quite nicely. My feet would have been hanging over the end. Victor was looking drawn and wan, a far cry from his usual dapper self. His face was ashen and his close-cut beard showed dark against his pale skin. That skin was drawn tight across his face, so tight that the cheekbones looked as if they were about to burst right through. Below his left eye, a muscle twitched. The only other time I'd seen a twitch like that on his face was when he'd been trying to restrain himself from killing someone. But he was still Victor, in complete control of his emotions even with a mangled leg. An ER doc stopped by for a quick look.

"Let's see what we've got here," he said, lifting the sheet.

He spoke with that practiced, casual air of competence good doctors have, meant to reassure the patient that however bad it is, it can be fixed. You know it's an act, but it's reassuring nonetheless. But his involuntary intake of breath when he saw the leg dispelled that illusion. He took only a brief look before shaking his head.

"I'm afraid you're going to need a plastic surgeon," he said. "That's a little beyond me." He looked at the leg more carefully. "You say a dog did that? Hard to believe. Looks more like that mountain lion that's been making news."

Victor didn't argue. He's a master at saying just the right thing to avoid problems with civilians.

"I know," he said. "Jim Schenkman is a personal friend of mine, and I'll be seeing him first thing tomorrow. All I need is some basic suturing until then."

I had no idea who Jim Schenkman was, but the ER doctor clearly did.

"That's a break," the doc said. "That's who I'd want working on me. But I'm afraid suturing won't be enough. You need to be admitted to the hospital. If we don't get you into surgery fairly quickly, you're going to lose that leg."

"It's not as bad as it looks," Victor said.

The doc stared at him as if he were insane. He tried to explain why going home wasn't an option, and another doc came by to back him up. Victor didn't argue, but he wasn't about to spend the night in the hospital. He just nodded agreeably and waited for them to run down.

Victor might or might not actually know this Schenk-man guy, but that wasn't who he was going to be seeing anyway. I'd already called Campbell, my ex, and she was on her way down from Soda Springs. She's the best healer around, and once Victor's leg was stabilized, she'd be able to do more for him than any plastic surgeon. Without her, he might well lose his leg, even with the best of surgeons available. She wouldn't be able to heal it overnight; the leg was too damaged even for her, but she could make it whole and cut his recovery time from months to a week or so. In theory. After I got a good look at the leg I wondered if the damage might not be too much even for her.

It was three hours before the staff was satisfied they'd done all they could for the present. They weren't happy when Victor insisted on leaving, and the ER doc actually swore at him, but there wasn't anything they could do keep him there. Despite what they like you to think, if you're determined to leave, there's not a thing they can do to stop you, even if it means you'll die soon after.

While they worked on Victor, I picked up a tattered newspaper from the lounge and spent some of that time rereading what I'd already seen that morning.

THIRD MOUNTAIN LION VICTIM DIES

Cathy Brougham, 22, is the latest victim to die from a vicious mountain lion attack. While hiking Tuesday in the East Bay near Mount Diablo State Park she vanished, failing to return home that night. Her body, mauled almost beyond recognition, was discovered early Wednesday morning by another hiker.

Two other hikers believe they may have seen her on a hiking trail at dusk on Tuesday.

Farther down on the page, an interview with a park ranger explained what to do if you meet a lion—wave your arms, yell, try to appear large, never turn your back—all useful bits of advice. But only if it's really a mountain lion. I knew better.

The ranger also said he'd never seen a lion do anything like that before. The injuries were more consistent with a bear attack, he said, but noted there hadn't been a fatal bear attack in California in more than a century.

Two of the attacks had been in the East Bay Hills, and one had been in Marin. Nothing in the city so far—maybe the creature was smart enough to know that would bring more heat than it could handle. Usually Lou could have tracked it down for us—he can find almost anything. But this creature was a distorted version of an Ifrit, with some of the same qualities. It was resistant to magical energy, and that messed with Lou's tracking radar. The only reason we'd been able to find it at all was a brief story in the paper about a man who swore he'd seen a wolverine near the Presidio. He'd been ignored, most people chalking up his story to mountain lion hysteria.

When we were ready to leave, my old battered van came in useful for once. A hospital orderly helped me load Victor into the back of the van where he could lie flat without having to bend his leg. The ER doc had given Victor a scrip for Demerol, which showed how serious he thought the pain was going to be. Victor wouldn't fill it, though. He thought using drugs to deal with a problem of any sort was a sign of moral weakness, although he wasn't above using talent to dull his pain. I didn't see the difference, except that while talent isn't available to ordinary citizens, drugs are. But that's Victor.

A half hour later we were back at his Victorian house out by Ocean Beach. It's a beautiful place, a mansion really, but it seems a bit out of place for the neighborhood. I didn't find out the truth about it until I'd known him quite a while. In reality, it had been built not that many years ago from plans Victor had brought back from England when he'd lived there. So it really was a faux Victorian, complete with gables, windows overlooking the Pacific, and authentic period furniture. It must have cost a fortune to build, but Victor has never had any money concerns.

I helped him up the stairs, moving one step at a time. He stretched out onto the couch in his study, extending the damaged leg and sighing with relief. For once neither one of us was sniping at each other—I was shaken by the viciousness of the attack on him, and even the usually unflappable Victor was subdued by the extent of the damage to his leg.

I called Eli, my best friend and Victor's as well, although Eli was more of a colleague to Victor, more of a mentor to me. He was away at a conference and not answering his cell, so I left a noncommittal message for him to call me back.

Maggie, Victor's Ifrit, stalked over and looked at me as if somehow I was responsible for the situation. Being a cat—well, sort of—she believed the proper assignation of blame is always the most important thing. Lou quietly backed out of the way. She and Lou don't get along particularly well, though they tend to set up an informal truce whenever there's real trouble.

The three hours we'd spent in the ER had given Campbell just enough time to make it down from her cabin in Soda Springs, up by Donner Summit. She breezed in ten minutes later, gave me an abstracted wave, and immediately went to Victor's side. His leg was wrapped in bandages from the ER, which had to be removed before she could assess the damage. She looked at the leg and drew in her breath exactly like the ER doc had done.

"Wow," she said, slipping off the backpack that carried the tools of her trade. "I'm surprised they let you leave."

"They can't actually keep you there against your will," I said. "And even if they could, well, it is Victor after all. Can you fix this?"

She threw me an annoyed glance. Campbell hates it when I referred to healing abilities as "fixing" things. She doesn't consider herself a practitioner as such, not the way Victor and Eli and I do. She's a healer more in the Wiccan tradition, although she'd fallen away from that lately. She couldn't create illusions or aversion shields. She couldn't animate the inanimate or perform magical forensics, or do any of the things Victor and I could. But what she could do was heal, using plants and a great deal of personal energy, and she was far better at it than I could ever dream of being.

But this time she was too shaken to even comment on how I'd phrased it. She kept shaking her head, looking doubtful. Campbell is confident in her own abilities, and rightfully so. And if she was worried . . .

"Well?" I said, suddenly a lot more worried than I had been. Maybe Victor really would lose the leg.

"Piece of cake," she said, almost bitterly, which was very unlike her. "That is, if we're talking about a five-tiered wedding cake that takes two days to create. I had no idea it was going to be this bad." Only Victor seemed unaffected.

"Do what you can," he said.

Campbell pressed her lips tightly together. Then she nodded slightly as if having an internal dialogue with herself, and the worry lines on her face smoothed out.

"I'm going to need some special materials I don't have with me."

"I'm guessing it's not anything that will be available at the local Safeway," I said.

"No, not exactly. But I do know where to get what I'll need." She turned to Victor. "Are you going to be all right alone for a while?"

"Of course," he said. "Timothy should be home soon, anyway."

Timothy, somewhat to my surprise, was still hanging in there—in fact, it was taking on all the aspects of a real relationship. After years of clueless twinks, Victor finally had met a real person. Now, Timothy wasn't exactly in love, as far as I could tell, but he did really like Victor. He refused to take any of his crap, though. Maybe that was the kind of person Victor had been waiting for.

I wasn't much of one to judge. My own relationships haven't turned out so well, Campbell being one notable example. But at least we were still friends, and there was clearly still something between us. We'd both been through some changes, and although we never talked about it, there was that someday possibility hanging around. And surely if Victor could find someone, there was hope yet even for me. At least I'm easier to get along with than he is. I think.

"Okay, then," Campbell said. "We'll be back in a while."

We took my van, and the place she had in mind was a botanica over on Church Street in upper Noe Valley, not far from where I live. I'd passed by it many times before but never had reason to go inside. The front display windows were dusty and crammed with every sort of object imaginable, all related in some way to religion or magic. Miracle candles. Statues of the Virgin Mary and various saints, all with copper-wire halos. A large statue of many-armed Kali next to an African wood carving of an ibis. Dolls with rose-patterned gowns hanging on wires from a tree branch. Scattered throughout, seashells and dried starfish from the sea. And tucked discreetly in a corner, something labeled herbal Viagra.

The woman behind the counter stared at me with a flat, impassive expression that darkened when she saw a small dog at my side, invading her precious sanctum. But when she saw who was with me a broad smile transformed her face. She rushed out from behind the counter and embraced Campbell, still looking suspiciously at me out of the corner of her eye.

"Campbell!" she said, with just a trace of an accent. She wore a white baseball cap perched jauntily over a grandmotherly face. I couldn't even begin to guess her race or ethnicity.

"Hello, Mama Yara. How have you been?"

"Good, good. And you?"

Campbell just shrugged. She noticed the eye Mama Yara was giving me.

"Mama, this is a friend of mine," she said. The suspicious look did not abate. Campbell altered her tone, almost as if she were reciting a ritual. "I have helped him and he has helped me."

Mama Yara relaxed and the suspicious expression faded, but I can't say it was replaced by any actual warmth. She turned back to Campbell.

"You are needing some herbs, I would guess."

"I do indeed. And I'm in a hurry. A bad wound, and a friend."

Mama Yara nodded and made her way back toward the counter, Campbell in tow. I looked around the store, politely keeping my distance. The floor was painted a sky blue, faded with age. A series of white lines, barely visible, delineated astrological signs. Fresh flowers abounded, along with plants, more statues, bronze censers, and bells of all different shapes and sizes.

"I could use some pau d'arco," I heard Campbell say. "And some white cobol."

"Some benzoin of Sumatra, you think?" Mama Yara asked. "It could help."

"Surely. It couldn't hurt. And most important, I need some . . ."

Her voice trailed off and I didn't catch the rest. Whatever she was asking for must have been special, because I could see Mama Yara's eyebrows go up and she lowered her voice. She glanced over at me again, clearly not happy to have me there despite Campbell's vouching for me. It felt like we were scoring dope from a particularly paranoid dealer.

The bell over the door tinkled as another customer came in, a woman. I glanced over briefly and then looked again. Tall, willowy, long red hair, and longer legs. A sleeveless top showing off two dragon tattoos, one red and one green, curling down each arm. A striking figure, but that wasn't why I gave a second look. I knew her.

It was Ruby, a practitioner I hadn't seen for years. I hadn't known her well, but she wasn't someone you forget. Also, I'd pursued her with some determination when we first met, oblivious to the fact she was gay, until she casually mentioned an ex-girlfriend to help clue in the clueless.

She noticed me the same time I noticed her, and her face lit up with delight. Apparently, all was forgiven and forgotten.

"Mason!" she said. "I've been meaning to look you up. How have you been?"

"Getting by," I said. "You? I thought you'd left the city for good—didn't you move to Paris or something?"

"Florence," she said. "Studying art. And some other things. Have you heard of Giancarlo?"

I certainly had. Giancarlo was not only in the same league as Eli in terms of magical scholarship but he also possessed the same innate level of talent as did Victor. Giancarlo was also a magical enforcer of sorts, although from what I'd heard, more like a Mafia don than a cop. He and Eli were great Internet friends.

"You were studying with Giancarlo?" I said, impressed.

"I was. The last five years, to be exact." She bent down as Lou rushed over to greet her. I remembered he'd liked her. "Louie. Good to see you, too." She pulled gently on his ears for a moment before straightening up.

"Are you back for a while?" I asked.

"Yep. Back for good, or at least that's my plan. Are you still playing music?"

"As often as I can."

"Still working with Victor?"

"Only when I have to."

She laughed. "Not much has changed, I see."

In some ways that was true, although a lot had happened in the last few years.

Campbell came out of a back room where Mama Yara had taken her, saw us talking together, and joined us. Introductions were made, and Ruby looked curiously at the herbs Campbell was holding.

"What's that root you're holding?" she asked. "That's new to me."

The conversation took off from there, and I was momentarily forgotten. I didn't blame Ruby—I'm sure she was interested in the herbs, but it didn't hurt that Campbell was hot; no doubt about that. She'd let her blond hair grow out, and even though she was wearing nondescript clothes and standing in a dingy herb store, nothing could hide her vitality and energy. A strong face and a toned, athletic body—she was an outdoors girl all the way. Unfortunately for Ruby, Campbell was also completely straight. Or at least I assumed she was from previous experience, but if anyone could make a woman think twice, it would be Ruby. She turned back to me after just a minute, though.

"I'm actually glad I ran into you," she said. "Apart from wanting to see you. You're still in touch with Victor, right?"

I certainly was, considering Campbell and I were at the botanica collecting herbs for his recovery. Ruby didn't know that, but she did know that the last time she'd seen me I had been working for him, and she knew that Victor is the chief magical enforcer for San Francisco and the Bay Area. It's his job to keep an eye on the magical practitioners living here, making sure they don't use their special talents to scam civilians, win beauty contests, fix elections, or any of the other things that might occur to an unscrupulous person who possesses magical talent.

Chief enforcer is an impressive title, but maybe less so once you realize he'd appointed himself to the job. Practitioner society isn't very structured—there are no official titles or positions. Practitioners are far too individualistic to develop any sort of hierarchical system. But without Victor and those like him, that society would soon devolve into chaos, with each practitioner doing whatever struck his fancy.

Then our existence would become widely known—already far too many people have at least an inkling that the world is not as prosaic as it seems to be. What would happen after that is anyone's guess, but judging from the history of mankind, it wouldn't be pretty. Laws passed against the practice of magic. Suspicion, envy, blame, and eventually lynch mobs. And although some of us do possess impressive abilities, our numbers aren't large and one army special forces unit could cause us a lot of grief. We'd put up a good fight, but you can't take on the whole world.

So, some type of magical enforcement squad, official or not, was a necessity. And for a while I worked for Victor as part of his enforcement group, along with Sherwood and Eli. Sherwood and I had been together for a time, but it hadn't worked out. Then, about a year ago, she had fallen victim to a bad practitioner. That loss had left its mark on me. Eli, my mentor and best friend, didn't exactly work for Victor—he acted more as an elder statesman and an adviser. Victor relied on Eli and seldom went against his advice. I was either a valued colleague or a low-level employee, depending on the day.

Eventually I'd got tired of playing cops and robbers and quit the group. I wasn't cut out for the job anyway. I started playing music full-time as a jazz guitarist, my true passion, and I was a whole lot happier, though poorer.

But then some unpleasant things started happening in the city. Ifrits were vanishing, and someone kept trying to kill me for reasons I didn't understand. Sherwood talked me into coming back to the group, and we eventually found out who was responsible—but there had been a price to pay. There always is.

Then, not long after, more trouble. Dead practitioners, and worse—others whose minds had been destroyed, leaving nothing but a husk behind. And finally, although the person responsible had eventually been stopped, there was one small matter that still needed to be taken care of—the creature we'd been hunting.

But all that history would take an hour to relate, so all I said was, "Of course. Just came from his house, as a matter of fact."

"That's good. I need to talk to him."

"You looking for a job?"

"You never know. Actually, he offered me one before I left for Florence. I didn't think I could handle it back then. But that's not it. There's something odd going on in this city, and I was wondering if he'd heard anything about it."

"What kind of odd?"

"The kind that Victor deals in. I've got an idea about something, but I'm not sure I'm on the right track. There's . . . Well, I don't know what it is, but I think there's some sort of creature wandering around these days, and I think it might be dangerous. Have you read about those hikers that have been savaged lately?" That got my attention.

"Yes," I said. "We're aware of it. There is something out there—in fact, we've been trying to hunt it down ourselves."

"What is it?"

"We don't know."

"Where did it come from?"

"We're not sure."

That wasn't exactly true. I didn't know what it was, but I did know it had come from an energy pool that I'd helped create. We had been testing the theory that Ifrits are actually creations of a practitioner's subconscious. The idea had been to create an Ifrit, and it had worked, sort of. Except, as usual, things didn't go according to plan—what had come out of that pool was no Ifrit, and it was dangerous.

Campbell had a puzzled expression on her face. She started to say something, then thought better of it. Ruby put her hand on my arm.

"Well, I'd like to talk to Victor about it. Maybe I could help. I learned a lot over in Italy."

"I can well imagine. Giancarlo's got quite the reputation."

The bell tinkled on the door to the shop, and Ruby looked up and waved at the person coming through it.

"I've got to talk to Mama Yara," she said to me. "Be back in a sec." She left my side and went over to the counter where Mama Yara stood.

It looked like Mama Yara's botanica was practitioner central today. I also knew the practitioner standing in the doorway. Everyone knew Ramsey, though few were glad they did. He might not have been the worst practitioner in the city, but he had to be the most annoying.

"Mason," he said, holding out his hand as he came toward me. I gave the hand a lukewarm shake and had trouble retrieving it.

"I've been meaning to call you," he said. "Ruby and I are onto something. I left Victor a message, but he hasn't got back to me."

No surprise there. Ramsey was a wannabe enforcer, always bugging Victor about a job, and providing bits of information about totally inconsequential things. He would have made a great enforcer, except for his lack of three small things: talent, judgment, and intelligence. To make up for that, his personality was nonexistent, except for the ability to clear a room at any party five minutes after entering it.

"Well, Victor's been busy lately," I said.

He nodded knowingly.

"Yeah, lots of stuff going on."

He spotted Lou and ran over to him. He bent down and picked him up, something Lou hates, even with people he likes, and Ramsey wasn't one of those. I saw Lou's mouth open slightly. He was going to bite him; I just knew it. For a second I thought about watching it play out, but that wouldn't have been very mature on my part. Amusing, yes, but not a good thing.

"Lou," I cautioned. He glanced over at me defiantly, but he closed his mouth. Ramsey continued pull on his ears, totally oblivious to the byplay. Finally he put Lou down and walked back over to me.

"So, did Ruby tell you what we're working on?"

"She mentioned there was something odd going on."

"Odd? Bizarre is more like it. This is something we really should look into."

I loved his use of "we." Ramsey was like those wannabe cops who can never make it onto the force, so they become security guards. They wear their uniforms, tailored to look as much like real cops as the law allows, with pride and a certain amount of arrogance. They put scanners in their cars to keep track of police calls and show up at unexpected times, always oh-so-helpful, always acting with an odd combination of contempt for civilians and obsequiousness toward real cops. They're a sad lot, but they can be dangerous as well—occasionally you read about one of them shooting a shoplifter who refuses to turn out his pockets on demand.

I was saved from having to answer by Ruby's return. Her arms were full of packages, and Ramsey leapt to take them from her.

"Be a dear and put those in the car, would you?" Ruby said.

Ramsey smiled happily and scooted on out the door. I looked at Ruby, who looked back blandly.

"Really?" I said. "Ramsey?"

"It's not what you think."

Whenever anyone says that, it's usually exactly what you think. But this was a mystery. First of all, Ruby was gay. Or so I thought—I had a moment's horrified suspicion that she'd been putting me on just to avoid my attentions, but then I remembered having met one of her girlfriends.

But if she was going to dip a toe in the other pool, why Ramsey? I could understand if she'd decided to hook up with some gorgeous man, or even some brilliant practitioner. But Ramsey was far from either—short and unprepossessing, with lank hair that always looked greasy and a perpetually unkempt beard. Plus, small talent as a practitioner and the aforementioned obnoxious and clueless demeanor.

"What, then?" I said. "His sparkling personality?"

"Don't be mean. He's not that bad." A smile flitted across her face. "Besides, he can be quite useful."

I didn't doubt that. Like many marginally talented practitioners, Ramsey did possess one area of expertise—he
was a consummate sneak. He could slip wards, unless they
were very strong, and had a way of remaining unnoticed
even if you were looking for him. He could indeed be useful, but putting up with him would be quite a challenge.

"I'll bet," I said. "But if you have any sense, you'll
keep him away from Victor. He's not as tolerant as I am."
She laughed and patted me on the shoulder.

"Actually, I'd just as soon you not mention this to Victor. He's a bit judgmental, you know."

"So I've heard."

Campbell had become increasingly impatient and finally
grabbed me by the arm.

"Mason. We have to go," she said.

"Sorry," Ruby said. "I'm keeping you. Anyway, I have to
go myself—I've got to pick up some things across town."
She went over to the counter, found a scrap of paper, and
scribbled down her number. "Call me. We'll catch up." I
tore the paper in half, wrote my number down, as well as
Victor's, and handed her the other half.

"Do give Victor a call," I said. "I'm sure he'd like to hear
from you. But not for a few days. He's going to be . . . a
bit tied up for a while."

As soon as we were out on the sidewalk, Campbell
said, "What was that about? Why didn't you tell her the
whole story about the creature and where it came from?"

"I'm not sure," I said. "Just habit, mostly. I'm not used
to confiding things, even to friends, and I haven't seen her
for years. I'll let Victor decide how much to tell her."

"You are one paranoid puppy."

"Maybe. But I've learned to be."

"I'm sure. But let's get back to Victor's before that leg
just falls off."

AS SOON AS WE GOT BACK, CAMPBELL UN-
wrapped her purchases and started pulling plastic baggies

containing various other plants out of her pack. Then a small glass bottle and a dish. She unstoppered the bottle and poured oil from it into the dish, adding a floating wick. As soon as she lit the wick, a thick chocolaty scent filled the room.

A medium-sized bowl of wood was next, and Campbell carefully measured out bits of plant matter and shredded them into it. She uncorked a flask and poured a different oil, thick and viscous, into the bowl. Again the aroma of chocolate filled the air. As she stirred up the ingredients, I looked at her questioningly. I hadn't seen her use anything like this before.

"Lwil maskrati," she said, indicating the oil in the bowl.

"Come again?"

"Lwil maskrati. From Mama Yara's. Something I learned about from Montague." A brief sadness passed over her face.

"Voodoo?" said Victor, with interest. I noticed that his hair was damp with sweat. He wasn't having as easy a time of it as he was making out.

"No," she said, shaking her head. "Same tradition, but not the same at all, not really." She applied the paste to Victor's leg, smoothing it over his leg from the ankle to just above the knee, wiping the excess off her hands with a soft cloth. "Almost ready."

I expected to feel a wave of healing energy coming off of her. That was her usual practice, and her healing powers had more to do with her personal abilities than the plants she used. Talent is about redirecting energy, not what objects are employed. The plants were just a focusing device to help enable her potential. That was my take; Campbell vehemently disagreed. She saw herself as simply empowering the intrinsic properties of specific plants. Who knows? She might even be right. She often was.

This time, however, she'd come up with something new. She started a slow, sinuous dance, using precise movements. It wasn't improvised; it was a carefully constructed ritual. It wasn't like any form of pagan dance I'd ever seen; it was suggestive, aggressively sexual, without being obvious. Whatever tradition it was from must have been one of emotion and feeling, not cold reason.

She kept it up until her eyes started to go glassy, then threw herself down next to Victor like a stage diva playing the dying swan. Finally, that familiar surge of energy rolled off her, but stronger than I'd seen before, and with a different tinge.

Victor hissed, drawing in his breath with a quick intake, and immediately after, a muffled grunt of pain escaped him. He prides himself on being stoic—he hadn't even flinched at the emergency room, so either this had caught him completely off guard or it had hit him like a ton of bricks. Campbell remained on the floor a few seconds before climbing shakily to her feet.

"That should help," she said, out of breath. "It will take a few more days, but when it's healed completely there won't even be any scars." A shadow of doubt passed across her face. "Hopefully."

Victor gingerly extended his leg. It was hard to see under the goop that Campbell had plastered over it, but from what I could tell, the skin beneath had already partially healed. In places it looked almost undamaged except for a network of fine red lines crisscrossing over it. Campbell had always possessed an aptitude for healing, but she now appeared to have taken a quantum leap toward being a major talent.

"Thanks," Victor said, slightly out of breath himself. It's not a word he uses often.

"You'll need to keep off of it for a couple of days," she told him. "And you'll need some rest. A major healing, especially a quick one, isn't entirely free, you know. It's taken something out of me, of course, but it's taken a lot more out of you—more than you probably realize. I think you might need some help with stuff for a while—where is Eli anyway?"

"Out of town for a few days," I told her. "Some conference of medieval history academics. He's due back tomorrow."

"You should call him."

"I will," Victor said. "But Timothy can take care of pretty much everything."

Victor was obviously drained and mostly just wanted to be left alone, so I suggested to Campbell we get a bite to eat. We stopped in at Marnee Thai, a small Thai restaurant in the Richmond, one of my favorites. We chatted over ample portions of Pad Thai and Mi Krob, catching up since we hadn't talked for a while. Campbell was in the loop and knew about the creature we'd been hunting, but she hadn't understood just how dangerous it was.

"What if you just left it alone?" she asked. "Maybe it would go back to wherever it came from, or just settle down somewhere."

"If only. It doesn't seem to have any desire to leave. And it seems to have a tremendous hatred of Ifrits—why, I can't say. Maybe because it's a distorted version of the true thing. In any case, Jasmine's Ifrit, Mercedes, came up missing a while ago. In the old days we would have just assumed she had abandoned her—it's sad, but it does happen. But then last month came an attack on Peewee, that little Ifrit/ferret who hangs with Jim Marvin. Jim was there and managed to drive it off, but it was a close thing. Then other deadly attacks, but this time on humans—by the supposed mountain lion that had been in all the papers. So it's become serious and Victor and I have been trying to hunt it down ever since."

"It never ends, does it?" Campbell said.

"Apparently not."

"You been seeing anyone lately?" she asked, changing the subject. I shook my head.

"After my last misadventure, I haven't much felt like dating."

"I can understand that," she said.

I didn't ask her the same question. What had happened to Montague was still too raw. When Campbell was ready to resume a seminormal life, whenever that might be, I was sure she'd let me know.

Lou was waiting patiently on the sidewalk when we left and accepted a spring roll with good grace. No peanut sauce, though. As we walked back toward where I had parked, a homeless guy detached himself from a doorway.

Lou took one look and started over to greet him, then stopped, then started again, then stopped again, as if he were a toy mechanical with a gear out of whack. It takes a lot to confuse an Ifrit, but I didn't blame him. This guy had long wild hair and a huge beard plaited in dreadlocks. He also flickered as he walked. And I knew him, all too well.

"Spare a quarter for a cup of coffee?" he said.

"What, you're living in the sixties now? Where are you going to find coffee for a quarter?"

"A buck, then," he said, smiling through discolored yet surprisingly strong teeth. And not just strong. Sharp, too. "Who's your lady friend?"

He wasn't threatening in any way, but he did project an unsettling aura of suppressed violence, as if he were a bomb that could go off at any moment. A year ago Campbell would have instinctively pulled closer to me, but she'd been through a lot since then. She gazed levelly at him and then walked over and offered her hand.

"I'm Campbell," she said.

He looked a bit taken aback, which amused me no end, but he put out his own hand and grasped hers. When he let go, he stepped back and considered her curiously.

"You're a healer," he said. "An important profession. I'm honored. My name is Rolf." She inclined her head gravely in acknowledgment.

I stared at him in astonishment. I'd know him for almost a year, and the only name I ever had for him was Bridge Guy, since that was where I'd first met him, living under the span of the Bay Bridge. He'd never shown any inclination to give me his name, and I hadn't been sure he even remembered what it was anymore. But he casually handed it over to Campbell like he'd met her at a party in the Mission.

I also wasn't entirely sure just how human he still was. He'd been the one who called up that creature we'd been hunting—with a little help from me.

"I've been looking for you," he said "You screwed up, I see."

I nodded, unsurprised. "That goes without saying. But you're going to have to be more specific."

"That thing you've been hunting? You're supposed to get it, not the other way around." Once again, he seemed to know more about my life than I was comfortable with.

"Maybe things would have turned out different if we'd had some help. You didn't seem that interested the last time we talked, remember?"

"True. I had other concerns at the time. But there's something else. That's why I was looking for you."

"Oh?" He shot a questioning glance toward Campbell. "She knows," I said. "I tell her everything." Campbell mumbled something I couldn't quite catch, but it sounded like "not everything." Bridge Guy, or rather, Rolf, nodded.

"Well, the creature that ran off that night wasn't the only thing that came out of the energy pool. And not the worst, either." Rolf could always be relied on to bring good tidings.

"How encouraging. What other things?"

"That's not entirely clear to me. But it's troubling." Rolf wasn't troubled by much, so this was also not great news.

"Yes, I can see how it would be," I said.

He smiled, showing teeth that were suddenly a lot sharper than they had been. One of the unsettling things about Rolf was that he didn't keep any one persona for any length of time.

"You could be of some help with this. You do owe me, you know."

That wasn't how I saw things at all, but I let it pass. But not completely. If I just went along with what he said, he'd be sure to take advantage of it.

"You got something to trade?" I asked. It wasn't that I needed anything, or even wanted anything, but bargaining was mandatory. That was the way Rolf operated. He smiled again, teeth sharper yet.

"Actually, I'm the one doing *you* a favor, but I'll let it ride this time. Meet me tonight, over by the bridge, same place. Don't be late." He nodded politely at Campbell and turned and hobbled off, just another street person.

"What time?" I called after him, but he didn't turn around.

"Charming fellow," said Campbell as we watched him shuffle down the street. "What was that about?"

"No idea," I said.

"Are you going?"

"I have to. He's not the sort to show up on an idle whim."

"You want some company?" I thought about it.

"Couldn't hurt," I said. "He can be very particular about who exactly has been invited, but I think he likes you."

"Oh, wonderful," she said. "At last, an admirer."

BY NOW IT WAS GROWING LATE, SO WE WENT back to my place. I was still living in my in-law apartment in the Mission, converted many years ago from a garage. It was a lot nicer than that sounds—blond wood paneling throughout, a garden in the back, and a landlord upstairs who traveled a lot. It was a good thing he was seldom home. If he'd been there full-time, he would eventually have noticed some very strange happenings indeed.

A dog door provides Lou with the freedom to come and go as he pleases, and the warding around the house, designed mostly by Eli, keeps out most unwanted visitors, at least those of the magical sort. It doesn't do much to keep away the occasional Jehovah's Witness or Mormon missionary, though.

I made some coffee and we sat at the little kitchen table. Campbell knew the basics of how the fake Ifrit had come into existence, but now that we were going to the very spot where it had happened, she wanted details. I could tell her what had happened, and how, but not why. I still didn't understand a lot about it.

"So the creature just formed out of nothing?" she asked.

"Not exactly. It's an embodiment of something, I think, brought into existence by that guy we met. As far as I can tell, he was once a practitioner himself."

"Like you?" That was a sobering thought.

"I guess maybe he was. But he's since evolved into something different. Or devolved."

"Into what?

"I'm not quite sure. The closest I can come to would be a troll."

Campbell looked at me, the corner of her mouth lifting slightly to let me know she understood I was putting her on.

"Folklore troll, or the kind you find in bars? Or the Internet sort?"

"Never mind," I said. "Anyway, he and a couple of friends like him tried to create an Ifrit, using Lou as a template and some strongly magical objects that I obligingly supplied."

"Why would you do that?"

"It's complicated," I said. That's what people usually say when they've screwed up and have no good explanation.

"I'll bet," Campbell said, well aware of that.

"The long and short of it is that something unexpected showed up, and we've been trying to deal with the aftermath. And now, apparently, there's another problem."

"Which is?"

"That's what we'll have to see."

We talked about other things until it was full dark, then headed downtown to the construction site on Harrison, under the shadow of the bridge, the place I'd first met Rolf and the place he'd held his ritual.

It had been a few months since I'd been there, so I expected at least some change, but it was like time had stood still. In the darkness I could make out the same pallets of lumber, the same piles of broken rebar and industrial trash, the same silent backhoe parked in the same place. Not unusual for a construction site, come to think of it. Construction time moves at a very different pace from normal time—like dog years.

But there was one difference. The fence and gate. Lou ran over to the place he'd squeezed through before, but it had been replaced with strong new mesh. The new gate was taller, with an even heavier chain and padlock and an extra strand of barbed wire all along the top of the fence. I hadn't counted on this.

A figure detached itself from the shadows inside the site and strolled over toward the gate. Rolf. He reached one thick hand through where the chain met the post and tapped the lock. There was a faint snick and the shackle moved a fraction. It was now unlocked.

"Show-off," I muttered. I wasn't good with metal objects myself; few practitioners are. Rolf wasn't exactly a practitioner anymore, though.

I unhooked the padlock, pulled the chain free, and swung the gate open. If Rolf was surprised to see Campbell with me, he didn't show it. He beckoned to us and led the way to a familiar area. We were right under an access ramp to the Bay Bridge at the base of the massive concrete pylons that supported it. The sound of traffic far above us was surprisingly loud.

I had no idea what he wanted to show me, and I wasn't sure what he expected me to do about it in any case. My strength is improvisational magic—I use my talent to pull together various threads gathered from the environment around me and weave them into useful spells. Much like the way I compose jazz tunes and play solos.

But as far as understanding things or investigating odd occurrences goes, I'm not the best choice. Victor is far better at that sort of thing, and so is Eli for that matter, despite his relative lack of intrinsic talent. But at least I could report back to them if there was anything worth reporting.

And there was. A faint glow was coming from the site of the area of the original ritual that had called up the beast we had been hunting. As we got closer, I saw what was causing it: an area about five feet across. A whirlpool of smooth swirling colors, one-dimensional, flat against the ground, but hinting at depths like a pool of water. The colors were separated into discrete bands of different widths, but they blended into each other at the edges and each band slowly changed color as I watched.

The colors moved with a slow, pulsating, hypnotic motion. The whole thing reminded me of the pattern I had seen while looking into certain jewels I once had the misfortune to find.

Lou walked up and stared into the center of the pattern with an intense yet curiously detached interest. That wasn't like him; he was usually all for something or all against it. There are few shades of gray in his world. Campbell came up and stood beside me.

"What is Lou so interested in?" she said. That surprised me. Campbell isn't technically a practitioner, but she does have talent. She wouldn't be the healer she is if she didn't.

"You don't see it?" I asked.

"See what?"

Rolf chuckled, although his voice was starting to slur as it sometimes did so it sounded more like a gargle.

"She can't see it," he said. "Just about no one can, except me and those like me. Even practitioners." He pointed down at Lou. "And him, of course. He's an Ifrit, after all."

"I can see it," I said. "Why is that? What is it, anyway?"

"I figured you might be able to see it, 'cause you were here when it was made. You helped, remember." Indeed I did. "There might even be a little bit of you in there."

Half the time I had no idea what Rolf was talking about. I bent down closer to the swirl. Raw power was coming off it, wild talent. The only other time I'd felt something like this was in the tunnels by the Sutro caves.

"You might want to take care," Rolf said. "I don't think touching it would be a good idea."

I appreciated the warning, but it wasn't needed. He might as well have been a shop foreman telling me, "I wouldn't stick my hand in that circular saw if I was you."

Lou was still staring intently, motionless. His eyes had gone vacant and were starting to take on a glazed expression. The edges of his fur were beginning to glow, ever so slightly,

"Lou," I said. "Back off."

He ignored me. I don't think he even heard me. I reached over and grabbed him by the collar, which I make him wear for just such situations. He gave a start, as if I'd rudely woken him from a nap, shook himself, and rapidly backed away from the lip of the swirling pattern.

"What the hell is this thing?" I asked Rolf.

"It's the energy pool," he said. "You remember; what that creature came out of? It was small at first. I never even noticed it; I thought it had gone, but it never went away. I think that has something to do with those stones you gave me. They had a lot of magic in them, and I think the power they contained may have caused the pool to become self-sustaining. After you left that night, after the fake Ifrit we called up ran off, it started growing. And then something else came out of it."

"Like the first creature?"

He shook his head.

"No, something else. I didn't get a good look at it, but it made me nervous."

"I didn't think there was anything that made you nervous," I said.

"There's not too much. Not anymore. But this was . . . well, different."

Campbell had been listening intently, at the same time scanning the ground, hoping at least to catch a glimpse of what we were talking about.

"How long ago was this?" she asked. Rolf looked momentarily baffled. I don't think he had much of a sense of time.

"A few months ago," I put in, helping him out. "About the same time as all that other stuff." She stared at him, quizzically.

"And you're just now getting around to telling someone about it?"

She spoke in a gently reproving manner, something I wouldn't have wanted to try myself. Rolf wasn't entirely human, not anymore, and I was always leery of pissing him off, which isn't difficult to do. But Campbell, for some reason, seemed to have a different effect on him. He shrugged, but at the same time shuffled his feet in embarrassment.

"I didn't think much about it," he said. "It wasn't doing anything to me. Live and let live is my motto. But a few days ago I was over in Marin with Richard. Richard Cory." He turned to me. "You remember him, right?"

I did. Richard was one of Rolf's circle, a man who had gone so far along that same strange path that he was now a walking embodiment of what used to be called the fey. He made me extremely nervous, and Lou even more so.

"Yeah," I said.

"Well, we were out at the Marin Headlands—"

"What were you doing out there?" I asked.

Rolf stared at me without answering, and what little I could see of his face in the dark started to subtly shift. Apparently I wasn't being given the same latitude as was Campbell. I put both hands up and ducked my head in the universal "sorry, my bad" gesture.

"We were out at the Headlands," he said again, pausing for just long enough to give me a chance to interrupt again. I looked at him with polite and attentive interest. "Richard was up a little ahead of me when he stopped and put up a hand as if he had heard something. All I heard was a meadowlark singing in the tall grass. Then he got this look on his face, kind of blissed out, you know? He took off running, crested the hill, and by the time I got to the top he was out of sight. I haven't seen him since."

"I don't get the connection," I said.

"Well, I never heard anything and I never saw anything, but I did feel something." He waved his hand toward the swirling pattern. "Feel that energy? I felt the same thing coming from the other side of the hill. I don't know what came out of that thing, but whatever it was, it took Richard."

"Maybe he just decided to leave," I said, hearing how lame that sounded the moment I said it.

"I can't do anything about it," Rolf said. "I can't mingle like you can, so I can't really look for him. I can't get around like you can. You were pretty good at figuring things out the last time you was here, though it took you a while." He straightened up and became oddly formal. "If you can find Richard Cory, or even tell me what happened to him, I'd be beholden to you."

That could be useful. It wouldn't hurt at all having Rolf owe me. Maybe he could even hunt down the Ifrit creature for us—if anyone was suited for the job, it was him. Besides, I was partly responsible for what had happened. I'd like to know what else we'd unleashed on an unsuspecting world.

"I'll see what I can do," I said. "Is there anything else you can tell me? Any idea at all what it is I'd be looking for?"

Rolf shook his head.

"If I knew what it was, I wouldn't have to ask you for help," he said.

We started back toward the gate. I was happy to get some distance between me and the color swirl. It made me nervous to stand next to it. As we approached the gate, I turned for one last look to see if I could find it from a distance now that I knew it was there. There was the faintest glow, more at the corner of my mind than my eyes, but it was there. And something, barely visible in the shadows, right behind it.

Lou had noticed it as well, of course. He was standing stock-still, focused, but without his usual warning growl to alert me to danger. He finally took a few steps toward it, but then stopped again, one paw off the ground, motionless. I can read him pretty well. He's as expressive as any dog in body language, and a lot more in facial expression. He was . . . "baffled" is the word that came to mind.

"What is it?" asked Campbell, looking at the two of us.

"I don't know," I said. "You might want to stay back, though."

I walked back toward the swirling pattern, Lou paralleling my steps. As I got closer, it became apparent there was a figure standing in the shadows, right behind the energy source. The closer I got, the more familiar it seemed. Then it stepped forward and the glow from the energy bands lit up its face for a fraction of a second.

My mouth turned dry and I had trouble catching my breath. Lou made a sound unlike anything I had ever heard from him—not a bark, not a cry, almost like a human gasp. The figure was no ghostly apparition; it was as solid and real as your next-door neighbor. It took another step forward, stepped into the swirling mass of colors, and disappeared, sinking through and leaving not so much as a ripple of disturbance in its wake.

It was Sherwood. But Sherwood had been dead for more than a year.

THREE

I DIDN'T TELL CAMPBELL WHAT I HAD SEEN—
mostly I tell her everything, but this was something I needed
to think about for a while. She didn't stay the night, even
though it was late and a long drive back to her cabin up at
Soda Springs. I dropped her off at Victor's, where she
could check on him and pick up her car.

I had no idea what it was I'd seen, but one thing was
for sure—it couldn't have been Sherwood. She and I had
been together for almost a year, and although it had ended,
it hadn't ended badly. We remained friends, and once we
stopped trying to be a couple, we became good friends.
But then she'd been murdered, killed right before my eyes
by another practitioner, and there was nothing I could have
done to stop it.

That practitioner was now dead himself. I had killed
him, but that hadn't helped Sherwood any. And although
I've come across my share of odd things and supernatural
creatures in my time, I've never seen a ghost and I never
expect to. A lot of my beliefs have been tested in the last
couple of years, but one thing I still do know: human, ani-

mal, or other, dead is dead and spirits of the departed do not return and walk this earth again.

But not surprisingly, that apparition by the energy pool had got to me. I didn't get much sleep that night, and the only thing that kept me from a complete meltdown was the knowledge that Eli would be back from his conference in the morning.

I'd been to a few of his lectures over the years. So I've seen him in his element and he's impressive. As an African American, he automatically stands out among the pale scholarly types that typically frequent history conferences. Plus, he's six feet four and two hundred fifty pounds or so, as befits a former football lineman. When he steps up to the lectern he dwarfs it. When he hunches over the microphone to speak, you half expect the lectern to collapse under the strain. Couple that with a professorial beard, wire-rimmed glasses, and a deep, mellifluous speaking voice, and he dominates any room without trying.

Eli's been my best friend and mentor for years, and not much throws him. He'd know what was going on here, or at least have an idea; that much I was sure of. At least I hoped he would.

I woke up early and had my usual breakfast of multiple cups of coffee, adding a toaster waffle to soothe my nerves. Lou, as usual, turned up his nose at breakfast kibble, so I relented and made him a toaster waffle of his own. I know that's not good for a dog, but he isn't really a dog, is he, now? Besides, if I held firm, he'd just duck out the dog door and disappear until he found a breakfast more to his liking. God knows what he'd find—for such a picky eater he's not picky at all once he's out on the street.

Eli was just on his way to Victor's house when I called him. By time I got there he was already upstairs, taking a close look at Victor's leg. Timothy was trying to get a look as well, hovering and trying not to get in the way. He was worried, but Eli didn't seem to be.

It had been several days since I'd last seen Eli, and he looked different. When you see someone almost every single day, you don't notice changes. They happen in such small increments that they're invisible to the everyday eye. But even a week's absence will give you a fresh perspective. He must have lost close to twenty pounds in the last few months, and although no one would ever call him svelte, he was looking good. He probably hadn't been this fit since his college football playing days, although I hadn't known him then.

He'd trimmed his usually scraggly beard as well, and had replaced his old wire-rimmed glasses with a more modern set of frames. He'd told me that he'd finally reached the stage of life where he realized he had to take care of himself. I took him at his word. I'm sure it was mere coincidence that for the first time in years he now had a woman in his life. Eleanor was her name, and although she wasn't a practitioner, she was a powerful woman. She'd have to be to get Eli to change his ways.

Eli finally straightened up from where Victor lay on the couch with a grunt of approval. Victor's leg already looked normal, except for some swelling and redness.

"I can't leave you two alone for even a few days," Eli complained. His relief at finding Victor in such good condition allowed his grumpiness to come out.

"That creature was faster than I expected," said Victor. "Next time I'll be ready."

"That creature isn't the only thing we have to worry about," I said. Victor gave a theatrical sigh.

"What now?"

"I'm not sure, but I think it's connected and I don't like the sound of it, not at all."

They were both familiar with Rolf, though neither had ever met him. I told them his story, the swirling circle of color and energy I'd seen, the fact that *something* else had come out of that circle, and the disappearance of the being he called Richard Cory.

"Interesting," said Eli, understating things as usual. Victor nodded his agreement.

"Yes, but that's the least interesting part," I said. "I saw something there, and when I went back for a better look, I saw something that couldn't be. And it was no trick of the mind, either. Lou saw it, too."

"And?" Victor prompted, after I'd waited long enough for the maximum dramatic effect.

"It was Sherwood. I saw her as clearly as I see you now."

I'm not sure what reaction I was expecting from the two of them. Victor would try his best to remain impassive and politely interested, as always, but Eli surely would be astounded. But the reaction I got was totally unexpected. The two of them instantly looked over at each other, then immediately looked away as if they shared a guilty secret they didn't want me to know.

"What?" I said. They looked at each other again.

"Are you sure about what you saw?" asked Eli, pretending nothing was going on. I wasn't buying it.

"What was that look?" I said.

He paused for a moment, thinking if there was a way to finesse it, then decided there wasn't.

"Victor and I have been doing some research," he said. He paused, started to say something, stopped, and finally came out with it. "We're not sure that Sherwood's actually dead."

I could say I was stunned, but that wouldn't be quite right. It was more like being totally blank. I heard the words, I understood what they meant, but at the same time they made no sense at all, as if Eli were talking gibberish.

"What?" I said, unable to muster anything else.

"We're not sure that Sherwood is dead," he repeated.

This time it sunk in, but it was the most preposterous thing I'd ever heard.

"What do you mean? You were there. You saw it. Christoph incinerated her before our eyes."

Eli took off his glasses and cleaned them with the corner of his shirt. At any other time seeing Eli at a loss for words would have been a rare treat, but not now. Victor hauled himself off the couch and stood awkwardly, favoring his bad leg.

"Not exactly," he said. "Christoph had those gems, remember, and that gave him an unholy amount of power. He threw a blast of energy at her, and it looked like she just melted away. But there wasn't any body. There wasn't even the slightest trace of any remains. Just a scorched spot on the grass from the energy burst."

I thought back to the charred circle on the grass, and her hand reaching out to me in a last desperate attempt.

"What else could have happened?" I asked. "She was there, she caught fire, and she was vaporized. With that much energy, there wouldn't be much left."

"Ahh," said Eli, recovering his voice, "but that's just it. There should have been *something*. But there wasn't. Nothing at all. Not a trace. I looked. So it's possible her body wasn't destroyed. She could have been transported to somewhere else, instead."

"You mean like another dimension?"

"Well, no, I don't think so, not precisely. But something like that, perhaps. I came across a couple of very similar accounts in some of my more arcane manuscripts, and it could be. In some accounts, the people involved eventually returned, but unfortunately the accounts are silent on where those people went or how they got back. So yes, it could be. But the problem is, I currently have no idea of how to find her or where she might be or how to get her back—if that's indeed what happened."

"And just when were you planning to tell me this?" I was seriously pissed, not just at Eli for keeping something so important from me, but for also sharing it with Victor and not me. It felt like a betrayal. Eli was supposed to be my best friend, as well as a mentor.

"Maybe I should have said something, but there didn't seem much point in mentioning it. It was just a theory, after all, and there wasn't anything I could do about it even if it were true. I didn't see any reason to upset you.

But now that you actually saw her, or some version of her, I think it's a different story."

I walked over to the front window that overlooks Ocean Beach and the Pacific and stared out at the passing gulls. I saw his point, sort of—Sherwood and I had been very close at one time, more than close for almost a year. But still, it was disturbing. I'm no kid anymore, and there was no excuse for treating me like a child who needs to be protected against false hope. Eli walked over and stood silently beside me. He didn't say anything, which was his way of apologizing. I decided to let it drop. For now.

"I don't understand," I finally said. "If this is true, why did she appear now, after all this time—if it really was her."

"That energy sink," said Eli. "It's already brought something uncanny out of God knows where, and it might have attracted her in some way. That, and the fact you were present there—she's probably more connected to you than anyone else, so your presence could have been the trigger. Your psyche might have been strengthened and enhanced just by your being so close to the pool—on the magical plane, that is. And it must have called to her, and the energy provided a bridge to wherever she is—not enough for her to cross over, but enough so that she could at least make a tenuous contact with our world again."

"Should I go back there again?"

"I don't think that would be a good idea. It sounds like the energy there is too powerful—whatever comes out of that place is twisted and distorted. Think of the fake Ifrit. If she really is somewhere, still alive in some sense, we might well be able to drag her back. But then, we might not like what returned."

That sent a chill right through me.

"So what now? Forget it ever happened?"

"No, we can hardly do that. In fact, were going to have to close down that portal eventually—it seems to be a vehicle for some uncanny things to enter our world. I'm surprised there haven't been more."

"Maybe there have been," said Timothy. "Maybe you guys just haven't run across them all yet." Another cheerful thought.

"But what about Sherwood?" I asked.

"She managed to establish some sort of contact with you, employing the channel opened by the energy pool. Now that the contact has been made, you should be able to reestablish it away from the pool."

"Well, that sounds simple enough. How, exactly, if I might ask?"

"One thing I can think of would be to use your emotional connection. Go to somewhere that had a special significance for both of you, for example. Try to re-create how you felt, then try to remember her being there with you."

I thought about it for a minute, but couldn't come up with anything. I'm not much for special places, and neither had Sherwood been. Our relationship had developed gradually, in part simply from spending so much time together working for Victor, so there wasn't even a first-date type of thing to use. There was another first, of course, but I don't think my bedroom would qualify as a special magic place.

"I can't think of anywhere," I said.

"You're such a romantic," said Victor.

"Well," Eli said after a moment, "there has to be somewhere, doesn't there? You've known her forever, and you practically lived together that one year. At least there must have been a place in this world she had a special connection to, even if it didn't directly involve you."

"Or if you have no special place, then somewhere like a graveyard would be best, of course," Victor said. "The veil between worlds. That sort of thing."

"Yeah," I said, not sure if it was sarcasm on his part. "Preferably at midnight, on a dank and foggy night with a chill wind swirling through the headstones." Then I stopped, memory flooding back. "The Columbarium."

"What's the Columbarium?" Timothy asked.

Eli looked at him in surprise. "How long have you lived here, anyway?"

He shrugged. "There are a lot of things I haven't heard of. I'm a computer guy, remember? I have no other life." Eli shook his head in resignation.

"A columbarium is a building or vault that is used as a storage place for the ashes of the dead. So it's a cemetery of sorts, and the Columbarium in San Francisco is one famous example. It's over in the Richmond, close to Golden Gate Park."

"I went there once with Sherwood," I said. "Her parents are both there. They were killed in an auto accident, remember? Their cremains are in one of the little niches."

"Perfect," said Eli.

"But what do I do once I'm there? Will Sherwood will be popping up out of a corner to embrace me warmly?"

Eli gazed at me with a fond tolerance. He knew me, and knew that when I get flip and dismissive it's because I'm either upset or worried.

"Who knows?" he said. "But if there's anywhere you might reestablish the connection, I think there's a very good chance it would be there. It's got all the requirements. Another thing that will help is if you could bring a keepsake with you—something that will help connect her to both you and the here and now. You must have something she gave you, some object, something special."

I didn't have to think about very hard about that one. I had just the thing.

"Okay," I said. "I'll give it a try."

ON THE WAY HOME I STOPPED BY MY FAVORITE taqueria to pick up a burrito. At Twentieth and Mission there's never any parking, but for once there was an open meter right in front, so I sprang for a couple of quarters.

I ordered a carne asada burrito to go. The burritos there are enormous, more than enough for me even sharing with Lou. He would have preferred an entire one to himself, but a few lunches like that and he'd be waddling instead of prancing down the street.

A few customers ahead of me picked up their orders and left. El Farolito was always busy at night, but afternoons could be slow. The only people left in the place were a trio sitting at one of the small Formica-topped tables along the side wall.

I watched them idly as I waited for my burrito, as one sometimes does in restaurants. An older couple, in their late fifties I would guess, and a young woman, probably their daughter. The couple had that indefinable air of out-of-towners, something that included the clothes they wore, the way they sat, and the curious glances they cast at everything around them. Natives, by the time they've reached that age, are blasé even about things they shouldn't be.

On the other hand, the daughter clearly was a city resident. Again, it's something hard to quantify, but you can always tell if someone belongs. She had short black hair, and when she turned her back I could see the top of a colored tattoo peeking out just below the neck of her red top.

So they were parents visiting their daughter, and she was showing them around the city. I gave her points for taking them to a Mission taqueria instead of Fisherman's Wharf, and bonus points for choosing El Farolito over classier and less tasty establishments.

Her parents were scarfing down their burritos with the gusto of intrepid explorers bravely indulging in some exotic cuisine. The daughter looked up and caught me staring at her, which was embarrassing because she was quite attractive, and the natural assumption would be that I was scoping out her obvious charms. Which was true, but not really.

I gave her my well-practiced open and nonthreatening smile, the one that says friendly interest but nothing more, and certainly nothing creepy. She stared back at me with a totally flat affect, giving me nothing. It was beginning to make me nervous when she made a decision and smiled back, jerking her head over at her parents and doing just the hint of an eye roll. It wasn't mean; in fact, it was done with fond affection, like a mother with unruly kids at the ice cream parlor. A real smile replaced my practiced one; I couldn't help it. And she saw that, too, and her own smile widened.

So far, I had established a deeper relationship with this woman than I'd had with any woman in the past year, with one notable and sad exception. Too bad I was unlikely to ever see her again.

Then her mother, who had been tearing into her burrito, stopped. She sat quietly for a moment before rising slowly to her feet and standing there, immobile and silent. He husband stopped talking to her and a look of concern appeared on his face. He jumped up and took her arm.

"Lily? Are you all right?" She didn't answer, just stood there hunched over slightly.

Shit, I thought. *That woman is choking.*

The husband realized it about the same time I did and started pounding her on the back, which never does any good. I took a quick peek at the door to see if perhaps a paramedic team might have decided to stop by for a bite, but no such luck.

I didn't have a handy spell available to dislodge a fat burrito from a narrow throat, but I had once taken a class in the Heimlich maneuver at Victor's insistence. That was ages ago, though, and I'd never had to use it. It looked like that long drought was about to come to an end.

I moved toward their table, not running, but close to it. The husband saw me coming, and God knows what he thought. He might have been leery of being in the Mission anyway, and now his wife was choking and a stranger was rushing toward them with unknown intentions.

I'm six feet tall, I hadn't shaved, I was wearing old disreputable clothes, and my dark hair was shaggy and unkempt. I must have looked threatening to him, like what he imagined a Mission gang member to look like, although the typical gang member is more often a baby-faced sixteen-year-old with a semiautomatic. But he didn't hesitate. He jumped in front of me, interposing his body between me and his wife, and stood ready to defend her. His daughter grabbed him and pulled him aside.

"It's okay, Dad. It's okay," she said. I hoped she was right.

I slipped behind the mother and put my arms around her. She didn't resist; she at least knew what I was up to. I took a moment to review what I'd learned. Find the xiphoid process. Check. Go two fingers below that. Check. Be careful not to be too rough; older bones are fragile and you can break ribs. Check. Make a fist, cover with your other hand, and give a sharp upward thrust. Nothing to it.

Except when I did, nothing happened. No rush of air, no wheezing gasp, no flying food. Nothing. I pushed down the beginnings of panic and thrust again, harder this time. Still nothing. I forgot about being careful and gave three more thrusts, each harder than the last, ribs be damned. On the third squeeze, a large chunk of burrito flew out her mouth and halfway across the restaurant aisle. She took a huge whooping gasp of air as I released her, and then it was over.

I backed off as the other two sat her down, making sure she was all right. She waved them off.

"I'm fine," she said, when she caught her breath. "Really." She looked up at me. "Thank you, young man. I thought for a moment I'd never see Cincinnati again."

"Glad I could help," I said.

The daughter came up to me and held out her hand. Up close, she was even more attractive, though she looked shaken at the moment.

"I'm Morgan," she said. "Thank you so much."

"Mason," I said, taking her hand. "Well, at least we'll have quite a story to tell our children."

Now that the crisis was past, I immediately reverted back to my default flip demeanor. Not an admirable quality, but I'm working on it. She looked at me with that same flat affect and I thought I'd gone too far, but then she smiled again.

"How do you know I'm not married?" she said. "Or gay? Or both?"

"We could still have kids." She moved back a step and looked me over.

"Possibly," she said, after a significant pause. "But I'd have to see how you clean up. Do you have a job?"

"I'm a musician," I said.

"Oh."

"No," I protested, "a real one. I get paid. Most of the time." She continued to look at me skeptically. "In fact, I'm playing tonight at the Glow Worm."

I wasn't sure if she would have heard of the club, since it's mostly for jazz aficionados, but she raised her eyebrows in appreciation.

"Oh, you play jazz," she said.

The way she said it didn't give a clue if she thought that was a plus or a minus, but at least she'd heard of the place and knew it featured jazz, which was something.

"I'm a guitar player—it's a trio gig. You should come by. Seven thirty for the first set."

"Maybe I will," she said.

Meanwhile, her father was looking at her with exasperation and disbelief. After all, her mother had almost choked to death, and here she was, flirting with a stranger, one bare minute later. He started to say something, but his wife put her hand on his arm and shook her head.

I retrieved my burrito and gave them all a wave as I left. I don't usually hit on nonpractitioners, no matter how attractive; it always turns out to be more trouble than it's worth unless you're talking a one-night stand, and that's something I haven't done in a couple of years.

But there had been an instant connection, even before the choking incident. If not for that, I would have just quietly departed, but this was a special circumstance. Surely I deserved some reward for saving a life.

Lou had his nose pressed impatiently against the window of the van. I'd been in there longer than I expected and the meter had run out. I was lucky there wasn't a ticket waiting for me. He looked at me expectantly when I climbed behind the wheel, but I made him wait until we got home. My van may be old and battered, but I still didn't want scraps of burrito strewn all over the seats.

"I just saved someone's life," I told him. "What have you done today?"

He stared fixedly at the paper sack with the burrito and ignored me.

At home, I ate my burrito slowly, pondering what Eli had said. Lou finished his portion in ten seconds and then expected more, but he gave up when it became clear I wasn't holding anything back.

By the time I finished my lunch it was close on three. Still plenty of time to get out to the Columbarium. I dawdled around for a while, reluctant to go. I wanted to know what that apparition of Sherwood signified, and yes, I had to know if there was a chance she was still alive; but still, the whole idea was creepy and unsettling. But I had to try. That wasn't even a question.

That thing she'd given to me, that special token with meaning, rested in the drawer of the nightstand next to my bed. Next to it was another token, a talisman Campbell had given me—a figure of ancient ivory and wood, a two-legged figure with the head of a wolf. The wolf was my totem, and twice now, that totem had called up help from God knows where and saved my hide.

But it had gone dead. Before, it had been alive, powerful, and a bit disturbing. Now it was inert, no more magically alive than any other antique curio in a dusty shop. I didn't know if it would ever operate again—it had been my security blanket, always there in the most dire of straits. Maybe I'd used it once too often.

I shoved the wolf figure back into a corner of the drawer and picked up Sherwood's gift, tossing it from hand to hand, contemplating. It was the only thing I had to remember her by—a figure of a guitar player made from one continuous strand of thick wire that she'd bought at a street fair one day, simple but clever. It reminded me of how it had been back then, when we were newly in love and took delight in the silliest of things.

I put it in my pocket, checked the Columbarium address on the Web to make sure I remembered it right, and five minutes later was on my way to the Richmond District.

The Columbarium sits at the end of a dead-end street, a large, neoclassical domed building, surprisingly light and airy. I parked a few blocks away and walked over, Lou by my side. It might have been more appropriate for my purposes if it had been dank and foggy, but the afternoon was bright and sunny, with a light breeze ruffling my hair.

Off to one side of the main building was a small courtyard with a fountain. Next to it, an immaculately groomed lawn, but behind the lawn was an untended field, overgrown with weeds. In back of the field were bushes of forsythia, bursting with color, but they, too, hadn't been tended to in quite some time. Maybe the contrast between the manicured lawn and the neglected field was some sort of philosophical statement about life and death, or maybe were just short on money.

I circled the outside until I reached the entrance. There wasn't a person in sight, so I gestured to Lou and we walked in. I'm almost positive dogs are not welcome in a shrine to the dead, but with no one around who was to complain? Certainly not the departed. And he'd come in handy if another apparition appeared.

Inside, it was deserted as well. Daylight streamed through the mandala of the glass dome at the top, throwing flickers of sunlight over the tessellated floor where tiled spokes radiated out from the middle, with marble columns surrounding the center. Boxes of Kleenex had been discreetly placed in small recesses next to each column. Large stained-glass windows glowed brightly, mostly depicting fierce winged angels.

Along every wall, recesses filled with urns or chests faced inward, like nothing so much as a room of safe-deposit boxes in a bank. I strolled by, reading the names: Saunders, Markey, Von Ronn, Hisieh, Silver, Yu. Several levels were visible, circular tiers like a wedding cake.

Sherwood's parents were in a niche somewhere up above, but I couldn't remember exactly where. From on high, hidden speakers poured out an old Jeff Buckley song, echoing eerily throughout the space. Someone had set the player on repeat so the song played over and over, but it wasn't annoying. After a while it was like Buddhist chanting, an integral part of the space, eternal and unchanging.

I had thought this time the place might feel odd, a bit creepy even, considering why I was there, but no. With the sun shining in and the music playing, it was light and pleasant. Peaceful, but not the quiet and weighty peacefulness of the graveyard—more like the quiet of a screened porch on a fine and lazy summer's day in the country, where the owners of the house had unexpectedly stepped out for a moment.

It was all quite lovely, but it wasn't getting me any closer to my goal. I found the stairs that led to the next level. More niches, some with personal items that clearly had meant something—a harmonica, a pair of reading glasses, ballet shoes, an antique dentist drill. It was surprisingly affecting—not sad, just touching.

Photographs were everywhere. Many showed young men, arms linked around friends, smiling at the camera. Others watched as dogs frolicked happily on the grass. Faces were licked; wagging tails were stopped midmotion, frozen in time forever. The men had all died young, disproportionally so for a place of the dead. I wondered about it until I noticed the ending dates, almost all in the early eighties. That was when the AIDS epidemic had raged through San Francisco, cutting short thousands of young lives. I gazed at these shrines, filled with mementoes. And thought of all the wasted potential, all the pain, all the sorrow of those left behind. I found myself in the odd position of missing people I had never known.

Up I went, circling around until I reached the top level,

where a side room caught my attention. A small window of stained glass was set in the ceiling, no more than two feet from the top of my head. Sunlight streamed in, casting a cheery glow over the room. Glass cases had replaced the usual niches, filled to overflowing with keepsakes. It was more reminiscent of an ancient curio shop than it was a final resting place.

Lou wandered around the room, respectfully subdued, sniffing at the glass cases. This wouldn't be a bad room for a final resting place, I thought. Light. Airy. Downright . . . pleasant. Although if things continued on as they had the last couple of years, it seemed unlikely I was going to be blessed with a peaceful end.

I watched Lou carefully for any signs he'd noticed ghostly activity, but he was relaxed and content to wander aimlessly. I took out the wire figure of the guitar player I'd brought and tried to concentrate on Sherwood, remembering when she'd given it to me, how she'd looked, how I'd felt when we were still close in that special way. Nothing.

The room was so peaceful I was loath to leave, but I wasn't getting anywhere. I beckoned to Lou and returned to the ground floor. The music was still echoing through the air, and through sheer repetition it had finally lost its nostalgic charm and taken on a melancholy aspect. I stood in the center of the main floor for one last look, then headed toward the door to the outside.

I'd almost made it to the door when I noticed Lou wasn't following. He had stayed at the center of the room and was staring at the back stained-glass window with an air of puzzlement. I walked back to see what he was looking at.

"What is it?" I asked.

Lou glanced over his shoulder briefly before turning his attention back to the window. The form of an angel, wings outstretched, filled almost the entirety of the stained glass. As random clouds outside passed over the sun, the angel alternately glowed and dimmed, pulsing with an internal life. The slight smile on the angel's face changed subtly each time the light varied, first soft and compassionate, then gently mocking, then sad, then almost cruel. The figure grew brighter as I watched, and at the same time the temperature in the room dropped twenty degrees.

Uh-oh. I'd wanted some indication of paranormal activity, but now that it was here it was making me nervous. I'd been hoping for a warm presence, or maybe a set of instructions appearing in bright glowing letters on a dusty wall. The angel in front of me was taking on a sinister aspect, awesome in the old sense of the word, not cool, but worthy of fear and dread.

The figure of the angel grew until it filled the room, so bright I could barely look at it. Its face began to seem familiar, idealized yet more personal than before. I could almost put a name to it, like a well-known but seldom-seen acquaintance. I closed my eyes for a second to get some relief from the blinding light, and when I opened them again I was staring into the eyes of Sherwood.

Her face grew brighter still, until all I could see was radiant light. I was adrift in a formless void, an impossibly bright fog without shape or form. The only sound was a faint susurration like wind or surf. I stood there for a while, at a loss. Then I heard the softest whisper of a tune, barely audible above the background noise. It was hard to locate—the sound came from all directions at once. I stood quietly, hoping it would increase in volume enough to provide a direction, but no luck. I could hardly start walking off into the featureless void; God only knew if I'd be able to find my way back. Where the hell was Lou, now that I really needed him?

A sharp nose poking into the back of my knee answered that question. I should have known. Another poke, more insistent. I bent down and grabbed hold of his collar, and the second I did, he started moving off in what I assumed was a direction. This wasn't going to work, though.

Since he's only a foot tall, the only way I could keep hold
of the collar and walk was to bend over almost double and
shuffle along like a very old man.

"Lou!" I said, letting go of the collar. "Go ahead. Bark,
so I can follow."

I had expected my voice to sound muffled, like it
would have been in thick fog, but it was surprisingly clear.
Lou gave a short bark and moved off. A few seconds later
I heard a strong bark up ahead, and as I moved in that
direction another bark, farther on.

We did this bark-and-follow routine for a while, until
the formless light began to ease, and I could see dim out-
lines of a landscape. At the same time, the song I'd been
hearing grew louder until I could make out the words and
tune.

It was an old Irish ballad Sherwood had dug up from
somewhere, one of her favorite tunes. I'd even worked out
a simple guitar arrangement for her so she could accompany herself when she sang. And it was her voice singing;
I'd heard her sing it often enough so there was no doubt.
The haunting tune echoed over the emerging landscape, or
maybe it was echoing in my head.

> *Won't you come from out that shadow,*
> *Will you turn your back on grief?*
> *You can lie down here beside me*
> *If that brings some small relief.*

I could hear it clearly enough now to follow the sound.
As I walked, the landscape solidified, slipping into focus.
I was on a high moor, with rocky crags and gorse and
heather stretching out to a distant horizon in every direction. A chill wind was gusting, whipping around my ears
and blowing through my hair, which had grown longer
than usual of late. Wisps of fog drifted over the ground,
blotting out some features and suddenly revealing others.
I could smell the odor of plant and peat, smoky and clean
at the same time.

Lou trotted along beside me, unflappable as ever. To him, this sort of experience wasn't that different from a trip to the burrito store. But this wasn't a real place. There were a lot of reasons it couldn't be, but I didn't need to be clever about it. There was one obvious clue, large enough even for me to get it. Everything was in black and white.

It wasn't a problem with my vision. Lou still had his tan chest patch and tan paws and those tan marks over his eyes. But everything else was like a black-and-white movie, *The Hound of the Baskervilles*, maybe. Or even better, *Wuthering Heights*. The minute I thought of that I knew it made sense. Why, I had no idea, but it was no coincidence. *Wuthering Heights* had been Sherwood's favorite movie, the one with Laurence Olivier and Merle Oberon. A strange, romantic choice for someone otherwise so practical, but there it was.

She'd made me watch it once, bringing over a DVD, and surprisingly, I liked it. But when I made a comment about what an asshole Heathcliff basically was, she looked at me sadly and said, "Yes, but it doesn't matter. It's about passion, you see."

Lou gave another short bark and pointed his nose toward the top of a nearby crag. A figure stood there, motionless, back toward me, long hair blowing in the wind. It stared out over the moor as I climbed toward it, oblivious to my approach. The slope was steep enough to get me out of breath, whether it was real or not. As I got close, I heard the last refrain of the ballad:

> *May your heart be freed from sorrow.*
> *May the heartbreak finally cease.*
> *May you wake in joy tomorrow.*
> *May you sleep tonight in peace.*

By now I was close enough to recognize Sherwood, even with her back toward me. She stared out over the film-set moor, hair swirling in the breeze. She was Cathy, waiting for Heathcliff to return. The only anachronistic detail was the familiar purple highlights in her dark hair. She, like Lou, was not part of this black-and-white world.

"Sherwood," I said quietly.

She broke off her song but didn't answer. For a long moment she was silent, then slowly turned her head in my direction. Her face was calm, but her affect was flat, as if she weren't fully engaged with the world. Her light gray eyes, usually gleaming with animation, were now cool and reflective. I had to look twice before I could convince myself it was really her.

"Mason?" she said.

I moved closer.

"It's me."

She stared right through me as if I weren't there.

"Mason?" she asked again.

I reached out to touch her arm but stopped at the last moment as Lou gave a soft warning growl. There was something uncanny about her, a noli-me-tangere quality. I withdrew my hand, took a step back, and spoke again.

"Sherwood. Where are we?" Again, the long pause.

"Come get me," she said, ignoring my question.

"How?"

"You can't." She turned her head away from me and I could barely make out her words. "When I go. He must call me. When I go. You can't." This was making no sense at all.

"Who must call you?" I asked. "Eli? Victor?" She mumbled something I couldn't catch, except for "when I go" once again.

I reached out for her again, ignoring Lou's warning. I couldn't just stand there trading cryptic remarks. But when I grabbed hold of her arm it was as if I'd seized an ungrounded power line. A bolt of energy shot through me. I was knocked to the ground, blinded, and it felt like every nerve was exploding out of my body. I lay there stunned for a second, until I heard the strains of familiar music echoing through the air. When I cautiously opened my eyes I was back in the Columbarium, lying on the floor. An elderly black man leaning on a cane was standing over me, face filled with concern.

"Are you okay?" he asked. I got shakily to my feet.

"Yeah, I'm fine," I told him. "Just a dizzy spell. I get them sometimes."

"You sure?"

"I'm okay," I said.

"Well, good." He nodded gravely. "I'm the caretaker here." Lou was standing quietly next to me, and he gestured at him with the cane. "Sorry, but you can't have that dog in here. It's not allowed."

"Sorry," I said. "I didn't know." He looked at me like he knew I was lying and he knew I knew he knew.

"I was just leaving," I assured him. "Come on, Lou."

I walked out the door to the outside, a bit shakily. The world outside was bright with color, blues skies and green trees, a far cry from the black-and-white moor I'd been on only minutes before. I hadn't a clue of what it had meant, but at least I'd have some time to mull it over, with Eli and Victor to help.

As we got up to the van, Lou stopped stock-still and began to growl. Not his warning growl; this was a snarl of pure hatred. Before I could even think, forty pounds of teeth and claws and strength streaked out from behind the van and launched itself at us.

FOUR

ANYONE WALKING BY WOULD HAVE SEEN ONLY a crazed pit bull launching an attack on an unsuspecting victim. But I knew better. It seemed to have gained some size or weight, probably from picking off unwary pets. It had learned to disguise itself; that was why we hadn't heard any reports of strange creatures prowling the city streets. But it hadn't done a very good job. Its ears still had little tufts of fur on them; the claws on its feet scraped the pavement as it came bounding toward us; its movements were quick and jerky, nothing like the smooth and fluid motion of a real dog's gait.

Naturally I didn't have a spell ready to deal with it— my magic doesn't usually work that way. I adapt, taking what I need from the environment around me, using sun and wind and bits of string and the sound of tinkling bells. It works for me; I'm flexible if nothing else, but right now I could have used some of Victor's raw power and clever presets.

The other problem was that this creature was resistant

to magic, much like a true Ifrit would be. So I also could have used one of Victor's extensive collection of firearms.

About halfway to us it slowed momentarily, having trouble deciding on who to attack first. I was the obvious choice; if it attacked Lou, I'd be able to intervene. If it attacked me, there wasn't much Lou could do about it. But it was cautious, and rightly so. One might assume that a puny unarmed human is no match for a wild animal, flush with sharp teeth and tearing claws, but that's not always the case. I'm one hundred and eighty pounds, in shape, and reasonably strong. A four-hundred-pound tiger isn't going to have any trouble with me, but a small carnivore, no matter how vicious, is another matter. Carl Akeley, a famous African explorer and hunter, once strangled an eighty-pound leopard to death with his bare hands after it dropped on him from an overhanging branch.

This creature could tear me up badly. If it got to my throat, it could kill me by ripping open an artery before I could get it off. But I could also kill it, grabbing hold of it and pounding its head against the pavement. It wasn't interested in a Pyrrhic victory.

In the end, I think its obsessive hatred of all things Ifrit was the deciding factor. It swung left and lunged at Lou, the jaws of its curiously flattened face snapping shut inches from his tail.

I didn't think twice. I glanced up at the Columbarium dome scattering sunlight through the air, twisted the refraction, and neatly divided Lou into five dogs. Not real dogs, of course; Lou and four illusions. Since the creature was related to Ifrits in some way, no illusion would fool it for more than a second. Not if they would obligingly stand still, that was. But with five small identical dogs running frantically in different directions, each one twisting and turning, it wasn't so easy to tell the real from the fake.

It picked one at random and went after it. Man, the thing was fast. It caught up to the fleeing dog and fastened its jaws on the back of the dog's neck, and I had a mo-

ment's sick fear that it had guessed right. But no worry;
Lou wouldn't have let himself be caught so easily. The
jaws chomped down on nothing at all, with the imitation
dog continuing its run as if nothing had happened.

I took advantage of the mistake by sprinting toward the
van. The creature saw and came after me, but I had too
much of a head start. I jumped in the front seat and slammed
the driver's door in its face an instant before it could reach
me. Leaning across the seat, I rolled down the passenger-
side window and put the van in gear before it could make
it around to the other side.

The fake dogs were still running in circles as I roared
off down the street, but the real Lou was easy to spot now.
He had stopped and was standing motionless, looking with
total disbelief at the van speeding away. I slammed on the
brakes and yelled at the top of my voice.

"Come *on*! Through the window. Get a move on!"

He came tearing across the street, running at full tilt.
Instantly the fake Ifrit was on his heels, no more than fifteen feet behind him. Without breaking stride, Lou launched
himself through the air like an Olympic hurdler, making it
through the window cleanly. The thing sprang through the
air after him, but I hit the gas, and by the time it reached
the window, the van had moved far enough so that it hit
the side of the van instead, making a satisfying thump.

The rearview mirror showed me its stunned form crumpled in the street. I swung the van around and gunned the
engine, aiming for it. Not nearly as subtle as a binding
spell, but I'm not picky. I thought I was going to get it, but
at the last moment it scrabbled off to the side and ducked
behind a parked car. Two seconds later, it was stumbling
off through a gap between two houses. Lou was staring
out through the open window, teeth bared. He didn't like
that thing at all.

I'd intended to go home and think through what had
happened with Sherwood, but instead I drove toward Victor's. This new development was worrisome. How the hell
had it known we were here? And if it could track me so

easily, what would prevent it from lying in wait outside my house?

What I needed was not a collection of handy spells; I needed one of Victor's useful collection of deadly fire-arms. Not that he would hand one over gladly. He'd taken me out to a firing range in the East Bay a month ago, but he still didn't trust me with guns.

"You never know," he'd said. "Magic's not always the best option. If you're working with me, I don't want you fumbling with the slide on an automatic while that rabid creature is busy tearing at my throat."

He had a point, but I wasn't as clueless about firearms as he assumed. And it was about time I started taking that thing seriously.

Victor was at his desk, working. He was usually work-ing on something—just sitting around and chilling doesn't seem to be part of his makeup, even with a bad leg. Timo-thy was there as well, which was unusual.

"Off work early?" I asked.

He ran his hand through dark, unruly hair. He'd recently added a couple of tiny gold hoops to his left ear to keep the others in it company. Pretty soon he was going to run out of ear, though.

"I quit."

"Oh? Is that good or bad?"

Tim worked for a dot-com, one of the few that was still in business. Long gone were the days where you could bring your dog to work and get rich at the same time. Mostly, people there were now happy just to have a job.

"Oh, it's good. I was getting bored. I made a lot of con-tacts there, though, and I think I can make a pretty good living just doing contract work, troubleshooting and stuff."

Lou ran over to greet him. Timothy was not a practi-tioner; he was just a normal person, but he was still one of Lou's favorites. Tim reached into his pocket, pulled out a Snausage, and offered it to Lou, who accepted it gravely. He was just being polite; he doesn't really care for them that much. In fact, his attitude toward all things dog food are about the same as mine about tofu—he'll eat it if he's really hungry, but it's no cause for celebration.

Victor looked up from his desk with a quick glance of inquiry. He knew I didn't stop by for random chats.

"I need a gun," I said.

"I seriously doubt that. What for?"

I told him about the fake Ifrit showing up at the Columbarium, as well as the vision of Sherwood I'd seen. Eli would have been more interested in the Sherwood story; Victor, ever the pragmatist, was more focused right now on the fake Ifrit. He had a point—Sherwood's apparition could wait, but the Ifrit was a serious and immediate threat.

"So how did it find me there?" I concluded. "Why hasn't it appeared before? And how about lending me something that will blow its head off next time it shows up?"

Timothy had been listening carefully. There was a time when I would have been more circumspect around him, since he's not a practitioner, after all, but by now he was one of the family. I trusted him as much as I did Victor. Maybe more.

"Think a moment. What did you do that was different today?" he said.

"You mean besides calling up a vision of a long-dead girlfriend?"

Then I got what he was saying. Of course. Whatever the vision had been, it had involved some sort of enormous magical dislocation. For a creature sensitive to such things it must have lit up the magical landscape like a fireworks display.

Victor looked over at Timothy and nodded approvingly.

"Good point," he said. "It was the evocation that drew it to you. And the last place we saw it was at the Presidio. It could easily have been hiding out in Golden Gate Park, right next door."

"Wasn't there a family of coyotes living there last year?" Timothy said. "They had to track them down and shoot them when they started attacking joggers, remember?"

"Okay, fine," I said. "So it's not going to be hiding behind every bush ready to leap out at me. But I'd still like something more than a couple of illusion spells for protection."

"Fair enough," said Victor, after a moment's thought.

He walked over to the giant safe in the corner of the room and spun the dial a few times. The safe is at least six feet tall and surprisingly deep, and you could cram a lot of stuff in there. Sometimes I wondered if he hadn't magically enhanced the inside space in some fashion. He was more than capable of something like that, and it always seemed there was way too much stuff in there, even for a safe that size.

Victor keeps his more potent magical tools in there, along with some rare artifacts. He also keeps an AK-47 assault rifle locked away, as I knew from experience.

After fiddling with the dial some more he swung open the safe door and rummaged around inside. Eventually he pulled out a long object swaddled in cloth. I could see a rifle barrel poking out of the top, and recognized it immediately.

"The AK- 47?" I asked. "I thought you didn't trust me with such things."

"Don't be ridiculous," he said. "You'd end up blowing off your own leg." He reached back farther into the safe and pulled out another weapon, giving a grunt of satisfaction. "This should fill the bill."

I was disappointed, but also relieved. I'd never shot an automatic assault rifle and a street confrontation is no time to be learning. But I did know how to use the weapon he had in his hand: a perfectly ordinary shotgun.

My grandfather was a man who had possessed quite a bit of talent himself, though I never knew it at the time. But he was also a hunter of small, inoffensive quail and large, strident geese, and by the time I was twelve he had taught me all I needed to know about those weapons. The one Victor held was a standard Remington 12-gauge pump, the workhorse of shotguns.

"I don't suppose you've ever fired one of these," Victor said.

"That Remington?" I said. "What is it, an 870? Actually I prefer the Browning over and under. But that's more for hunting birds. This one will do just fine, I imagine. Holds, what, five rounds?"

Victor looked at me suspiciously, sure I was putting him on. I gazed back blandly, then took the shotgun out of his hands, pressed the slide release catch, and cycled the pump a couple of times to make sure it was unloaded.

"What do you think?" I said. "Buckshot or slugs?"

For once I had Victor at a loss for words. His notions about me didn't include my having familiarity with firearms of any sort, even after the session at the range. I couldn't blame him, but it was nice for once to throw him a curve. Timothy watched, grinning, making no effort to hide his amusement.

Victor struggled for a moment with the desire to ask me where I'd acquired such expertise, then decided to pretend it was no surprise at all.

"Both," he said, as if it were the most obvious question in the world. "You might miss with slugs; load four buckshot and one slug. Lead, not steel. Load the slug in first, keeping it for the last chance in case the buckshot doesn't do the job."

"Got it," I said.

He stared at me again, shaking his head almost imperceptibly before reaching back into the safe. He brought out two boxes of shells, one of double-ought shot and one of rifled slugs. I closed the slide so there wouldn't be a round chambered, slid a slug round in first, then the four buckshot shells so the slug would be the last to be fired. First in, last out. I clicked on the safety, just to be double safe, hefted the gun, and smiled.

"Thanks," I said. "This might come in handy."

I HAD JUST ENOUGH TIME TO CATCH A QUICK bite and make it to my gig at the Glow Worm. Now that Jazz at Pearl's had closed once again, the Glow Worm was the only place left trying to uphold the tradition of quality jazz in North Beach. It was too bad about Pearl's; it had been a great venue with a lot of tradition and history. But it had closed before—it's not an easy task to make a jazz club financially successful. It always seems to resurrect itself from the ashes, though.

I debated about whether to take Lou along and decided not. I like having him nearby but he couldn't hang out at the club, and North Beach is a tough place for a dog on the streets—the sidewalks are often crowded with tourists, and someone would eventually decide he needed a home and try to scoop him up. I didn't want him biting anyone. Besides, I had the shotgun now, just in case. I couldn't take it up on the bandstand, but I could at least have it handy in my van.

The Glow Worm is on Columbus Avenue, not far from Pearl's. You'd think that since jazz clubs tend to struggle anyway, having two of them on the same street wasn't the smartest move. Maybe that had been a factor in the demise of Pearl's. So far, the Glow Worm seemed to be holding its own.

I parked in a nearby lot that had a discount arrangement with the club for the musicians, which is another indication they're a class act.

Weekends usually feature an out-of-town big name, with the rest of the week dedicated to locals. It's as much a supper club as it is anything else—appetizers are served at the front tables closest to the bandstand and full dinners farther back in a raised portion to the rear. The food's excellent, and a lot of tourists frequent the place for the food as much as for the music. The live jazz being played up front serves mostly as high-class Muzak to accompany the meal.

I didn't mind. The club paid well and a working musician can't afford to be a snob. Besides, there were always a few people down front who came for the music.

I got there about seven and set up. I'd been gigging fairly regularly with Dave, the bass player from Oakland,

and Roger Chu, the wunderkind drummer I'd gigged with at Julio's at few months ago. After a couple of gigs he'd got over his pathological shyness, and he turned out to be a great kid with a wicked sense of humor. Except, he called me "Gramps" all the time, which I didn't find all that amusing. He was an amazing drummer, though, energetic and subtle at the same time.

There was a good supper crowd, and we started right at seven. Just as we launched into the first tune, Morgan walked in wearing a black long-sleeved top and loose-fitting jeans. I hadn't really expected her to show up, so it was a pleasant surprise. She had her parents in tow, which meant either she was a dutiful daughter, or she had no interest in me, or she felt she needed protection from possible lecherous intentions. Or all three. They took one of the free tables down front and ordered drinks. I caught her eye and she gave a little wave hello.

We played a relaxed set. People at dinner don't want discordant and "interesting"; they want melodic and relaxing. We played mostly standards but did slip in one of my own tunes right before the break, a ballad based on a re-harmonization of "What Is This Thing Called Love?" and I did manage to throw in some outside playing.

After the set, I joined them at the table and asked the waiter for a Calistoga water.

"A wonderful set," said the father. "Outstanding. That last tune—one of yours? Based on 'What Is This Thing Called Love?' wasn't it?"

"But reharmonized," Morgan added.

Okay. Actual jazz buffs. What were the odds?

"Do you play?" I asked, looking at them both. The father shook his head.

"No, not me." He waved a hand at Morgan. "Now, my dad, her grandfather, he played in swing bands all through the thirties and forties. I grew up on that music and never stopped listening. Morgan's taste is a bit more modern, but she still caught the jazz bug."

The mother held out her hand to me. "I'm Lily," she said. "I just want introduce myself properly and thank you again for this afternoon."

"And I'm Frank," the father said. "That goes double for me."

They both sat there beaming at me. Nice, friendly, very normal people, totally unaware of the world I lived in, the world of deadly creatures and dangerous practitioners. I had a moment of envy, nostalgia for a life I'd never had and never would.

Of course, it wasn't a life I wanted. It wasn't a life that would have made me happy. But sometimes I thought about how much simpler things would have been if I hadn't been born with talent. Then again, if I hadn't been blessed with talent, I'd never have known Lou.

"Right place, right time," I said, acknowledging their thanks. "Just luck." I changed the subject quickly. "Are you in San Francisco for a visit?"

"Oh, yes," said Lily. "Morgan here's been a little down lately, so we thought we'd visit and cheer her up." She looked over brightly at her daughter. "She just broke up with her boyfriend."

Morgan was in the act of lifting a glass of wine to her mouth. She froze, glass suspended inches from her lips. Her head slowly turned until she was looking directly at her mother. There was going to be a reckoning after they left, without doubt. Lily blithely continued on as if unaware, though I doubt she was.

"She was too good for him anyway."

I hastily excused myself and off off to the bar to get another Calistoga. It was getting uncomfortable at the table, and I thought I'd give them a few minutes to sort it out. Dave was standing at the bar with a beer in his hand. I try not to drink at gigs, but Dave has no such rule. Wunderkind Roger had no such option, being all of seventeen.

"Who's the lady?" Dave asked.

"Just someone I met recently."

"Lucky you."

"Well, unlike you, I'm not married."

"As I said, lucky you."

Dave liked to play the long-suffering married man tethered to a ball and chain, but it was all an act. He's happily married with two kids, and the last time a woman had hit on him, he'd run into the men's room and hid.

I snagged my water and returned to the table. Morgan's face was set, and her mother seemed a bit subdued. This posed something of a dilemma. I didn't know if they'd be staying for another set, so I wanted to take my chance and ask her out. But asking out a young woman while she's sitting at a table with her parents is not the easiest task, even for someone adept at such things, which I'm not. And the residual tension at the table made it even more difficult.

So I indulged in the usual small talk with her parents—how they liked San Francisco, what they did back home, how tough it was being a musician these days—until it was time for the second set.

"Time to play," I said. "Can you stand to hear another set?"

"Wouldn't miss it," said Morgan, smiling. So she was interested. Or maybe she just liked my playing. Hopefully, both.

I concentrated more on my playing for the second set. Now that I knew she was a knowledgeable listener, I wanted to impress her with my ability. Pitiful, really, like a high school jock hoping to score a touchdown so he'd have a better chance of scoring with the cheerleader after the game. But there you have it.

When I rejoined their table after the set, Morgan smiled approvingly. "Very nice," she said. "Very nice indeed. And I love that drummer."

Of course. Everybody loved that drummer. Partly because he was so young, but mostly because he was the best drummer around. Pretty soon other musicians in town were going to catch on to that, and he'd be snapped up by a big name. New York or L.A. would be beckoning.

"He is good," I said.

"He looks so young—he really surprised me."

"And Morgan's difficult to surprise," her mother said. She beamed proudly. "Morgan's a psychic, you know."

Again, the glass of wine was suspended halfway to Morgan's lips, and her head turned slowly with a glare terrible to behold. I was never going to get a date out of this.

"How interesting," I said quickly, hoping to deflect her. It worked. The glare became fastened on me. "How does it work? Can you tell something about me?" I was babbling inanely, digging myself an even deeper hole.

"Go on, show him, hon," her mother said, ignoring Morgan's glare.

It was hard not to laugh, and Morgan could see it. This was going from bad to worse. She would be thinking I was laughing at her, when I was laughing at the whole dynamic between her and her well-meaning, clueless parents.

I threw up my hands in wordless supplication, hoping she'd understand. If she was psychic, maybe she'd pick up on that. She looked at me with that same flat affect I'd noticed at the taqueria, then looked at her mother, then back at me. The corner of her mouth twitched, and a small snort of laughter escaped. Which of course set me off, and then we were both laughing uncontrollably. Her parents looked at us in bewilderment.

"What's so funny?" her dad asked, which naturally set us off again.

"Nothing," she said.

"Are you really?" I said. Now that the ice was broken, it seemed the most natural question in the world.

"Sort of. I don't usually talk about it, because people then think I'm a New Age kook, which I'm not." She sent a significant glance over toward her mom. "But, yes."

She looked at me not with a challenge, but with resignation, like she knew what I was thinking.

"I've seen a lot of strange things in my time," I said.

She had no idea how true that was. "I'm not about to dismiss any possibilities."

"Show him, why don't you?" her mother repeated.

She cocked her head to one side, shrugged in defeat, and said, "Okay, why not? Give me your hands."

I did so, reaching across the small table, palms down. She slid her hands under mine and grasped my wrists. Her hands were long and slim, and cool even in the hot atmosphere of the club. She closed her eyes, took a deep breath, and let half of it out, just like a shooter on a target range. After a pause, she started breathing again, slow and measured. I wondered if I would feel any surge of energy coming off her. Many times, those who are termed psychics have a small bit of unfocused and untrained talent. They just don't realize what it is.

I felt nothing, though. Just a sense of calmness and peace. Morgan's deep and even breathing was oddly soothing, and my mind started to wander. Then, with no warning, she gasped and abruptly released my wrists, jerking back in her chair so violently that it almost overbalanced.

Her mother reached over and touched her arm in concern. Morgan took a deep breath to steady herself.

"I'm fine," she said. "But it's getting late. Why don't you and Dad get the car, and I'll settle up here and meet you outside? My treat tonight."

Mom and Dad both looked dubious, but they knew their daughter. They got up without too much protest, shook hands with me, and made their way toward the door.

Morgan didn't get up right away, just sat staring at me across the table.

"You look like you want to say something to me," I said, smiling, still trying to keep it light, though that ship had long since sailed. The smile was not returned.

"Okay, listen," she said. "I know how weird this is going to sound, believe me. And I know how it makes me look. But I've got to tell you.

"Sometimes, when I do readings for people, nothing

comes. When it does, mostly I get flashes and images, and a lot of what I can tell is just putting together those hints with what I already know about the person. But sometimes, I get a hit of something so strongly, it's almost like being there. And when that happens, I'm never wrong. Well, almost never. And I got something when I grabbed your hands, the strongest images I've ever had. So whatever you think of me, no matter how crazy you think I am, I've got to warn you. I've just got to."

"About what?" I said, genuinely curious. "What did you see?"

"You were in the woods. Tall trees were all around. In fact, I saw the place so clearly I even recognized where it was—I've been there. Muir Woods, and not too far from the entrance, I think. You weren't alone—you had a companion, something like a dog, but it wasn't a dog, not exactly."

I sat up straight in my chair. That was not something I'd expected to hear from her.

"And there was something else. The wind was rushing through the trees, making a sighing, moaning sound. And high up in the branches, something odd—maybe dangerous."

"What was it?"

"I couldn't tell."

"Then how did you know it was dangerous?" I said.

I realized she might think I was pointing out a logical flaw, but I really was seeking information. I'm not as skeptical as I used to be, and her reference to Lou, whom she'd never even met, gave her vision a lot of credibility. She paused a moment, thinking.

"I'm not sure it was. But it was the most peculiar thing I've ever felt. I didn't like it—it made me very nervous. It wasn't an animal, but it didn't feel like a person, either. I know how that sounds, but if I were you, I'd stay away from there, really." She reached across the table and took my hand, slightly embarrassed but determined to make her point. "You don't have to believe me. Just stay away to ease the mind of this crazy woman you met, if you want to look at it that way."

"I don't think you're crazy at all," I said. "In fact, you may have helped me more than you know." She let go of my hand and leaned back in her chair, suddenly suspicious.

"What do you mean by that?"

I really needed to work on my social skills. Instead of making things better, every time I opened my mouth, I made them worse.

"Nothing," I said. "Sometimes I just say things." She didn't believe me, I could tell. But what else could I say?

"Well," she said. "I've got to go. At least be careful."

"Always."

She walked away from the table without looking back. This could have gone better. I hadn't got her number. I didn't know where she lived. I realized I didn't even know her last name. If Lou had only been around, he could have found her anytime, anywhere, but he has to have come in contact with a person before he can track them. Besides, I don't like to use him for that. It feels too much like a cop running the license plate of an attractive woman to find out where she lives.

And I still had a third set to play. Dave and Roger were already up on the bandstand, waiting for me. But as I got up from the table, Morgan returned. She handed me a scrap of paper.

"My number," she said. "Call me and let me know you're all right. When I see something like this, I feel responsible, as if somehow my seeing it makes it come true."

"I will," I said, folding the paper and putting it carefully in my wallet. "But don't worry about me. I'll be fine, honest."

"Yeah," she said. "Call me anyway." She turned and walked away, leaving me looking after her.

The last set was uninspired, but no one noticed. Customers coming in to eat that late were starving and tended to concentrate on their food, and the ones who had been there for a while were three sheets to the wind and couldn't care less about the music.

I played on autopilot, thinking. It was ironic. The vision Morgan had told me about was meant to warn me off, but its effect was just the opposite. I knew the fake Ifrit had come out of that swirling pool of color and energy we'd created, but now, according to Rolf, there was something else roaming through the Bay Area as well. I'd promised to look into what it might be and what might have happened to his friend Richard Cory. Now I thought I knew where to start. Muir Woods was my next destination.

FIVE

IT'S ONLY ABOUT A FORTY-FIVE-MINUTE DRIVE over the Golden Gate Bridge to Muir Woods. Next morning, as I pulled into the parking lot entrance, the sun reflected off the leaves of the high trees, throwing a dappled pattern on the forest floor. There were only a few cars parked there, which was a relief. Usually it's crowded, even on a weekday, and if anything odd were to happen, a bunch of freaked-out civilians was not something I wanted to deal with.

Since the parking lot was deserted I was able to check the shotgun without worry. The slug first, then the buckshot, five rounds in all—the mantra of first in, last out. I could have squeezed an extra round in if I'd racked a shell into the breech and carried it loaded, but I preferred to keep the breech empty for safety's sake. Not to mention that the ugly sound of a round being racked in is enough in itself to discourage all sorts of potential threats. There's a gut reaction to that distinctive sound, one that makes the mouth go dry, and even the bravest tend to freeze in place.

Another minute was all it took to put a concealment

spell on the shotgun. I was getting better at that sort of thing; it didn't take much energy or thought anymore. It helped that I made it appear to be a fishing rod—same general shape and proportions, and in a way, similar in purpose as well. If I'd needed to make it look like a back-pack or a picnic basket, it would have been a lot more difficult and less believable.

The gun was no problem, but Lou was. Dogs aren't al-lowed in Muir Woods, even on a leash. I suppose I could have made him look like a raccoon, but a tame raccoon trailing along beside me would draw even more attention, which was the last thing I wanted.

I decided to rely on his ability to blend in and go unnoticed—not a strictly magical ability, just something he's good at. If we ran into a park ranger, Lou could al-ways slip away into the underbrush before he was noticed.

The woods were cool and quiet, hushed, with the huge, overarching trees providing an atmosphere of almost reli-gious calm, like an ancient church. There's even a favorite spot named Cathedral Grove, so it wasn't just me who felt that way.

I would have loved to relax and enjoy a walk through some of the most beautiful woods in northern California, but I was there on business. The trail that leads up to the falls was surrounded by the logs of giant fallen trees, still covered in mossy green from the winter's rains, and thick brush stretched out beyond them. I kept a wary eye out, constantly glancing from side to side, on alert for the slight-est sound. I wasn't sure what I was looking for, but ac-cording to Morgan's vision it wasn't anything pleasant. And although the fake Ifrit was safely on the other side of the bridge, you never know. I wasn't confident it would stay there. Lou was trotting along nonchalantly, but every so often he would cock his head to one side and twitch an ear, so I knew he was on sharp lookout as well.

It was a beautiful day. Even with Morgan's vision of danger sitting in the back of my mind, the woods were lovely and serene. I followed the main trail through twists and turns, gradually becoming more comfortable. Maybe there wasn't anything here after all. Visions, like oracles, are notoriously unreliable.

The sound of the breeze swirling through the tops of trees was pleasant and hypnotic. I fell into a rhythm as I walked and, even though I knew I should stay alert, found my thoughts drifting.

It wasn't until I'd gone a couple of miles that I noticed the wind had picked up. The soothing music of fluttering leaves and swaying branches had become harsh and grating. A high keening sound echoed through the treetops, setting my teeth on edge. The sun went behind some clouds, and the forest now felt less cheerful, more uncomfortable, and somewhat threatening.

The keening of the wind increased, and underneath it was a low groaning sound, almost subsonic. I was finding it hard to concentrate, and gripped my disguised shotgun more tightly.

A feeling of malaise and dread washed over me, for no reason I could fathom. But it was strong, strong enough to make me break out in a sweat and feel sick to my stomach. Lou stopped moving forward, doubled back past me, and headed back the way we had come. He flashed a glance over his shoulder to tell me it was time to get the hell out of there, and for once I agreed with him. I followed him, and as he broke into a sudden trot, I did the same. But it was too late.

As we hurried back down the path, the feeling of dread didn't fade; it grew stronger. And as I passed around a bend in the trail, I saw why. On the left, on a branch high in the tallest tree, a figure sat casually dangling its legs in the air. It was too far away to see clearly, but I still did. It was a man, of sorts, dressed in greens and browns, almost like one of Robin Hood's merry men. But he was not merry.

His hair was curly, tangled, and colorless, like dried grass. There were stains around his mouth, which was wider than it should have been. His eyes were black and his face narrow and vulpine, blank and expressionless. Except, when he saw me he smiled, and that smile was the most horrible sight you could imagine. All around him a faint aura glowed, shot through with shifting colors, just like the energy pool at the construction site under the bridge. I'd found what I was looking for, or maybe he had found me.

My heart was pounding and my mouth dry. I didn't even think of using talent. Without hesitation I racked a shell into the breech of the shotgun, just in case. He jumped up nimbly, now standing on the branch, and beckoned to me.

"Come," he whispered, and I heard him as clearly as if he had shouted at the top of his voice.

I automatically took one step forward before I could stop myself. Then I started backing away, never taking my eyes off of him. He beckoned again.

"Mason. Follow!" The word reverberated in my head, repeating on an endless loop. He sprang off the branch and onto the branch of an adjoining tree, like some giant mutant squirrel. I started walking toward him; I couldn't help myself. My skin was itching all over and my feet felt like they were on fire. I wanted to stop and pull off my boots, but I couldn't.

It wasn't that I was in thrall. There was no feeling of control; it wasn't like I was struggling against a will more powerful than my own. It wasn't like I felt compelled to follow, not exactly; I just couldn't seem to think of anything else to do. As I walked, I started feeling oddly light. My steps became higher and longer and it took more time to touch earth each time, like gravity was growing weaker and I was walking on the moon.

Lou was unaffected, unsurprisingly, and he was barking constantly, using that high-pitched yelp that cuts through anything, nipping at my heels, trying to distract me and break whatever hold that thing had on me. But it was useless. I was barely conscious of his presence, as if he were some distant and long-forgotten dream.

I still held the shotgun in a death grip. I would have let it fall uselessly to the ground, but I no longer had control

of the muscles needed to open my hands. Lou was growing ever more frantic, and I felt a momentary twinge of
sorrow for him.

Finally, in desperation, he threw himself under my feet
so that one foot came down directly on him. He squealed
in pain as I stumbled and went down, sprawling full length
on the ground. I was still holding the shotgun, and my finger must have remained on the trigger, because it went off
with a roar inches from my head, momentarily deafening
me. At the same time, the butt kicked back and caught me
on the jaw, stunning me.

There was a ringing in my ears, but it broke the spell. I
had about fifteen seconds before my hearing would return,
and with it, my relentless march toward God only knew
what.

I gathered my wits and reached out to the quiet of the
forest. Then I took my own temporary deafness and wove
it into a feedback loop, cutting off all sound. The ringing
faded, but in its place was blessed silence.

The man was becoming impatient and looked somewhat
puzzled. I saw his mouth form words, but heard nothing,
safe in my cocoon of silence. He shrugged and lowered
himself to the next branch down. Agile as he was, it
wouldn't take him more than a moment to reach the forest
floor. I thought about using talent, trying to come up with
some sort of spell to deal with him, but I didn't think about
it for long. Whatever it was, this thing was quite possibly
resistant to magical operations, much like Ifrits are.

Instead, I aimed and squeezed the trigger. The recoil
slammed into my shoulder, but I didn't stop. I racked in
another round without taking the gun from my shoulder,
then another. He was still standing on the branch, one leg
dangling idly to the side. Every shot had missed. Or worse,
maybe they hadn't. I jacked in the last round, the slug, and
aimed more carefully before firing. I thought I saw him
flinch, but I could have imagined it. But he clearly was way
out of my league.

Before he could make it out of the tree I had sprinted

past and was hightailing it back toward the parking lot and my van. Lou was well out in front; I might have knocked the wind out of him, but he could still move faster than I could.

I made it to the van, and was roaring back down Highway 1 in no time. I drove in ghastly silence until I realized I'd neglected to take the hearing spell off. As soon as I was back over the bridge I turned the van toward Victor's. Checking out something for Rolf was one thing, but this was serious and I needed help.

Victor was at his desk in the study, scribbling notes about something. Eli was also there, as usual, and he was annoyed.

"I've been calling you all day," he said. "Were you going to tell me about the Columbarium and Sherwood, or just wait until I asked?"

"Sorry," I said. "I figured Victor would fill you in."

"Well, he did, of course. But I want to hear it from you."

"Okay, but there's something else going on. Something important."

"More important than Sherwood?"

"Well, no. More urgent, though." He regarded me skeptically until I began my story. "You remember how Rolf said something else came out of that energy sink?"

"Rolf?"

"Bridge Guy. His name is Rolf."

"Oh. Of course."

"Well, I found what that was, or at least I think I did. And it's bad."

After I finished the tale, Victor sad, "So it never actually did anything to you, then? I mean, before you tried to kill it?"

"You weren't there. You would have done the same."

"Possibly. But I wouldn't have missed."

"I don't think I did."

Eli had walked over to the window and was staring out at the ocean as if Victor and I didn't exist. I started to ask him a question, but Victor put his finger to his lips and shook his head. We sat there in silence for a good five minutes. The only other thing that happened was that Lou curled up and went to sleep.

"The world is a strange and wondrous place," Eli finally said, turning back from the window. Not a statement that required comment, but I tossed one out anyway.

"Strange, yes. I'm not so sure about the wondrous part." Eli smiled, but in an abstracted fashion. "So what do you think? Apart from it being wondrous and strange?"

"I think we're in very deep waters indeed." He turned to the window, staring out again, his back toward us when he continued. His voice took on that familiar professorial tone, as if lecturing in a classroom. "Now, you'll remember a few months ago, when I posited that some of the creatures you were dealing with were archetypes— werewolves, trolls, and the like. Or rather, their uncontrolled talent had caused them to take on those aspects." I nodded, but of course he couldn't see me. "Well, I think we're dealing with the same thing here, except on a far more powerful level. The energy that helped bring it into existence was enormous—not only from your friend under the bridge and his cohorts but from those rune stones. The fake Ifrit, that horrible creature, was bound by the invocation—limited in scope. Dangerous, but not any more so than any predator with near-human intelligence. But what came next was not a result of a focused spell—so it took on the aspect of legend, and I'm afraid it's very powerful indeed."

"But what is it?" I asked. "I can't recall anything about tree-dwelling men with hypnotic powers.

"It wouldn't have to be an exact replica of anything from mythology," said Victor. "It could be an amalgam of legends—including more modern tales, works of fiction."

"Like H. P. Lovecraft?" I scoffed. "You mean we're lucky they didn't call up Cthulhu, lord of the universe?"

"No," Eli said. "But there are also ancient legends that got a modern makeover. Native American myths, for one."

He turned back and pointed a finger at Victor. "A creature who lives in the forest. When it calls your name, you have to go with it, over the treetops. 'Oh, my burning feet of fire!' Do you recognize that?"

I hadn't told Eli about my feet feeling like they were burning up. This was too close to the mark for my liking. I didn't get Eli's reference, but Victor did.

"Algernon Blackwood. *The Wendigo*," he said.

"A Wendigo? Isn't that a spirit that possesses people? Turns them into cannibals?"

"There are many diverse legends, from different tribes," said Eli. "Blackwood took a little here, a little there. He also got ideas from his unconscious, I'm sure. And the unconscious certainly taps into that Jungian archetype pool. Haven't you told me that sometimes when you're playing at your best, the ideas aren't so much yours as they are channeled from somewhere outside you? As if you're tapping into something—much like accessing talent, by the way."

"Well, sure, but that's music. That's a different thing."

"Is it? Maybe, but whatever the mechanism, I think that's what we're seeing here." He turned away again to continue his contemplation of the ocean, so his next words were muffled. "Who would have thought. A Wendigo."

At least, that was what he'd obviously said, given the context. But he'd spoken softly, and the words were obscured. What I actually heard was "a wennigo." Wennigo. When I go. Oh, my ever-loving God.

"When I go," I said. "That's what Sherwood said, out on the moor. It made no sense. 'He must call me. When I go.' She was talking about a Wendigo."

"I don't know," said Victor. "That seems rather far-fetched, don't you think?"

Eli walked back over to the big desk where Victor sat.

"No, I don't think it is," he said. "Not that much of a stretch at all. The Wendigo came out of the energy pool. Sherwood made her first appearance, after more than a year, at that same pool. And what did she say? 'He must call me'? As Mason found out, when this creature calls, you have to go. Quite the coincidence, no?"

"And that raises an interesting point," Victor said.

"Which is?"

"Your name," Eli said. "How did it know your name, Mason?"

"Well, I certainly didn't tell it. But what does my name have to do with anything? Do you think that's what gave it power over me? That whole nonsense of knowledge of names giving another power over you is ancient superstition." I paused. "Isn't it?"

"I used to think so, but if you'll think back on the events of the last year or so, I think you'll find a lot of our former beliefs have been tested. And as to how it knew your name, and whether that knowledge bestows power— I have no idea, but I think it significant. Maybe it knows all names, just by virtue of what it is."

"That's a comforting thought."

"Okay," said Victor. "Assuming, hypothetically, that you're right, where does that leave us? If it could really call Sherwood, bring her back from wherever, how does that help us? We can hardly go up and say, 'Excuse me, Mr. Wendigo. I have a favor to ask.'"

"I don't know. Maybe we could strike a bargain," I said. Victor snorted.

"You don't strike bargains with elemental archetypes."

"Quite the contrary," Eli said. "That's exactly what one does. Think of the literature."

"But we have nothing to trade."

"Coercion, then," I said. "Compel him in some way. Could we trap him?"

"Doubtful," Eli said. "It would take far more power to control something like that than any of us possess, singly or in concert. Now, if we had a magical enhancer, something like those rune stones, the ones that gave us so much trouble, that might be a different matter."

Those stones, the petrified bones of long-dead creatures, were of immense magical potency. They'd come from another time and place, or dimension, or something—I'm not very good with the cosmology of such things. A black practitioner had discovered them and brought them back, and they'd caused all kinds of trouble. The stones acted as enhancers—with them, even an ordinary practitioner could achieve extraordinary things, and they'd been used in unpleasant ways. When it was all over, I confiscated the lot of them. They were too dangerous to be left lying around.

I should have destroyed them, or given them to Eli for study, but I couldn't bring myself to give them up. At least I knew better than to use them myself, but I did it anyway. I'd given a few to Rolf, who thought he could employ them to create his own Ifrit. That hadn't worked out so well. But maybe the stones could be used to help fix the very problem they'd caused. Eli and Victor might be able to keep that magic under control.

"How many of those stones do you think we'd need?" I asked, trying to be casual about it.

"A lot. In effect, we'd have to use them to build a metaphorical cage to contain it." As soon as I asked about how many would be needed, Victor's head swiveled toward me. He stared, thoughtfully at first, then with growing suspicion.

"Why do you ask?" he said.

"Just curious."

He was on it like a bird dog on a quail. Damn him for being so sharp.

"Curious? I'll bet. You kept some of them when you found them, didn't you?" He shook his head in exasperation. "There were more of them than you let on, weren't there? I should have known."

My first instinct was to deny it, but what was the point? Technically I hadn't done anything wrong.

"Yes, I still have a few," I said. I expected Eli would be angry at this, but all his face showed was disappointment.

"Why didn't you tell me about this, Mason?" he said. I shrugged.

"I don't know, really. I was going to toss them, but

when it came right down to it I couldn't bring myself to get rid of them. And I knew how you'd feel about that, so . . ."

"They do get a hold on people. That's one of the reasons why they're dangerous. You use things like that too much, and before you know it, they control you instead of the other way around." His face hardened. "You haven't . . . been using them for anything, have you?"

I shook my head.

"No. Honestly, I was afraid to, and Lou would have taken my hand off if I'd tried. He really doesn't like them."

"That's because he, at least, has some sense." Eli came all the way across the room and peered into my face from a foot away. "Are you sure you haven't been using them?"

"I'm sure. I think I would have remembered something like that."

After a long moment, he clapped me on the shoulder, almost knocking me off my feet.

"Well, that's all right, then."

Victor pushed his chair away from the desk and rocked back on its two legs, teetering precariously. He often did that, and I always hoped he would overbalance one day and flip backward ass over teakettle. But he never did. He pointed a finger at me. There was a lot of finger-pointing going on.

"Okay," he said. "Again, let's assume we can use the stones, and we can build a trap. How are we going to find this Wendigo thing. Lou?"

"I don't think so. He couldn't track the fake Ifrit, and I don't think he'd have any better luck with this."

"Too bad. But how did you find it in the first place, then?"

"Well, that's an interesting thing," I said. "Basically, a woman I met told me where to look."

"Oh? Who? And how would she know that?"

"She's a psychic, or something like that. I met her accidentally."

"How do you meet someone accidentally?"

"It happens. But that's irrelevant. She had no idea what she was telling me."

"Could she tell you where to find it again?"

I considered that. It hadn't entered my mind, but it was possible she could.

"I don't know. But it's worth a try, I guess."

"First things first," said Eli. "I want those green rune stones."

"I'll bring them by tomorrow, I promise."

"Why not right now?"

"I've got things to do. I want to talk to my psychic friend, for one." I also wanted some time to get used to the idea of giving the rune stones up, but I didn't say that.

"All right," Eli said. He looked at me hard. "Just make sure you bring them. *All* of them." I wasn't fooling him. I got up to leave, but Victor held up a hand.

"Hold on a minute," he said. He reached into the desk drawer and pulled out a standard 12-gauge cleaning kit— cleaning rod, patches, and Hoppe's No. 9 solvent. "By the way, you fired the shotgun, so make sure you clean it thoroughly. A dirty gun is a lazy man's weapon, and a lazy man is a liability."

I took the kit, but I didn't need the advice. My grandfather had drilled that into me long ago. As I drove home, I actually felt a sense of relief. I hadn't touched those stones since I'd picked up that fateful bag, but they had been weighing on my mind for a while. Nothing ominous, just a low-level combination of curiosity and unease. I hadn't been entirely forthright with Eli, which he was well aware of, but he had decided to let it pass. I think he understood those things could take hold of the imagination.

At home, I took a quick shower to wipe off the grime and nervous sweat that had piled up. Then I spent a while figuring out what I was going to say to Morgan. I could ask her out for coffee, but she would likely say no. She'd asked me to call her, but it was because she was worried, not because she was looking to hook up. My call might be misinterpreted. Not that she would have been altogether wrong.

Telling her over the phone that I wanted her to help me track down the mythical Wendigo wasn't going to go over well, either. That approach could well lead to a restraining order. So I needed a use a different slant.

The first time I called, her machine picked up. I didn't leave a message; this had to be finessed, and that takes talking in person. When I tried again a few hours later she answered on the first ring.

"Morgan? This is Mason. The jazz guy, remember?"

"Of course," she said. "How are you?" Her tone was non-committal, and I couldn't tell if she was happy to hear from me or regretting giving me her number.

"Getting by. Just wanted to check in and tell you the news. I did end up in Muir Woods, despite your warnings."

"What?"

"Don't worry; I'm fine."

"How could you?"

"I had to. You were absolutely right, though. I'm lucky I got back okay."

"What happened?" she asked. "You sure you're all right?"

"Positive. But it's a bit complicated. I'm not really sure what I found there, and I'd love to talk to you about it. Maybe you could help clear it up for me. Could we meet for coffee somewhere?"

There was a long pause as she thought it over. What she had seen in her vision had shaken her, as well it might have, and she wasn't sure if she wanted to get involved any further. But she was curious—who wouldn't be? And it never hurts to just talk. That's one of the great lies people tell themselves.

"Uh, yeah, we could do that."

"I've got my van, so you pick the place," I said.

Another moment, then, "How about Martha's? There's one on the corner of California and Divisadero. It's not too far from where I live." It would take me about twenty minutes to get across town.

"Great," I said. "Half an hour okay?"

"Fine," she said. "See you then."

The area around California and Divisadero lies between the tony Upper Fillmore and the posh Pacific Heights. It has no real identity, instead sort of bleeding off into each one without having the cachet of either. And unlike its wealthy neighbors it's middle class, at least as much middle class as you can find in San Francisco. Some places in the city, like North Beach, could only be in San Francisco. Others could be transplanted into any good-sized city in the country without seeming out of place, and this area is one of them.

A few outside tables were clustered outside this Martha's, right by the door. I left Lou to hold a table and went inside for a latte. Morgan wasn't there yet. I hoped she hadn't changed her mind. Ten minutes later, I saw her crossing the street toward us. She was wearing those same loose jeans again, but with a shapeless sweatshirt on top. I got the feeling she'd changed into it before coming over, trying for aggressively neutral. She gave me a quick nod and passed by the table, going inside inside to get her own cup of coffee. While I waited, I called Lou over.

"We need her help," I said. "So put on the charm—don't lay it on too thick, though. Let her think you're just an ordinary dog. For now."

Hopefully she was a dog person. Lou could charm almost anyone, but there are people who simply don't like dogs, period. Go figure.

She came out, carrying a tiny cup of espresso, and slid into the opposite seat. Lou glanced up at me and I gave a slight nod. He stretched, sidled up to her, and sat up in his cute begging position. She smiled over at me, a good start.

"Yours, I assume?"

"Remember your vision where I was with something like a dog, but not quite? Well, you were right. This is Lou. Lou, this is Morgan. Say hello."

Lou sat down and offered a paw in the standard doggy-shake fashion. She reached down to take it, and at the last moment he whipped it away and gave a short bark.

"Psych!" I said.

"Well, that's just rude," she said, laughing. "I suppose you taught him that."

"Not at all. He has his own sense of humor, and the canine variety can be rather juvenile." Lou walked back to her and offered a paw again.

"This is like Charlie Brown and the football, isn't it?" she said.

"No, he's apologizing."

She reached down again and this time he gravely accepted her hand. Then he jumped up in my lap, curled up, and pretended to go to sleep. All of this had a purpose, of course. Not only did it humanize me and ease the tension, but the byplay would get her mind off any suspicions she might be having. Small, friendly dogs are so reassuring.

We looked at each other over the table for just long enough for it to start feeling uncomfortable. She took a sip of her coffee and made a face.

"For what they charge for espresso at these places, you'd think they might do better." She emptied a packet of sugar into the coffee and tried again. "Worse," she said. "So what happened to you? And why did you go up there the very next day? Did you want to see if I perhaps was a fraud? That's a long ways to go just to out me as a fake psychic."

"Not at all. I didn't doubt you for a moment. But I've been looking for something, something odd. I didn't know where it was, but your warning at least pointed me in the right direction."

"Well, that's ironic."

"Yeah, that's what I thought."

"Did you find what you were looking for?" She took another delicate sip of espresso and her hand trembled slightly. "What I saw made me nervous. I wouldn't have gone up there myself. I did warn you, you know."

"I'm afraid I had to. It was something that needed checking out."

She leaned forward, putting her cup down with a clink. "And that's the whole point, isn't it? What exactly was it, and who are you, anyway? And what do you want from me?"

This was the tricky part. Usually I don't tell nonpractitioners anything about the world of practitioners, or about my talents. I prefer they think of me as nothing more than a guitar player, which is what I am, really. There's no rule about telling civilians, and sometimes it works out fine—look at Victor and Timothy.

But there's a certain reluctance, as if the whole thing is just a bit unseemly. Mostly people don't believe you anyway. Even a slight demonstration isn't enough to convince hard-core skeptics—they'd rather deny the evidence of their own eyes than change their comfortable view of the universe.

Morgan might be different, though. She obviously had psychic ability—she'd not only known about Lou ahead of meeting him; she had guided me to the exact place where the Wendigo had taken up residence, and had felt its disturbing presence. Accepting that there might be others with unusual powers shouldn't be that much of a leap for her.

"Well, first of all, you know I'm a jazz musician," I said, treading carefully. "But there's another side to me. You're a psychic—and thanks for the warning, by the way. I'm a—well, let's just say that I possess certain powers of my own." She looked skeptical.

"Such as?"

"It might be easier to show you," I said. "Lou?" His ears pricked up. "Up on the table."

He uncurled himself from my lap and stepped delicately onto the tabletop, being careful not to spill any coffee. He sat there stoically. He doesn't much care for being put on display.

I glanced around to make sure no one was paying attention. Doing magic in public is frowned upon, at least by Victor. It obviously could lead to complications. But if anyone noticed my little demonstration, they'd just think they were seeing things and needed to get their eyes checked.

I spotted a woman walking across the street with a cocker spaniel. Every time it stopped and tried to sniff at something she would impatiently pull on its leash. This would be easy—not spectacular, but simple. I reached out, took the spaniel essence, and let it flow into Lou.

This kind of spell is easy. A static spell, one where you change something's appearance and it stays that way for an extended period, does take some energy. But a fluid spell, one where you basically act as a conduit so the spell lasts only as long as you pay attention and keep the flow going, takes very little effort.

Lou's coat changed from his normal black and tan into a mottled brown and white, thick and furry. His ears grew long and floppy, his muzzle squared off, and he put on a few pounds as well. In five seconds he'd been transformed into a friendly, smiling cocker spaniel.

Morgan stared at him in disbelief and put out a tentative hand to see if he was real. Then she pulled it back. She wasn't sure she wanted to touch him. If she had, she would have felt a short coat and a sharp muzzle; I hadn't gone to the trouble of making a tactile illusion as well—those are tricky and there wasn't any point.

"Holy crap," she said. "How did you do that?"

"Just an illusion." I stopped the energy flow and Lou reverted back to his original form. "That's just a parlor trick. But there are other, more serious things I can do."

"Like what?"

"That vision of me you had? I was hunting down something that shouldn't be in this world at all. I found it, but that didn't go well. This time we're prepared and I need your help to find it again."

"We?"

"I have friends."

"Friends like you?"

"Sort of."

She digested this awhile. So far, things were going well. She hadn't broken out in a cold sweat and quickly departed. Lots of people would have. The next step was more difficult. Would she accept me or fixate on the apparent supernatural? Ordinary citizens can go one of three ways. Morgan wasn't quite in that category, but she was close.

One, remain skeptical, and insist it's all some kind of trick. Another is to believe, and get the hell out of there as fast as possible. A third is to become so enamored with the whole concept of magic being real that they can think of nothing else.

If you build up a relationship with a nonpractitioner before you spring it on them, it usually works out okay. They know you, so they're not as freaked out or blinded by what they see. But if you have just met someone, who you are gets lost in what you can do.

"So, what is it exactly you want me to do?" she finally asked. Her voice was steady, but she wasn't nearly as calm as she was pretending to be. Nobody could be, not after something so flat-out weird had been sprung on them.

"Do another reading for me," I said. "Maybe you'll see me again, somewhere different. I think the nature of what I'm looking for will make it easier for you to see when we intersect."

"That might be difficult right now. I need to be centered in order to get anything, and right now my psyche feels like it's been scattered into little pieces."

"Have another espresso," I said. "That always calms my nerves."

She smiled, but it was strained. I gave Lou another slight nod and he walked over and put one paw on her knee. She automatically put a hand down to ruffle his head, and when she did he rubbed against her calf like a cat. She smiled again, and this time the smile was real. Lou and I make a great team at running cons, even if they're for a good purpose.

"Want to at least give it a try?" I said, holding out my hands.

Morgan took both of them in hers, just like before. She closed her eyes and breathed in, then half out, just like before. This time, though, there was no dramatic conclusion. She simply sat there, breathing evenly for a couple of minutes, before opening her eyes and releasing my hands. She shook her head with a quick back-and-forth motion.

"Sorry," she said. "I didn't get anything this time."

"Nothing?" I had been counting on at least something.

"Just some images. The only thing I could recognize was the Golden Gate Bridge, for what that might be worth."

"Could you tell which side?"

"This side, I think. It was close to the tower, and I could see sunlight just hitting the top of the tower, so it must have been late afternoon."

"And could you feel the presence of . . . well, whatever it is?" She shook her head again, slowly this time.

"No, just the bridge and you. There might have been other people with you." That wasn't much help.

"Well, it's better than nothing," I said. "I appreciate the effort."

"Anytime." She got up from the table and pushed the chair back in.

"I'll give you a call if anything else comes up," I said. "Or call me if there's anything I can do for you." I wrote my number on a napkin and handed it to her. "Or for any reason."

Lou hopped into my lap and looked up appealingly at her. He makes a great wingman. Or wingdog.

"Sure," she said, smiling more at him than at me. "Why not?"

SIX

NEXT MORNING I DUMPED ALL THE STONES into the original black-and-white messenger bag they'd come in. Lou looked on approvingly until I took a bunch of them back out, wrapped them in a piece of silk, and put them back in my trunk. When we left the flat, he stalked out ahead of me, stiff-legged and disapproving.

Half an hour later I walked into the study with the distinctive-patterned bag slung over one shoulder. Eli looked at the bag with frank curiosity, while Victor barely looked up from his seat behind his desk. Lou stayed a good distance away from me, and as soon as we entered the study he trotted over to the far wall, as far away from those things as he could get. He didn't like anything about those rune stones, not one bit. If he could talk, he would have ratted me out for still holding some of them back, I'm sure.

I spilled them out dramatically on top of Victor's desk, marring the pristine finish. Victor abandoned his casual demeanor as they cascaded past him. Usually he would have been pissed at my cavalier treatment of his precious desk, but in truth he was too awed by the aura of power emanating from them to do anything but gawk at that pile of ancient bones.

Maggie had been curled up under the desk, but when I dumped them out, she shot out of there like her tail was on fire. She ended up next to Lou, and they stared at me with both canine and feline disapproval. The feline variety was a lot more obvious, complete with lashing tail.

Eli bent over to examine the stones. He picked up one and gingerly held it between his fingers, where it glowed softly like a dying firefly.

"I had no idea," he said, after a moment.

"Yeah," I said. "They're special all right."

"You really shouldn't have kept these."

"I know," I said. I tried to keep my voice neutral, but Eli was good at reading me. For a moment I thought he was going to pursue the matter, but finally he shrugged and placed the stone back into the pile.

"Well, you never know about these things. Maybe it was just as well you did keep them."

"Do you think these are enough to do the trick?" I asked. Victor had quickly overcome his initial sense of awe and was examining one particular stone that was slightly larger than the rest.

"With this kind of firepower?" he said. "If they don't, we're in trouble. These stones are the magical equivalent of RPGs."

"But we still have to figure out how to harness the power, and what kind of trap to set up," Eli said, "so we might as well get started."

Victor opened his safe and hauled out an impressive array of magical props—powders, a copper bar, shavings of various other metals, a few bottles of liquids, a twelve-volt battery, and as always, salt.

"What are you trying to do?" I asked. "Build something that can trap and hold it?"

"Building a cage will be comparatively easy," said Victor. "Getting it into the cage might be another matter."

"Then what? Why would it help us?"

"We can bargain. If that doesn't work, there's always Bertram."

"No," said Eli. "That's not a good idea."

"He's effective. He can be very persuasive."

"Doesn't make it right."

"Why not? This Wendigo is a monster, after all."

"We don't know that. And no, we're not using Bertram. End of discussion."

Eli doesn't say things like that very often, but when he does there's no arguing. Victor shrugged and turned away. I was just as glad we weren't calling on Bertram for help—his methods were unpleasant in the extreme, and he enjoyed using them.

Eli returned his attention to the large tattered book he was thumbing through, the kind of book you usually see in the rare-book room at the library or in specialty bookstores.

"We'll need to find a way to compel it to enter. Ironic, is it not, considering how it operates?"

He closed the book and knelt down on the floor where Victor was arranging items according to some criteria I couldn't even guess at. My improvisational use of talent has served me well, but it was at times like this that I realized how little I know. And how useless I was in this type of endeavor.

The two of them discussed strategies. Victor wanted to grind up a few of the stones and incorporate them into a larger matrix. Eli thought that too dangerous and unpredictable; he wanted to use the stones themselves to form a template. Neither one asked for my opinion, which was just as well since I didn't have one.

Finally Eli won out on that point. They took half the stones and arranged them in a rough circle, not much larger than it would take to contain a person. I wasn't sure if half was all they needed or if they were saving the other half in case something went wrong. A layer of salt was poured out, snaking in and out between the stones, and each stone was dusted with a small amount of iron shavings.

Most of the folk knowledge about magical operations is laughably wrong, but there are two items that crop up in myth all the time: iron and salt. And those two are real. Salt is practically a universal substance in any ritual designed to bind something, and iron is almost as common. All metals, except silver and sometimes gold, are difficult to work with. But iron is by far the most difficult; it's almost as resistant to talent as is an Ifrit.

Victor spoke a command and let energy flow into the circle. He didn't need much; it was like lighting a match to a bonfire of kindling. Power welled up, strong and fierce. Eli took a step backward, and even Victor seemed slightly intimidated by what he'd done.

"Now the attraction spell," said Victor. "Mason, I could use your help here."

At last I felt useful. Eli knows more about the operation of magical constructs than anyone I know, but he personally has only a minor amount of intrinsic power to work with. It's too bad; if he'd been able to combine his knowledge with Victor's power, he would have been one of the most powerful practitioners on the planet. But maybe he wouldn't have been Eli then.

Victor reached over for the battery, connected a length of copper wire to each terminal and the other end of the wires to one of the green stones.

"He's making an electromagnet," Eli explained, "or at least that's what it would be if it were hooked up to a metal rod. Same principle, though."

Victor took hold of one of the wires and gestured for me to take the other one.

"We don't want to try pouring energy directly into the stone," he said. "That could cause problems. When I speak the code word, just feed it into the wire and it will flow into the stone. Got it?"

I nodded and grasped the wire firmly. Victor had one

hand on his wire and the other on the stone. "Attract," he said, and I let loose with a surge. Then he took his hand off the stone, saying, "Release." I dropped the wire, but as he spoke he released another small pulse of energy into the circle. I understood what he was trying to do—set up code words that would activate an attraction spell or release it on command. I wasn't sure it would work, though.

"How are you going to isolate its effect?" I asked.

Victor reached over to the circle of stones, took one out, and rearranged the others so that a circle remained. He then reached into a desk drawer and pulled out a flashlight. A quick consultation with Eli, a drop of liquid from one of the bottles rubbed on the lens, and then a few words spoken while holding the rune stone up to the flashlight. When he turned it on, the flashlight beam passed right through the stone, casting a green light on the far wall.

Back to the desk drawer, this time for some duct tape. He neatly taped the stone onto the front of the flashlight, securing it in place.

"Very elegant," I said, looking at the duct tape.

"It works," he said, shortly. Eli looked over at Lou and Maggie, who had uncharacteristically been looking on with great interest.

"We should test it on one of them," he said.

"Why them?" I asked.

"Because Ifrits, as you well know, are immune to all sorts of magical compulsions. Aversion spells mean nothing to them. If this works on them, it will work on anything, even our tree-dwelling friend. It won't hurt them any." Victor looked a question at me.

"Why not?" I said. I pointed over to where Lou and Maggie were sitting. Maggie took one look at me and stalked over to the other side of the room. She was having no part of it. "Lou. We're going to try something. If you feel a pull, resist. Fight it."

He licked his lips nervously, but didn't make any other protest. Trying to prove he was braver than a mere cat, perhaps. Eli nodded and Victor said, "Attract." The runes around the circle flashed once. The he turned on the flashlight and played the beam of green light over Lou's body. Lou stiffened, then started walking stiffly toward the circle. It wasn't like what the Wendigo had done to me; this was more of a physical compulsion and Lou was fighting it all the way. He twisted his head around to look at me, either in supplication or disgust, but his steps didn't slow for a moment. Seconds later he was inside the circle, and Victor turned off the flashlight.

"Can you get out?" I said to him.

He circled the perimeter once and sat down in the middle of the circle. He wasn't even going to try.

"So far, so good," said Victor, and he released the power flowing through the circle.

Lou trotted out, ignored my outstretched hand, and joined Maggie on the other side of the room. Showing that he preferred even her company to mine at the moment was his way of letting me know he was seriously pissed.

"Now you," Victor said to me.

"Me? Why not you?"

"I need to check for possible flaws."

After offering up Lou as a guinea pig I could hardly say no. I shrugged and walked into the center of the circle. When Victor activated it, I understood why Lou hadn't even attempted to get out. I'd expected lines of force, or even a dome of energy blocking any escape, but nothing like this. It was like being locked in a bank vault with nothing but a butter knife to pry the door open. No magical energy could escape, either, and hopefully that would include the seductive power of the Wendigo's voice.

Sheer force wasn't going to do the job, but that's not the way I handle things anyway. I probed for weaknesses, but there weren't any. Those stones held immense power, and Victor had been his careful self in crafting it. There was no way out. Except, there's almost always a way around things if you're clever enough. Sheer force isn't everything, and there was one weakness Victor hadn't thought of. The circle couldn't be affected from the inside, but what about from the outside? I signaled to Lou, who was still sulking on the other side of the room.

"I need some help," I said. He looked at me sourly. "Bacon for breakfast tomorrow?" His ears perked up. When all else fails, bribery is usually a viable option with him. He stood up alertly, awaiting instructions.

"The circle. The stones. Grab one, pull it away."

Victor turned to intercept him. But it was too late. Lou ducked around him, grabbed the nearest stone, and tossed it aside with a quick flick of his head, as if he were killing a rat. The circle was broken, and an opening appeared in the space the stone had occupied, just wide enough for me to squeeze through. I stepped out of the circle and tapped Victor on the shoulder.

"You're it," I said. "Or maybe, you're dead."

He started to say something, probably along the lines of accusing me of cheating, then realized how lame that would sound. Instead, he gave a reluctant nod.

"Good catch," he said, grudgingly." We'll have to be alert for outside interference—we don't know what else may be out there. Now all we have to do is figure out where our Wendigo might be." He paused, remembering. "Did you have any luck with your psychic?"

"I'm afraid not. Something about the Golden Gate Bridge, and dusk; that's about it. What are we going to do, set up the trap out by Baker Beach until it makes an appearance? And not to be difficult, but how are you going to tempt it to come to where you've set up the trap, anyway? What if it shows up a couple of miles away from the circle?"

"We're not going to set it up beforehand," Eli said. "We don't have to. All the hard work has already been done. When—if we locate the Wendigo, we'll set up the circle—it shouldn't take more than a minute or so. But we can't depend on finding it. What we need is some way to attract it to us." Victor suddenly sat up straight.

"The shotgun," he said. "Have you cleaned it yet?" My God, the man could be anal.

"Haven't got around to it yet," I said. "I was going to do it this morning, but I thought building this trap might be a tad more important."

"No, no," said Victor impatiently. "The residue in the barrel. We can use the residue if you haven't cleaned it yet."

"I don't see it," Eli said. "The powder has no connection to the creature."

"Yes, but the barrel isn't just fouled with powder residue. It also contains traces of the lead pellets which passed through it—a tiny bit of the lead sloughs off each time it's fired."

"Ah," said Eli. "And those same pellets struck the Wendigo. Creating a connection between the lead pellets that hit the Wendigo and the lead residue they left in the barrel. Very good, Victor."

"Unless you missed it," Victor said to me. "Are you sure you hit it?"

"I'm sure," I said. "It's hard to miss something at that distance with a shotgun. And I fired four shots. I damn sure didn't miss with all of them."

"Excellent," Eli said, rubbing his hands together. "Admittedly, the connection is weak, but I think we can work with it."

Most magical operations are simply about utilizing talent to redirect and transform energy—everything from simple illusions to complex spells involving time and space. But there are some constants that help to enable such spells. The principle of similarity, for example. Using nearby water to effect fluid changes, or rock to draw energy for a protective shield, or the emotions of hate and fear to fashion a killing spell.

Or the rule of contagion—things once part of a whole but which are then separated retain an affinity for each other—like the shotgun pellets leaving part of themselves as lead residue an the rest of them striking the Wendigo.

I brought the shotgun in from my van and broke out the cleaning kit. Twenty minutes later I had a collection of cotton patches, damp with solvent, the first one black with fouling and each subsequent one progressively lighter. While I pushed the patches through the bore, Victor was busy pulling out additional magical tools from the safe.

"What do you think?" he asked Eli.

"A paste, a salve would be best, I think. We can apply it to Mason, and that should attract the Wendigo to him." I didn't like the sound of that.

"So not only am I the sacrificial goat, staked out to tempt the tiger, but I'm basically going to have hamburger rubbed all over my body? Why not just pour a bottle of steak sauce over my head and be done with it?"

"If we have to," Victor said.

"If you're going to be making up a magical potion, maybe we should give Campbell a call. No offense, but she's really better at that sort of thing." And at least that way, I could be sure whatever it was Victor came up with wouldn't cause me to break out in boils.

"That's not a bad idea," Eli said. "Why don't you call her, Mason?"

So I did, and after being filled in on everything, she was eager to come down. I spent the next few hours doing a magical refresher course with Eli. I'd been lazy of late, not keeping up with even the basics. I wouldn't dream of playing an important gig without some practice time, and the same principles apply in magic. And we would be playing a very important gig indeed if this worked.

We went over the basics—like how to utilize talent in the most efficient manner so you don't exhaust yourself in the first minute. How to narrow focus, like a lens, and not spray energy all over the place. The less talent you use to produce an effect, the more energy you have in reserve for the inevitable unforeseen circumstances.

Then a run-through on which materials work best for implementing which spells. You can use anything for any-thing, but some things are easier to work with than others, and again there's no point in wasting valuable energy. Metals are hard to use; living things easy, since they have their own energy. But even with metals, there are degrees. Silver and moonlight go together like bread and butter. Copper is very useful for specific types of work, and iron, of course, is almost impervious to magical talent. But that makes it ideal for defense.

And finally, concentration exercises. I used some talent to keep a tennis ball suspended precisely twelve inches off the floor while Eli asked me a series of increasingly difficult questions. The ability to concentrate on more than one thing at once is crucial to magical operations.

Lou had turned these sessions into a favorite game. As I tried to answer Eli's questions and keep the ball steady, he would harass me. Sometimes it was mock attacks; sometimes he even nipped me unexpectedly. Or he'd do back-flips, each time almost landing on his head, distracting me with worry. I did pretty well this time until Maggie threw herself on the back of my neck. The tennis ball dropped as I lost concentration. Eli frowned, but I thought I'd done pretty well by simply not jumping up with a scream. Maggie bounced off and retreated across the room, tail waving. Cat humor.

When Campbell showed up a few hours later she shook her head at me.

"You're determined to get yourself in trouble, aren't you?"

"Not my idea. But worth a try, I think."

She brought out her familiar copper pot and a can of Sterno and set them up on the floor. While the pot heated, she placed the plants she'd brought next to Victor's various props while carrying on an animated discussion about how to blend her plant properties with his inorganic power objects. One of the plants she pulled out was unlike anything I'd seen.

"This is a sundew," she said, noticing me looking at it with curiosity. "It's hard to come by, but useful. It's incredibly sticky for one thing. Great for attraction."

"Isn't that a carnivorous plant?" I asked. "Insects and stuff?" The idea creeped me out.

"It is. Usually it's only used for potions that aren't entirely beneficial, but I think it will do fine." She set out what looked like beeswax, and a pale yellow bar that smelled faintly of chocolate. "Cocoa butter," she explained, and next to it she placed a couple of more familiar plants, herbs familiar to anyone who cooks at all. "Thyme and rosemary. Traditionally used for attracting the fey." She smiled. "Not that there's any such thing, of course."

"No," I muttered. "Of course not." I bent down for a closer look. "Do you really think you can summon a Wendigo with savory herbs and chocolate?"

"No, but from your description I'm not so sure it's a Wendigo. In lore, they're evil, evil creatures. It should have made your blood run cold."

"It did."

"But it didn't do anything to you."

"It didn't get the chance."

"That's true, but it just doesn't fit. What you described sounds more amoral than evil, if you get my drift—more like an elemental woodland spirit. That fear you felt might have been simply your own fear, projected out and returned in a feedback loop."

"That could be," said Eli. "And if that entity came out of the energy pool, it might have taken on several archetypal attributes. It wouldn't necessarily be exactly one thing or another. But the parallels to the Wendigo—the calling by name, for example—are too strong to discount."

Campbell put a small amount of water in the pot and crumbled in the thyme and rosemary. Victor handed her the dirty gun patches, which went in soon after. While the concoction simmered, she kneaded the beeswax and cocoa butter together. Victor, meanwhile, took out some braided copper wire and, as Campbell cooked up her concoction, arranged his tools. He laid the ring of copper wire around the pot and, at carefully measured intervals, some highly polished stones. I recognized an agate, rose quartz, and a black stone that might have been obsidian, but there were several others I hadn't a clue about.

"Magnets?" I asked, thinking of the other circle. Victor shook his head briefly.

"Wrong type of attraction," Eli said. "We want to attract it to you, not bind it."

"What about using one of the rune stones? If the connection between the lead and the Wendigo is weak, it could give it quite a push, couldn't it?"

"It could, but we don't know much about those stones. I don't know what the effect might be, and if it turned out badly, I'd rather not have anything made with its help going onto your skin."

After that, I was quiet and just watched. Campbell fussed over the pot but was unhappy with what she saw.

"It's not coming together properly," she complained. "I'm not sure why."

Victor peered into the pot.

"It's the cleaning patches. They have gun solvent on them; that's why it won't bind properly."

"Ah," she said. "Of course."

She added a little of this and a bit of that, and finally was satisfied. Leaning across the pot, she blew sharply across the top, and I could feel the energy come off her from across the room. That was how strong she'd become. She snuffed out the Sterno and sat back.

By the time the gunk had cooled down it was late afternoon. I had expected we were done for the day, but both Eli and Victor were gung ho to get started.

"We may as well try it out," said Victor. "It's at its strongest when it's fresh."

"Now what?" I asked. "I slap the stuff on and we wander around blindly, hoping what's-his-name will show up?"

"No, we do have a starting point," Eli said. "Your psychic friend was right once. I'm thinking over by Fort Point, right by the bridge, would be a good place to start."

Victor picked up the pot containing the salve.

"Strip down, Mason."

"In your dreams, Victor."

Campbell took the pot from him.

"I'll apply it," she said, looking at me expectantly.

I took off my shirt and she rubbed the goo all over my back, arms, and chest, working it into the muscles like a sports trainer would. It was actually rather pleasant. The balm smelled faintly of chocolate and rosemary, with just a whiff of astringency. It was a bit weird, though, like getting a professional massage from a former girlfriend. Talk about your mixed messages.

When she was done, Eli asked if she wanted to come along, but she demurred.

"Chasing monsters is your thing, not mine. I'm happy just to stay in the kitchen and whip things up."

"Sure," I said. "I'll bet."

"But be careful, Mason. I'd miss you, you know."

"So would I." I looked around. "Okay. Let's do it."

SEVEN

FORT POINT SITS JUST UNDER THE SOUTH END
of the Golden Gate, hunkered down in the shadow of the
bridge. It was built during the Civil War to fend off invading fleets—from whom, I'm not sure, and I don't think they
were, either. It's become a big tourist attraction, crowded
on weekends not only with tourists but with locals as well.

A footpath, several miles long, runs east toward Crissy
Field. Most of the path is clear of brush with great views
of the bridge and the ocean, but there are parts of it that
wend closely through overhanging trees. Overgrown lanes
occasionally branch off the main path, where concrete bun-
kers have reverted back to the wild, almost unrecognizable
as man-made constructions.

Eli carried the messenger bag containing the stones.
Victor had the iron shavings and the salt, as well as the
flashlight with the duct-taped stone. He was also carrying
a shotgun. He didn't even bother to disguise it; if we ran
into anyone, he'd use enough of an aversion spell so that
they wouldn't care to look at him.

The shotgun might not be much use against the Wendigo, but Victor hadn't forgotten about the creature that had savaged his leg. This was smack-dab in the middle of where it had been hanging out, and any display of unusual magical power would bring it running. I wasn't carrying anything. My job was simple. I was bait.

Dusk is a dicey time of day to be hunting anything. Your eyes play tricks on you, and you can never be quite sure what you're looking at until it's right up on top of you. But that was when Morgan had seen me here, so that was when I was here.

I still wasn't happy with the setup. Too many assumptions were being made, way too many for my comfort. What if the Wendigo wasn't here? What if it wasn't a Wendigo at all? What if it was, but could manage to call us all at once—who was going to set up the circle and trap it? Eli assured me that it could focus on only one individual at a time. He seemed quite sure of that, but what if he was wrong? He'd misjudged things in the past. Not often, but he's not infallible.

And once we had it, what were we going to do with it? Could it really call Sherwood back from whatever place she was? Then what? Did we let it go to continue on its merry way? What if it were bent on wreaking havoc? I don't mind playing things by ear; in fact, mostly I prefer it. But this was going out on a very long limb without a paddle, so to speak.

It was a warm evening by San Francisco standards. The sound of ocean waves blended pleasantly with the muted sounds of traffic from the opposite direction. The sun had just set, and the last of the evening rays lit up the tops of the bridge towers. I felt strangely at peace, relaxed and happy, even though we were on a dangerous mission with unknown consequences. Lou was trailing along right behind me, looking remarkably at ease himself.

Too much at ease. This was not normal. I looked behind me, and sure enough, Victor and Eli were ambling along lackadaisically, as if they hadn't a care in the world. I roused myself enough to point out this disturbing state of affairs, but something else caught my attention. This time it wasn't someone calling me. It was a whisper in the depths of my brain, right at the edge of conscious thought. *Come,* it urged. *Come, Mason.*

I knew where it wanted me to go. I stopped by the side of the trail, letting Victor and Eli drift by, lost in their own thoughts, then walked back up the path the way we'd come. Again, it was an odd sensation, a feeling of compulsion that wasn't compulsion at all. I didn't *have* to come to it when it called; it just seemed there was nothing else I could do, really. I went because I was supposed to go. Makes no sense, I know, but it's the best I can explain it.

A ways farther up the trail I heard Lou's high-pitched yelp, warning Eli and Victor something was amiss. About time, I thought, but I wondered if they'd get the holding circle up in time. It didn't worry me either way.

Twenty feet ahead of me, about ten feet up in a small tree, barely visible against the darkening sky, he waited. Eli and Victor would be too late. I felt a vague sorrow about that, and an even stronger regret that I'd never see Lou again, but it wasn't enough to throw me off stride. What would be, would be.

I'd almost reached the Wendigo's tree perch when his face lit up with a green glow. Immediately my mind cleared, and I backed off rapidly, almost stumbling over my feet. Apparently Eli had been right about him; he couldn't keep his mind focused on more than one thing at a time. He sat without moving for a long moment before toppling off the branch and falling to the ground with a heavy thud. He wasn't hurt, though, and immediately got to his feet with a jerky, uncoordinated motion.

He'd shown a fluid grace while sitting in the tree, but now he was staggering along like a recalcitrant mario-nette, stumbling and lurching toward the circle. So they'd pulled it off after all. Victor kept the flashlight trained on him until he was completely in the circle. When he switched it off, we all held our breath, waiting to see if the circle would hold.

The Wendigo did a complete three-sixty, examining every aspect of the trap. He put his hands up near the interface of the power grid produced by the stones and the space outside the circle, shook his head, and then calmly sat down.

He looked about the same as the first time I'd seen him—same curly hair, same woodland clothes, although the colors shifted as he sat there, so maybe they weren't really clothes at all. He was smaller than I remembered, though, only five-eight or so. People who scare you are often smaller than they seem at the time. But this time he seemed more human, less scary. Maybe it was something he could control. Anyone passing by on the street wouldn't look twice at him.

And now that we had him what were we going to do with him? I wasn't even sure we could communicate with him, much less get across complex ideas. I needn't have worried. He looked at each of us in turn and said, "Now what?"

His voice was light and pleasant, with a hint of a Southern twang. I had no idea what to say, but thank God it wasn't up to me. I was more than happy to let Eli and Victor do the talking. Eli got up close, right to the barrier of stones, before he spoke, and when he did, his tone was mild.

"What do we call you? Have you a name?"

"Many," he said. "Most of which are hard to pronounce. But you don't need a name. You seem to know who I am."

"I know *what* you are, which is not precisely the same," Eli said.

"A nice distinction. What is it you want?"

"What makes you think we want something?" said Victor. He was never one for standing on the sidelines.

"You've trapped me here. There must be a reason for that." He waved expansively at the circle. "I don't know how you did it, I'll admit. Most things don't affect me much. But trapping me took a lot more thought and planning than simply trying to kill me, for example. So you want something from me, no?"

He sounded reasonable enough, but I'd been under his thrall twice now. Maybe his reasonableness was another, more subtle form of the same thing. The sky had grown dark, and the only illumination came from the ring of rune stones that glowing faintly as they pulsed with power. The Wendigo's face was half hidden in a greenish shadow, giving him a diabolical cast. The devil's a smooth talker, they say. Eli slowly nodded.

"True enough. We want you to find someone and bring them back."

"Oh? From where?"

"If we knew that, we wouldn't be talking to you. She's . . . somewhere, not quite in this world but not quite out of it, either. Something you might be familiar with."

"What's her name?"

Eli hesitated. It seemed dangerous information to be giving out, but if we weren't willing to do so, what was the point of catching this thing, anyway?

"Sherwood," he said.

"Sherwood," he repeated softly, caressing the name softly. It set off echoes in my mind.

He closed his eyes and for a moment his entire form blurred. When he opened his eyes, he shook his head. "Too many possibilities. I'm going to need more information."

"She reached out to me," I said. "At first she was in a featureless void, but then it resolved into a specific place, like a movie set from *Wuthering Heights*." The Wendigo looked at me blankly. "Her favorite movie," I explained. "Moors, fog, stunted bushes, bleak vistas—that sort of thing."

"Ah, I see. A construct. That makes it easier." He closed his eyes again, and this time when he opened them, he nodded. "I see her. I can call her."

"What does she look like?" I asked, not trusting him.

"Dark hair. Pretty. She's sitting on a rock, high on a

hillside, overlooking the moor you described. Not really, of course, but that's the way she perceives it." So he might not be trustworthy, but he wasn't faking it, either. "The question now is," he continued, "what are you going to do for me in return?"

"Well, there's a problem about that," Eli said. "You tried to take Mason from us once already. I don't think it would have been a good thing for him if you'd succeeded. What's to say you wouldn't try the same sort of thing once you were free? A lot of innocents walk through the woods. It was hard enough to catch you once, and I don't think it would be easy to catch you a second time." The Wendigo chuckled, deep in his throat.

"No, probably not."

"So you see the dilemma."

"I do. Well, first of all you seem to have the wrong idea about me. I have no use for ordinary humans. Although I find them interesting. Especially their music." He looked over at me. "You're a musician, yes?"

"What does that have to do with anything?" I said.

"Everything, but you should know that. Practitioners, now, that's a different matter. I absorb energy from them. But as far as people go, what do you think I'd do with them? Eat them?" He made it sound like a joke, but that was exactly what I thought he'd do. "The energy is what keeps me strong. But it doesn't hurt them any—in fact, afterward they usually forget they ever met me."

"Richard Cory," I said.

"Ah, you know him? Delightful fellow. I got enough from him to keep me going for a month."

"And where is he now?"

"Back with his friends, I imagine. Have you checked with them?"

I hadn't, and of course there was no way to do that now. But it wasn't impossible. Rolf wouldn't have bothered to tell me if Richard had returned. He just didn't think that way.

"What about those hikers," Victor said, "the ones who

were torn to shreds. We've been assuming it was something else, but now I'm beginning to wonder."

The Wendigo gave him what was supposed to be a bright and cheery smile, but under the glow of the rune stones it looked more like a satanic leer.

"Oh, come, now. All of you seem strangely eager to jump to conclusions, based on nothing at all. Now, that beast, yes, it's possible. It's a vicious animal, though not truly intelligent." He gestured over at Lou. "And although it hates everyone and everything, it especially despises Ifrits."

"Why is that?" Eli asked. Once again, academic curiosity had overcome the practical problem in front of us.

"Because of how it came into this world. It was pulled in by an overload of talent—I would guess from these very stones you used to trap me. The magic has run wild, coursing through its bloodstream, and that's made it sick, almost like a rabid dog." He looked over at me. "So it's not really the beast's fault—it's yours."

"Never mind that," Victor said. "Mason, you're the one this fellow first called—you must have some idea of his nature. Do you buy it?"

I thought about what Campbell had said, about it not really being a Wendigo the way Eli had assumed. More like an elemental, with unknown motives. And I realized I had indeed made a lot of assumptions about it. But letting it out of the circle did not seem safe.

"Could be," I said slowly. "But there's no way to know for sure."

"Well, how about if you call up Sherwood for us," Victor said. "If you can. Then we'll talk about what's to be done with you."

"I have a better idea. How about you let me out of here, and then we'll talk about getting this Sherwood person back."

Classic impasse, a Mexican standoff. I don't know how it would have been resolved, but then the unexpected happened, as it often does.

We'd all been focused on the Wendigo, not surprisingly. So when the fake Ifrit burst out from behind the closest bush, it caught us all by surprise, even Lou. It ran right by, ignoring me, and sprang at Victor. That made sense; he was the one holding the shotgun. Victor spun around, but he didn't have time to line up the barrel for a shot. The creature launched itself at his throat, snarling with a thick, guttural roar. Victor did just manage to get the shotgun up to protect his throat, using both hands, but instead of blocking the creature's charge, he threw himself backward. He used the length of the gun as a lever and flipped the creature over his head as he went down. It was like watching a goddamned ninja movie.

He sprang to his feet as if he were made of rubber, leveled the shotgun, and pulled the trigger. The sound was enormous in the quiet. Before I could even react he'd pumped off four more rounds. The creature dodged, incredibly fast, and despite Victor's vaunted marksmanship and competence he only managed to graze it at best. The creature screamed as if it had been hit and dropped to the ground, where it flopped around like a dog's chew toy. But it was on its feet almost instantly. Victor was out of rounds and would need to reload, but it didn't know that. It decided it had had enough on this particular night. It bolted past me, whipping out a passing claw in an attempt to slice through Lou, but he ducked it easily. Then it was gone, bounding off into the night. The whole thing had lasted no more than ten seconds.

But there was one small unintended consequence. Between the flying pellets and the creature thrashing around, the circle of stones was in ruin. Not that it was a circle anymore; it was now merely a random collection of stones. The Wendigo casually stepped forward out of what was left of the circle, kicking a few of the remaining stones out of the way.

"Well," he said. "This certainly changes things."

EIGHT

WE ALL HAVE DIFFERENT WAYS OF HANDLING such situations. If I'd been alone, I would have run without a moment's hesitation. Hell, it had worked once. Victor automatically crouched into a fighting stance. I don't think he even knew he had done so; it was just a reaction as unconscious and natural to him as breathing. Eli simply walked forward until he was two feet away. He gestured toward the darkness where the fake Ifrit had vanished.

"Was that your doing?"

The Wendigo smiled, but it wasn't bright and cheery this time.

"Not at all. I would imagine your clever stone circle attracted it."

"Quite possibly," said Eli. "So, you're free. What now? Are you going to help us or not?"

You had to admire him. Eli just assumed, matter-of-factly, that there was no danger now that the Wendigo was free. He just carried on as if nothing about the situation had changed. I've seen him do that before. Mostly, it works, but that's because it's Eli. If I tried something like that, I would most likely end up as lunch. But the Wendigo seemed more than happy to play along. Maybe he'd been telling the truth after all.

"Again, what's in it for me?" he said. "You don't seem to have as much to offer now."

Eli pointed at the stones scattered on the ground. After the test runs and the trap, they were barely glowing.

"You absorb magical power. Those stones have enough to keep you going for I don't know how long—months, at least, I'd say."

The Wendigo glanced down at them.

"Not anymore, they don't. They're almost used up."

"Yes, but we have more of them. We'll trade you—stones for Sherwood. You bring her back and we'll give you enough of them to last quite a while."

"Now, that is tempting."

"He claims Richard Cory is back safe," I put in. "If he is, if he's telling the truth, great. But if not . . ."

"You'll hunt me down like a dog?"

"We can at least make your life difficult," said Victor.

"I'm sure you could. And if I just take care of you all right now? I could, you know."

"Possibly," said Eli. "But to what purpose? You wouldn't get any stones that way. And maybe it wouldn't turn out for you as well as you might think. Those stones are not our only tools."

Eli seemed to grow in size and bulk, and his voice became quietly menacing. He was an impressive figure, and anyone or anything would think twice about taking him on. What the Wendigo didn't know was that it was entirely a bluff. Eli of course has great intellect and presence, but no real intrinsic power. Victor would put up a fight, but even with my help I had a feeling we'd be badly outmanned. But it worked. I don't know if the Wendigo was unsure of our powers, or if he simply had no bad intentions, or if he really wanted those stones, but it worked.

"Deal," he said. "I'll be at your house tomorrow morning. I'll call back this Sherwood for you, and you'll hand over the stones."

"My house?" said Victor. "You don't know where I live."

"Don't I? I'll see you there."

He walked off, brushing by me. Lou looked over at me, asking if I wanted him to follow, but I shook my head no.

I WAS AT VICTOR'S EARLY NEXT MORNING. IT hadn't been a bad night's work. We'd found the Wendigo and got him to agree to do what we wanted. The fake Ifrit had been a surprise, but at least no one had got hurt.

Victor was eating breakfast and grudgingly provided me with coffee. Lou didn't even bother to beg; he knew it was useless. Victor looked tired as well, which was unusual for him. His earlier leg injury must have taken more out of him than I'd thought. He hadn't even got around to reading the morning *Chronicle*, still secure in its orange plastic wrapper.

"Do you think he'll show?" I asked for the third time. Victor had thrown open the tall front windows, and the early sunlight was streaming through. A pleasant breeze came off the ocean, uncharacteristically warm for so early in the day. For once there was no morning fog. I was sipping coffee, Eli was pacing back and forth, Maggie was sitting by the window, and Lou was lying on a rug, hogging a patch of sun and catching up on his interrupted sleep. He hated mornings almost as much as I did.

We'd got home late, since as soon as we'd left Fort Point I'd driven down to the Bay Bridge to try to find Rolf. He wasn't around, and even Lou had some trouble tracking him down, so it was a while before we'd run him to ground. And yes, it turned out Richard Cory had indeed returned.

"Was he okay?" I'd asked. "Can I talk to him? He must have some information about this Wendigo."

"Depends on what you mean by okay," Rolf had answered. "Weirder than ever—he's finding it hard to keep a human form these days. And I'm sure he could tell you a lot, but I don't think he'll talk to you—I'm not sure he could even if he wanted to. But otherwise, yeah, he's fine."

I didn't bother to complain that he might at least have informed me. It wouldn't have done any good. But if that much had turned out to be true, there was a good chance our Wendigo would be showing up. And if he did, there was a good chance he could do what he said he could. Otherwise, why bother to make an appearance?

I don't know what I expected. Maybe for him to materialize in the middle of the study with a puff of smoke, or something equally dramatic, so when the knock on the front door came it was an anticlimax.

Victor answered the door, and there he stood. His forest garb had been replaced by a colored tee with a picture of Elvin Jones behind a drum set and a pair of jeans. He stood in the doorway and looked around appreciatively.

"Quite the warding system," he said. "Very impressive. I'm not sure even I could get in here without your permission."

That was something of a relief. The wards around Victor's house were not strictly his own—Eli and a lot of other knowledgeable practitioners had helped design them, as well as contributing their own power into keeping them strong. The wards around my own house are clever and subtle, strong enough to do the job, but nothing special. Victor was protected by state-of-the-art constructions, utilitarian, sleek and gleaming, and composed mostly of lines of sheer and forbidding power. It was reassuring they could block even a magical creature of power.

Victor reached out and touched him on the shoulder. An almost invisible spark of energy passed between them, providing the Wendigo with the magical equivalent of a key card. Once he was inside, Victor led the way up to the study.

"Very nice," said the Wendigo, looking around at the

dark paneling, huge fireplace, and tall windows. "A bit too faux Victorian for my tastes, but nice, nonetheless."

"Thank you," said Victor without the slightest trace of sarcasm. "Let's get down to business."

"You have the stones?"

Eli opened the old messenger bag and showed the stones to him, then closed it firmly. Like at Mama Yara's botanica, it reminded me of nothing so much as a dope deal, complete with suspicion on both sides. The Wendigo turned to me.

"I'll need your help," he said. "Or rather, it will be a lot easier if you're involved."

"Okay," I said. I still didn't trust him, though. "Are we actually going somewhere, physically, or is this just a psychic journey?" I remembered asking Eli the same question when I'd gone seeking the origin of the rune stones, more than a year ago.

"Ahh, well, that depends on how you look at it," the Wendigo said. I should have known.

"Let me guess. It's not an either/or question."

"Exactly. I'm glad you understand."

"Yeah, me, too. But on the practical side, what if something happens to us there?"

"Well, then the question becomes academic, but we won't wake up safe in our beds; that I can assure you." He held out his hand, impatiently. "Here, just relax; take my hand. Envision the place where you were when you saw her." I wasn't that eager to let him touch me, but I did it. His hand was warm, pulsing with magical energy. Nothing else happened. "It might be easier if you close your eyes and block out your present surroundings."

I did what he asked, concentrated on my breathing, and one by one blocked out the distractions around me. It wasn't that hard; it's a basic of both yoga training and magical discipline. The last senses to go were touch and smell, the breath of salt air on my face coming through the open windows.

It grew stronger, and the tang of the ocean was replaced with the slightly musty odor of gorse and bracken, and the breeze had turned cold and damp. When I opened my eyes I was back on the moor.

But this time it was different. It was dark, as if the winter sun was just sinking under the horizon. Patches of thick, evil-looking fog closed in around us, obscuring the landscape one moment, swirling away the next to reveal a barren and desolate scene. Before, the moor had been dramatic and full of mystery. This time it gave off an aura of evil and danger.

The Wendigo was standing next to me, but Lou was nowhere in sight. I had a moment of not quite panic—he'd never failed to follow me anywhere before. But then he burst out of a nearby thicket and stood there, tongue out and panting as if he'd run a long way. The Wendigo looked surprised.

"I didn't think that was possible," he said. "He didn't come with us, and there's no way he could have followed us here—there isn't any 'here' to follow us to, strictly speaking."

"He is a talented creature," I said. "So, what now?"

"Your part is done. Now that we're here, all I need to do is call her home. It won't be a problem."

I could have told him that was the wrong thing to say. It's a form of unconscious hubris, poking your finger in the eye of the gods. Sure enough, the minute he finished talking I heard a long-drawn-out, muffled howl in the distance, sounding like a hound from hell.

"What in God's name is that?" I asked. For the first time since I'd seen him, the Wendigo looked ill at ease.

"Oh, shit," he said. Not a reassuring response.

"I didn't hear anything like that the last time."

"Last time, you were pulled into Sherwood's construct. This time, it's partly yours as well. You mentioned that the moor looked like a movie set. *Wuthering Heights*, I think you said."

"Yeah."

"This isn't exactly the same place, is it? Have you ever actually been on a moor?"

"No," I said.

"But this is partly your own construct. So where did you get your idea of it from? What do you think of when you imagine a moor?" I didn't have to think about that one.

"*The Hound of the Baskervilles.*" Another howl, closer, punctuated my remark.

"And that is?"

"Sherlock Holmes. A story about a gigantic, spectral hound who roams the moors, killing people."

"I see."

"But in the story it wasn't really anything supernatural," I explained. "It turned out to be a huge, vicious, but quite ordinary dog."

"Maybe in the story. But not in your construct—trust me on that."

Another howl, long-drawn-out and definitely closer. Now it sounded less like a hound and more like some creature from hell. Lou flinched involuntarily and started picking up first one paw, then the other, the way he does when he's nervous.

"What are you worried about?" I said. "You can take a shotgun blast without it bothering you, and you can control things with just your voice. A ghostly hound shouldn't pose much of a problem."

"You'd think. But you mostly missed me with that shotgun. You only thought you hit me. A couple of pellets nicked me, but that was all. Misdirection and illusion are my true strengths." So we had something in common after all.

"Your voice is no illusion," I said.

"Sure, it is. It doesn't control anyone. It just makes them think they have no choice." That seemed like semantics to me, but this was no time for a philosophical discussion.

"So use it, then," I said.

"Believe me, I would if I could. But things work differently in places like this. I can call Sherwood; that's what I came here for. But other than that, I'm as vulnerable as you are. Maybe more so—it's your place, and you at least should still have your talent here. So it's up to you, I'm afraid."

Another howl, worse than before, and considerably nearer. My throat got dry, and this time it wasn't only Lou who flinched. For the first time since I'd met him, the Wendigo had lost his self-assured demeanor.

About twenty yards to the left of us the ground cover thinned out and dissolved into a small patch of swampy bog, no bigger than a double bed. I reached out to see if I could feel talent working, and it was. I didn't have enough power to expand it to a useful size, at least not directly. But I could gather swamp essence from the small patch and flip it over, effectively doubling it in size. Then again, and again once more. With the power of geometrical progression, it wasn't long before I had created an area some fifty yards square. Technically, I wasn't using enough power to transform a large area, but it worked. That's why it's called magic, at least by those who don't fully understand it. Which would include me, though I usually don't use that term.

I called Lou over and worked on his paws, expanding and flattening them until they were like tiny snowshoes, which took more energy and skill than creating the entire swamp did. When I was done, he ran back and forth, trying them out and stumbling a few times. Twice, he even fell over his feet before he got the hang of managing them. He wouldn't be nearly as agile as usual, but he wouldn't have to be. He'd just need to make it to the swamp.

I used the rest of my energy to put a deflection spell around myself and the Wendigo, using the fog and the bleak and featureless landscape as my model. It wouldn't fool the hound for long—for one thing, dogs rely on scent as much as they do sight, but it would make us hard to locate at first. I hoped it would work. If it didn't, we were in trouble, since I'd now used up most of my power. I would have been a lot more confident if I could have somehow brought along the Remington 870.

Just as I finished, the hound materialized out of a patch of fog. It was close to two hundred pounds, looking like a cross between a mastiff and a wolf. Muscles rippled under a short coat of hair, and it bounded toward us, light on its feet. No clever dodging aside was going to work with this one. Its eyes glowed a deep phosphorescent green, and its muzzle was full of strong and sharp teeth, covered with foaming slobber.

If the Wendigo was correct, it was a creature created in part out of my own subconscious. Which didn't say much for my imagination. It was a stock Hollywood monster, a stereotype. But that was just its physical appearance. It also projected an aura of inevitability—it was going to kill us all, rend us limb from limb, slashing muscle and crunching bone. When things created from the unconscious take on an independent existence, they're always worse than your everyday monster.

Despite my attempt at masking, it instantly zeroed in on our location and swerved toward us, uttering a bay of triumph. The closer it got, the larger it looked, and there was nowhere to hide. It didn't notice Lou, discreetly standing behind me, and just before it reached us, Lou bolted out from behind me and ran right under the beast's muzzle. It snapped at him out of reflex, like a dog after a fly, but Lou knew what he was doing. He dodged just as the muzzle lowered, and the teeth snapped shut on empty air.

Lou squealed as if mortally hurt, and the thing couldn't resist. Prey drive kicked in and it spun and went after Lou as if he were a wounded rabbit. Lou took off toward the swamp area, occasionally uttering that wounded cry. The hound was faster in a straight line than Lou was, especially a Lou with altered paws, but it couldn't change direction like he could. Lou zigged and zagged, always just a little out of reach. At one point he stumbled and nearly went down, and my heart skipped a beat. But he was just playing the beast, making sure it wouldn't abandon the chase, like a mother duck who pretends to have a crippled wing to draw a predator away from its brood.

When Lou reached the boggy area he flew right over it. At twelve pounds with magically altered paws, he barely sank into it at all, skimming over the bog like a water strider on a summer pond. The hound was right on his tail, and its momentum carried it well into the morass before it realized the danger and started to sink. In seconds it was floundering helplessly, each desperate struggle trapping it more securely in the mire. Lou doubled back, making sure not to get too close to the mire, and ran up to where I waited.

"Good job," I said to him. It looked like he was going to be living on bacon instead of kibble from now on for quite a while. I returned his paws to normal, and he stood there shaking them out like an athlete after a hard training run.

"Nice work," said the Wendigo. "I wasn't sure you had it in you."

"I'm full of surprises." I watched the hound struggling, sinking inexorably deeper with every effort. I felt kind of sorry for it. It must have shown, because the Wendigo picked up on it immediately.

"Not to worry. It doesn't really exist, you know, any more than this place does."

"Are you trying to say it couldn't have hurt us after all?" That didn't jibe with what I knew about such things.

"Oh, no. Just because it isn't real doesn't mean it couldn't have torn us to shreds."

"Glad you cleared that up," I said. "Now, any chance you can do what we came here for, before something worse shows up?"

"Of course." He spun in a circle, sniffing the damp air, like Lou on a scent. "This way."

We trudged over the moor, through the drifting fog. I immediately lost all sense of direction, but the Wendigo seemed sure of his direction. We walked for fifteen minutes or so, until a break in the fog revealed a rocky crag in the distance. It was familiar, and I thought I could see a misty figure blending into the rock.

"Close enough," said the Wendigo. He faced in that direction and called softly, "Sherwood." At first I could barely hear him, but the sound grew until it filled the landscape as strongly as if he had shouted at the top of his lungs. He spoke again. "Sherwood. Come."

The Wendigo wasn't speaking to me, but I still felt the pull. I wish I knew how he did it. The fog had closed in again and I could no longer see the crag, but he turned and began to walk away. He headed directly for a particularly dense area of fog, where the vapor turned to water the moment it touched your skin and you couldn't see more than five feet in front of your face.

"Home," he breathed, again the word barely audible. The fog closed in thicker than ever until it was almost as disorienting as the featureless void I'd entered at the Columbarium. A bright, diffuse light source appeared, illuminating the fog from the side, further disorienting me. A faint shape loomed ominously right at the limit of my vision, then another. The rocky ground softened under my feet, and as the fog thinned, the shapes resolved themselves into the figures of Eli and Victor. The rocky floor became a carpet, the bright light became sunlight streaming through tall windows, and then we were back in Victor's study.

Sherwood lay crumpled on the floor. Eli bounded over toward her, but I beat him to it. I put my fingers on the side of her throat and felt warmth, but no pulse. Then I moved my fingers slightly and found it, reassuringly strong and steady. She was alive. I didn't want to let go of her—I could hardly believe she was back, solid of flesh and breathing easily, but Eli shouldered me aside, looking worried.

"What's wrong? Why is she unconscious?" he asked the Wendigo, putting his large fingers where mine had been.

"Don't worry," said the Wendigo. "She'll be fine. Remember, she was suspended in that place for a very long time. The psychic shock of returning has just temporarily short-circuited her consciousness, that's all."

I moved around Eli to the other side. I needed to touch her again, to feel her, to make sure this wasn't just a cruel illusion. Eli scooped her up in his massive arms and laid her gently on the couch, and Victor joined us at her side. We all just stood there, staring silently down at her.

"Ahem," said the Wendigo, with a fake cough. "I hate to break up this touching reunion, but I believe you have something you want to give me."

"Not until she comes to," Victor said.

As if on cue, Sherwood opened her eyes, looked up with a puzzled expression, and then closed them again. Eli leaned over and looked at her closely.

"I think he's right," he said. "She'll be fine. Give him what he wants." He glanced over at the Wendigo. "And if she isn't . . ."

Victor picked up the messenger bag, now half full of rune stones, and handed it over, a bit reluctantly. A quick look inside, and the Wendigo was satisfied.

"Nice doing business with you," he said and headed toward the door, then stopped.

"By the way," he said, "did you get a chance to look at this morning's paper?"

"No," Eli answered. "Why?"

"You might find it interesting."

Victor picked up the paper from the desk and slipped it out of its orange plastic bag. He unfolded it with a snap of his wrist, and I could read the headline from across the room: "Another Hiker Dead!" The Wendigo smiled and turned back toward the door.

"Just a moment," said Victor sharply. He read down a ways. "This says it happened right at dusk. In Marin County."

The Wendigo stopped and stared back at him.

"I hope you're not thinking of welshing on the deal," the Wendigo said. "That would be a very bad idea, I guarantee you."

"No, not at all," said Eli, and I knew he meant it. He'd warned us often enough about the dangers of reneging on promises made to uncanny creatures. "But you knew about that headline. It couldn't have been the fake Ifrit; it was stalking us at the time. It couldn't have been you; you were trapped in the circle. So what was it, then?"

"That does seem to be the question."

"You want to tell us what's been going on?"

"Why should I?" he said. "I'm not real fond of any of you." He pointed at me. "You tried to kill me, remember, the first time I saw you." He pointed at Victor. "And then you trapped me in that cage. What would have happened to me if I hadn't escaped?" He shook his head. "No, I'm not overly fond of any of you."

"You and the Ifrit creature aren't the only things that came out of the energy pool, were you?" I said, finally getting it.

"Brilliant," he said. "Right on top of things, I see."

"But you won't tell us what it was? Can you at least tell us what it looks like? I did save your ass out on that moor, after all."

"Yeah, and your own as well." He laughed, suddenly, sounding very human indeed.

"How about a hint? Just to show there are no hard feelings."

"But there are. Just stay close to home and I'm sure you'll figure it out, anyway. Eventually. But of course by that time it will be too late."

Without another word, he walked through the door and down the stairs, and this time Victor didn't try to stop him. A moment later, the sound of the front door slamming shut echoed up to us.

Eli turned his attention back to Sherwood. He bent down close and took her hand.

"Sherwood?" She opened her eyes briefly.

"Grmff," she said, and closed them again.

"She's coming out of it," Eli said.

Victor meanwhile was skimming through the rest of the article in the paper.

"Damn," he said. "Another girl. They pinpointed the attack to eight in the evening—just about the time we were catching the Wendigo, and fighting off the fake Ifrit. So it really wasn't the fake Ifrit and it wasn't our Wendigo, either. Damn."

Sherwood interrupted whatever else he was going to say by opening her eyes and sitting up suddenly and speaking.

"What happened?" she said in a clear and lucid voice. "Where's Christoph? How did we get back to Victor's?"

For a moment I thought she was asking about her return from the moors, but Eli nodded in comprehension and a second later I caught on as well.

"What's the last thing you remember?" he asked, still holding on to her hand. She shuddered.

"We were up at McClaren Park. Chistoph had hold of me. He'd taken over my mind, somehow—I was fighting all the time, but he was too strong. Then he let go and made a gesture in my direction. I felt a blast of energy, everything went white, and then suddenly I'm here with all of you staring down at me solemnly. Am I hurt?"

"Not exactly," Eli said. "But there's a lot to tell you. You had better get comfortable—this is going to be rather a long story. Victor, some tea perhaps?"

"I could use a cup of coffee," I said. Victor ignored me, and Sherwood said tea would be nice.

It took all of an hour for Eli to explain what had happened during the last year while I'd thought she was dead. Sherwood took it all in, interrupting only a few times with questions. At the end of Eli's tale, she only said, "What about my apartment?"

"Gone. You can stay here, though."

"And my stuff?"

"Also gone. There didn't seem any point in keeping it." She was silent for a moment.

"Well, thank God my parents are dead. I never thought I'd say that, but it would have killed them." Another moment of silence. "I should be thankful, I guess, but to me it's like nothing happened. Except that I've lost a year of my life. What a total drag."

"Not really," Eli said. "We've all aged a year, but you haven't. Think of it as if you had traveled into the future."

"Exactly," I added. "You're looking at it the wrong way around. You haven't lost a year—you've gained one. Like Eli said, it's as if you were a time traveler. You're only a few days older than you were that day up in McClaren Park, but Eli and Victor and me have aged since then. You've gained over a year on all of us—you're in the future."

"I suppose you're right," she said.

We spent what was left of the day filling her in on the state of the world these days. One of the things she was most interested in was Timothy and how long Victor and he had been together. By afternoon, she was exhausted and crashed in one of Victor's spare rooms. She may not have remembered anything about her yearlong sojourn into the netherworld, but it had affected her nonetheless. She kept losing her train of thought and asking us to repeat things. It was worrisome, but Eli thought she'd be fine in a few days.

By the time I got home, I was drained as well. But when I entered my flat, there was something waiting there for me. Not a ravenous ghoul or ghostly apparition, but something far worse. The goddamned message light on the phone was blinking again.

NINE

"MASON, THIS IS MORGAN," THE MESSAGE RAN. "Sorry to bother you, but I had this weird dream . . ." Her voice trailed off and I heard a muffled curse as she put her hand over the phone. She took her hand off. "Okay, I didn't realize how lame that was going to sound. But considering, I thought we could at least talk. Call me when you get a chance."

Most of the messages I get aren't anything I want to hear, but this wasn't so bad. Not bad at all. I flopped down on the bed and picked up the phone.

"Morgan? Mason," I said when she answered.

"Oh, God. I'm so embarrassed. A bad dream, for Christ's sake, and I call you about it."

"Hey, you're a psychic, and a real one. Dreams are important."

"Well, this one was. Or I think it was. There are dreams and dreams, you know, and this was the other sort. Scared me half to death to be honest."

"So tell me."

"You were walking along a street, somewhere in the

city, I think. Two people were with you—a large black man, middle-aged. And another man, smaller and very intense, or at least that's what I got." So far, so good. Me, Victor, and Eli. "But your dog? Louie? He wasn't around." That didn't sound good. "And here's the weird thing—the reason I almost didn't call. There was a sense of danger, worse than the vision I had last time, way worse. But there was nothing else there. Or if there was, it was invisible."

"Was it a specific danger, or just something general?" I asked.

"Both. Very specific, but nothing I could put my finger on. Have you ever had one of those dreams where everything is perfectly ordinary, but for some reason you're terrified? Like in the dream, you know if you go into a house, something dreadful will happen?"

"Sure," I said.

"Well, this was like that. I have no idea what is waiting there—it might not even be something physical—visions rely on metaphor, you know. But whatever it is, it's bad, really bad. How ridiculous is that?"

"Not ridiculous at all," I said. "I know who you're describing. Those two others are friends of mine, and if we were out together, it's a good bet something nasty was waiting around the corner."

"But why couldn't I see it?"

"A good question," I said. "Don't worry. Between the three of us, there's not much we can't handle. But thanks. It's always good to be on guard."

After she hung up, I considered what it might mean. Despite my assurances that we could handle anything, I was disturbed. If her vision showed some awful thing awaiting us, where was Lou? He wouldn't let me go off alone like that. And why couldn't Morgan see what was threatening us? Bad enough to be searching for a monster, but an invisible monster just wasn't fair.

But what was it? An invisible beast was possible, I supposed—anything was. But that seemed unlikely.

I pulled out my guitar and ran through some tunes,

standards that I know so well I don't have to think about them. It's a form of meditation for me—it requires a conscious attention to detail, but at the same time, part of my mind is able to wander and free associate. Sometimes it works; I've gotten some brilliant ideas that way. Well, some useful ones, anyway.

But this time, nothing came. Lou sat in the corner, listening. That's the way I like to imagine it—I doubt very much if he has any ear for music other than the occasional drawn-out howls from his canine brethren. But he usually sits there attentively, so who knows? Who knows anything about Ifrits, anyway? But after a while with no success, I gave it up and went to sleep.

When I woke up next morning, though, an idea did come to me as I was pouring my morning coffee. Nothing brilliant, something rather obvious, but an idea is an idea. The only real clues, the logical place to start, was with the murdered victims. So if I could find out more about exactly how those hikers had been killed, it might reveal something about what had killed them, or at least point us in a direction.

The cops weren't releasing a lot of details to the papers, just using phrases like "mutilated" and "torn up." And if those were the phrases they were using to *prevent* panic, the reality must be far worse. Specific information wouldn't be easy to come by—you can't just call up the cops and ask what the real scoop is. Only, sometimes, you can.

A few years ago there had been a rash of burglaries over in Cow Hollow. There were never any signs of a break-in; apparently the victims had simply neglected to lock their doors when they left their apartments. But after a while, that theory started to look unlikely. The residents there became so paranoid that many installed additional locks, and a few even changed their locks out completely. Still, the thefts continued.

The cops were baffled. For a while they focused on a locksmith who ran a small key-and-lock store on Chestnut

Street, but that didn't pan out. Somehow Victor got wind of this and we did some investigation of our own. It turned out that the person responsible was a teenage kid with a flash of talent. Usually we find out about these kids early, before they get into any real trouble, and mentor them. Sherwood in particular was good at this. She spent a lot of time working with these kids, and almost without exception they loved her. And were scared of her. Sherwood has enough talent to be scary indeed to a novice, and none of them wanted to cross her.

But once in a while, one slips through the cracks. Jenna, the teenage girl we'd taken off the streets over a year ago, was one of those, although that hadn't worked out well for anyone, especially her.

These untrained talents can't control their abilities most of the time. They accidentally find something they can do, and it never occurs to them they might be capable of more. The parlor trick they've learned is all they know and all they do. But interestingly, sometimes they stumble onto something that even an experienced practitioner can't manage.

All metals are difficult to work with, and especially iron. Trying to affect an iron lock, for example, using magical talent is almost impossible, even for the strongest practitioner. But this kid could unlock any door, defeat any lock, with only minimal effort. He was a one-trick pony— like an idiot savant who can instantly tell you the day of the week for any date in history, but that's all the math he can do. Even so, that's a feat outside the realm of the possible for even the most brilliant of ordinary mathematicians.

So this kid would wait until he saw the resident leave, defeat the lock with a snap of his fingers, unlock the front door, and stroll in to take whatever he wanted.

That was how we first met Macklin. He was in charge of the makeshift task force the cops threw together to solve the rash of burglaries—this was Cow Hollow, after all, not Bayview, and thus worthy of police notice. And although we obviously weren't about to turn the kid over to the cops, we did take him off the streets and the burglaries stopped. Also, we were able to help Macklin out by doing some magical forensic work on an unrelated burglary, one where a cool half million in jewelry was taken. It helped to solve the case, and although he couldn't figure out how we'd come up with the information, he was glad to have it just the same. So he was well-disposed toward us, as they say. But he was never entirely sure about who we were.

He was a sharp guy, and he knew there was something not quite right about Victor and me. I think he decided Victor was some sort of government black op. I have no idea what he thought I was about, but we got along.

It also turned out he was a jazz buff, and we ended up keeping in touch afterward. Not exactly friends, but more than casual acquaintances. He liked hanging with musicians, and for my part, well, having a cop as a friend is never a bad idea. Besides, he was a good guy.

I hadn't bothered to call him before, because for one, Victor didn't like the idea of having a sharp cop becoming interested in us and our doings. Besides, I'd thought I already knew what was killing those hikers—the fake Ifrit. But I'd been wrong. And civilians were dying—so getting some useful information was worth the risk of making him curious about us.

When I called his extension he picked up on the first ring.

"Burglary."

"I want to report a crooked cop."

"Which one? We got hundreds to choose from."

"Some guy named Macklin. A real thug, if ever there was one."

"I know him. A bad apple. We've been trying to get rid of him for years." He laughed. "What can I do for you, Mase? Played any good gigs lately?"

"All my gigs are good. The audience occasionally sucks, though."

"You want a tough audience? Try being a cop sometime."

"No, thanks. I don't possess the people skills or the superb intelligence necessary to do that job."

"Hold on a second. Let me find my shovel."

"I mean every word."

"Oh, I see. You want something."

"Of course. Why else would I flatter a stupid—I mean, not at all, Inspector, but now that you bring it up . . ."

"Shoot."

"You know those animal attacks? The ones that have everyone in a panic?"

"I seem to recall hearing something about them," he said dryly.

"The paper just says the victims were all torn up. I know you're not directly involved, but cops talk. Have you heard anything else about them?"

"Why the interest?"

"Let's just say I'm a concerned citizen."

"Sorry, Mason, but you know I can't talk about an ongoing investigation. Wish I could help, but them's the rules."

"That's okay," I said. "I understand. Thanks anyway."

We talked another couple of minutes about other stuff and I invited him down to my next gig before hanging up. Thirty seconds later, my phone rang.

"That was quick," I said.

"Cell phone. It's not a good idea to talk on department lines, I assure you."

"I know, but I couldn't find your cell number."

"Well, it doesn't matter. So what's your interest here?"

"Just an idea I had. But I need a description of what really happened to those hikers."

"I don't have access to any official reports, but I can tell you this. If the state of those bodies was common knowledge, there'd be more than just panic."

"Why's that?"

"Well, from what I've heard, they weren't just mauled; they were completely eviscerated. And the internal organs were missing—heart, liver, kidneys—even the brain. The heads were all cracked open and it looks like some animal just scooped them out and ate them."

"Are you sure it was an animal?"

"What makes you ask that?" he said, his tone sharpening as the cop sense kicked in. Then it softened. "No, it's an animal, all right. One of the victims was seen being attacked. His friends were hiking with him and they were lagging back a ways, which is probably what saved their lives. They saw something come out of the bushes and drag him off. It happened so quick they couldn't give a good description, just that it was large and dark in color, but they swear it wasn't a mountain lion. But it certainly wasn't a person. Whatever it was tore the boy apart, just like the others. The wildlife guys are saying it can't have been a mountain lion, either—about the only thing that could do that to a person would be a bear. But there aren't any bears around these parts. And even if one escaped from captivity, bears don't act like that anyway. The whole thing is just spooky."

"Hmm," I said. "Interesting. Well, thanks for the info."

"No problem. Does any of it mean anything to you?"

"Not really."

"Right. Like you said, just a concerned citizen. And speaking of which, I do remember hearing about another guy asking very similar questions a while back, offering to help. Homicide was very hot on him for a while. They thought he was just a bit too curious. But that was before the animal was actually seen. Turned out he was just another nutcase." Warning bells went off in my head. Macklin might think it just an odd coincidence, but I didn't.

"Huh," I said. "Curious. You don't remember his name, by any chance?" Now warning bells were definitely going off in Macklin's head.

"What's going on here, Mase?" he said.

"Nothing. Just thought it might be someone I know—a lot of my friends have been discussing this case."

"Yeah? Well, I can't remember his name, but it was something like Rocky or Rambo."

I almost blurted out, "Ramsey?" but caught myself in time. One more coincidence and Macklin would start paying me serious attention, animal sighting or no. Cops hate things that don't add up. I guess all of us do, for that matter.

"Well, it's not important," I said. "Thanks for the help, though."

"Anytime."

After I hung up for the second time, I did some serious thinking. What was Ramsey doing sniffing around the cops? Was it just his general clumsy attempt at investigation, or did he want to find out how much they knew? Maybe Ruby had put him up to it, but she had to know how lame and ineffective he was. The only thing he'd accomplish would be to draw unwanted attention. I'd have to check with her.

The information from Macklin was interesting, but it hadn't really helped at all. Instead of narrowing down possibilities, it opened up even more of them. Such as, what if the killings had nothing to do with any theoretical entity wandering around? Nothing kills just because it's evil. Everyone and everything acts from motive, even powerful beings with unknown abilities. Power. Fear. Simple hunger.

And missing organs? That smacked of a more human agency—a black practitioner gone bad, for example. I had no idea what those organs might be used for, but it wasn't a random happenstance. But the witnesses had seen an animal. Or something not human.

I thought some more, then pulled out the scrap of paper with Ruby's number on it and called. After a few pleasantries, slightly less juvenile than the ones I'd traded with Macklin, I got down to business.

"Have you talked to Victor lately?" I asked.

"I have—in fact, I'm on my way over to his house later this afternoon. I've got some ideas I want to run past him."

"Does that include any ideas from the cops?"

"Beg pardon?"

"The cops. Did you know Ramsey's been bugging the cops about these murders, stirring up interest?"

"Oh, fuck. I'm sorry. I'll talk to him."

"You do that. He can cause trouble for us all, you know."

"I know. He's been helpful, but he's beginning to wear on me anyway. It might be time to send him on his way." She paused. "I'd appreciate it if you didn't have to tell Victor about that, though. It makes me look like a flake."

"Tell Victor about what?"

"Thanks," she said. "Why don't you come by, too? We can run some ideas past each other."

"That would be great, if I had any. But sure, I'll be there."

"About one, if that's okay? If I can get some other stuff done by then."

RUBY WAS STRETCHED OUT ON THE COUCH IN the study when I arrived at Victor's. She unwound herself from the couch, slinked her way over to me, and held out a cool and dry hand, giving me a little squeeze as she did. I think she knew the effect she had on me and enjoyed teasing me, but not in a mean way.

"Ruby's got an interesting take on this," said Eli. "She doesn't think there's a creature out there at all."

"Why not? We didn't dream up the fake Ifrit," I said. "Or the Wendigo, either."

"No, that's not what I mean," she said. "I'm talking about there being another creature."

"Well, something's been killing people, and it's not the two we know about."

"Something or *someone*."

"Like a black practitioner, you mean?" Her face took on a grim expression.

"That's exactly what I mean. I've been casting some scry-ing spells, ones designed to locate uncanny things. Something Giancarlo taught me. That's how I tumbled to that Ifrit creature, the one you've been hunting. I can't use my talent to actually locate it, but I can feel its presence.

"And there's another being I've felt as well—I had no idea what it was until I heard about your 'Wendigo'— although I don't think that's really what it is. But here's the thing—nothing else like that is out there. If there were, I could feel it, I'm sure."

"Maybe it's invisible to you," I said, thinking about Morgan's vision.

"No, I'd still sense it, even if I didn't know what it was. But if it were a practitioner, now . . ." She shook her head. "That wouldn't register. But what I don't get is why any practitioner would do such a thing."

"Well, it's worse than that," I said. "I did some digging, called a cop friend. You remember Macklin, Victor?" He nodded. "He told me that not only were the victims torn apart but all their internal organs were missing—heart, liver, kidneys—everything." Ruby spun around and smacked her hand on her forehead.

"Of course. The organs." She grabbed my arm. "The skulls. What about the skulls? Were they cracked open?"

"They were. And the brains were sucked out as well."

"Son of a bitch." She started pacing back and forth, muttering, until Eli stuck out a large hand and corralled her.

"This means something to you, I'm assuming."

"It does. It's typical, I'm sorry to say, of a very specific type of spell work."

"Black practitioners? Again?"

"Not necessarily. It's a spell used to extend life. Through the ages there have been more than one practitioner who's tried it, and they weren't all dark arts guys—mostly older practitioners, though, ones who thought they could cheat death that way. You take the organs and the life force from young men and women, transfer it into your own chi, and gain a few years of youth and vitality. Theoretically you could continue that way forever, although each time it takes a little more to get the same effect."

"Is that possible?" I asked, glancing over at Eli for confirmation.

"Supposedly," he said. "I have read about such things in my researches, but it's all been speculation. It would take a strong practitioner. I've never met anyone who's run across an actual case."

"Well, I have," Ruby said. "Or at least Giancarlo has—it was before my time."

"Maybe," said Eli. "But it seems an incredible coincidence that something like this would surface at exactly the same time as the fake Ifrit and the Wendigo. Are you saying there's no connection?"

"There are coincidences in this world. But maybe here's the connection. Consider this: When Mason found the Wendigo, it knew his name. Now, sure, it could have found out with a little research, or even by just hanging around. But until Mason showed up at Muir Woods, it would have had no reason to know he even existed, am I right? But not only did it know Mason's name; it was almost as if it was waiting there for him."

"Exactly. So?"

"So, maybe a practitioner told it about him—as soon as he and Victor figured out the fake Ifrit wasn't responsible for those attacks, you'd start looking around for another suspect. A preemptive strike, perhaps."

"Maybe," said Eli. "But consider this: Mason, before you ran into the Wendigo, who or what did you and it have in common?"

"Rolf?"

"Rolf never saw him, didn't even know what he might be, much less where you would be." I thought for a few seconds.

"Well, there isn't anything else."

"Are you sure? How did you know where to find him?"

"Through Morgan's vision, of course. But . . ."

Now, that was interesting. She'd seen me; she'd seen Lou; she'd seen the woods. And although she hadn't seen the Wendigo, she'd certainly felt his presence.

"Exactly," Eli said, seeing the look of dawning comprehension on my face. "Morgan saw you in the vision. She saw where you would be. She sensed the Wendigo. And the Wendigo has showed himself very comfortable in dimensions of the mind, places that are both of the spirit and of the flesh, places not exactly one or the other. He had no trouble finding Sherwood, remember.

"Visions, true ones, operate on a psychic plane outside of our ordinary space and time. And clearly, that outside perspective is something very familiar to our Wendigo. So when she saw him, and you, he also saw her. And you. And he knew what she knew—your name, for example."

"And the Wendigo isn't the only thing she's had a vision of," I said, slowly. "She's seen something else— actually, she didn't see it, but she sensed it, and it scared the crap out of her, far worse than the Wendigo did. No offense, Ruby—she couldn't see what it was, either, but unlike you, she could feel it."

"So either way if there's something else out there, it's not only aware of you; it's aware of her as well," said Victor. "That's not good."

"No, it's not," Eli said. "I think this woman might well be in need of some protection."

"She's going to be thrilled about that."

"Can't be helped. The least we can do is ward her house, so she'll have a safe haven. Even if it turns out to be a rogue practitioner after all, it can't hurt."

"And we'd better get on it," Victor said. "Ruby, do you want to come along?"

"No," she said. "I've got things to do. But I'm sure you guys can handle it. I still think it's a practitioner—no matter what this woman saw in her vision, if there were a monster prowling around, there's no way I wouldn't feel it. Still, I guess I could be wrong, and it certainly couldn't hurt to give this woman some protection."

She left, looking thoughtful and worried.

• • •

THE PHONE CONVERSATION WITH MORGAN WAS as awkward as I'd expected. Not surprisingly, the idea she might be in mortal danger didn't sit well with her. She wasn't upset with me, however. She was mostly mad at her mom.

"If she hadn't started spouting off about my being psychic, I wouldn't have done a reading for you and I wouldn't be involved with this now," she said.

"True, but a very close friend of mine wouldn't have been rescued, either," I told her. She was less than impressed.

"Good for her; not so good for me," she said.

She did like the idea of making her home safe, though. Who wouldn't? When she gave me her address, I was surprised to learn it was over in Bernal Heights, not so far from my own place.

"I thought you lived on the other side of town," I said.

"Yeah, well, I wasn't so sure at first I wanted you to know where I lived. I picked a coffee shop over in my old neighborhood to meet."

"And I reassured you?"

"Not really, but Louie did. That's one of the things he's good at, right?"

"Yes, it is," I said. "We need to get this done right away. We'll be over in an hour or so, if that's all right."

"You and Louie?"

"Me and my friends. They're very good at this sort of thing."

HER HOUSE IN BERNAL HEIGHTS WAS RIGHT ON Holly Park Circle, across from Holly Park itself. Bernal was once a working-class neighborhood and in many respects still is, although houses there, like everywhere in San Francisco, are now out of the price range of true working people. Way out of the range of a working musician.

At one time Bernal Heights was a favored spot for motorcycle clubs and other counterculture types seeking to keep a low profile. It hasn't been yuppified as much as the Mission, but it's getting there. Jimmy's bar, one of the sketchiest in the city, is located there, as well as the Wild Side West, perhaps the oldest lesbian bar in the city, although it's hard to tell anymore since the clientele has become so diverse.

There was frantic deep-pitched barking from inside Morgan's house when I rang the bell. Lou looked interested. The door opened and a huge Rottweiler pushed its way into the doorway, guarding its turf, growling softly. Lou bounded over to sniff noses and it jumped back three feet.

"Beulah, calm down," she said. Beulah whined and sat down. Morgan sighed. "I originally got her for protection, but that turned out to be a joke. She's a sweetie, but she's afraid of her own shadow. Small dogs make her nervous, and she's terrified of cats."

Beulah whined again as Lou greeted her. He's very good with real dogs. He actually enjoys playing doggy games on occasion, and it's the rare dog who realizes that he's not really one of them. After the appropriate amount of sniffing, both tails began to wag.

"Morgan, this is Eli and Victor," I said as we walked inside.

"I recognize you two," she said. "You're the ones—" She broke off and glanced over at me.

"The ones you saw in the vision," I finished. "They're here to help set up wards around the house, for protection."

"Oh. How does that work, anyway? Will I feel it, like an electric fence?"

"Not at all," Eli assured her. "You won't even be able to tell the wards are there. But they will keep out things that shouldn't be allowed in."

Eli and Victor continued their walk-through, examining the back door and the windows. The house was a two-story wooden structure, probably built in the twenties or thirties. Inside, art deco furniture and original artwork crammed every room.

"Very nice," I said.

"It is, isn't it. I wish I could take credit for it all, but I inherited the place from my aunt Aida about five years ago." That explained how she could afford such a place.

"She had excellent taste," Victor said, looking around approvingly.

"Didn't she? Not a very nice person, actually, although since she left me the house I shouldn't say that, but she did have a great eye for things."

We walked through the house to the kitchen, where the back door opened out onto a wooden deck and stairs ran down to a garden below. Victor was the one who would set up the wards—lots of practitioners can contribute, but the actual warding tends to be a one-man job. Everyone has their own style in setting up protection, and often two people working together don't mesh. Two differing approaches can result in discontinuities, and the warding often ends up weaker than it would with either person working alone. Victor was the logical choice to do it; his talent is better suited and he's a stronger practitioner than I am anyway. Eli's expertise is invaluable, but he doesn't always have the power to implement his own ideas.

Sometimes practitioners can work together. Victor's mansion is the best-protected house on the West Coast, a fortress of interlocking grids of energy. Nothing gets in or out unless he wants it to. It has to be that way, since he's made serious enemies in his day, practitioners who bear him no love at all. That's what happens when your job is chief enforcer of magical behavior, and your moral code leans toward the ethically rigid.

Quite a few practitioners worked on the warding of that house, and it now looks like a power substation when viewed on the psychic plane. But they'd had weeks to work on it, plenty of time to fine-tune and check every magical seam and rivet where there was a possibility of conflict.

Victor started on the front door, throwing out a line of energy that limned the edges of the doorway with pale green. Of course it wasn't really green; it wasn't strictly a

color at all. Green is just a metaphor for what could be
perceived on the psychic plane. He wove in several other
lines, mostly in blacks and grays, then moved on to the
windows. Around the back, upstairs, and finally the fireplace in the front room, something I might have overlooked
if I'd been doing it.

Morgan followed him around, wide-eyed, although of
course she couldn't see anything of what he had done.
Except, she could.

"Why are most of those lines black?" she asked. Eli
looked at her sharply.

"You can see them?"

"Well, not really see them, not with my eyes. More like
what happens when I get a vision."

This was unexpected. She was a psychic, to be sure,
but she shouldn't have been able to see the wards. Unless
she had more than a touch of the talent herself. This was
an interesting development.

"When this is settled, we'll need to have a talk," Eli
said.

Victor finally finished sitting up the wards and sat down
heavily at the kitchen table. Warding an entire house on
short notice will take a lot out of you, even if you're Victor.

"Is it safe now?" Morgan asked.

"As safe as I can make it," Victor said. "Nothing's getting in here."

"Nothing?"

"Well, nothing of the magical variety. No practitioners.
No creatures. You'll still need locks against burglars."

"What about Mason? Can he come in if I want him
to?"

"Sure, as long as you invite him in. The wards are at-
tuned to you."

"You mean like a vampire movie? He can't come in
unless I invite him?"

"Not the metaphor I would have chosen," I said. "But,
yes, basically."

"That's kind of cool, actually." She looked out a window at the backyard. "What about the backyard? I spend a lot of time out there, in the garden. Do I have to stay in the house all the time?"

"It's hard to properly ward an open area," Eli said. "We could make it safer, though, strong enough to slow something down and give you time to get inside."

Victor looked over at me.

"Do you think you could handle that?" he said.

I was stunned. First, that he was admitting, at least implicitly, that he was worn-out. And second, that he would even think of trusting me to do something like that. Luckily, both he and Eli had taught me a lot about warding last year when my own place had needed serious protection. And since the yard was a separate area my work wouldn't interfere with Victor's house wards.

"Sure," I said.

I wasn't sure at all, but it wouldn't help Morgan's peace of mind if I hemmed and hawed. I walked down the back stairs, and I liked what I saw. A tall ivy-covered fence surrounded the entire yard, no breaks, nice and even. On either side, the fence came right up to the house. I could attach the wards in the yard to the warded house, and the even height of the fence made warding the rest of the yard an easy task.

Most of my talent is the improvisational sort, but I have learned some other skills. I didn't have enough power to properly ward the entire fence, so I laid a tiny line of force around the top of it, like a guide wire. I poured all the energy I had into one corner and bound it up with the ivy growing on the fence. It sat there quietly glowing. So now, although the rest of fence was basically unprotected, the minute anything tried to climb over or break through, the bound force would travel along the guide wire to the appropriate spot and stop it cold. In effect, the entire fence was now protected as strongly as the small section where I'd put all my focus. Eli was observing, and he smiled approvingly.

"A very elegant solution. You're learning, boy."

Morgan was appreciative of our help, but at the same time was understandably disturbed. Eli assured her it was just a precaution.

"You don't have to hide inside the house all the time," he said. "Just be careful—don't go out alone late at night, for example."

"Like as if I had a stalker."

"Yes, something like that. And if you're spooked about anything, give one of us a call."

"Oh, don't worry," she said. "I will."

I WENT HOME FOR A WELL-DESERVED REST, BUT had barely managed to sit down when Ruby called.

"Good, you're home," she said. "I think I'm onto something. Or maybe something's onto me. I'm sitting at a café, over on Valencia and Twentieth, enjoying a soy latte."

"I'm not sure that counts as a grand discovery, but it does sounds nice."

"At a table in the back, there's a practitioner watching me. He's been shadowing me all day, but he's been shielding and I could never get a good look at him—until now. He's still shielding, but just hiding his talent, so I wouldn't spot him as a practitioner."

"You think he knows you're hip to him?"

"I doubt it. He's just reading the paper, pretending to be just another Mission hipster."

"What does he look like?"

"Quite striking, actually. Medium height, youngish, with a mass of flaming curly red hair."

"Like yours?"

"No, his hair is dyed."

"And yours is natural?"

"Something you'll never find out; that's for sure. But his isn't meant to look natural. It's a fashion statement, bright scarlet, but with heavy black eyebrows."

"Does not ring a bell at all," I said. "Maybe Victor's

heard of him, or maybe he's new in the city. What made you pick up on him?"

"He wasn't shielding that well—I could hardly have missed him."

"Maybe he wanted you to notice."

"Maybe. Anyway, you live close. I thought you might want to drop by and then we could have a talk with him."

"Give me five minutes," I said.

"Hold on," she said. "He's leaving. Got to go."

"Wait, wait," I said quickly. "That might not be the best idea. If he's letting you notice him, he probably wants you to follow. People have been dismembered, remember? If your idea about a practitioner is right, you don't want to be confronting him alone."

"I can take care of myself."

"I'm sure you can, but it's not worth the risk. Use your head. I'll be down there in a few minutes."

I got a reluctant agreement out of her, and by the time I got to the café she was drinking another latte, sitting at an outside table.

"I should have followed him," she said.

"Not worth it. If you're wrong, it doesn't get you anywhere. If you're right, it could be a big mistake."

"I guess. But I don't think I'm wrong about this."

"So why do you think he was following you?"

"Well, if I'm right, and a practitioner is behind this, he's got to be aware of me. I've been asking a lot of questions, poking my nose all over town. Maybe he wants to see what I'm up to, whether I'm a threat to him."

"Or maybe he was trying to get up the nerve to hit on you."

"Aren't you sweet? No, there's something going on with this guy."

We tossed a few ideas around but didn't get anywhere, and eventually Ruby finished up her latte and headed home. I got a cup of coffee and sat there with Lou for a while, watching the Mission denizens stroll by. The demographics of the Mission were changing—fewer Hispanics, more yuppies and faux hipsters. And it was a younger crowd these days, most of them younger than I was. Then I realized they were the same age as they'd always been. I was the changing demographic, growing older every day, imperceptibly but inexorably. After ten minutes or so, Lou nudged my knee, in that deliberate fashion he uses when he wants to alert me to something.

I scanned the area, and it didn't take long to see what he had scoped out. Across the street, staring intently into the front display window of a bookstore, was the redheaded stranger. His back was toward me, and he was using the reflection of the street in the window to keep an eye on me—a trick he'd no doubt picked up from countless bad TV movies. But even though his back was turned, there was no mistaking him. He had a mop of curly red hair, dyed an entirely unnatural red. Not the ideal appearance for trailing someone on the q.t. Which meant that I was supposed to see him. Which meant . . . what?

Abruptly, he turned away from the window and walked away, moving at a good clip, but not fast enough to keep me from following if I wanted to. The advice I'd given Ruby was perfectly sound. There was no reason to follow him, except curiosity, since I didn't see a practitioner being the answer to our murders. And if by chance I was wrong, the downside could be considerable. I pushed my chair back, beckoned to Lou, and took off after him.

He ambled casually down Valencia, to Sixteenth, then over to Mission. Without so much as a backward glance, he descended the stairs to the BART station. I always carry a ticket with some money left on it for just such situations, so I inserted my ticket and breezed through the turnstile, not far behind.

Lou scooted under, staying close to my feet. Dogs aren't allowed on BART, and whenever I take the train I use a small backpack for him to ride in, layered over with a minor concealment spell to make him look like an old sweater on casual inspection.

That wasn't an option, so I used some talent to cast an aversion spell over my feet and told him to stay close. It wouldn't hide his presence, but it would keep people from glancing down to see him as long as he stayed close. Casting the aversion spell directly on him would have been better, but it would have taken time I didn't have and a lot more energy. I could maintain the spell on my legs without much effort; if I had to make it a discrete spell and attach it to him as he moved along, it would have been a more difficult thing to maintain. Besides, except for the BART police, nobody cared.

The redheaded practitioner got aboard a southbound train, which was crowded as rush hour wound down. I squeezed in at the back end of the same car, Lou crowding close so he wouldn't get his paws stepped on. One thing was now clear—this guy was playing a game with me. I had an impulse to push through he crowded car and confront him on the spot. That would throw a monkey wrench in his plans.

But that wouldn't be the best idea, for the same reason a cop wouldn't confront an armed suspect in the middle of a crowded subway car. A lot of things could go wrong and probably would, with serious consequences for innocent passengers. And bad guys seldom care about collateral damage.

The car was crowded, with that eclectic combination of passengers you get only in a big city. Neatly dressed Asians with briefcases. Teens with piercings, carrying skateboards. Rough-faced men with callused hands, on their way to work or on their way home. Stolid-faced women of indeterminate race. Each of them has a life, happy or sad, unknown to their fellow travelers. Eight million stories in the naked city. Or a few hundred thousand, in any case.

Right across from me sat a young Hispanic couple with a baby and a toddler. The man had one of those serious faces, with a faraway look, thinking his unknown thoughts of unknown places as the train moved along. The toddler noticed Lou and stared at him, fascinated. He looked up at me, and when I smiled at him he hid his face in the man's lap, but he was unable to resist peeking out.

When the train reached the Glen Park station, the red-haired practitioner got off. I followed him up the escalator, not getting on until he had reached the top. I was staying well back in case he was preparing a surprise for me. I had no fear I'd lose him—he'd make sure of that.

He headed up Bosworth, away from the commercial area around the station. After a few blocks it was clear where he was headed: Glen Park itself. The park isn't one of those manicured showplaces; it's an urban wildlife area nestled right in the middle of a thoroughly developed neighborhood. Set in the bottom of a tiny canyon, it's hardly a park at all—more an overgrown area choked with trees and brush, with a stream running through that provides a miniature riparian environment for frogs and snakes and small mammals and even a coyote or two.

I followed him into the park, letting him still keep a good lead, until eventually he came to the loop that runs along the far end. It was getting chilly, and apart from a few hardy dog walkers, the park was almost deserted. As he disappeared around a bend, I stopped to take stock of the situation.

He was obviously setting up a confrontation. And he had chosen the time and the place, giving him an immense advantage. You never want to fight someone on their own terms or on their own turf, unless you have no choice.

A couple of years ago I would have let it go. But lately I'd developed a macho streak, a reluctance to avoid a challenge, along with the feeling I could take care of myself under any circumstances. Looking back over the last couple of years, a case could be made for that being untrue—most of the things I'd handled had been as much about luck as skill. But sometimes, confidence is as important as ability. Unless you let it overwhelm your judgment, at which point you're sure to crash and burn.

So I wasn't about to blunder ahead totally unprepared.

Being able to improvise has its advantages—there is an infinitude of situations and threats, many of which you cannot possibly foresee. A well-crafted spell is useless if it doesn't address the problem at hand. Sometimes I have to scramble, but in the end I usually come up with something that works.

But I had learned to prepare when it was appropriate. I had only enough energy to set up one prepared spell, though. Any more than that, and I wouldn't have enough power left to deal with the unexpected. And there were two things to worry about. One was a magical attack, but since I wasn't going to be caught off guard, I figured I could handle that. But those poor victims had been torn apart in a purely physical manner. When you deal with magic every day, you sometimes forget how deadly a mundane attack can be.

What I really needed was my shotgun, but it was resting uselessly at home. So, a magical equivalent might be in order. I looked around for a branch or other straight section of wood, and found just what I needed a few feet off the trail, a six-foot branch with the leaves stripped off long ago. I broke off the little side branches until I had a relatively smooth staff. I worked some dirt into one end, letting some energy flow out into it, forming a magical barrier. Then I squatted down by the small creek that ran through the park and dipped the other end into the water. Again, I let energy flow, but this time I kept it up. The water flowed into the staff, filling it up as it backed up against the dirt barrier. I held it there until the pressure built up to the breaking point before pulling it out. I capped the other end with a binding energy woven into more dirt. Now if I needed it, I could quickly rub that dirt off, release the energy, and the pressurized water would spurt out like a fire hose.

That may not seem impressive, but fire hoses and water cannons are what get used for crowd control. A stream from a two-and-a-half-inch hose will knock you off your feet and send you tumbling along the ground. With enough pressure, the stream can even break through a weak brick wall. And my enhancing would provide at least twice the pressure of an ordinary hose.

At that pressure, an ordinary hose would pick me up clear off the ground. It would be like trying to hold an angry anaconda. But magic does have its advantages—I'd be able to direct the flow as easily as I would a simple stick. Now I was set—a wizard with a staff, at long last.

Lou was shifting back and forth on one paw and then the other, not exactly nervous, but keyed up like a boxer before an important bout. I motioned him over toward where the path exited after looping around.

"Stand guard," I told him. "Bark if he comes out this way." He looked at me and moved closer to the entrance. "Other side," I said. He ignored me.

That made me think again. Lou knows a lot more about tracking than I do, and he wouldn't ignore me for no reason. Maybe he felt is was too dangerous to separate. He did have a point; it was a lot like those slasher films where the idiot teen says, "Let's split up. You check out the attic. I'll head down to the basement."

Then I realized there was no point in leaving him to guard the exit anyway. This charade had been designed to set up a confrontation. Whoever this was, he wanted to engage me. He wasn't going to slip out the back the minute I got close. That would have made the entire charade pointless. I nodded to Lou and we started along the path together.

It was narrow and closed in. After a short quarter mile, the path started to curve around and head back. Lou was walking a few paces ahead of me, nose twitching, acting more like an actual dog than a magical companion, seeking out danger on a practical level. When he stopped, one paw raised halfway up, I knew we'd reached the crucial place, and I gripped the homemade staff tightly, one hand on the dirt cap.

Even so, it almost got me. It burst out of the bushes and launched itself toward me with a noise like an explosion of frightened quail. Time shifted down into slow motion—not the magical kind, but the type that happens in a car crash. It stood upright on two legs, and was huge, at least six feet four. I saw dark fur and long arms with claws the size of a grizzly bear's. I saw teeth, gleaming white. They were almost the last thing I ever saw.

I tore the dirt off the end of the staff and simultaneously pointed it in one motion. A stream of water gushed out and struck the creature full in the chest, sending it flying. My idea had been to knock down whatever attacked me, then use talent to bind and neutralize it if I could. But the water hose worked too well. It went head over heels back into the bushes, and it must have hurt it and scared it as well, because instead of attacking again it took off. I heard the sounds of crashing branches as it bolted through the tangled undergrowth. Round one to me.

Lou took a couple of steps forward and looked back at me to see if I wanted him to follow. He didn't seem that eager. From the glimpse I'd got of the creature, I wasn't, either. I shook my head.

"Not this time," I said. "Let's not push our luck."

We made it back out of the park without any trouble. There was no sign of our red-haired practitioner. Glen Park is close enough to my flat so that I could walk home, though it took about forty minutes. On the way, my mind churned. Too many questions, which was rapidly becoming my default state of mind every time things got weird.

But I had learned something, and it was important. The question of whether these murders had been done by a creature out of the energy pool or by a mad practitioner was no longer one of either/or. It was both. But was it a creature like the fake Ifrit, but under magical control? Or was it a sentient being, like the Wendigo, working in partnership with a practitioner? And if so, why? One thing was clear—unless and until I figured it out, more people were bound to die.

TEN

"I CAN'T SHAKE THE FEELING THAT EVERYTHING is slightly off, slightly askew," Sherwood said.

We were having a celebration dinner at Angkor Borei, a neighborhood Cambodian restaurant on upper Mission Street, in honor of Sherwood's return. All of us—Sherwood, Eli, Victor, myself, and even Timothy—were gathered around a small table. Timothy had begged off, since he hadn't even met Sherwood before her return and so felt he'd be an intrusion. But Eli was having none of it.

"You're family now, boy," he said. "Like it or not. Your presence is required at all such events."

There was hardly room on the table for the various dishes and the steaming mounds of sticky rice. Cambodian food is just like Thai food, only different. Not much of a description, I know. Lou was wandering around somewhere outside, being unwelcome as usual in restaurants. There was going to be plenty left over for a doggie bag, though. It would probably end up making him sick.

"Feeling that things are askew is to be expected," Eli said. "Considering."

"I know, but it doesn't even feel like I've been through anything unusual. To me, we were fighting Christoph only a few days ago. Whatever happened between then and now simply doesn't exist."

"Maybe not consciously. But you were gone quite a while, and something in you knows that—maybe not in your mind, but certainly in your body."

"I guess. But I don't like the feeling. And I'm still pissed about losing a year of my life—I know, I know, it's the wrong way to look at it, but that's the way it feels."

We talked between bites of food, catching up. Eli told Sherwood about the recent events in his best storytelling style—all the practitioners who'd died in the past year— the whole thing.

"I'm glad I missed it," she said. "Sounds like no fun at all."

"No, it wasn't," said Timothy. "I was only involved in part of it, but Mason managed to scare me half to death."

"One of his specialties," Sherwood said, punching me playfully on the arm.

This was different. In the old days, she never would have done such a thing. One of the reasons we broke up was that she felt I was too flaky, though fun, while I thought she was too inflexible, almost rigid sometimes. She'd come to a complete stop at a four-way stop sign even if it was two in the morning out in the boondocks and there was no other traffic. Ironically, the only time she'd ever got a ticket was when she was driving me to a gig and rushing to get me there on time.

If this was the new Sherwood, I approved. But maybe it was just my own perception. It's not often you get to have dinner with someone newly returned from the dead, and that's bound to make you view them in a different light. Not that she had actually been dead, but for all intents and purposes, she had. But maybe she'd always been somewhat playful and I'd just never noticed.

I heaped some more fish and sauce over rice, and everyone ate quietly for a time.

"You don't remember *anything*?" I asked, after a while. "About . . . well, you know."

"No. Not a thing. But I have had some odd dreams the last few nights, and every once in a while I get a quick flash of something—like someplace I can't quite remember. But one thing that's changed—I seem to have a much clearer view of people."

"In what way?" asked Victor.

"People seem more open to me now. I've always tried to be empathetic, but now it's a lot easier to sense when something's going on with someone, even if they're trying to act cool and calm like there's nothing wrong." She laughed at my nonchalant shrug, not fooled for a moment. "Don't worry, Mason. For some reason it's clearest when it's someone I don't know well, or even at all. You, fortunately, remain as opaque to me as ever."

"Thank God," I said. She turned to Timothy.

"Now, you, on the other hand—" A panic-stricken expression crossed Timothy's face, and she laughed again. "Hey, you don't have to worry, either. Victor doesn't begin to know how good he's got it with you."

Timothy relaxed.

"See?" he said to Victor. "I told you."

"Opinion is not fact," Victor said, but he gave one of his rare smiles.

I couldn't remember the last time we had all just sat around and relaxed, having fun for once, putting aside the usual strategy and planning that went with most of our get-togethers.

"Speaking of knowing people, here's a question," Timothy said, now totally at ease. "If an angel appeared to you—" He stopped as Victor made a face. "What if God or karma or whatever, something that knew you down to your very core, gave you this choice: your life could continue on pretty much the way it's been, or it could be changed and you would receive exactly the lot in life you truly deserve—which would you take?"

"Easy," I said. "Leave well enough alone."

"Absolutely," said Eli. "Get what I deserve? Not a comforting proposition."

Victor shook his head.

"I'd go with option two," Victor said. "Maybe I'd end up worse off, but that's hardly the point. It's the moral choice."

Pure Victor. But I didn't believe him. I'm sure he meant it, but not as a moral issue. He was secretly convinced he would immediately be elevated to ruler of the Western world.

"Sherwood?"

Sherwood wasn't paying attention. She was staring at the front of the restaurant, where a young Asian kid had just come through the door and was standing at the front counter. A red bandana was wrapped around his forehead.

"That boy is up to something," she said. I looked, but he seemed normal to me.

"Are you sure?" Victor said.

"Pretty sure. He's as nervous as a cat."

The hostess approached the boy, smiling. He hunched over slightly and thrust his hands deep in the pocket of his jacket.

Sherwood sighed, lifted her hand, and twisted her fingers in the air. The boy froze, then suddenly screamed, jerked his hand out of his pocket, and ran out the door. The hostess looked after him in bewilderment.

"Problem solved," Sherwood said.

"What did you do?" Eli said, in an almost demanding tone.

"He had something in his pocket—maybe a gun, I would guess. I think he was going to rob the place. I just changed its feel to that of a giant spider." She laughed, a bit uneasily. "I imagine it gave him quite a start when it started squirming around."

"What if he decides to hit some other place?" Victor asked. "If he really was going to pull a robbery."

"I don't think he will. He was scared to death when he came in. And after feeling that spider in his pocket? He'll never try anything like this again—I got the feeling he's the superstitious type to begin with."

"And you got all that just from looking at him?"

She shrugged.

"I could have been mistaken; it was just a feeling I got. But I don't think so." Eli was looking very thoughtful indeed.

"And how did you accomplish that little trick with the spider illusion?" he asked. "You didn't used to be able to simply wave your hand and accomplish a transformation like that."

"I don't know. I didn't think about it—I just did it."

"Curiouser and curiouser," Eli muttered. Sherwood put her arms on the table and rested her head on them.

"Wow," she said. "That took a lot out of me."

We all made a show of splitting up the bill, which was our usual ritual, though pointless. Victor always offered to pay and we always let him. The man is rich, after all. Not just well-off—rich. And unlike many rich people, he's a generous man. Victor has his share of flaws, but stinginess is not one of them. I'll give him that.

Sherwood took a quick trip to the restroom, and Timothy reached over and picked up a section of newspaper that had been left at the adjacent table by a solitary diner.

"Look at this," he said, pointing to the obituary section. "They're holding a memorial for one of those hikers who was killed."

"Or what was left of him," Victor said. Timothy shot him a disapproving look.

"It's sad," he said, skimming a long article. "He was apparently quite a guy—an athlete, a musician, a top student with a bright future." He pointed at the picture next to the text. "Cute guy, too. What a shame."

I glanced over at the picture and did a double take. It showed a young man with curly hair, looking into the camera and smiling, his whole life ahead of him. The photo was black and white, but there was one thing about which I had no doubt. The last time I'd seen that mass of curly hair it had been died a brilliant, artificial red.

ELEVEN

BACK HOME, I FOUND MYSELF IN AN ALL-TOO-familiar state of mind—being utterly baffled. What the hell was going on? Had the practitioner I'd followed been a doppleganger? Had our mysterious practitioner taken on the dead boy's aspect as a disguise, and if so, why? There were a thousand people he could have picked to copy, and a thousand more faces that would be entirely made-up. Was it some bizarre sense of humor, or was it a deliberate challenge? He had led me into a trap where that creature waited, but why? And why was he stalking Ruby? And what was that creature anyway?

I couldn't answer any of these questions, and Eli and Victor hadn't been much better at coming up with a logical theory. Maybe it was time for a visit to someone who might be able to provide them—if he felt like it. Rolf. He wasn't much for answering questions unless there was something in it for him, but he owed me. I'd helped him out when he was worried about Richard Cory—or at least I'd tried. Rolf was unpredictable; he might ignore my questions, but he might just as easily decide to answer them simply because it was a full moon on a Tuesday.

I called Sherwood and asked if she'd mind coming along. I was interested to see what her take would be about Rolf—I didn't trust him much, although he'd never actually crossed me. Yet. And he had a fondness for good-looking women; that much was obvious by the way he'd reacted to Campbell. It might help make him more amenable, and every little edge helped.

I picked up Sherwood a little after dark and we headed down to his stomping grounds under the Bay Bridge. To Rolf, that was home. I think he was psychically drawn to the bridge, which was a good thing. It meant I didn't have to search the city every time I wanted to talk with him. Of course, for all I knew he had a cell phone. It wouldn't have surprised me.

The street in front was all parked up, but I found a spot a couple of blocks away. When we reached the gate I could see the faint glow of a small fire way in the back of the site, next to one of the massive bridge support pylons. I could barely make out three figures crouched around the fire. So Rolf had company. I didn't want to go through the whole drill of climbing over the new gate, and I didn't want to come up on the group unexpectedly in any case. Rolf was used to me, but his friends might not be.

I found a corner of the new wire mesh fence where the bottom didn't quite meet the ground and pried it up a fraction, giving Lou just enough room to wriggle through.

"Tell Rolf he's got company," I said. "And be careful of those other guys."

Lou gave a quick tail wag and was off. He didn't look worried.

"Who exactly is this guy?" Sherwood asked.

"He used to be a practitioner, just like you or me. But over time, for reasons that Eli seems to get, but I don't quite understand, he changed into something less human, something more like a magical creature."

"You mean, like an Ifrit?"

"Not exactly. More like an archetype of some magical being—the stuff legends are made of. It's something that's been going on for years, centuries, probably. People eventually noticed, and made up folk tales about what they saw. Werewolves. Vampires. The fey. Rolf has friends even less human than he is. And there are still others, ones who have passed entirely over. They can be dangerous—I ran into a few of them last year.

"So you're essentially saying that such things as vampires are real?"

"No, but there must be former practitioners who have taken on some of those characteristics. I've haven't seen anything that matches up with a vampire yet, though. I don't think I'd care to meet one, either."

Sherwood looked skeptical, especially when Rolf strolled over to the gate, looking remarkably like any other homeless man. Lou wasn't with him.

"Where's Lou?" I asked.

"He's fine. Hanging out by the fire." He gave Sherwood the once-over. "You've brought another lady friend, I see."

"This is Sherwood."

"Ah, yes. Of course. The rescued damsel."

Once again, Rolf seemed to know an awful lot about my life. He did his little trick with the lock again and swung open the gate. He bowed low in an exaggerated fashion, sweeping one hand out to the side. Then he turned and walked back toward the fire.

Lou was sitting close to the flames, staring intently into them. On the opposite side, Richard Cory sat on an overturned plastic bucket, looking incongruously elegant. Lou gave a start as we came up, backed away from the fire, and shook himself as if he'd just come out of a rainstorm.

Right outside of the range of the fire's glow stood a third figure, blending into the shadows and piles of broken concrete rubble. I could see him only out of the corner of my eye; whenever I tried to focus on him my eyes played tricks on me and his figure vanished. Rolf followed my gaze and chuckled in that deep way he has.

"Kind of hard to see, ain't he? It's just as well, believe me." He picked up a long narrow board and poked at the fire. "I don't suppose this is just a social visit. What's on your mind tonight?"

"The usual. I've got a couple of questions. I thought you might have a couple of answers."

"Could be. You got something to trade?"

"You owe me," I reminded him. "You asked me to find Richard, remember?"

"And did you?"

"Well, no, but that's hardly the point. You asked; I tried. Got myself into a bit of trouble over it, I might add." Rolf thought for a moment before nodding.

"Fair enough, I guess. Okay, ask away." I told him about my encounter with the redheaded practitioner and the beast in Glen Park. "What I can't figure out is the connection between the two and why he chose the aspect of the mur- dered boy," I said. "What do you think?" Rolf looked at me with an expression that was hard to read.

"I think you've wasted a question," he said. "It doesn't take any special talent or knowledge to answer that one."

"What do you mean?"

"Well, think about it a minute. You have a practitioner that's taken on the aspect of one of the victims, right? Which indicates first of all that he was involved in the murder, and second, that he can alter his appearance. You follow him, and he vanishes. Suddenly, a creature springs out at you. You don't see the connection?"

"You mean he was able to transform himself into that creature?" Rolf let out an exaggerated sigh.

"You're not getting it. There was no practitioner. There's only the creature, the one who killed all those people. It's a shape-shifter; it took on the persona of its victim, that's all, and then reverted back to its natural self when it got you alone."

"Oh."

"A shape-shifter? How can that be? Does that mean it could imitate anyone?" Sherwood asked. "Even one of us?"

"I don't know. I know it can take on the aspect of its victim, but I don't think it can imitate just anyone, at least not as successfully." He pointed at Richard Cory, who was blithely paying us no attention at all. "I'm sure Richard could tell you. He knows all about such things. But he doesn't talk to people anymore. Ever since he came back from his time with the Wendigo, as you call it, he barely talks at all, even to me." He smiled, showing teeth as usual. "And by the way, it isn't a Wendigo, not a real one. If it had been a real one, you wouldn't have come back."

"Yeah? Well, thanks for pointing me in that direction, then."

"Maybe Richard will talk to me," said Sherwood. Rolf started to shake his head, then looked at her closely.

"You know, he just might. There's something different about you. I can't put my finger on it, but it's there." I'd been thinking much the same thing myself, ever since her return. "Just remember, he's not all there these days. And don't look in his eyes—that can be a disturbing experience."

Sherwood walked around the fire and squatted down on her heels next to Richard. He ignored her, but then she started talking in a low voice, almost whispering. I instinctively leaned forward to try to hear what she was saying; her voice was oddly compelling, almost like the Wendigo's. Richard Cory turned his head as if seeing her for the first time and answered in a low, mellifluous tone that rose slightly at the end, clearly asking a question.

Rolf stroked his dreadlocked beard, obviously impressed.

"Let's give them some privacy," he said, moving off farther under the bridge. Cars rushed past on the bridge access ramp high overhead, sounding like far-off surf. The figure in the shadows followed us, coming closer, soundless and menacing. Rolf turned toward him, his aspect changing in an instant, revealing the gnarled and leathery troll-like persona that was always lurking right below the surface.

"No," he said, in a thick guttural voice. "Not for you. Nor the other." The figure drew back, disappointed.

"Who is that?" I asked. "Or maybe 'what' is a better question."

"Vlad," he said. "He's almost all the way gone. Soon he'll be too dangerous to be around, even for me."

"Vlad? Is he Russian?"

"No."

We turned and watched Sherwood and Richard Cory, deep in conversation. Several times, Sherwood nodded her head, and once she shook it, definitively. After a while, they stopped talking, and Richard Cory leaned forward, put his hands on either side of her face, and stared intently at her.

"Uh-oh," Rolf said.

Lou appeared from the other side of the fire, circled around, and started creeping up behind them, moving one paw at a time, slowly, like a stalking cat. Sherwood reached up, gently took Richard's hands from her face, and held them for a moment. Then she patted him on the shoulder and stood up, motioning to me. Rolf whistled, or he tried to. It sounded more like a horse with asthma.

"That's quite a woman," he said.

Rolf walked us to the gate and again made a bow to Sherwood, but this time it was very short and not at all mocking. Sherwood's expression was grim.

"Did you learn anything?" I asked, as we walked back to the van.

"Quite a bit. More than I wanted to, actually. Richard Cory is an interesting . . . person."

"Could you get a read on him?"

"Not really. He's hardly human anymore, just like you said. There's just enough left to be able to communicate with him. He's not an evil person by any means, but he is spooky."

"How about Rolf? Can he be trusted?"

"Depends on what you mean. He's basically okay, but he has a different idea of right and wrong than we do, I think."

"That much I'm aware of," I said.

"Yes, I would think so." Sherwood stopped for a moment, thinking. "I think the best way to put it is this: if he thought he could gain some personal advantage by pushing you into a raging river, I don't think he'd do it. But if you fell in on your own, and that benefited him in some way, I'm not sure he'd try to pull you out, either." That sounded about right.

"And Richard? What did he have to say?"

"It's not good. You were right; there was another creature that came from the energy pool. And what it needs to survive is life force—it kills people and devours all their internal organs. Then it's fine for a while, until it has to feed again."

"Sounds like a bad horror movie."

"It gets worse. It's protean—the creature that attacked you is its natural form, but it can shift and imitate almost anything."

"It's got to have a tell," I said. "I can't see how anything like that could fool Lou."

"Yes and no. If it copied someone you know, a friend, it wouldn't be totally effective. It could fool you for a while, but you'd catch on sooner or later. And it wouldn't fool Lou for a second. But when it kills someone, I think that's a different matter. It absorbs their essence, somehow."

"The brains."

"The what?"

"The brains. It cracks open the head and sucks out the brain tissue, leaving an empty skull."

Sherwood shuddered delicately.

"How delightful. But however it does it, it can then replicate its victim right down to the last detail. Appearance, memories, skills—in essence, it can *become* its victim. I doubt even Lou could see it wasn't the original person."

"So if it killed me and took my place, would it be able to play guitar?"

"Apparently. It might lack your creative spark, but it could play."

"Could it use talent?"

"That he didn't know, but it's not unlikely. It is a magi-cal creature itself, after all."

"And Lou would never know the difference? That I don't believe."

"Well, that's different. Lou's almost part of you; there's no way he wouldn't figure it out the moment he saw you. But if it were me who was being copied? Or Victor or Eli? I'm not sure he could tell there was anything wrong."

A sharp clatter from right behind us made us both jump and spin around. Talking about this had set our nerves on edge. A metal garbage can lid was lying on the sidewalk, knocked off a can next to a doorway. Lou had scented something he thought might be edible. He poked his head around from the back of the can with a sheepish expres-sion and a slight tail wag that meant, "Oops, sorry."

AFTER I DROPPED OFF SHERWOOD BACK AT VIC-tor's, I went home. But on the way back to my flat, I started thinking. If there was a shape-shifter out there, it was targeting not only random victims to keep itself go-ing. It was also targeting those who might threaten it. Like Ruby. And me. And people who might be able to help track it down. Like Morgan.

That was why we'd warded her house, of course. And that was why we'd told her not to let anyone in that she didn't know. But what about someone she did know? Or someone she thought she knew. Someone who looked like me, for example. Like a shape-shifter.

I made a U-turn and headed toward her house. Chances were she was fine, but I had a bad feeling. Warding her house was not enough; she was going to have to get out of town for a while. A nice return visit to her parents might be in order.

There were lights on at her house, so she was home. When I rang the bell, deep woofs came from the other side of the door. Beulah was standing guard, in her own ineffective way. But Morgan didn't answer the door. I rang the bell again and knocked loudly. The woofs turned into whines. Maybe she was afraid to answer the door. Maybe she'd gone out for a moment to the store. Maybe she had been taking a nap and didn't want to get up. And maybe it was something worse.

Lou was standing very still, never a good sign. I got a sick feeling in the pit of my stomach. I didn't bother trying the door to see if it was unlocked. Victor's useful wards were great protection, but they'd keep me out as surely as they would anyone else. But I had warded the backyard, including where it touched the back door. I should be able to get in there.

As I edged my way to the back, along through the narrow gap that separated Morgan's house from her neighbors, I hoped no one would see me and call the cops. That would be all I needed.

My own wards were solidly in place, but since I'd made them, it was no trouble to circumvent them and create a small opening by the gate. I slipped through into the garden, and looked up at the back deck. The door to the deck was open, making entrance easy. Beulah had come out onto the deck and was staring down at me. She saw me and started up whining piteously, bobbing her head up and down and throwing in an occasional bark. Worse and worse.

She backed away as I came up the back stairs but kept whining, wanting help but also afraid of me. I tried to pet her as I passed by, but she ducked under my hand and retreated into the house.

In the kitchen I found a plate with a half-eaten sandwich on it. The water in the sink was running. I turned it off, and when I called to Beulah again she screwed up her courage and crowded up against me as if I were now her best friend. "Morgan?" I called out. Nothing. Beulah bolted suddenly, running to the bottom of the stairs that led to the second floor, and then started barking again. Lou joined me at the bottom of the stairs, glanced up, then glanced back at me. He showed no fear, but no inclination to go upstairs, either.

So whatever was up there wasn't good, but whatever danger there had been was now gone. I didn't want to go up those stairs, but what choice did I have? I walked up the stairs, and every step was an effort, as if my feet had turned to stone. At the top of the stairs was a small landing with a bathroom directly in front and two bedrooms on either side. The door to one of them was open, possibly a guest room, with a colorful comforter on the bed and everything neat and in place. The door to the other room was closed.

I knew what I would find before I pushed it open. My hands started shaking and the walls of the room brightened and rippled, seeming to move in and out as if they were breathing. I heard with perfect clarity the faint sound of Lou quietly panting.

Morgan would be lying across her bed, clothes soaked in blood, chest torn open, eyes open and staring. Her organs would be missing and her skull cracked open, with traces of gray matter around the edges of the wound. Every detail was etched into my brain before I ever saw it. I couldn't catch any air, and a metallic taste filled my mouth.

But I was wrong, thank God. No one lay across the bed and there was no one in the room, alive or dead. Lou started forward but I held him back. It still wasn't all right. There was blood on the floor, quite a lot of it. Morgan might be lying crumpled in a corner, out of sight, and if so, the cops would be on this one eventually. They might not connect it with the other murders, so they would start investigating. They'd start with her boyfriend, or ex-boyfriend, and then expand out into her friends. Peer groups, they call it. Sooner or later the ripples would cross mine and they'd be coming to talk to me.

There were a lot of physical traces of me lying around the house. The principle of transference would make sure of that. Whenever someone enters a crime scene, they leave something of themselves—hair, skin cells, lint from their clothes—something. And they pick up and take something away as well. It doesn't matter how careful you are; with today's high-tech forensics there's always some trace to be found.

But that wouldn't be a problem for me. Morgan was a friend; I'd been there with Victor and Eli, and any traces of my presence in the house would be entirely natural. But if some of my DNA, or Lou's for that matter, ended up mixed in with her blood, that would put an entirely different slant on things.

In the far corner an armchair was pushed against the wall, clothes strewn carelessly over it. And something behind it, barely visible. My heart stopped. It was long and thin, furry and black and tan in color and red at one end. It took me a moment to make sense of what I was seeing, then all at once I saw what it was. It was a leg, but not a human leg. The leg of a dog, separated from the rest of its body. A black-and-tan leg, like that of a Rottweiler. Poor Beulah. All her fears had come true at last.

But wait, Beulah was downstairs. It took the clicking sound of dog nails on hardwood coming up the stairs to jolt me out of my confusion. Lou got it about the same time I did and took up his guard position directly behind my knees. A shape-shifting creature doesn't have to take on human form. An animal form could be a very useful change of pace.

The Rottweiler's head appeared, peeking over the landing. Its head looked heavier than I'd remembered, and the teeth looked stronger and larger. It wasn't as impressive as the shape-shifter in Glen Park had been, but a giant Rottweiler with human intelligence is frightening enough. I took a step back, almost tripping over Lou, and let loose my talent, reaching into the room behind me. This one was easy. That room was full of death, and death was what I gathered. I used poor Beulah's leg to direct it specifically toward the Rottweiler. There was an ironic sense of justice in using it to strike down its killer.

I focused and let loose a burst of deadly energy, striking the shape-shifter square in the chest just as it leapt toward my throat. It collapsed in midflight, but as soon as it hit the floor it was up again. That blast should have killed anything, but as I'd feared all along, this thing was immune to magical energy. Or if not immune, highly resistant, like the fake Ifrit. The staff I'd constructed when I met it in Glen Park, using a water stream, had been far more effective; this shape-shifter was something that needed to be fought on a physical level. But it had teeth and I didn't. I'd put everything I had into the strike, and now it was shaking off the effects as if it had been merely hit in the nose with a sharp blow. Painful and surprising, but not lethal, and not even that effective.

I vaulted over it before it could get its bearings and tore down the stairs toward the back door. Lou was well in front of me and was already at the back door by the time I had reached the bottom of the stairs.

"Yeah, but you can't open the door, can you, now?" I said, sprinting over and throwing it wide. I heard the shape-shifter barreling down the stairs after us. It seemed to have recovered completely. We made it through the door, but we were never going to make it down the back steps or out of the backyard in time.

I looked around for something to use as a weapon as I reached ground level at the garden. There was a shovel leaning against the back wall, but I wasn't going to be able to reach it quickly enough. But next to the shovel a small bit of ivy, glowing brightly in the psychic realm, clung to the back fence. That was where I'd wrapped up the energy of the wards, compacting it into that one little space. The energy I'd locked up there was concentrated, containing all the effort I'd expended in the half hour it had taken to set up the wards. As a result there was four times as much power waiting there as I could have summoned up on the spot. I reached out and unlocked the energy, and as it flowed out I redirected it toward the Rottweiler on my tail.

It sprayed out like a fire hose, and this time it had a sizable effect on the shape-shifter. Resistant is not invincible. It stumbled and went glassy-eyed, as I sprinted over to the back wall and grabbed the shovel that was leaning there. Before it could recover, I was at it, swinging the shovel like a baseball bat, hitting its skull with the sharp edge. It staggered to its feet and snarled. I hit it again. It was tough, but it was still shaken.

Lou, seeing how unsteady on its legs the shape-shifter was, took heart and darted in, trying for a hamstring. Lou's not very big, but his jaws are twice as strong as an ordinary dog his size, and if he got in there, he could easily cripple a leg. The Rottweiler whipped around to get him, and when it did, I hit it yet again. It turned to face me and Lou was at its back legs again. Tag team.

Not surprisingly it was still confused from the effects of the two previous energy blasts. It should have been dead. Unexpectedly, it decided it had had enough for the day, turned, and bounded off toward the side fence. The fence there was a good six feet high and I didn't think it could make it over, but as it sprang upward its body elongated and its front legs became rudimentary arms and its paws almost hands. It grabbed the top of the fence, pulled itself over, and dropped to the other side.

I waited ten minutes to make sure it was gone, peering cautiously through the gate every couple of minutes. The adrenaline surge was fading rapidly, leaving me exhausted with a headache and a dead feeling in my legs. I went back inside and sat down heavily at the table in the kitchen. I was so burned out that when I heard a noise from the front of the house, I reacted in slow motion. Fortunately, it didn't cost me.

The front door opened, and there stood Morgan. She looked at me in puzzlement, and I looked back at her in some surprise.

"When did you get here?" she said. "Where's Molly?"

"Molly?"

"My friend Molly. She must have let you in. I just had to run out for cigarettes."

I hadn't known she smoked. I didn't know anyone smoked anymore. That explained why she was still alive—cigarettes had saved her life. How ironic. That also explained how the shape-shifter had got in. Molly, a trusted friend. No reason not to invite her in. Except, it hadn't been Molly at all, of course. Morgan noticed my disheveled appearance.

"Is something wrong?" she asked.

"I'm afraid so. That wasn't Molly who came over to visit you."

"Of course it was. I've known her for years."

"Come in the kitchen," I said. "This is going to take a while to explain."

IT TOOK MORE THAN A WHILE. I TOLD HER about the shape-shifter, but I'm not sure she really believed me until she saw Beulah. That was the worst part. She cried, and I didn't know her well enough to comfort her.

We buried what was left of Beulah in the back garden. Then she took a wire scrub brush, some Ajax, and bleach, and cleaned up the blood that stained her bedroom floor, as much as was possible. While she worked, her mouth was set in a thin line and her face was pale and drawn, but she was now dry-eyed.

"I don't know if I can stay here tonight," she said.

I'd been thinking the same thing myself. I wasn't sure how safe it would be for her, even with the wards up and her forewarned.

"Maybe you should stay at my place for the night," I said.

She looked at me dubiously, not comfortable with that idea. But even less comfortable about spending the rest of the night alone in that house.

"I have friends I can stay with," she said.

"You'd have no protection at all somewhere else. At my place, at least you'll be safe." If the shape-shifter tracked her down to a friend's house, she might not be the only one in danger.

"Maybe you're right," she said. "I'll get a plane ticket tomorrow. I can get out of state, go home, visit with my parents." She thought a moment longer, then nodded her head. "Let me get a few things."

I'd assumed she would ride over with me, but she followed me home in her own car. She might be willing to spend the night, but not without an escape option. Wise beyond her years. I called Victor as soon as I got home.

"We've got more trouble," I said. "It went after Morgan. Killed her dog, and she escaped through sheer luck."

"What happened?" Victor said.

I told him. Things were getting out of hand, I was one step behind again, and I had no idea what the next step should be. As I talked on the phone, Morgan wandered around my small space, idly picking up things and putting them down again.

"I'd better call Ruby," Victor finally said. "Like Morgan, and yourself for that matter, she's also walking around with a bull's-eye painted on her back right about now."

"Ruby at least can take care of herself."

"Yes, she can. But both of you need to be extremely careful."

"We need to kill this thing, and quickly."

"Yes, we do."

"Any ideas? It can look like anyone, according to Richard Cory, and as I just found out, any*thing* as well."

"Yes, Sherwood told me. Not offhand, no. Maybe Eli has some thoughts. Its ability to imitate people must have some kind of limit—some flaw. Nothing's perfect."

I nodded to myself, half listening. All I wanted to do right now was to fall into bed. Tomorrow I could start thinking again, but for now all I could think of was sleep. When I hung up, Morgan came over and stood next to me.

"One bed?" she said.

"Sorry. Forgot to mention that. You can have it—I'll sleep on the couch in the back room."

"No need. I don't want to kick you out of your own bed." She smiled. "A warm body nearby would be some comfort anyway. Beulah used to sleep on the bed."

"You sure?"

"I'm sure."

We were both tired and emotionally spent. A quick trip to the bathroom, and when I crawled into bed I could hardly keep my eyes open. Morgan joined me five minutes later, wearing some loose pajama-type bottoms and a tee. She grabbed my wrist and examined my forearm, where my own tattoo of intertwined wreaths showed.

"Secret society?" she asked.

"I can't say. It's a secret."

"Huh."

She turned on her side, back toward me, and I could see half of her own tattoo, spreading down from her neck in a complex pattern of reds and greens.

"And yours?" I asked.

"No secret there. But a long story."

I turned out the light and closed my eyes. For once, Lou wasn't wedging himself between us, or trying to worm his way under the covers. He lay sedately at the end of the bed, on the very edge, as if keeping guard. Maybe he expected the shape-shifter to come bursting through the door at any minute.

It was nice having a woman lying next to me in bed, even if it was under less-than-ideal circumstances. I slipped into a reverie about having a real girlfriend, a partner, someone to comfort and be comforted by. It felt nice, in a dreamy way, but I knew from experience that in the harsh light of morning it would seem very different.

I dropped off almost immediately, but I didn't sleep well, plagued by dreams that were not quite nightmares. Images of Morgan and Beulah ran through my head as I ran through clichéd dream corridors, being chased by something I could never quite see. Sometime in the middle of the night I was awakened by the feel of a warm body and a head pressed against my chest. I made an inquiring sound, and Morgan whispered, "I'm scared."

"I don't blame you," I said and pulled her closer to comfort her. We lay without moving for a while until a subtle shift in her breathing told me that comfort was changing into something else. My own breathing changed, and I slowly stroked her back. Her hand eased up to the back of my neck as she gently pulled me down until we faced each other in the dark.

Not a word was spoken. Morgan was reaching out to me for comfort, and maybe a way of forgetting, or a desire born from fear, a reassurance that she was still safe, still alive. And that was strange—it's not uncommon for men to react that way in times of stress or danger, but not women, not so much. Men can use sex as a means of connecting, of achieving an intimacy that's otherwise difficult for them to acknowledge. Sex for women tends to be just the opposite, to grow out of intimacy, not as a search to achieve it.

Maybe that's just stereotyping, though. Not all women are like that, nor all men. But it's certainly not common for a woman to jump into bed as a reaction to trauma, at least not from what I've seen.

But whatever the reason, there was no frantic need involved. It was slow, and sweet, and sad and nostalgic all at once, like making love to someone you care about but you know you will never see again. Even when she finally came, it wasn't frenzied or desperate, with groans and screams and thrashing. Which was a considerable relief, considering how my last romantic encounter had gone.

Instead, she was still for a moment, and then moved with a quiet intensity. At the last moment, she made a sound in the back of her throat I'd never heard before, a trilling sound almost like a hummingbird, surprisingly loud and oddly erotic, enough so that it swept me along with her.

We lay together and she fell back asleep in my arms. I'd started to drift off, too, when Lou appeared by the side of the bed and gently nipped my hand to get my attention. I came fully awake and sat up carefully, disengaging and trying not to wake Morgan. She made a few mumbled sounds and turned over on her side, leaving me free.

Lou was staring fixedly at the window. I wondered if the shape-shifter had somehow found me, and I wondered if the wards would hold if it had. But Lou was alert, not nervous or excited. I got up cautiously, and as I did so, he relaxed. So odds were whatever had been out there had already taken off.

I grabbed a flashlight from the bedside table drawer and slipped outside, just to check. Nothing was there, but near the window I could see definite impressions in the dirt. Someone or something had been right outside the window.

Maybe a burglar looking for an empty flat. Maybe a pervert looking for a thrill. Maybe a flesh-eating monster. Maybe they were old marks I'd never noticed. There was no way to tell.

I managed to slip back into bed without waking Morgan and drifted off soon after.

The next thing I knew it was morning and I woke up to the sound of Morgan's voice in the back room. As I sat up yawning, she walked back into the bedroom holding a cell phone.

"Morning," she said. "I got a flight out today. I hate to rush off, but I've got to get moving if I want to make the flight."

"You need a ride to the airport?" I asked. She shook her head no.

"Thanks, but no. I'll take BART."

I got up and made some coffee, but she wouldn't even stay for a cup. She didn't seem ill at ease, not at all, but she didn't mention a thing about last night. Being a gentleman, I didn't bring it up. Maybe she wanted to pretend it had never happened. Maybe she thought it had been a dream. Maybe it was just one thing too many to deal with right now. In ten minutes she was gone, and I was left drinking a cup of coffee with only Lou for company.

TWELVE

I MIGHT WELL HAVE SPENT THE REST OF THE day just hanging out in the house, pretending to think, avoiding actually doing anything, but Sherwood was having none of that. She didn't call; she knew I'd just let the machine pick up. So she arrived at my flat at noon.

"Lunch," she said.

"I don't feel much like eating."

"Maybe not, but I do, and you're taking me out."

"Really, I don't—"

"Where do you want to go?" she interrupted.

I gave up. Once Sherwood's set on something, there's no denying her. But my favorite Mexican place, El Farolito, where I'd met Morgan, was ruined for me. It would just remind me of what still needed to be done. My favorite Japanese place, Takai's, was another that brought back bad memories. If enough bad stuff continued to happen to me and my friends, eventually I'd run out of places to eat.

"You choose," I said. "You're the one who wants lunch."

"Herbivore," she said. "It's nice out, and it's walking distance."

"Since when are you a vegetarian?"

"Since my 'return.' I can't bear to even look at meat."

There's nothing wrong with being vegetarian. I converted for a few months once when I was going out with Amy, a practitioner who was serious about the concept. The things we do for love. Or for something. Lou was not pleased with the new regime. He started disappearing at dinnertime, returning a couple of hours later looking well satisfied. He was not unhappy when Amy and I inevitably split up.

So I'd been to Herbivore a number of times. It was not only vegetarian; it was vegan. It was Amy's favorite restaurant. But I never cared for it. A bit bland for my tastes—it takes more than a few months to shed the carnivore habit.

We walked down Valencia, Lou trotting dutifully behind. Until we reached the restaurant, at which point he looked at us with an unmistakable expression of "You have got to be kidding." I wasn't the only one who remembered the place. He did a U-turn and trotted back the way we'd come.

"I'll save a doggie bag for you," I called after him. "Seitan. Your favorite." He didn't bother to even glance back.

The decor inside Herbivore's is pretty cool—minimal, almost Japanese in feel, the bare off-white walls sparsely adorned with understated prints. The small front portion of the room looks out on the street, and a narrow line of tables runs alongside the wall next to the kitchen area.

I ordered a grilled portobello sandwich and Sherwood got a salad with odd things in it. After a few bites, she put down her fork and stared at me.

"What?" I said.

"So, what are we going to do about all this?"

"If I knew that, we'd be doing it instead of having lunch. The first thing, obviously, is to find this thing. But I can't think of how. Lou's no use—it's immune to his tracking sense, just like the fake Ifrit was. Morgan might be able to help, but she's left. Involving her any further would be criminal, anyway."

"What about the Wendigo? I'll bet he could find it. Maybe even call it."

"Hmm. Possible, I guess. But he wouldn't help us, not without something in it for him. And anyway, I have no idea how to find him again, either."

"I think I might be able to."

"Really? How?"

"I'm not sure how. But when he pulled me back, it established a connection between us. I don't know what it consists of, but I'm sure it's there. I can feel it."

She resumed eating her salad, and I took another bite of sandwich. If she still had a connection to the Wendigo, in theory that might be enough to locate him. But the gap between theory and practice often looms large. That's why Eli and Victor work so well together; Eli has a deep understanding of the principles of magical operations, while Victor is a master engineer—he's the one who actually implements the spells, and sometimes designs the specifics as well.

But finding the Wendigo would just be the first step. I'd need something to bribe him—he wasn't going to help us out of the goodness of his heart. If he even had a heart. But I did in fact have something to offer—more of those magically imbued stones. Problem was, if Victor and Eli found out, they'd both be outraged, for different reasons. I'd lied to both of them, telling them I'd handed over all the remaining stones, and I wasn't eager to come clean about it. But without their expert help, I wasn't sure I could come up with my own solution for finding the Wendigo again. Catch-22. Whenever you lie to friends, it comes back to bite you on the ass.

I did have Lou, though, with his marvelous tracking ability. It might not work on beings like the Wendigo, but maybe I could isolate his ability and, using the rune stones as enhancers, transfer that ability to Sherwood. I turned my attention back to her and caught the tail end of her sentence.

". . . Eli could figure it out," she was saying.

"Sorry. I was thinking. What?" She looked at me in exasperation.

"I said, 'I'm sure Eli could figure out a way to use my connection to find it.'"

"I'm sure he could. But I've got another idea."

She looked at me suspiciously. Sherwood knew me far too well, knew that taking things into my own hands and cutting Eli out of the loop was not my usual operating procedure. Something was up. But she let it pass.

"What, then?"

"Louie. He's got that tracking ability, and even though it won't work with the Wendigo, I'll bet I could channel it through you. Then, with the connection you already have, you might be able to track him down yourself."

"You think?"

"Certainly worth a try," I said. I thought it probably wouldn't work, not without some extra help—like those stones—but I didn't mention that.

Halfway back to my flat, Lou reappeared from under a parked car. He must have found something good to eat, because he was holding no grudges. He trotted along happily next to Sherwood and me, taking the occasional side excursion. He'd always liked Sherwood and was happy to see us together again, even if we weren't really together.

As soon as we got home, I opened the trunk where I kept the rest of the stones and pulled out five of them. The minute Lou saw what I was doing, he jumped up in Sherwood's lap and turned his back on me. He did not approve of those things. He was probably right.

I stuffed four of them into a pocket and held on to the fifth. Poor Lou. He thought he was showing disapproval by jumping up on Sherwood, but it was exactly where I wanted him to be.

"Concentrate on the Wendigo," I told her.

I let out a pulse of talent, directing it though the rune stone. Then I bent it and sent the enhanced energy through Lou, who sneezed violently as it coursed through him, then through Sherwood and back through Lou, creating a feedback loop. Sherwood straightened up suddenly, almost throwing Lou off onto the floor.

"I'll be damned," she said. "It worked. I can feel him."

"Can you tell where he is?"

"No, not exactly, but I'll bet I can find him. It's like a heat source in a cold room—diffuse, but you can tell what direction it's coming from. And he's fairly close by. I can tell that much. Somewhere south, I'd say."

"Great," I said. "Let's go."

"Shouldn't we let Victor and Eli know?"

"We don't need to. We're not going to be doing anything. We're just going to talk to him."

Sherwood got that I didn't want to involve the two of them, although she didn't know why. The old Sherwood would never have let that pass, but now she just shrugged her acceptance. But when she stood up and Lou hopped off her lap, she stopped.

"It's gone," she said.

"Pick Lou up." Lou submitted with good grace, although of course he didn't care for it.

"You're right," she said. "It's back. I've got to be holding Lou for it to work. Good thing he's not a Great Dane."

We climbed into my van, Sherwood in the passenger seat and Lou in her lap. She directed me with hotter and colder, like the children's game. Finally she got a handle on it; west on Cesar Chavez, then south on San Jose, winding through the city. We passed Geneva, then a couple of blocks later, Sherwood said, "Go back. We passed him." At the corner of Niagara Street I stopped and looked around. Nothing seemed promising—no parks, no wooded area, just the usual collection of houses, and a Muni yard down the block.

"There," she said, pointing over to the right. "Somewhere there."

I could barely see a long low building painted a sickly green, half hidden by some trees. It clicked suddenly and I knew where we were.

"That's Bluestone Studios over there," I said. "A cou-

ple of floors, lots of little rooms for bands and artists—
forty or fifty, as I remember. I was here about five years
ago, checking out a friend's band. What the hell would the
Wendigo be doing here?"

"Maybe he likes music," Sherwood said.

"Or musicians. I'm still not sold on his being harmless." We got out of the car and walked over toward the
building. Sherwood was carrying Lou, who had given up
squirming.

"He's definitely inside," Sherwood said as we approached the building. The entry door was propped open
with a metal folding chair, and musicians carrying instruments were passing in and out.

We walked in and down a long hallway, listening to the
muffled sounds of guitars, keyboards, and drums, all behind
closed doors. From the hallway, all the sounds blended
together like some enormous modern performance piece.

When the corridor crossed another hallway, Sherwood
turned left without hesitation, passed a few more doors,
and stopped in front of a door painted a bright red. She
put Lou down and gestured at the door.

From behind it came the sound of a highly distorted
guitar running fast scales and a drummer doing speed rolls.
I knocked on the door, loudly enough to be sure I would
be heard over the instruments.

The room went instantly silent. We waited a moment,
but there was no sound of movement from inside. Sherwood looked at the door, then back at me.

"What's that about?" she whispered. The silence from
behind the door was contagious, as if we had been caught
doing something illegal just by knocking at the door.

I shrugged and knocked again, and now that the room
was silent, it sounded twice as loud. There was the sug-
gestion of movement inside, then the door opened a crack.
I could just see a young stocky guy whose face showed a
pitiful attempt at a beard. The faint sweet whiff of high-
quality dope wafted out past him.

"Yeah?" he said, suspiciously.

I put my foot over the doorjamb in the best PI movie fashion so he couldn't slam the door on us. On second thought, he still could, and if the door was heavy enough, it would probably break my foot. I withdrew it as unobtrusively as I could.

"We're looking for a friend," I said.

"Who?"

Good question. He saw me hesitate and the suspicion on his face deepened into paranoia.

"Are you guys cops?" he said. Sherwood laughed.

"Are you serious?"

"Hell, yes. If you're cops, you gotta say so. If I ask you directly, you have to tell me the truth. That's the law."

An enduring urban legend. Generations of brain-dead dope dealers believe this as a matter of faith. It never occurs to them that if it were true, there would never be such a thing as a successful undercover operation. But it was a useful misapprehension—for the cops.

"Dude," I said. "Do we look like cops?"

"Yeah, sorta." Fair enough. We were cops, sorta, when you came right down to it.

"No way," I said. I pointed down at Lou. "Does he look like a police dog to you?"

Lou got tired of this exchange and wriggled his way through the opening, squeezing past the attempt to block him. The guy turned and stepped back, unwilling to let a strange dog in, unwilling to step away from the door to get Lou, but also unwilling to close the door and trap Lou inside. Stoned as he was, he still realized that would not go over well. I took the opportunity to push the door all the way open and step inside.

A huge drum kit filled up one corner of the room, with three different toms and seven or eight cymbals. Sitting behind it was a familiar curly-headed fellow, wearing forest green. I thought for a second the guy at the door was going to tackle me, but the Wendigo sighed and said, "It's okay, Zack; they're friends of mine." He eased out from behind the kit and walked over to us.

"Give us a moment, would you, Zack? We've got some business to discuss. Get me a soda, will you?"

Zack nodded knowingly. Private "business" was something he could understand.

"This is a surprise," the Wendigo said.

"Yeah, we're full of surprises. I didn't expect to find you behind a drum kit, for that matter."

"Music is my life. Or I hope it will be."

He looked strong and healthy, bursting with energy. Those stones must have pumped him up considerably.

"Why didn't you tell us we were looking for a shapeshifter?" I asked.

"So you finally figured it out. Who was I to spoil the surprise? I wasn't that happy with you guys in the first place, if you'll remember."

"And in the meantime, a friend of mine nearly died." A look of concern crossed his face, but I couldn't tell if it was real or not.

"Sorry to hear that," he said. "But telling you what it was wouldn't have made any difference in the long run. She's pretty focused once she sets her sights on someone."

"She?"

"You assume all monsters are male? Kind of sexist, don't you think?"

"Whatever. How do I find her?"

"Again, assuming I knew, why should I tell you?" I pulled the four green stones out of my pocket.

"Four?" he said, unimpressed. "That's hardly worth my while." The greedy look in his eyes belied his casual tone.

"It's not like before; I'm not asking you to actually do anything. Just some information, that's all. Still, if it's not worth it to you." I started to put the stones away.

"Hold on," he said. "Hold on. Maybe we can do business here." He really was a junkie for the stones. He could have a thousand of them and he'd still want more. I carefully laid the stones out on top of a speaker cabinet.

"How do I find it?" I repeated. "Or her."

The Wendigo sat back down on the low stool behind

the drums, picked up a pair of sticks, and started tapping idly on random drum surfaces.

"Why a drummer?" I asked, suddenly curious. "With your peculiar voice talents, I'd think you'd be a natural as a singer."

"What fun would there be in that? Music is all about rhythm, anyway, at least the kind I like. Rhythm is what calls to the blood—it was the first music, before humans were humans. Believe me, I know."

"So you've been around for a while," said Sherwood, who had been silent up to now.

"Indeed I have."

"Fascinating," I said. "Once again, how do we find this creature?"

"Well, she's in the city. I can tell you that much."

"That much I already know."

"And she's taken on an aspect. Not the way I have—the aspect I have is pretty much the aspect I'm stuck with. But not her—she can steal the identities of normal people." I was getting impatient.

"So far, you're not telling me anything I don't know," I said.

"How about this, then. She's got to kill every three days or so if she wants to keep strong. If she goes more than a week without a fresh infusion, she'll revert back to her normal state and eventually end up as a mere mindless beast."

"Anything else?"

"Well, this should be obvious, but she's got a strong survival drive. Not just blind instinct; anyone she thinks could possibly be a threat to her she will target and murder—and feed off them as well, killing two birds with one stone, if you'll pardon the pun?"

"What about your own abilities?" asked Sherwood. "You called Mason. You called me back from the dead, or close enough. Could you call her?"

"No, and I wouldn't if I could. She's not very pleasant. And calling her up wouldn't fit in with my new lifestyle." He did a couple of quick drum rolls. "But I can't affect her, anyway. We cancel each other out, at least as far as special abilities go. But if you really want to locate her, you do have an obvious method."

"And that is? "

"You're clearly someone who's a threat to her, and she knows that. All you need to do is to put yourself in a particularly vulnerable position and she'll show up, believe me. Guaranteed."

Bait. Once again. That seemed to be my current function in life. Still, not such a bad idea. Between Victor, Eli, and Sherwood, we surely could come up with a plan that would tempt her into showing herself but still keep me safe. Relatively. I scooped up two of the stones and put them back in my pocket. I didn't think what he'd told me warranted any more, and in truth, I was loath to let them go anyway. The Wendigo got a weird look on his face and for a second I thought there was going to be trouble, but then Zack came back in carrying a couple of cans of soda.

"Everything cool?" he said, nervously, picking up on the tension.

"Totally," I said. "We were just leaving."

Zack stood in the doorway and watched us walk down the hall, still feeling paranoid, I'd guess. When he went back inside, he slammed the door and the sound of the dead bolt being aggressively shot home was audible all the way down the corridor.

"I thought musicians were supposed to be mellow," Sherwood said.

"Jazz musicians are. Mostly. They have to be, just to get gigs. Heavy metal guys are another matter. Mostly Satan worshipers, I believe."

We headed back to Victor's. If we were going to set up a trap with me as the tempting morsel of cheese, I wanted to get started on it right away, before anyone else died.

We met Ruby coming out the front door of the mansion as we pulled up. She walked over to the driver's-side window and reached in, putting a hand on my shoulder. She looked exhausted, with dark lines showing under her eyes.

This thing was taking a lot more out of her than she'd admit.

"I'm sorry about the trouble with your friend," she said. "And her dog. That's sad. I'm glad you're okay, though. But we really do need to do something about this, you know, before it gets worse."

"We will," I said. She looked past me inquiringly at Sherwood. "I'm sorry; I forgot you two haven't met. Ruby, Sherwood." Ruby smiled at her, and Sherwood nodded a bit distantly, which was unlike her. Weird.

"Let me know what you come up with," Ruby said. "You know I'll be glad to help any way I can."

"Thanks," I said. "We'll be in touch. And be careful. I have a feeling one of us could be next on the hit parade."

"You know me," she said. "Always."

She got into her old VW Beetle, waved, and putted off down the street. Lou and I jumped out of the van, but Sherwood remained seated, looking at me oddly.

"What's up?" I asked.

"I'm not sure," she said. "As I told you, ever since my return I see people more clearly. They seem almost transparent at times—that's the best analogy I can come up with. Some people's goodness shines through; others . . . Well, let's just say not so much."

"And Ruby's one of those others?"

"Not exactly. It's like there's no one home, nothing there. I get no feeling at all from her."

"That's odd," I said. "But she's a strong practitioner. Maybe she likes keeping her private thoughts private. I know I do."

"Maybe. But it doesn't feel like she's shielding, or hiding anything. She's just . . . blank."

"And you think that means something?"

"We're looking for a shape-shifter, right? What if that's not really Ruby? What if that's not anything human at all?"

THIRTEEN

"WHAT DO YOU THINK?" I SAID TO ELI. "IS IT possible?"

Sherwood had dropped her bomb of an idea on Victor and Eli the minute we got inside the house.

"Oh, quite possible. The real question is, is it true?"

"But how could she fool us all so easily? It's not just that she looks exactly like Ruby; she *is* Ruby, for all intents and purposes."

"Remember what Richard Cory told me?" Sherwood said. "That once it consumes its victim, it becomes that victim? Not just the looks, not just the memories, but all the quirks, all the habits—everything that makes someone what they are."

This was wandering into territory too deep for me. I could see Eli's eyes light up behind his glasses, though. This was what he lived for.

"In essence, it is the victim, but at the same time, of course, it's not. That makes for an interesting metaphysical speculation. What is it that makes us what we are? Does it have a soul?"

"Who cares," said Victor. "As long as we can kill it. Let's leave the speculation for another time and look at the facts. We're looking for a shape-shifter, one so good it can fool even Lou. Ruby shows up at an opportune time, and tries to convince us that there is no creature wandering around. Instead, she points Mason in the direction of a mysterious 'practitioner.' One that lures Mason to an out-of-the-way corner. He attacks him, turns out to be a shape-shifter himself."

"And she describes the supposed practitioner for me, but is conveniently missing when he shows up," I said, slowly.

"Exactly. One and the same, perhaps. Add to that the fact that Sherwood finds her oddly opaque, and you've got a hell of a lot of coincidence."

The chain of logic was flimsy, but it was one of those things that felt right—it had the ring of truth on an emotional level, and that's often more reliable than cold fact. I wondered why I hadn't thought of it before.

I offered a few halfhearted objections, but it was more just to excuse my own lack in not even thinking of it in the first place. It was still hard to believe that none of us, even Lou, couldn't tell the difference between a child in a *Lion King* costume at Halloween and a real lion.

Timothy had been listening quietly, but he had a puzzled look on his face.

"I have a question," he said. "You were over at your friend Morgan's yesterday, right? When the shape-shifter was there?" I nodded. "But Ruby was over here almost all of yesterday. So how could it have been her?"

Damn. The idea had made perfect sense, only to be torpedoed by an inconvenient fact.

"That is a problem," I admitted.

"It would seem so," said Victor, "but something's not adding up here, and I think at the very least we need to pay Ruby a visit. Unannounced and unexpected. Mason?"

"Now?"

"When better? After the next person dies and we figure out the details?"

Point taken. We decided just Victor and I would go—maybe we could catch her by surprise. If we all showed up en masse, she'd know something was up right off the bat.

A half hour later we were looking for a parking space for Victor's silver BMW. Ruby's place turned out to be on the second floor of a small apartment building in the Richmond, not far from where Eli lived.

Victor wasn't relying on any use of talent this time. Anything that involved talent would be up to me—he was going with firepower, a Glock .40 that he had taken out of his safe and put in a shoulder holster.

When we arrived in the area he parked two blocks away, as a tactical move. We walked over to the building separately, a half block or so apart. If true, it was entirely possible Ruby had realized she'd been outed—Sherwood might be as transparent to her as she was opaque to Sherwood. No point in providing her an opportunity to take us both down at once. I wasn't that worried, though—between Victor and myself, I thought we could handle her. But we didn't know the extent of her powers, and it never hurts to be cautious.

Victor entered the building first, and I entered behind him a few seconds later. It was an older building, with three apartments on the ground floor and three more up above. We climbed up the stairs to the upper landing and stood outside Ruby's door, listening. Victor knocked, loudly. It was silent inside. Either she hadn't got home yet or she was very sound asleep. Or she was quietly awaiting us.

Lou gave a little snort and wrinkled up his nose as if there was a bad smell in the air. I took a deep breath, but couldn't smell anything. But when I took another, I could just sense the faintest whiff of something, sweet and cloying like rotten fruit. Or meat. It sent an atavistic chill up my spine to the back of my neck. The reaction to that particular smell is rooted deep, and is never good.

"No wards," Victor said quietly.

I checked; he was right. No practitioner leaves their home unguarded. But perhaps Ruby wasn't precisely a practitioner, was she, now? He tried the door. Locked, of course. That wouldn't be a problem for Victor, however. Mechanical devices are very difficult to affect using talent, but in addition to his talent, Victor was a regular James Bond. I had no doubt but that he carried a handy collection of precise lock picks in his wallet.

He reached inside his jacket, pulled out the Glock, and held it six inches away from the striker plate where the lock met the doorjamb. So much for precision and subtlety.

"Muffle the sound for me, will you?" he said. "We don't want to disturb the neighbors."

He half expected me to have trouble with that, at which point he'd sigh and whip out some preset spell and do it himself. But a thick carpet covered the hallway, and overhead, a cone-shaped metal shade held a ceiling lightbulb, the kind you slip over the bulb and then screw the bulb into the socket.

I used the funnel shape as a template and curved a line of talent around the gun, then another line spreading out into the floor of the landing. When the gun fired, the sound would bleed off into the carpet. People in the adjacent apartment might feel a slight vibration, but in San Francisco occasional tremors are hardly worth remarking on.

Victor put two silent shots next to the doorknob. Splinters of wood flew off, one almost gouging my face. He shoved the door open and stood in the doorway, gun ready, scoping out the inside. After a few seconds, he motioned to me and eased his way into the apartment.

Inside, it was a mess. Half-eaten pizzas falling out of their boxes littered the floor, along with crusted cartons of takeout. Clothes strewn about, dirt everywhere, empty wine bottles collecting dust on the floor. A mattress had been shoved into the corner of the living room, up against a wall. On each end, blankets and sheets had been torn into strips and jumbled together into a nest, with indentations at either end where a heavy body might have laid at rest. The lair of the beast. The whole room smelled like the big cat house at the zoo, overwhelming that first faint whiff of corruption I'd noticed in the hall.

A bathroom, surprisingly clean, was off to one side, and next to it a closed door, apparently to a bedroom. Victor crossed the room, crouched down so that his head was below the level of the doorknob, and reached up for it. Anyone inside the room would be expecting someone outside to be standing erect, and the most common attack is focused at chest level. The split second it takes to adjust can make all the difference.

I moved out of the line of sight from the bedroom door. A couple of years ago Victor would have needed to remind me, but I'd at least learned the basics by now. He swung open the door, whipped his head into the doorway for half a second, then whipped it back before anything inside could react. None of these precautions turned out to be necessary. There was nothing in the room. At least, nothing alive.

Ruby was there, of course. The real Ruby. Parts of her. She lay crumpled on the floor next to an unmade bed. Her chest had been torn open and there was an empty cavity where her heart had once pumped merrily away. Her head had been detached from the rest of her body, and the skull had been cracked open like a walnut. What was left of her face was swollen and barely recognizable, smeared with blood and gray brain tissue. Her long red hair was clumped and matted, like stuffing in an old pillow, and its once-vibrant color was dull and washed out. Everywhere, flies swarmed greedily around the carcass.

I walked over to the doorway but didn't go in. With the bedroom door open, the distinctive sickly sweet odor of rotting flesh was now evident—not overwhelming, but enough to make my gorge rise. I had to swallow several times to keep from throwing up. Lou backed away and went over to the front door, pretending to stand guard. I wished I'd thought of that first.

Victor walked into the room and knelt down by her body as if this were something that happened every day.

But he straightened up quickly and got out of there before very long. He wasn't anxious to linger any more than I was, and there was little point in performing forensic tests. It's not like there was any mystery about what had happened here. We took a brief look around the apartment to see if there was any indication of where Ruby, or rather, the shape-shifter, might be now. Papers were strewn over a table in the living room; handouts promoting bands and clubs, a brochure from a show at the Asian Art Museum, a flyer titled: "Open Studios at Hunters Point."

"Not much here," Victor said. "She's probably gone for good."

"You think? Maybe we should wait here in case she returns."

"No, I don't think she will. She knew her game was up as soon as she met Sherwood. We won't see her again, at least not in that guise, and definitely not here. She wouldn't have had just this one spot—she must have known it might be discovered at some point, and a predator always has a backup lair, just like prey will have more than one bolt-hole." He glanced through the door into Ruby's bedroom. "If they realize they're prey, that is."

"So how do we find her?" Victor pointed at Lou, but I shook my head.

"I don't think so. It's like the fake Ifrit and the Wendigo—anything from the energy pool seems to be immune to his tracking sense."

"Yes, but he's a dog, remember?" Lou whipped his head around and fixed Victor with a disbelieving stare until he amended his statement. "At least, he's got some of the same capabilities. He doesn't have to use his Ifrit sense. If we can narrow down her location, he can track her by scent alone."

I wrinkled my nose, smelling the overwhelming cage odor permeating the apartment. Victor had a point; I could almost track the scent myself.

"Maybe," I said. "But how are we going to do that?"

"First things first. He needs to fix the scent in his mind."

Lou looked up at me inquiringly. He can't really follow conversations, but he gets the gist of most things. But he wasn't taking directions from Victor.

"Go ahead," I told him.

I walked over to the corner where the nest of blankets and sheets lay, bent down, and took several deep breaths to illustrate the point. I instantly regretted it as the musky odor made me gag again. Lou followed me over and sniffed delicately. He probably didn't need to, with a sense of smell as sharp as his, but he enjoys humoring me occasionally.

"What now?" I asked.

Victor didn't immediately answer; he just looked at Lou and then back at me, as if considering something.

"Wait here," he finally said. "I need to get my bag."

Before I could say anything he was out the door, leaving me and Lou alone with a rotting corpse, slowly decomposing ten feet away. The room seemed suddenly hotter than before, closed in and claustrophobic. My chest felt tight, and I started to get dizzy. I'd been unconsciously breathing in shallow pants, trying to ignore the combination of feral reek and dead flesh. Carbon dioxide had been building up in my blood and I needed to get out of there before I passed out. I stepped out and waited in the hall until I heard the downstairs door open and Victor's footsteps on the stairs. Then I ducked back into the apartment— I wasn't going to show weakness in front of him.

He came in, carrying his old black doctor's bag, the one he keeps in the trunk of his car when it isn't in his safe. Pushing papers aside, he set it on the living room table. Out came a knife, an old-fashioned mortar and pestle, and a vial of yellowish powder.

"Okay," he said. "Now, Lou can't track a shape-shifter, but he doesn't have to. We can use the same method that we used with the lead and the shotgun pellets—a little more subtle, but the principle is the same."

"Something in common?" I thought for a moment. "I can't think of anything."

"Well, the shape-shifter devoured part of Ruby, and imprinted her essence on itself. But the rest of Ruby's body is still here in the apartment."

I didn't like where this was going. Victor's knife implied some use of blood, and dealing with a corpse as well had definite overtones of the black arts. But I still didn't see what he was driving at.

"How does that help us?" I said. "You can't very well . . ." I stopped, feeling sick. The stench of the apartment wasn't helping.

"Yes," said Victor. "I can. A drop of blood. Some magnetized filings, and a bit of Ruby's flesh. And Lou's help."

"No way," I said. "He won't stand for it, not if there's blood involved. Especially his."

"Not his; mine. All I need from him is a bit of his hair, taken while he's focused on finding someone. Then I can track the shape-shifter myself."

I saw what he was doing—it was like what I'd done when I ran energy through Lou and into Sherwood so that she could borrow his tracking ability. Victor had his own ways of doing things, though. He picked up the knife and handed it to me before walking to the door.

"I'm going down to the street. Tell Lou to find me, and then slice off a bit of his hair while he's focused. Put the hair in the mortar bowl. Got it?"

This sounded a bit convoluted to me, but I shrugged my acceptance. Victor nodded, stepped outside, and a moment later his footsteps echoed down the stairs. I sighed.

"Lou," I said. "Find him. Find Victor." Lou slowly turned his head toward me, checking to see if I was serious. Didn't I know this was no time to be playing hide-and-seek?

"Just do it," I said. He stared at me long enough to let me know he thought I was deranged and started toward the door. I caught him by his collar and brought the knife close. He stopped and half opened his mouth. He didn't like knives, not at all, and was letting me know that if I tried for a blood sample, I was going to lose a couple of fingers. He's a patient guy, but there are limits.

"Take it easy," I said. "I just need a snip of hair." He let me saw off a little tuft, but didn't relax until I moved the knife away. "Okay. Relax. Forget Victor." Now he knew I'd gone off the rails. He walked over and sat near the door, keeping an eye on me, as if I might start dancing and gibbering at any moment.

Victor was back in the apartment a minute later. He took the knife back from me, used the tip on his finger to get a drop of blood, picked up the mortar bowl, and mixed it in with Lou's hair. A sprinkling of powder from the vial was next, and he mashed it all together. He started at the mixture blankly, then took a deep breath.

"One final ingredient," he said and moved off toward the bedroom where Ruby's body lay. I'd seen all I wanted to see.

"I'll wait outside," I said and headed toward the hall. Lou was out the moment I opened the door. If Victor saw this as sign of weakness, fine. It was better than throwing up all over the potion he was mixing up.

Just mixing it was bad enough. I didn't know how he meant to employ it and I didn't want to, although I could make a guess. I sat on the stairs and waited, trying not to think about it. After a while, Victor joined me, bag in hand. He looked a little green around the gills.

"Did it work?" I asked.

"Oh, yes."

"You know where she is?"

"Not yet. Ruby's body is too close and its proximity too powerful; it overwhelms everything else. It's like trying to see a candle flame in the distance while you're standing next to a bonfire. I need some distance."

We left the apartment. The shattered lock was going to present a hell of a problem for the police department when they discovered the body. Their theory that an animal was responsible wasn't going to hold up much longer, but they'd never come close to understanding the true state of affairs. I was beginning to regret having called Inspector Macklin earlier—Victor was right; it would make him wonder what

I knew about it and why I was so interested. Maybe homicide would hush it up, though, put it on a need-to-know basis. If I was lucky, maybe Macklin would never even hear about it.

Once back on the street, we walked for a block and then Victor stood, concentrating.

"No good," he said. "Nothing in this direction." We retraced our steps until we were well past Ruby's apartment in the other direction.

"Got it," he said. "East. Maybe across the bridge."

We got in his car and he started driving east. Victor drove almost as if he were in a trance, sitting stiffly erect, following his new sense. I hoped he wouldn't crash the car, but there was no point in offering to drive. We ended up continuing east on Cesar Chavez, but instead of heading for the bridge, he angled off onto Third Street and through the Bayview district.

"Hunters Point," I said, suddenly. "There was a flyer in the apartment, remember, about the open studios there."

"Good guess. Out of the way, lots of space. That wouldn't be a bad choice for her."

Hunters Point Shipyard lies at the end of Bayview, right on the water. At one time it was a thriving port and shipyard, but those days are long past. Now it's mostly a toxic waste site, with a huge power plant that dominates the landscape. The old buildings of the shipyard have been converted into artists' studios, where painters and sculptors work in happy isolation.

Bayview is almost entirely African American, an urban slum rife with drugs and gangs, like Big Block and Westmob. Shootings are common, and it's a dangerous place. But it doesn't look dangerous, and it doesn't look like what people think of as a slum, either. Older, detached houses sit on tree-lined streets, businesses dot the landscape, and people go about their daily life. It looks peaceful and rather pleasant. Appearances can be deceiving.

At the very end of Bayview, right up against the edge of the bay, the old shipyard sprawls out across the shore.

Victor drove partway down the sloping driveway that leads into the complex, then stopped. Spread out down below were the studio buildings, looking more like military barracks than artists' studios, which is logical since that's what they once were. Off to the north side a large expanse of tangled scrub and low bushes covered a steep slope, crisscrossed by narrow gullies. A perfect place for the lair of a beast, or maybe Ruby had taken on the persona of a random artist in one of the studios. That would be more likely, considering her habits so far.

"She's here," he said. "But exactly where, I can't tell. My locating sense is too diffuse."

"It's a pretty big area," I said. "It's not going to do a lot of good to wander around there hoping we'll bump into her."

Victor gestured at Lou.

"This is where he takes over."

"Ahh. You have a plan."

"Lou picks up her scent and pinpoints her exact location. You follow him, keeping an eye out for her."

"Great idea."

"But I don't think he'll have to track her for very long—I imagine she's already aware you're here."

"Why?"

"Because you were present when the energy pool was formed and helped in its creation. That provides her with a connection to you—not a strong enough one to track you down, but enough to feel your presence as soon as you get close."

"But if she senses me closing in, won't she just take off again?"

"Not necessarily. I might be wrong on the connection part. And anyway, I think it more likely she'll try to ambush you and rip you apart."

"I see. And what will you be doing when this ripping apart thing is taking place?"

"Well, that's the rub. I'll have to stay up here. The point is to tempt her into an attack, and I don't think she'll take on both of us at once. After all, she didn't have much luck even when she caught you alone, so she'll be cautious. So I'll hang back, far enough away so she doesn't sense me, but still close enough to jump in when she attacks. You just have to fight her off long enough for me to get to you."

I thought about the body in the next room, torn apart and partially dismembered. Then I thought about Morgan and Beulah.

"Okay," I said. "But I'm going to need that gun of yours. She's resistant to talent, remember."

"The gun could pose a problem. If you're armed, she might be able to tell. And then she'll slink away and wait for a better opportunity. You need to make her feel confident enough that she can take you so that she'll launch an attack."

"Maybe you should just truss me up hand and foot and dump me somewhere she can find me," I said. "Then, while she's busy eating my brain, you can sneak up on her." A ghost of a smile flitted across Victor's face.

"That has crossed my mind. Anyway, try to keep an open line of sight between us. And if you have to move behind a building, do it slowly and I'll angle over to where I can keep you in sight."

This seemed like a haphazard plan to me, but I didn't really care. I'd driven the shape-shifter off once already and I could do it again. I nodded and headed into the compound with Lou. We reached the bottom of the access road, where there was a large parking lot of gravel and dirt, muddy, with pools of standing water that had nowhere to drain. Across from it was where the first buildings started.

"Do your stuff," I said to Lou. "See if you can sniff her out."

He put his nose to the ground and started searching, moving out in concentric circles, adroitly avoiding the areas of mud and water. It wasn't long before he raised his head slightly and moved off toward one of the buildings on the far side of the parking lot.

I looked up to make sure Victor was still in sight. He wasn't. I cursed quietly, trying to figure out where he'd disappeared to. If I'd pulled that kind of sloppy backup on him, he'd have ripped me a new one. I hesitated a moment, then followed Lou. I was going to find this shape-shifter, whether Victor was paying attention or not.

Then, as we passed by the first building, I saw Victor come out from behind the rear of it. He put his finger to his lips in an exaggerated fashion and motioned to me. As I turned toward him, his body was violently jerked back around the corner as if something had grabbed him from behind. I heard a triumphant sound, somewhere between a snarl and a roar. Holy shit.

They say a sudden shock or fear can paralyze you into immobility—the body just shuts down. Not so. My legs were carrying me toward the building, sprinting at top speed, before my mind fully took in what had just happened. Lou was right alongside of me. With his speed he could easily have outpaced me, but he's no fool.

Right before I rounded the corner of the building Lou let out with a volley of warning barks. Kind of superfluous, I thought. But then he sprinted ahead, turned on a dime, and launched himself through the air at me, striking me square in the middle of my chest. At twelve pounds that wasn't enough to knock me back, but it certainly slowed me up for a second, long enough for my brain to start functioning again. Why had I assumed that was really Victor?

I was going too fast to stop, but I swung wide and sprinted past the corner of the building, angling away in a straight line. When the shape-shifter waiting there for me sprang, it missed me by a good six inches.

It hadn't had time to completely transform itself back from its Victor persona. Maybe being in the midst of a change had made it clumsier than usual. What I saw was a caricature of Victor, twice life-size, claws like a bear, but with a face almost unchanged. That typical, somewhat supercilious expression remained fixed on the shape-shifter's face even as its arms grew longer and its teeth lengthened.

I didn't stop running. I sprinted toward the adjacent building, and by the time it saw what I was doing I had a good head start. It bounded after me, now on all fours, its transformation almost complete. I ran through the door at the end of the next building, a long, low structure with a corridor that ran all the way through. Before I was halfway down the corridor, it had appeared in the doorway behind me. I wasn't going to make it out the other side before it caught up with me, and even if I did, what then?

I frantically tried several doors until I found one that was unlocked and ducked inside. It was a sculptor's studio, and thank God the artist wasn't home. The room was full of large twisted metal sculptures, elongated figures that were all sharp angles and rough surfaces. Interesting, perhaps, but of no use to me. I can work with metal, but barely, and it takes me forever to accomplish anything.

But there was clay there, too, bags of it, and that I can work with. The first thing I needed to do was buy some time. That's always the case—every time you really need a moment to come up with a clever spell or elegant solution to a problem, something's just about to rip your heart out. So first things first—block the door and keep it from getting in until I was ready to deal with it.

I grabbed a lump of clay and threw it toward the door. Then I poured some talent into it, expanding both its properties and its size, until the entire door was covered with a thick, gluey coating. More energy, not quite heat, but a magical analogue. It was like having a giant kiln operating at unheard-of temperatures. In seconds, I had the door layered over with a hard shell of baked enamel.

She didn't even try to open the door. She hit it full force like a grizzly separated from her cubs. The door splintered, and the hardened shell I'd so cleverly constructed shattered like a vase dropped on a stone floor. Shards of hardened clay flew everywhere, and then she was inside, standing in front of me, finally in her true form and glory.

She stood on two legs, like a bear, six and a half feet tall. She was thick, long fur covered her, and long claws grew from the ends of powerful arms ending half in paws and half in hands. Her muzzle was narrow and elongated, like an anteater's, with an almost perfectly circular mouth like that of a giant lamprey. Useful for sucking out the brains of her victims, I would imagine. A long snakelike tongue flicked in and out the mouth, and when she opened it a double row of teeth gleamed wetly. Where the hell was Victor?

Lou took one look and dove under a workbench, hiding behind a rolled-up tarp. I scrambled behind one of the sharp metal sculptures, putting some cover between her and me. She made a keening sound and reached out with those half-paw-half-hands, hooking a claw over one of the metal struts of the sculpture. Lou came out from under the bench and bolted past her through the ruined door and was gone. So much for the faithful dog defending his master to the death.

The sculpture toppled with a crash, and then she was scrambling over it to get to me. I reached out with talent to the fluorescent light fixture and diverted the flow of electricity into the metal sculpture. The effect wasn't much; fluorescents don't use much current, but it was enough to make her howl and jump away as if she'd landed on a hot stove. She stumbled back and tripped on a pile of scrap wood in the corner.

Without thinking, I reached out and gathered up the wood, using one of the metal sculptures as my pattern, and fashioned a creature of my own, one to rival even her. It was tall and spindly, but full of jagged wooden edges and sharp points, and it projected an aura of power and menace. Several of the wood pieces were studded with nails, and I turned those into jaws capable of rending flesh. It was a golem, insensitive to pain, neither alive nor dead, and a formidable creature indeed.

Not really, though. It was all bluff. At heart it was nothing more than random pieces of wood, and one good blow from her paw would scatter it over the room. She didn't know that, however. I moved it toward her and it creaked noisily forward like a clockwork monster in an old horror film. The bluff wasn't going to work for long, though. She automatically backed away until she came up against a wall, and I could see her tensing for a desperate spring.

But the distraction worked. I took my chance and was out the door in two seconds. I was halfway down the corridor before she figured out the golem was no real threat at all, destroyed it, and came after me again. She was no more than fifteen feet behind me when I heard a volley of high-pitched barks from up ahead, and then the door at the other end of the hallway flew open and Lou came charging through, followed closely by Victor, Glock automatic in his hand. I stopped short and plastered myself against the corridor wall, giving Victor a clear shot.

The sound of the Glock going off in the confines of the corridor wasn't nearly as loud as I'd expected. More of a flat cracking sound, a quick series of pops that seemed almost harmless rather than lethal. But that was deceptive.

The shape-shifter jerked, stumbled, and went down snarling. She got back up to her feet, took a few more hesitant steps, and crumpled to the floor again. Victor ran right past me up to where she lay and put two more shots into her head from close range. She jerked twice, quivered, and lay still.

I expected doors to fly open at any moment, questioning heads to appear, and horrified screams to start echoing through the hallway. None of that happened. Maybe there was no one in the building right now, or maybe anyone working there was too immersed in creative throes to notice. Or more likely, they had developed a finely tuned sense of urban self-preservation, and well understood that when you hear gunshots in the hall, sticking your head out of your door to see what is going on is not the smartest thing to do.

But now we had another problem. We were standing in a hallway next to the body of a monster out of a Hieronymus Bosch painting. Somebody was bound to wander in before too long, and we could hardly leave it there to be found. Victor had obviously been thinking the same thing. He straightened up from where he had been crouched down examining the body.

"We need a tarp," he said.

I remembered the tarp I'd seen in the sculpture room, under a bench. I ran back, squeezed through the ruined door, and pulled it out from under the bench where it had been stashed. We spread it out in the hallway next to the shape-shifter and rolled her onto it. Then we rolled it a couple more times until it was covered up. The shape-shifter was hidden, but now it looked exactly like what it was: a tarp containing a dead body.

Victor bent over the tarp, made some gestures, and tensed with effort. The tarp shimmered briefly and then I was looking at an old spruce tree, like something left over from a long-ago Christmas. It was a perfect illusion—the needles were brown halfway along their length, and little piles had apparently fallen off and onto the floor. The man has ability.

We grabbed the corner of the tarp and pulled it along the hallway and out the door.

"I'll get the car," Victor said. "Watch the body." He disappeared around the corner of the building.

"Try to make it back this time," I called after him.

With a little effort I could cut through the illusion and see the tarp, bulging in the middle. I watched it anxiously, afraid beyond reason that it would start to move. I was sure the shape-shifter was dead, but that didn't stop me from obsessively checking every few seconds.

I was starting to get nervous when Victor returned. I didn't think there was going to be enough space to cram the body into the small trunk—a BMW M5 is not a family sedan, after all. But she hadn't stiffened up yet—that takes a number of hours—so we were able to force it in with some judicious pushing and folding. Squishing sounds could be heard from under the tarp as we squeezed her in, which made me queasy. Once we got the body stowed securely we drove slowly away, as if nothing out of the ordinary had happened.

"Okay, where the hell were you?" I said as we drove away from the shipyard. "That thing almost got me, you know."

"That was unfortunate. Just after you walked down the driveway I got a call on my cell. From Eli. He said to wait, he was almost at the front gate and it was crucial to meet him there."

"And you just left me to fend for myself?"

"He said you'd be in no danger. He had Ruby in sight."

"That's insane. What was he doing here? And how the hell did he know where we were? And why—" I broke off. Victor turned his head and favored me with a quick glance, and didn't answer. "Oh," I said, after a few seconds.

"She was a perfect mimic. A voice is even easier."

"How did she get your number?" This time I didn't have to wait for Victor's look. "Oh, right. She had it from when she was Ruby. She had all the info she needed, including your cell number."

"I should have realized," said Victor. "The number came up on the display as blocked, which should have been the tip-off it wasn't really Eli calling. But it wasn't until Lou came tearing up the road that I knew I'd been had."

That's about as close to an apology as Victor's capable of.

"What are we going to do with the body?" I asked.

"I'll take care of it," he said. We drove in silence the rest of the way until we finally reached my house. I turned to him before I got out.

"One thing still bothers me. When Ruby was at your house, the shape-shifter was at Morgan's house at the same time. How did she pull that off? Did she leave for a while? Was she around where you could see her the entire time? Did she split herself in two somehow?" The minute I said that, I got it.

"Oh, shit," I said. Victor looked at my face and knew I had something.

"What?" he said.

"Think back. Think of what we saw in Ruby's apartment. The mattress."

I flashed back to the scene there, the mattress in the living room with two piles of torn sheets and two piles of wadded-up blankets and sheets and two indentations. Victor looked off into the distance as he did the same. His visual recall was as good as mine, possibly better.

"Two of them," he said. "Goddamn it. There are two of them."

FOURTEEN

I CALLED MORGAN TO LET HER KNOW IT STILL wasn't safe to come back, but her phone went straight to voice mail, and her message box was full. She hadn't called me, either, which was a bit worrisome. Ruby had been taken care of, but what about the other? Still, as long as Morgan stayed away, she should be safe.

Meanwhile, I had a message of my own—an unexpected gig. The booker at Rainy Tuesdays had called to ask if I was available tomorrow night. I was. I needed the money; even with shape-shifters roaming the streets, rent still comes due every month.

The club's scheduled draw, the Scott Harkins quintet, had unexpectedly cut short their tour and abruptly canceled. Thus the call. I haven't worked hard enough at self-promotion to be a headliner and I probably never will, but I did have enough of a local reputation to be on the short list as a fill-in. I was even getting enough of a name that occasionally people came out to specifically hear me play. Who'd have imagined?

I called the booker back and assured her we were ready

to go. Then I started making calls, and it took until the next afternoon to get hold of everyone. Dave's always the easiest—he's a family man and he returns calls, especially if there's a paying gig in the offing. But Roger is liable to be off skateboarding and he keeps temporarily losing his cell phone. And Bobby Clemens, whom I wanted to add, is drunk half the time and can't be bothered to check his messages. But I finally got them all on board.

It was nice to be setting up at Rainy Tuesdays again. There are other clubs that are more fun to play, but few classier and few that pay as well. Of course, there's Yoshi's. They'd opened up a sister club in San Francisco, not yet quite with the cachet of the Oakland original, but it was getting there. But I'd been temporarily banned from playing there after an unfortunate situation that was none of my making. Nothing official, but effective. It would blow over. Things always do in the jazz world.

Rainy Tuesdays sits in the middle of the Mission District. Ten years ago the Mission was still a sketchy enough neighborhood to discourage nighttime business, but these days the main danger a patron faced was getting scalded by an errant latte. It's a nice space—medium-sized, very trendy and hip, lots of small tables, and a great sound system to pipe the band's music into the front room.

The long curved bar with its black leather rail at one end has taken on an iconic status in only a couple of years, and other places are starting to copy the look. They'd recently softened the original industrial retro look, adding some color and giving the place a warmer feel. They'd kept their trademark logo—an umbrella with three raindrops, done in blue neon tubing. The stage is still a bit too small, because they want to squeeze in as many tables as possible. But it's raised only about half a foot, and the nearest tables are close enough to almost touch the players, giving it that intimate touch. Jazz was never meant for the stage or the concert hall; originally jazz was club music, meant for people who dance and drink and party. And the best jazz hasn't abandoned those roots.

Dave, the bass player, and Roger Chu, the wunderkind on drums, had become my go-to guys, and this time I'd added Bobby Clemens. Bobby was the finest organ player in town, one of the best anywhere, actually. He didn't work as often as he should, because frankly, he was a total asshole. Unless he was drunk, and then he couldn't play. The only reason he ever got a gig at all was that he was just that goddamned good. But he did manage to suck most of the joy out of playing music, simply by his very presence and attitude.

But I thought he'd work out for us. Dave is so laid-back he can get along with anyone, and Roger lives in a world all his own. The only thing that matters to Roger is the music—except for his skateboard. And it's hard to insult someone who doesn't even realize they've been insulted. When Roger's not playing drums he's mostly in an impervious teenage fog that nothing penetrates.

Bobby and I get along fairly well, considering. He never hassles me, not because I'm so easy to get along with, but because he's slightly afraid of me. He'd once seen something he wasn't supposed to, when a couple of street thugs tried to rip off my guitar one night. He'd managed to convince himself he'd been high that night, but there was just enough doubt remaining in his mind to treat me with a certain amount of caution and respect. Whenever he started getting out of line, I'd throw something minor his way, like quietly turning the ice cubes in his drink blue, then red, then back to normal. He never could be sure if it was real or not, and that certainly put a damper on his aggressiveness.

The draw that evening was light, since the original show had been canceled, but we were all on our game. For the first time in a long while I put everything out of my mind, refusing to worry about such mundane issues as carnivorous shape-shifters. My playing was assured; my lines inventive and flowing. Roger was a monster on drums, as usual, and the sound of Bobby's B3 Hammond was so sweet that it makes every tune seem to groove even if it really doesn't.

So temporarily life was good—right up until the moment I noticed who had taken a seat behind the first row of tables. Our curly-headed friend, the Wendigo.

I immediately went on autopilot, comping behind Bobby's solo without even paying attention to what he was doing. No one in the audience noticed, but Bobby did. He started to throw me a dirty look, but quickly changed it to neutral and puzzled when he saw the look on my own face.

The Wendigo ignored me, focusing on Roger playing drums. He hunched forward, drumming his fingers on the table, jerking with a little tic every time Roger hit the snare.

Maybe he was just here to listen to an up-and-coming drummer. Maybe he wasn't here to cause any trouble. Maybe he was just a jazz fan. And maybe pigs really can fly.

We played a couple more tunes before I signaled for a break, a little early. I wiped down my guitar, unhurriedly, watching the Wendigo out of the corner of my eye. He seemed totally at ease, striking up a conversation with a couple of women at a nearby table, throwing back drinks like the original party boy. I quietly sidled over to his table and sat down. He turned to face me, feigning astonishment at my sudden presence.

"Ah, Mason. How good of you to come down and mingle with the hoi polloi."

I was in no mood for snarky humor. He'd managed to turn a great evening into a bad one in two seconds, just by showing up.

"What are you doing here?" I said.

"What, I can't go out and hear some music, just because I'm not like other people? I thought you'd be more tolerant, being a musician and all." I wasn't buying it for a moment.

"What do you want?"

"Well, for starters, how about an intro to that drummer? He's incredible." I got up from the table and started to walk away. "Now, hold on," he said, grabbing at my arm. "You're right. I didn't just come down for the music. I came here to help you."

"Of course you did," I said. "Why wouldn't you?"

"No, really."

"And in return?"

"You've still got some more of those stones. At least a couple; you didn't hand them all over the last time."

"You're really hooked on them, aren't you?" I said. "You've become a junkie, basically."

"And whose fault is that? You're the one who introduced them to me."

"So I did. I'll just have to live with the guilt, I guess."

"It's not just about the magic; it's about the music," the Wendigo said. "Surely you can understand that. You see, I discovered that with them I'm a great drummer. Without them, just very ordinary."

"Jesus," I said. "You might as well be mainlining crystal."

"What?"

"Never mind."

"Music's important, in a way that other things aren't. You know that. How do you think you found me in the first place?"

"I was following a vision, as I remember."

"Sure, but a vision just tells you what may happen, and where. It doesn't tell you why. It's the creativity that connected us—yours and mine." A philosophical Wendigo. What next? "Anyway, I thought I'd trade you some more information for the rest of those stones. I know you've still got a few of them left."

"Sorry," I said. "You're a junkie. You'd say anything for a taste. Information from you would be worthless."

"Not a problem. I'll tell you, and you decide if it's worth it or not. If so, then you give me the stones. If not, you don't. Fair enough, right? You see, unlike you, I'm the trusting sort."

"Right," I said. We sat looking at each other for a minute. "Well?"

"Well, you managed to kill the shape-shifter that was causing so much trouble, I see."

"We did. How did you know that?"

"I know things."

"And you have a problem with that?"

"No, not at all. She, and those like her, aren't really individuals like you or me—they take on the aspect and intelligence of others, and without a host of sorts they remain basically just animals. But there's something else interesting about them that you don't know."

"They rise from the grave at the new moon?"

"Don't joke about things you know nothing about. But no, nothing like that."

I waited patiently. I was fairly certain he was bluffing, trying to pull some sort of scam to get his fix, but he might have valuable information. Or rather, he might be willing to share it. I had no doubt that he knew more than he ever let on.

"All those shape-shifters have their little differences," the Wendigo said, "but there is one thing about them that's a constant, that always holds true."

"And what might that be?" I asked warily. I had a feeling I wasn't going to like the answer. The Wendigo smiled, almost gleefully.

"Just this. They seldom enter the world alone, and they never stay alone. They exist in pairs. Always."

He leaned back in his chair with a satisfied smile, proud of the bombshell he'd dropped. When he noticed I was looking at him with no change of expression, he frowned.

"You don't believe me?" he said.

"No, I believe you. But you're a day late and a dollar short."

"Beg pardon?"

"It's an expression. Not to burst your bubble, but I already figured that out."

The Wendigo looked positively crestfallen. He'd expected his news to knock me off my feet. Maybe it would have if he hadn't waited so long.

"Okay, so you know about that." He paused and thought for a moment. "What about the energy pool—the one I came out of? And the others?"

"Yeah? What about it?"

"It's an open conduit, you know. Other things can come out of it as well. You really need to shut it off."

"Yeah, we figured that out as well. But we've had more pressing issues lately." I shook my head. "Anyway, that's not information. That's advice."

"Oh, I know. I was just trying to be helpful, that's all."

"And pick up some stones."

"Well, yes. But you don't want them anyway, not really. And I did want to help."

I left the table and played the rest of the gig in a funk. When the Wendigo came into the club, he mixed the two worlds that I tried so hard to keep separate. It was hard to concentrate on the music when the sight of him was a constant reminder that there was unfinished and unpleasant business waiting for me. The simple life of an ordinary musician had never looked so good.

NEXT MORNING I WAS BACK AT VICTOR'S. PROBLEM was, we had nothing to go on. If we waited for more dead people to start turning up, that would give us a place to start, but it would be a little hard on the victims.

But one thing that the Wendigo had said was true—we needed to close off the energy pool. So far, four things had come through—the fake Ifrit, the Wendigo, and apparently two of the shape-shifters. And perhaps even other things we didn't know about yet. And as long as it stayed open, there was always the chance that something even worse might appear. In fact, I didn't understand why we hadn't already been inundated with uncanny apparitions.

Eli thought there must be specific circumstances governing it.

"You mean like the new moon falling on a rainy night?" I asked.

"Something like that, but nothing that simple, I imagine," he said. "It would take a lot of study to figure it out. It will be a lot quicker just to shut it down."

Easier said than done. I had no idea about how to go even get started, but Eli and Victor were in their element. We decided to wait until dark, since the construction site was active during the day, and there was no way to operate until it shut down. The energy pool was more apparent at night anyway, easier to locate and isolate. They spent the rest of the day poring over books and arguing about the best way to dissolve the pool. I stayed out of the way for the most part. About seven, we headed out.

Eli was disturbed at the turn things had taken, but he was thrilled to finally be able to meet Rolf. Eli was the one who had figured out what he and those like him were—practitioners who had changed over time so that they were no longer quite human, but instead incarnations of myth and lore, magical beings themselves. But with one thing or another, he'd never met any of them.

Rolf was alone, though, which was a disappointment for Eli. He'd particularly wanted to get a look at Richard Cory. Rolf let us in, sizing up Victor and Eli. He immediately took to Eli, but didn't seem to care much for Victor. I guess he hadn't yet lost all his human reactions.

"What brings you here tonight?" he asked.

"We need to close down the energy pool," I said, getting right to the point. "We think there might be other things that could come through it, and the ones that already have weren't too friendly."

"Be my guest. You may be right, but it's not something I'd care to mess with, myself."

"What gave you the idea to create it in the first place?" Eli asked. "And how exactly did you manifest it?"

"We didn't mean to," Rolf said. "It just happened."

Eli immediately started in speculations about the unconscious and its relation to talent. Which led, inevitably, to the subject of Ifrits, and why Rolf and his friends never acquired them.

Rolf became instantly wrapped up in the discussion, and the two of them ended up sitting cross-legged on the ground next to scraps of concrete and lumber, chattering on like two unkempt chess-playing codgers in a city park. Victor waited impatiently, then gave up temporarily and wandered back to where the energy pool shimmered and sparkled in the darkness. When he almost walked right into it, I realized he couldn't see it. That was a complication.

Eli finally joined us, still talking to Rolf, and he couldn't see it, either. Rolf seemed to be amused by that.

"Any ideas?" I said to him. Rolf nodded and draped his arms around both their shoulders.

"Ahh," said Eli. "Now I see. Amazing."

Rolf removed his arms from their shoulders, but once they'd seen the pool they could keep their vision of it. Victor walked around to the other side, taking care not to get too close.

"Hmm," he said. "Now that I actually see it, I'm thinking we might have to change our strategy."

"It's too strong to push it back," Eli agreed. He walked around the pool and joined Victor on the other side. "Perhaps we could speed it up, instead. Add some additional energy and destabilize it that way."

"Hmm. Could work. What about the Coriolis force? Can we adapt that?"

"No, but there should be an analogue we could use."

As usual, they were talking way over my head. I wandered away and joined Rolf.

"Quite the professors, ain't they?" he said.

"Not a bad thing, actually. It doesn't hurt to be smart."

"Never said it did."

We watched them measuring and discussing. After a time, Victor reached into his traveling bag and took out four crystals, placing them around the perimeter of the circle, evenly spaced. Next came a series of wooden rods, and he enclosed each crystal with a triangle of three sticks, like a little tent. Finally, he nodded and stood next to Eli.

"Will it be enough?" asked Eli, and Victor shrugged.

I walked over slowly to where they stood. Eli in particular wasn't going to like this, but I had no choice.

"These might help," I said, taking the two rune stones that I'd been carrying around out of my pocket. Eli looked at them, then at me.

"How long have you had those, son?" he said quietly.

"All along. I kept a few back when we used them to trap the Wendigo."

Victor just shook his head and reached out a hand for them, but Eli stepped forward and took them instead.

"How many more do you have at home?"

"Some."

"My fault. I should have known. A junkie doesn't turn over all his drugs just because you ask for them. Well, time for that later. Right now we can certainly use these." He handed one of the stones to Victor, who circled around to the opposite side. Eli lifted up his own stone, and a rueful smile broke out upon his face.

"I forgot how it feels to hold these," he said. "This is what it feels like to have real power. Very seductive, I must say." He called over to Victor.

"Ready?" Victor raised one arm in the air. "Now," said Eli, and there was a crackling sound as a flash of phosphorescent green light arced between the stones. The crystals flashed in unison and began to pulse with their own light of swirling color, reflecting the colors of the pool. The swirl of colors in the energy pool started to move more quickly, and a high-pitched hum like a jet turbine filled the air, making my teeth hurt. Lou had been sitting by the edge of the pool, gazing into it, fascinated as always, but now he jumped back in alarm.

The pool revolved even faster, like a maelstrom in a horror tale. Bits of color broke free and washed up onto the ground, like nothing so much as a whirlpool throwing off rainbow-colored spumes of spray. The colors blended together as it spun faster; then, when it seemed as if it could no longer hold together, it folded in on itself like multicolored Silly Putty. One final spasm rocked through it, and just before it collapsed, a long streamer of viscous energy snaked out, falling right across one of Lou's front paws. As it contracted, it dragged him toward its center and pulled him under, almost as if it had a malevolent consciousness. There was a horrible slurping sound like a clog becoming unstuck in a bathtub, and then the entire construct dwindled into nothingness. Then, at the last possible moment, it surged back, gyrated wildly, and finally settled down into its familiar rhythm. The humming cut off abruptly, and the only sound left was the roar of traffic on the access ramp overhead and a far-off ambulance wailing.

I ran over to where it pulsed, seemingly eternal. It was back, but Lou was gone.

FIFTEEN

IT WAS HARD TO BELIEVE A SPACE SO SMALL could feel so empty. My flat is great, but it wasn't suited for pacing, and I couldn't sit still. Four strides and I was up against a wall; four more brought me to the opposite side of the room.

This wasn't the first time Lou had gone missing. But the previous time I'd thought he'd simply left, abandoned me. That happens sometimes with Ifrits; it's a lurking fear felt by every practitioner who's blessed with one. It had plunged me into a depression and paralyzed me, but this time it was different. He'd been taken, swept up by the energy pool, and I didn't even know if he was alive or dead. And if he was alive, I had no idea how to locate him. Neither did Eli or Victor. It was like watching someone fall into a raging river, swept away by the current. You stand on the bank, watching helplessly as the torrent sweeps them away. You feel you have to do something, but there's nothing you can do.

Which was ironic. If it had been me that had fallen into

that thing, Lou could have found me, and he would have, come hell or high water. But I wasn't as clever.

Victor wanted to try closing the pool again, but Eli nixed that idea. He pointed out that if we closed the pool now, Lou would be gone forever. The chances of his finding his way back were slim, but if the pool were destroyed, those chances would drop to zero.

Besides, he was worried. Trying to close the pool had instead made it even stronger. Another attempt might have unintended disastrous consequences. A lot more research and thought would need to be done before the next attempt, and that would take some time.

I didn't care about any of that. I wanted Lou back. The only person I could think of who might be able to help find him was the Wendigo, and the only way that I knew to find the Wendigo involved using Lou's talents. Catch-22.

For once, the knock on the door came as a welcome distraction. When I answered, the Wendigo stood outside. I'd never been so glad to see an untrustworthy supernatural entity in my life. But why was he here? Of course. He was still hoping to get the remaining stones.

"May I come in?" he politely asked.

Normally I wouldn't have wanted him to. But now I treated him like an honored guest.

"Of course," I said.

He nodded and walked in, looking around with curiosity. He wandered back and forth, picking up things and putting them down again before sitting down at the kitchen table, much like Morgan had done. With him it seemed rude and out of place, though. I guess he hadn't quite got the human conception of appropriate boundaries yet. But a lot of normal people are the same way.

"Sorry about what happened at the energy pool," he said. Once again he seemed to know everything, which saved some time and explanation. "You've got to be careful with those things."

"I get that. And it was pointless, anyway; it's still there. But Lou's not."

"I know. A shame, really."

"Yes, it is. I don't suppose you have any ideas?"

"About what?"

"Locating Lou. Bringing him back—if he's still alive."

"Oh, he's alive all right, unless something on the other end got him." Relief flooded over me at hearing the word "alive," but I didn't like the rest of the sentence.

"What other end?" I said, suspecting I wouldn't like the answer. The Wendigo looked at me patiently.

"The other end of the energy pool. It doesn't work quite the way you seem to think it does."

I regarded him sourly.

"I have no idea how it works."

"Take a guess," he said. I thought about it.

"Well, Eli thinks it creates things based on archetypes, bringing them into existence in some fashion."

"With all due respect, Eli is totally clueless about that. The pool doesn't create anything. It pulls things from other places, things that already exist elsewhere. Sometimes the things it pulls up have entered this world before—that's why I seem so familiar, and mimic legend and myth in some manner. It's not that I was 'created' by some archetypal template; it's because others like me have visited before and people remember."

"So the pool could never have created an actual Ifrit, then?"

"Of course not. It simply pulled in a creature from somewhere else that resemble Ifrits in some ways."

"And how did you get sucked into it?"

"That's a little different. I wasn't an accident—I was just waiting for an opening. When someone like myself gets into this world, we gain some powers, ones we don't ordinarily have. That's why I like it here, and that's why I intend to stay."

"And the shape-shifters?"

"Same thing. In their world, nothing but mindless beasts. Here—well, you can see how clever they become."

"So Lou wasn't swallowed up and dissolved by the energy field?"

"No. He just went somewhere else, much like I came here."

"Goddamn it," I said. "I should have gone after him." The Wendigo shook his head.

"If you had, you might well have ended up somewhere entirely different, and I doubt you'd ever have found your way back."

"Why hasn't Lou found his way back, though? That's something he's very good at, after all."

"That I couldn't say. Maybe the pool took him somewhere his tracking sense doesn't work. Different places, different rules. Maybe he's trapped by something and can't get away."

"And maybe he's dead."

"Maybe."

"But if he's alive, you could find him," I said, making it into a statement. "And bring him back, like you did for Sherwood."

"Possibly. I'd like to help, if I could." That didn't sound very believable.

"In return for what?" I asked bluntly.

"Maybe I just would like to help. Is that so hard to believe? Of course, if you wanted to show your appreciation . . ."

"By handing over the rest of the stones, for instance?"

"That would indeed be a handsome gesture."

"And I'm supposed to trust that you'll do your part?"

He smiled, but it wasn't triumphant, or knowing, or smug. It actually seemed a bit sad.

"What choice do you have?"

And that was the truest thing he'd said since I'd met him.

"Deal," I said, walking over to the trunk where I kept them. I pulled out the remaining stones, placed them on the kitchen table, and pushed them across toward him. I was breaking one of the cardinal rules of bargaining—never front the money. But he had the upper hand, and he knew it. Now that he had what he wanted, there was no reason for him to renege on the deal, though. If I tried to play hardball with him instead, he'd feel obligated to find a way to screw with me. At least, that was how I read him. He let them sit there, as if afraid I'd change my mind if he tried to pick them up.

"What now?" I asked.

He didn't answer right away and I thought he was thinking, but then noticed he had focused on a drawing on the wall over my computer, a sketch of me at a gig done by an artist friend. A Wendigo with ADD. How perfect. I rapped on the table, making him start.

"Sorry," he said, pulling his attention back to the subject at hand. "Tell you what. I won't try to track him down myself—that could be very difficult."

"But you said you could do it."

"I said it was *possible*. But not only would it be difficult; it could be dangerous. You never know what you'll run into, or how the place you end up in may affect your powers. Remember that beast on the moor?

"So no, I won't go there—I'm just getting used to it here. But what I will do is help you get there on your own, if you like. Getting back will be up to you, though."

"That will do just fine," I said.

"It's got to be at night," he said. "So I'll come back this evening."

He swept up the stones on the table with an exaggerated flourish and tucked them away in an inside pocket. "Again, a pleasure doing business with you."

WHEN HE KNOCKED AT MY DOOR THAT EVE-ning, I was ready. I had a ham sandwich, matches, a heavy shirt, my old semiwaterproof leather jacket, my hiking boots, and of course, the Remington. If I ended up in some exotic city full of God knew who or what, I was going to feel rather foolish, but there are worse things than feeling foolish.

I also had my Buck knife, and Lou's rawhide chew toy. Or rather, part of it. I'd sawed it in half, and part of it was now in the corner of the room, while I set the other half on the kitchen table. This was the most important thing I was taking—Lou might not have his full abilities, not enough to find his way home, but there's nothing stronger than half of a once-undivided whole. They call to each other, magically speaking, and I had confidence Lou could use half his favorite toy to find his way to the other half. If not, we might spend the rest of our lives in a foreign dimension, amidst the alien corn.

I felt bad about not telling Eli about what I was doing, but he would have gone ballistic on me, at least as much as he ever does. He would have pointed out how stupid it was to go off half-cocked, and he would have been right. No doubt he would have tried to stop me. But Lou had vanished once before, and I had sat around feeling sorry for myself. If Campbell hadn't been there to kick my ass in gear, I would have been too late to help him, and that wasn't going to happen again.

When the Wendigo finally showed up, he looked at the half chew toy on the table and nodded approvingly.

"Very clever," he said, getting it immediately. "It might even work." He looked around and then shook his head as he spotted the shotgun. "Bad idea."

"What is?"

"The shotgun."

"I don't see why. Talent may not work when I get to wherever Lou is. You already said his own abilities probably aren't working right. It just might save my butt."

"It might," he said. "But it also might not. You're not going into battle, after all. You're not hunting anything. You're on a rescue mission, and you want to get in there and out of there as quickly as you can. You don't want to go in with guns blazing; you want to be invisible."

"Sure," I said. "But it never hurts to have a backup, just in case."

"If you say so. But when a person has an option, most of the time they end up using it. No shotgun and you run. If you have it, you stand and fight, and that can be a fatal mistake. It's your funeral, though."

I hated taking advice from the Wendigo. For one thing, I didn't trust him, and I never would. But when I thought about it, it made a certain sense. The problems I was going to run into weren't going to be solved with a convenient blast from a shotgun.

I put my knife in one pocket and the chew toy in the other, crammed the ham sandwich in with it, and looked longingly at the Remington that was leaning against the wall.

"Okay," I said. "I'm ready. What now?"

The Wendigo gave me a sardonic stare.

"Well, great, but I can't just transport you out of here."

"What, then?"

"Back to the energy pool. You're going to have to go through it yourself. How else did you think you were going to get there?"

ROLF WAS NOWHERE TO BE SEEN WHEN WE GOT to the construction site under the bridge, so I had to clamber over the gate, barely avoiding cutting my hands on the barbed wire, even with my usual hardening spell for my hands. The Wendigo watched with amusement, then bounded over himself, skimming over the gate without so much as touching it, like a low-gravity moonwalker. I had got so used to him I'd forgotten he wasn't human at all.

The faint glow of the energy pool, still going strong, was visible at the back of the site. We walked up to the edge, right where the shifting bands of color swirled and pulsed.

"What do I do now?" I asked.

"Go ahead," the Wendigo said. "Just walk right into it."

"You're joking, right?"

"Not at all. How else do you think you're going to find him? I'll provide the psychic push that will determine where you'll go and make sure it's the same place your Ifrit ended up."

I took a step forward, then stopped. Talking about it was one thing, but plunging right in was not something I relished, any more than diving into a midwinter lake through a hole in the ice. I remembered Lou's startled yelp as he was pulled into it, but it didn't make me feel any more determined. The Wendigo came over and stood beside me.

"Changed your mind?" he said. I shook my head, and he smiled. "Well, let me give you a little push, then."

He took a step back, placed his hand on the small of my back, and gave a powerful shove. The promised push turned out to be more than metaphorical. Instead of bravely stepping forward into the unknown, I was propelled, stumbling and flailing, into the center of the maelstrom.

SIXTEEN

IT FELT LIKE I WAS BEING TORN APART, AND FOR a long moment I feared I'd been tricked, murdered by the Wendigo for some obscure motive of his own. But then the world stabilized around me, and I found myself lying facedown in dirt.

It was cold. I had my leather jacket and a heavy shirt, but I felt the cold anyway, and the dirt beneath my hands was rock hard. I sat up and looked around. It was dark when I'd been pushed into the energy pool, but it was daylight now. No signs of civilization. Trees, stretching out for as far as I could see, scattered far enough apart to give a good idea of the landscape. Low-spreading conifers dominated, with only the occasional towering tree to break the pattern.

Lou was nowhere to be seen. I hadn't expected I would just drop down in his lap, though. Things are never that easy. And there was still the possibility that the Wendigo had sent me on a wild-goose chase, for whatever reason.

My first priority was to find out whether talent operated here, wherever here was. I broke off a few twigs from a nearby tree branch, set them on the ground, and tried a basic ignition spell, the default operation I always use when I'm trying to assess the magical climate of a place. It worked, all too well. The twigs went up in flames, instantly alight as if they'd been wrapped in flash paper, and a few seconds later all that remained was ashes.

This was an unexpected and not unwelcome development. If this held up, I was suddenly a powerful talent, no longer dependent on cleverness and guile. With a wave of my hand, all opposition would wither before my awesome power. There was bound to be a catch, though. There always is.

But one thing was worrisome. If this place enhanced rather than blocked talent, why hadn't Lou been able to find his way back? The more I thought about it, the more troubling it became. The chew toy I'd brought, which I thought so clever, now seemed irrelevant. Come to think of it, Lou should have been able to find his way back home based on his connection to me—we were more strongly bonded than any rawhide strip. Hopefully.

But as long as my power had been enhanced, I was going to take advantage of it. I've never been very good at locating people or things; that's a specialized talent.

Still, if I had enhanced power, it was worth a try. I pulled out the rawhide toy, concentrated on it, and concentrated on Lou at the same time. Immediately I could feel something, partly like the heat of a campfire on your face when your eyes are closed, partly like a puff of wind blowing from the north, and partly like neither of those things. But it gave me a direction, and there was no doubt about it.

I started walking, always uphill, and as the elevation increased, spotty areas of snow sprang up around the bases of trees, like a late-spring thaw breaking through a winter landscape. Soon I found myself slipping and sliding on the now-unavoidable snow cover.

I was walking as quietly as I could, but there was nothing to be done about the snow crunching under my feet. But whatever sound I was making was soon drowned out by a commotion coming from just over a small ridge. I heard animal snarls, which is never good, and some loud thumping as if someone was beating on a drum. The pressure that indicated Lou's presence was increased, which meant it was a good bet that whatever was happening up ahead had something to do with him.

I crested the ridge, almost running now, and emerged through the trees. Below, a small clearing opened out in the middle of tangled brush and trees. The impulse to rush down and see what was happening was strong, but I held back. It wouldn't do either Lou or me any good to blindly charge ahead and blunder into something I wasn't prepared for.

I slid behind the cover of a tree and peered around. At the far end of the clearing, I saw a large animal standing at the end of a huge log, two or three feet in diameter. For a moment I thought it was a bear, but when it turned sideways I saw a thin elongated muzzle with a familiar anteater profile. A shape-shifter.

The log it guarded must have been partially hollow, and from its actions it looked like something was trapped inside of it. I had a feeling I knew who it was. Wood splinters littered the ground nearby, and there were long score marks where the creature had tried unsuccessfully to rip open the log.

It prowled from one end of the log to the other, then pounced on one end, pounding and roaring. Then it ran around to the other end, waiting for the terrified prey to rush out the other end, like a cat trying to outwit a panicked mouse. Lou was no mouse, though, and though he was probably scared, he wasn't one to panic. He hunched down farther back in the log, safe for the moment. He wasn't going anywhere.

No wonder he hadn't been able to find his way back. God knows how long he'd been trapped there. As I watched, I realized the beast was exactly that—a beast. It was a clever animal, nothing more. In its own dimension it was a natural predator like a bear or a lion. Only when it entered our world did it morph into the shape-shfter it was, stealing not only bodies but memory and personality and intelligence as well. And although it was resistant to talent back home, there was no reason it would be resistant here, especially with my newly minted strength. For once, I wasn't worried.

I calmed my mind as best I could and concentrated on gathering the elements of a spell. Use its massive physical strength against it. Use the patches of snow dotting the ground, and the cold in the air. I gathered up the cold, added in some essence of grit from the sandy forest soil, used my nervousness to add a dollop of paralysis, and let my strength flow into the mixture.

"Louie! Lou!" I shouted, my voice echoing in the chill sunlight. "To me, now!"

If there's one thing Lou doesn't lack, it's decisiveness. In a similar situation I might well have stood there for a moment gawking, until it was too late to move. Sometimes Lou acts without thinking and ends up getting himself in trouble. But all in all, the ability to act quickly is a good quality. Anytime you deal with violence and danger it's better to be wrong than indecisive.

He bolted from the log and flew up the slope toward me. The creature had looked up at the sound of my voice, and by the time it looked back toward Lou, it was too late. So far, so good. Only, as usual, there was something I hadn't counted on. Goddamn it! I'd forgotten what the Wendigo had said. They operated in pairs, and just like Ruby, there were two of them here.

The second one burst out of a thicket to the left, and in a few ground-eating bounds it was right on him. Lou dodged left, then right, but the thing was also quick, and it reached out one powerful arm and sunk its six-inch claw right above Lou's right haunch. It lifted him up off the ground and brought him up toward its mouth.

Now what? If I cast out the spell I'd been preparing, it would catch Lou as well. But if I didn't, he'd be dead in about a second, so there really wasn't much thought involved. Maybe his natural Ifrit resistance to talent would provide him some protection, and it wasn't precisely a killing spell anyway. I cast my spell hastily outward. With any luck, the creature's joints would now seize up like a piston deprived of oil, and when it tried to move it would simply topple over like an ancient dinosaur with paralyzed feet.

The creature had turned slightly sideways, inadvertently protecting Lou with its body as it reached toward his skull, stretching out its long neck for the killing bite. When the spell hit, it froze in midstride. It stood there, unmoving, like a grotesque statue. Lou squirmed his way out of the thing's grasp, giving a sharp yelp of pain as he did so. He dropped onto the ground and staggered, unsteady on his feet. It wasn't just the wound that was affecting him. A light layer of hoarfrost rimed his fur, and he shook himself vigorously trying to shake it off, then collapsed on the ground. The motionless creature above him was rapidly glazing over with ice, as was the ground around him.

Spells are mostly about accessing power, and my spells usually employ some form of similarity for their effectiveness. Not everyone does it that way, but it works for me. Every culture from the ancient Sumerians to current voodoo priests acknowledges the power of similarity in magic. It's one of the few things they have right, although you do have to possess some inborn talent to make it work. But it's not supposed to be literal. The cold was a template for the spell, enabling me to metaphorically freeze the creature where it stood, but it wasn't supposed to literally freeze it solid. Unfortunately, my newly enhanced talent wasn't entirely under my control. I'd let loose with a broad wave of unbelievable cold, close to absolute zero I'd guess, and if Lou hadn't been shielded by the creature's body as well as being naturally resistant, he would have ended up as stiff as a frozen trout himself. Even so, he must have been suffering from frostbite at a minimum.

Before I could decide what to do next, a gust of wind breezed through the clearing. It caught the frozen creature, toppling it ever so slowly onto the hard ground, almost on top of Lou. With a tinkling shivery sound, it broke into a thousand pieces, as if it had been dipped in liquid nitrogen. Shards of frozen creature scattered everywhere.

I looked over to where the first creature had been standing at the other end of the log, but it was gone. It might not possess intelligence here, but it had enough animal cunning to understand that I was a danger. But like any true predator, whether a tiger or wolf or an otherworldly creature, it was still dangerous. I had no doubt it was lurking nearby, waiting for a careless moment on my part. We needed to get out of here as quickly as possible.

I ran over to check on Lou. He lifted his head and fixed me with a ferocious glare. You'd think he would have been jumping up and down slobbering with gratitude at being saved, but I hadn't done such a great job of it. He's not that way, anyway. It was a compliment, actually. He assumed that if he was in trouble, sooner or later I'd show up to help. After all, that's what he would do. But he expected more from me than almost letting him get eaten and then freezing his tail off, almost literally. If my blast of cold had been just a little stronger, he'd now be a miniature dogsicle himself. He knew that, and he didn't appreciate it.

"Sorry," I said, bending down to examine him. "It got out of control."

The layer of frost had dissipated from his coat, but he was still shivering. Considering what had just happened, I was afraid to try a warming spell. It might end up incinerating him by mistake. His right side was covered in blood, and when he tried to stand he had trouble staying on his feet. I needed Campbell; I'm not that skilled in the healing arts, and with my out-of-control power I was afraid to try anything in that direction, either.

I stripped off a couple of broad, coarse leaves from a nearby bush and used them to staunch the bleeding from his wound. The leaves were distinctive, bright red along the edges, thick and serrated. I hoped they weren't this world's version of poison oak. After I'd stopped the bleeding, I stuffed them into a pocket. I didn't want to leave any of Lou's blood in this place—it's never a good idea, and blood could help something track us, even all the way back home.

I picked him up and put him under my coat, using body heat to warm him. The wound from the creature's claw looked serious, and I had to get him out of here, back home where it could be taken care of. The problem was, I had been depending on him to find the way back, and the way he does that involves a lot of physical movement.

When he'd warmed up some, I put him down and offered the ham sandwich from my pocket—he must be starving by now. He probably hadn't eaten in twenty-four hours—he could survive on the streets of any city with no problem at all, but the wilderness was not his thing. After a brief sniff he turned away, though. Not good. Not good at all. I would have put money on him eating even on his death bed.

Lou was sitting quietly now, watching me, listing slightly to one side as he tried to keep the weight off the injured side of his body. If we stayed here, he might not recover. I didn't want to push him, but there was no hope for it otherwise.

"Can you get us back home?" I asked.

He gave a little doggy sigh, pushed himself slowly to his feet, and started off back the way I'd come, limping badly. There was a path of sorts, but after a few minutes he began to lag. There was no way he was going to be able to lead us back; he was too badly hurt.

I wasn't skilled enough to try healing him, but the other option was an infusion of magical energy. That I could do; it's a relatively straightforward process, and the enhanced power I had would make it easy. But that comes with its own price. It would be like pumping a bunch of painkillers and meth into a sick and exhausted person. Useful in an emergency, and it will keep them going, but it takes a serious toll. When the body is pushed to its limits it eventually collapses, but when it's magically pushed beyond those limits, the consequences can be serious and even deadly. If we didn't get back soon enough, it could easily push Lou over the edge. But if we stayed here, he might not make it, either. And there were the creatures to consider. I doubted that the two we'd seen were the only ones around.

So either way we might end up screwed, and in that situation it's always better to do something than nothing. I called him and he limped over, unsteady on his legs. I reached out and gathered living energy and life force from the trees around us. At least the natural base of the energy boost would make it less toxic. I directed the flow into him, as the needles on several surrounding trees turned brown. It took only a few moments before he perked up considerably, gave a bark both confident and halfhearted, and took off down the path again.

At first he was fine, trotting down the path with only a slight limp, but as time passed the limp became more pronounced and he was getting noticeably more tired, stopping every few minutes. I was beginning to think it was hopeless when he suddenly took a detour straight through the underbrush. This was more like it. We were lower in elevation now, and thick bushes were beginning to clog the path. Tired and injured as he was, he slipped through the massed thickets as easily as a greased seal. I stumbled behind him, with branches whipping across my face and tree roots grabbing at my feet. He seemed to be describing a large circle, and sure enough we eventually arrived back on the path. He sat down to rest, then five minutes later, he took off through the brush again and repeated the entire procedure.

I wasn't sure what he was doing—it was typical of how he finds his way, the way he operates, but I'd never seen his path so convoluted. By the fourth go-round he was panting heavily. I was just about to bend down and pick him up when I noticed that the landscape had subtly

altered. The path looked the same, but the scattered patches
of snow were gone and the trees surrounding us were different.

The next time he angled off the path, the undergrowth
had become less tangled and the bushes now seemed more
like broad-leafed plants and less like low-spreading conifers. It was definitely growing warmer, and Lou started
moving faster. Soon I was loping awkwardly, having trouble keeping up with him despite his injuries. I yelled at
him to slow down before he killed himself, but he didn't
even turn his head. Maybe the pace was as important as
the twists and turns.

Soon, he located a small ravine and plunged in. By the
time we reached the bottom, it was so overgrown I couldn't
even see the sky above me, and the tangle of undergrowth
made moving fast impossible, at least for me. Lou pulled
himself up the opposite side and, when he reached the top,
gave a couple of weary barks and collapsed. Pushing my
way on up, I emerged onto a scene of broad hills dotted
with spruce and fir.

A deep breath brought the faint but unmistakable stink
of diesel fumes. A constant rumble from my left caught
my attention and when I turned my head, I could see, a
half mile away, a line of cars and trucks headed up a freeway incline. I was back, but I wasn't sure exactly where I
was.

The sun let me know it was late afternoon. I picked
Lou up and headed over to the highway, hoping to find out
where I was, and maybe catch a ride. Most of the passing
vehicles had California license plates, so coupled with the
landscape and the familiar freeway, it was a good bet I
was looking at I-80 as it wound through the Sierras. As far
as I could tell I was on the west side of the summit,
maybe twenty miles from Soda Springs, where Campbell
lived. That made sense, too; if Lou hadn't been able to
find the exact way home, he might have found a way to a
place he was familiar with, somewhere similar to where
we had been. And Campbell's was the best possible place

we could end up. Maybe that had something to do with it as well.

I stood by the side of the road and stuck out my thumb, trying to look harmless. Trying to hitch a ride on the interstate is never the easiest thing to do, and the leather jacket and my disheveled appearance weren't going to help. I might have to try a masking spell that would make me seem clean-cut and harmless. It turned out to not be necessary—not a whole lot of drivers will stop for a solitary male alongside the road, but add a very small dog, pitifully curled up in his owner's arms, and you have to beat them off with a stick.

In less than five minutes a young couple pulled over, the wife obviously being the one who insisted they stop. Lou of course climbed into the woman's lap and looked up at her adoringly. He was trembling from exhaustion and the dried blood on his coat shocked her.

"What happened to him?" she asked, face wrinkling up in concern. "Is he hurt?"

"We were out hiking," I said. "He ran off and tangled with something, maybe a bobcat. By the time I found him I'd got turned around and couldn't find my way back to my car."

"Doesn't he need a vet?"

"There's one in Soda Springs," I said. "If you could drop me off there, I'd really appreciate it."

"Of course," she said. "Poor baby."

The husband was curt and barely civil until he heard we were going only as far as Soda Springs, at which point he warmed up considerably. He was so relieved to be rid of us quickly that he detoured off the highway, followed my directions, and dropped me off right at the driveway leading up to Campbell's cabin.

The first time I'd ever seen Campbell's cabin it had been wintertime, surrounded by snow, and that was the way I always saw it in my mind's eye. Snug and warm, smoke coming from the vent connected to the old iron wood-burning fireplace, windows frosted up like an old-time

Christmas card. We'd had our problems, but some very fond memories lived there.

But today it was surrounded by greenery, with scattered alpine wildflowers tucked in the shadow of the building. Campbell was sitting on the front porch, looking down curiously at the unfamiliar car dropping off its passengers. When she saw me climb out carrying Lou, she rushed down the driveway.

"What happened?" she asked. "Was it that creature—the one that tore up Victor's leg?"

"No, something else. It's a long story. He got caught by a much larger creature—it caught him with its claw."

She took him out of my arms and started back up the driveway. Lou didn't protest—despite his dislike of being carried. He was now beyond caring.

"Victor told me about another Ifrit that had been attacked—that's why I thought of it. An Ifrit named Jackie—do you know him?" I did. Jackie was a weasel, or maybe a stoat.

"Sure," I said. Vikki's Ifrit. "Is he okay?" I asked.

"Apparently. He was too quick for the creature, I guess. Escaped out a window. But Victor was worried because for the first time that thing actually came right into a practitioner's house, I guess. That practitioner wasn't home at the time, but still . . ."

That was disturbing. It was getting bolder. Right now I had more important things to worry about, though.

Inside Campbell's cabin, all was calm. The sun streamed though the windows, lighting up dust motes in the air, sending them twinkling and sparkling throughout the room. Campbell's collection of colored-glass jars where she kept her herbs and plants glowed merrily as the sunlight hit them, deep blues and greens and ambers. The patterned spread on the corner futon was new and colorful, and as always, the room was neat and tidy without being anal. In comparison, my own little basement apartment, scattered and disorganized, was sad indeed.

Campbell set Lou down on a coir mat on the floor and

ran her hands over him. When she glanced up at me I put my hands out, palms up, in that universal gesture that asks a question.

"He'll be all right," she said. "The injury's bad, but not as bad as I thought. Lou's tougher than he looks. But he's almost completely used up."

I explained why that was, and she briefly pursed her lips in disapproval.

"No choice," I said.

Campbell busied herself among the jars of plants, choosing a few at what seemed like random, although I knew it wasn't.

"I can heal most of the damage," she said, "but after that energy boost, to really heal up he's going to need an awful lot of rest." She started a kettle on the stove, laid out a small collection of the plants and herbs, and shot me a brief look. "You look tired, too. Coffee?"

"Bless you, yes."

I threw my jacket in a corner and sat by the window, watching as she measured out coffee into the coffeemaker and poured water over the plants she had mixed, steeping them like tea. As she moved back and forth, the sun coming through the window struck her blond hair and lit it like a halo. It was such a scene of domestic tranquility that it made me nostalgic, and a bit regretful. *I could live here,* I thought. *I could live with this woman.*

Well, maybe not. After all, it hadn't worked out the last time. Still, a lot had happened since then, to both of us. I wasn't the same person, and neither was she.

Campbell turned to ask me something and caught me staring.

"What?" she said. I shook my head.

"Nothing. Just thinking."

She regarded me for a long moment. "Yeah. Sometimes I do some of that thinking myself." She smiled thoughtfully, but not sadly at all.

When her concoction of herbs was ready, she put it aside to cool, then looked down doubtfully at Lou.

"He needs to drink this, but it's bitter. Downright nasty, in fact. How are we going to get it down him?"

"Not a problem," I said. "I'll trick him into thinking it's a plate of your pancakes."

Campbell's pancakes were a special treat, Lou's favorite. Mine were definitely second-rate in comparison. Campbell looked at me as if I'd lost my mind.

"You'll what?"

"Just kidding. He'll drink if I tell him it will make him well. It's not like he's only a dog, you know."

"Ah, yes. Sometimes it's hard to remember that."

As we drank coffee, waiting for the infusion to cool, I filled her in on everything that had happened. She listened intently, leaning forward in her usual position, elbow on the table, chin in hand.

"So Ruby wasn't really Ruby? She was this shape-shifting creature?"

"So it would seem."

"When did that happen? Before I met her at Mama Yara's store, or after?"

"Before, I think. But I don't really know."

"Weird," she said. "And creepy."

"Very," I agreed. She thought for a moment.

"And there's still another one of these things running around?"

"Apparently."

"And it can look like anyone?"

"Pretty much. Although to become a perfect copy, it has to kill and eat part of its victim."

"Yuck." She was silent again, turning it over in her mind. "So what if this isn't really you sitting here? I wouldn't be able to tell, right? It's hard to wrap my mind around that."

"I know," I said. "It's very existential."

"Must be hell on someone with trust issues to begin with."

"Well, don't worry," I said. "Lou wouldn't be fooled, not about me. Besides, if I were a monster, I'd have already killed and eaten you."

"Very reassuring," she said, "but I wasn't talking about *me*." She looked at me pointedly until I got whom she meant.

"Oh."

Now I remembered one of the reasons we'd broken up. Campbell was a lot quicker on the uptake than I was, and that sometimes made me uneasy. But that no longer bothered me. I couldn't remember why it ever had.

Campbell got up from the table and tested the liquid she'd prepared, then poured it into a bowl. It looked vile, and I wondered if I had spoken too soon about convincing Lou to drink it. She put the bowl down next to him, and he looked at it without interest. I crouched down next to him and pulled gently on an ear.

"Lou," I said. "It's medicine. Drink it. It'll make you better." He appeared unconvinced.

"It's not that bad." I put a finger into the bowl and took a taste. It was that bad. "You really want to die?" I said. "There's no bacon in heaven, you know." That might be an exaggeration, at least the part about dying, but I couldn't afford to have him out of commission for a month. And with things like infection lurking, it might even be true.

He hauled himself to his feet, took a couple of weak licks at it, retched convincingly, and then started lapping it down like it was beef gravy. He got about three quarters of it down before he stopped and retched again. I was afraid he was going to throw up, which would make the entire ordeal useless, but he managed to keep it down. He looked at the rest and turned away. Clearly he would sooner die than drink another drop.

"That should be enough," Campbell said, took the bowl away, and sat down cross-legged on the floor beside him.

She placed her hands over the wounded part and slowly stroked it with a circular motion. As she did, she softly hummed a wordless tune. Lou's eyes half closed, then his muzzle sank down on the floor, then his eyes closed the rest of the way. Campbell continued on for about a minute more, then gently removed her hands and carefully stood up. She smiled at him and suddenly clapped her hands together, making me jump.

Lou jumped as well. One second he was snoozing on the mat; the next he was standing on all fours. He took a couple of steps forward, stopped to assess things, and then walked deliberately across the room and back. He still had a slight limp, but other than that he seemed fine. He lay down and closed his eyes again.

"He'll need to sleep for at least twenty-four hours before he'll be back to normal," Campbell said. "It took a lot out of him."

"What about you?" I asked. I knew Campbell would be worn-out as well, since healing can take a lot of energy, especially when it's something major.

"Me? I'm fine. Remember, he's not very big, so it didn't take all that much energy."

"Good," I said. "And thanks." I got up and stretched. "We hate to eat and run, but we've got to get back to the city. While we're sitting here in the sunshine, one of those shape-shifters is stalking the streets back in the city. Any chance you could drive me back?"

"Sure," she said. "But it's too late for a long round trip. I'd have to stay over."

"Of course. My clever plan is working."

"You mean all this drama was just a cover to get me to stay overnight? How flattering."

Interesting. Somehow, Campbell and I had started flirting again. I wasn't sure what that meant, if anything.

"You do remember there's only one bed?" I said.

"How could I forget? But I'm not worried. Lou will protect me."

Indeed he would. His usual place to sleep is under the covers—he's cold-blooded and San Francisco gets chilly at night, even in summer. If I'm lucky enough to have company, his favored position is to be wedged between me and my guest, a living bundling board. He'll discreetly withdraw if things start to get serious, but it can make spontaneity difficult.

Campbell threw a few necessities into an overnight bag. I called Eli, got his voice mail, and let him know I'd found Lou. Ten minutes later, we were in Campbell's old Land Cruiser, headed to San Francisco. By the time we made it back to my place it was just past nine.

Campbell unpacked her travel bag and settled in. Lou was still dead to the world but I had managed to catch a few winks on the way back, so I was awake enough that we could go out and grab a late bite to eat. Lou attempted to come along with us, bleary-eyed and yawning, but it didn't take much convincing to get him to go back to sleep.

Dinner was fun, even with the specter of the second shape-shifter hanging around the corners of my mind. We talked about this and that, nothing heavy, comfortable and at ease, connected in that way you can sometimes be with an old girlfriend when the post-breakup tension is finally gone.

When we got back to my place, I did wonder if it was going to lead anywhere, but the inevitable ringing of the phone made the issue moot. It was Victor, and he had news.

SEVENTEEN

"WE'VE GOT A LEAD," VICTOR SAID. "GET OVER here."

"Right now?"

"Yes, now. Why else would I call?"

"What have you got?" I asked.

"Never mind that. Just get over here." He hung up the phone before I could ask anything else.

"Who was that?" Campbell asked.

"Victor. Duty calls." I looked over at Lou, dead to the world again. "I hate to go out without him, but he doesn't look in shape to do much."

"He's not," she said. "Something dangerous, I assume."

"Maybe. You going to be all right here?"

"Of course. I'll keep an eye on Lou." She shook her head in resignation. "Hanging out with you is like Groundhog Day, Mason. Monsters. Midnight missions. Death-defying feats."

"It's all Victor's fault," I said.

"Of course it is. Be careful, will you?"

• • •

WHEN I REACHED VICTOR'S HE WAS OUTSIDE waiting for me, pacing impatiently up and down. Eli was leaning against the side of Victor's Beemer, looking tired.

"Took you long enough," Victor said. It had been all of twenty minutes.

"Where's Lou?"

"He's home, recovering. He got hurt."

"Ahh," said Eli, looking at me strangely. I waited for some further elucidation, but that was all he said.

"Get in," Victor said, opening the passenger-side door. I got in and sank into the comfortable seat.

"Where are we going?" I asked.

"Telegraph Hill. By Coit Tower. "

"You think it's up there? How do you know?"

"We have information," said Eli, "from Bertram." He lapsed into silence. This was odd. Neither one of them asked anything about what had happened to Lou, or how he was doing. They were focused and intense.

Bertram. I didn't know how I felt about that. He had been an enforcer for a while, but after a number of unfortunate incidents, Victor had stopped using him for anything. Bertram had a take-no-prisoners attitude, and could easily escalate a minor situation into a major one. Cops have a phrase for that—"badge heavy."

Eli had already vetoed his involvement once before, when we trapped the Wendigo. But apparently things had got desperate. Bertram could come in handy when results were needed and the methods used to get them weren't a primary concern. His specialty was intelligence, which in his case meant leaning on people in creative ways until they told him what he wanted to know. I didn't like him much.

Victor pulled up at the Pioneer Park lot, right next to Coit Tower. Coit Tower is an iconic San Francisco landmark, and although the surrounding Pioneer Park is small, it could provide plenty of cover for something to be lurking in the dark.

Before Victor got out of the car, he checked his fanny pack, the one he carries on many magical sorties, a mini version of his usual black doctor's bag. Most of the stuff it contains is for magical forensics, but it also contains objects for enabling those spells that need magical props. It contains crystals, small bars of different pure metals, things I can't identify, and other, more prosaic items such as duct tape and a hunting knife. Finally satisfied, he zipped it shut and exited the car.

"No shotgun?" I said.

"We won't be needing it."

Again, no explanation, no conversation. I shrugged and followed him out of the car. I'd seen him like this before, but never so bad. There wasn't any point in pestering him with questions; he'd tell me what was going on when he was good and ready.

We headed down Greenwich Street in the direction of Bertram's place over on Montgomery. Victor led the way and Eli brought up the rear. I had a sudden sense of déjà vu. Of course. Morgan's dream, the one where she had seen Victor, Eli, and me walking down a darkened street. And no Lou. She'd felt an overwhelming sense of dread and danger, but she couldn't see anything. All she had seen was the three of us.

I hadn't been feeling very comfortable anyway, but now I was filled with my own sense of foreboding. I kept glancing left and right, expecting something to leap from out the shadows at any moment. When Victor suddenly stopped, I almost ran up on his heels.

"What is it?" I whispered, unwilling to make any noise that might bring something down on us.

He held up a hand for quiet. We had just passed an alleyway, and he turned back to examine something lying on the ground, hidden in shadow. He squatted down to examine it more closely, then whistled softly.

"I'll be damned," he said. "Look at this."

I walked up obligingly, and that was when Eli grabbed me from behind in a bear hug and lifted me off my feet. Once you're off your feet, you have no purchase and there's nothing you can do, especially when your opponent is bigger and stronger. You can try a head butt, snapping your head back with as much force as you can muster, but that's easy to counter just by keeping your head tucked down behind the other guy's shoulder. None of that mattered, though. I was too stunned to even struggle.

"What the fuck!" I yelled, but that was all I got to say. Victor had his handy roll of duct tape out and whipped a few turns around my head and mouth in no time flat. Eli pushed me facedown onto the pavement, knocking the wind out of me, and Victor looped more turns around my hands and feet. I was neatly trussed up like a Thanksgiving turkey, and all I could do was glare and make muffled sounds.

I stopped making even those when Victor put a knife blade up to my throat.

"Not a sound," he said. "I'd as soon cut your throat as not, and the minute you start to change, that's exactly what I'll do. Understand?"

Now it started to make sense. Victor and Eli thought I wasn't me—that I was the shape-shifter. But where in God's name had they got that idea? However they'd come to that conclusion, I was in trouble. With the duct tape over my mouth I couldn't explain, and I doubted that Victor would listen anyway. Since the shape-shifter could do an almost perfect copy, complete with memories, nothing I could say would convince him. No wonder Morgan had seen only the three of us. There wasn't anyone else, but that didn't mean I wasn't in serious trouble.

Eli hoisted me up and tossed me over one broad shoulder. With his professorial demeanor, it's easy to forget just how strong he is. I felt a tickling sensation as Victor laid a slight illusion over my body to make it look like an innocuous pile of coats or some such.

"Bertram?" Eli asked. Victor nodded.

This was getting worse by the moment. Obviously they wanted some information from the shape-shifter. Bertram was notorious about getting answers, but his methods were not for the squeamish. And I was in the unenviable position of having no answers to give. No matter what he did to me, I couldn't give information I didn't have, and any insistence that I was really me would just be taken as stubborn intransigence, inviting further unpleasant interrogation.

"Do you think Mason's still alive?" asked Victor as we walked along. Rather, they walked. I rode.

"I don't think so," Eli said. "But it's possible. Remember, it wouldn't have had to kill and consume Mason to do a good enough copy to fool us, at least for a while. It wouldn't fool Lou, of course, but you'll notice Lou is conveniently missing. Bertram will be able to get the answer."

"Still, I would have never suspected. Are you positive?"

"Oh, I'm positive, all right. Remember, I saw his hands change when he thought I wasn't looking. If not for that, he'd have fooled me, too. We've got the son of a bitch, all right."

Saw my hands change? What the hell was he talking about? When had my hands changed? As usual, I was a little slow on the uptake, but in my defense it's hard to think clearly when you're trussed up, hanging upside down, and on your way to an "enhanced interrogation."

What tipped it was simple, though. "Son of a bitch" was not a phrase I'd ever heard Eli use before, and there was a reason for that. It's not a phrase he would ever use. A shape-shifter was present all right, but it wasn't me.

The shape-shifter must have assumed Eli's identity and used that guise to convince Victor it was me who had been replaced. You'd think after that phony phone call out at Hunters Point Victor would have been more skeptical, but apparently not.

One good thing, though—the shifter had used a phrase Eli never would have uttered. Which meant it hadn't got him down quite right. Which meant Eli possibly hadn't been killed—it was just aping him.

It was hard to see Victor clearly since my head was hanging upside down, but I was sure I saw a momentary stiffening. He'd picked up on that out-of-character phrase as well. The Eli shape-shifter might have temporarily fooled him, but Victor was no dummy. He hadn't lived as long as he had by ignoring little things that seemed out of place.

The fake Eli seemed to sense he'd made a false step and went for a distraction. He eased me off his shoulder and dumped me roughly onto the sidewalk. Another atypical behavior that I hoped Victor would notice. I lay there among trash wrappers and unpleasant smells.

"Maybe we should search him," Eli said. "He might be carrying something."

Victor nodded and rolled me over so that I was face-down on the pavement and started going through my pockets. He took my folding knife, loose change, and then he came across those leaves I'd stuffed in my pocket. I'd forgotten all about them. He held them out to show to Eli.

"Here's something interesting," he said. "These leaves are unusual, and they're sticky with dried blood."

"Interesting. Have you got enough in your forensics bag to test them?"

Victor nodded again, but he didn't look happy. Something was bothering him, but he couldn't put his finger on it. I made a couple of muffled grunts, trying to get his attention, but he ignored me.

He took off his fanny pack and moved out of my range of vision. A couple of minutes later, he walked back and handed the leaves to Eli.

"Not from this world," he said. "No doubt about it." How damning was that bit of evidence? Victor had no idea I'd been through the pool to another world. He turned to look at me, and his face was as hard as I'd ever seen it. "And the blood on them is from an Ifrit." For a moment I thought he was going to shoot me right then and there, and so did he. I realized with surprise that he was fond of Lou in his own way.

"I can explain," I said, desperately. Actually, I didn't say anything; I could only make grunting sounds again.

The fake Eli saved me by interrupting, although he didn't realize he'd done so. He couldn't read Victor like Eli would have.

"Let's get him up to Bertram," Eli said, and after a moment, Victor turned on his heel and walked away from me.

Victor really should have known better, but he put great store in measurements and numbers and tests, things that could be quantified. He knew in his heart there was something not right about the whole thing, but the damning evidence of the leaves and blood was powerful, enabling him to brush aside his inner reservations. He's always been a head-over-heart guy.

The fake Eli walked away from me, following Victor, and I took the opportunity to roll over on my side to where I could see. I kept testing the duct tape bonds, but they held fast. Victor had done his usual competent job.

You'd think I could have used talent to free myself, but it's not that easy. I don't have any preset spells in hand; I don't operate that way. And although I could gather what I needed from the world around me, with no ability to speak or move or even gesture, I had no way to actualize anything. It was like having a loaded gun in your pocket, but with no way to use it.

Eli casually strolled over to where Victor was stuffing items back into his fanny pack. He slipped in behind him, and as I watched, I thought I saw his hands start to change. I looked again and this time I was sure—the hands began to gradually lengthen and change shape. Familiar six-inch claws spurted out in slow motion where fingers once were. The rest of him didn't change; that would have taken too long. He was the same benign, reassuring presence I'd always known. Victor heard him come up and glanced back over his shoulder. Eli's familiar presence reassured him, and he turned his attention back to his pack.

There was nothing I could do. It would get Victor first, then me. To make things worse, if possible, a movement in the shadows caught my eye. A rat, maybe, coming to investigate my helpless position. It loomed out of the darkness and poked its snout toward me an inch from my face. Only, it wasn't a rat's snout at all. It was a sharp black-and-tan muzzle, as familiar as my own face.

Lou disappeared behind me, and I could feel sharp teeth working on the duct tape that held my wrists. It was going to be a race. Would he be able to free me before the fake Eli grew those talons and sank them into the back of Victor's neck? Lou should have ignored me and warned Victor first, but he doesn't think that way. I was his first priority, and if Victor's fight with the shape-shifter gave him some extra time to free me, so much the better. If Victor bought the farm as a result, it would be unfortunate, but war always has collateral damage. He'd help Victor if he could, but not at my expense. Better Victor than me, was his opinion. Or maybe I was being too harsh—Lou has trouble keeping more than one thought at a time in his mind, anyway.

He chewed through half the tape, and with that start, I was able to rip the remainder in half. I reached up with fumbling fingers to rip off the tape across my mouth, but my fingers were numb and I couldn't get a grip. Eli's arms came up toward Victor. I looked down at Lou, pointed at the two of them, and grunted wildly.

He got the message and charged toward them, rattling off his usual volley of high-pitched barks. Victor spun around immediately, just in time to see the claw at the end of Eli's arm descending toward his face. He threw himself sideways, landing on one shoulder and rolling, bouncing immediately back to his feet. You had to admire the guy.

The Eli shape-shifter lunged at him, but Victor was too quick for it. If the shape-shifter had been in its natural form, it might have been a different story, but it was limited by the form it had taken. I had finally managed to tear the tape off my mouth, but the band around my feet was still secure. I couldn't move from my spot on the ground, but I was no longer helpless.

I wasn't much help, though. I knew from experience that it would be hard to affect the shape-shifter directly, and if I did something simple, like making the pavement as slippery as an ice rink, Victor would be affected as well. The two of them would go down together, and only one of them would get up.

Victor didn't wait for me to weigh in. As he dodged to one side, he pulled the Glock out from under his jacket. The first round missed as the shape-shifter dodged sideways, surprisingly quick, and there wasn't time for a second. A sweeping claw knocked the pistol from Victor's hand, and now it was Victor's turn to dodge again.

It leapt toward him. But before it could reach him, I struck. I reached out and swept all the trash I could find up into a swirl—wrappers, paper, leaves, and dirt—then mixed in the sticky properties of duct tape and threw the entire mess into its face. The trash stuck fast, effectively blinding it. It pawed at its face, trying to clear the mess away. The mask of gunk it wore wouldn't last long, but it gave Victor his opportunity and he scooted over to retrieve the gun. The fake Eli realized what was happening and stopped trying to get rid of the trash covering its face and eyes. Instead, it darted away, blindly but with determined speed. It didn't want to face firepower. It bounced off a couple of cars it couldn't see and disappeared into the darkness before Victor could level the gun and get off another shot.

I took a deep breath and started working on the tape that still bound my feet. Lou flopped down next to me, looking exhausted. For a moment Victor started to go after the shape-shifter, but saw it was hopeless. Finally he shook his head and walked over toward me, gun still in his hand.

"Finally, your chance," I said. "Shoot me now. I'm helpless—my ankles are still taped together."

"Sorry about that," he said, in a tone that lacked any contrition. He looked down at Lou. "Nice work." No mention of my role in fighting off the shape-shifter. We stared at each other for a few seconds, until he looked away and muttered something.

"What?" I said. "I didn't catch that."

"I might have been a bit hasty on this one," he said. "All things considered."

I waited, but that was all he had to say. I had a feeling that his almost killing me had shaken him considerably, but he couldn't bring himself to say it out loud. But there were more important things to worry about. I asked the question that I didn't want to.

"What about Eli? Is he dead, do you think?"

He sighed and dropped down on his heels beside me. He put the pistol away back under his jacket and pulled out the knife that had so recently pressed against my throat. It took only a few seconds to slice through the tape around my ankles.

"No, I don't think he is. I'm betting he's alive. This shape-shifter's incarnation of him was off, not quite right. So I think the shape-shifter was just imitating him—if it had actually killed him, the masquerade would have been perfect and undetectable." Victor took out his cell and punched in a speed-dial number.

"Eli?" I asked. He nodded, then gave me a thumbs-up and relaxed slightly as the call was answered.

"Eli? Where are you?" There was a brief silence as he listened. "No. It wasn't me who called." More listening. "No, everything's fine. Just go home, but be careful. It's still out there." Another pause. "I don't have time to tell you the whole story. But you could still be in danger, so keep a sharp eye out, and get yourself home. Better still, go back to my house and we'll meet you there." He snapped his cell shut.

"I still don't get it," I said. "So you did notice something odd about him at the time, but you never even thought twice about it?"

"Actually, I did, but I put it down to his being upset. He's very . . . protective of you, after all, and when he told me what he saw, I figured that would have been enough to throw him off stride completely."

"And he saw what? Supposedly."

"Right before I called you, he showed up at my house." He waved vaguely at the street stretching off into the darkness. "Or, rather, the not-Eli. He told me he'd seen you earlier and, when you thought he wasn't looking, seen your hands change. He was sure you were the shape-shifter and

thought we should capture you—it—and find out where
the real you was and if you were still alive.

"Then, when you showed up without Lou, which is
unheard of, any doubts I might have had vanished. You
never go anywhere without him." He looked over at Lou
again. "Which is just as well. But your excuse that Lou was
sick seemed all too convenient at the time."

A sound plan, psychologically speaking. By naming me
as the shape-shifter, all the focus had been put on me. Victor would be watching my every action and thinking about
my every word. He'd never think to put the same scrutiny
on the supposed Eli.

"I see. The real Eli thought you had called him. But it
wasn't you; it was the shape-shifter again."

"Exactly. Before it came by my house, it called Eli,
imitating me. It told him to meet me over in Berkeley.
Eli's been waiting for me there, safely out of the picture.
It's a clever beast."

Speaking of clever, how the hell had Lou found me?
Well, that much was a given, but how had he got across
town so quickly?

"You've got Campbell's cell number, don't you?" I
asked. Victor nodded. "Give her a call for me, will you?"
He punched in another number and handed me the phone.

"Campbell?"

"Mason! Are you okay?"

"I'm fine."

"Where are you? Did Lou find you?"

"He did. He's here with me now, over by Coit Tower.
Where are you? How did he get here?"

"I'm fairly close, actually. About an hour after you left
the house, I was just dropping off to sleep when Lou jumped
up on the bed and started barking at me. I thought there
was something wrong with him until he ran to the door and
kept barking. So we got in the Land Cruiser and I started
toward Victor's house, but he wouldn't stop barking until I
turned north. Then he quieted down for a bit, then started
barking again until I changed direction. It was like play-

ing the hot-and-cold game, but with barks. Eventually we ended up somewhere on Telegraph Hill, and when I stopped at a stop sign, he jumped out the window and was gone. I was beside myself, terrified something bad was going down. I've been driving around looking for him ever since."

"Well, we're over on Greenwich Street," I said, "just down from Coit Tower. Come on by." I handed the phone back to Victor. "I see a problem here. If this shape-shifter can imitate us all, how can we trust anyone to be who they seem? I've got Lou to vouch for me, but what if he's not with me, like tonight? And how would I know you're really Victor, for that matter?"

"A good question," he said, which of course was no answer at all.

"And another thing," I said. "The original shape-shifter knew us all—she'd have had no problem in imitating us. But this one did a pretty good job on Eli, so wouldn't it have to be someone who knew him? Someone besides Ruby? And you, as well. It imitated your voice. And me, since it knew quite a bit about who I was. Who knows all three of us?"

"Half the practitioners in the city," said Victor dryly. "And all of the ones who cause trouble."

"Ramsey," I said

"Ramsey? You must be joking. Why him?"

"Ruby was hanging around with him when I first ran across her at Mama Yara's. It made no sense to me at the time, but it does now. The shape-shifters travel in pairs, the Wendigo said. You know Ramsey—the man is a walking disaster. Why else would Ruby keep him around—unless it wasn't Ramsey?"

"Backup rations? A kind of walking larder if things got too lean? And Ruby could have been using him as an information source—a gofer or a sneak. How could he have guessed she wasn't what she seemed? We certainly didn't. And why didn't you mention this before?"

"Well, when I thought Ruby was Ruby, she asked me not to. At the time, I thought she was just embarrassed to have you think she was with a total geek like Ramsey. After, with everything that was going on, I just didn't even think of it."

Victor muttered something under his breath, and I don't think it was a compliment on my brilliance. "But think about it," I said. "What better disguise?" Victor was not impressed with my reasoning.

"This is another of your unwarranted leaps in logic," he said. "The shape-shifter that was Ruby could have provided her partner with all the information she'd need."

"Okay," I said reluctantly. "Maybe it is a stretch. But it's still worth checking out."

"Agreed," said Victor. "I don't suppose you know where he lives?" Fortunately, or maybe unfortunately, I did. Ramsey had invited me over so many times that I eventually relented and once showed up against my better judgment. It wasn't much fun.

"He lives over on Sutter Street, around Fillmore," I said. "Not that far from here, actually."

"Good. We'll head over there."

"What, right now?" I had the feeling I was repeating myself. Hadn't I just said that the other day?

"If you're after someone, you don't want to give them time to catch their breath if you can help it. If Ramsey is the shape-shifter, which I doubt, it won't be expecting us so soon."

CAMPBELL'S LAND CRUISER CAME INTO VIEW, driving slowly up the street. She caught sight of us and pulled over. I looked over toward Lou, who was stretched out on his side, sound asleep again.

"Can you take Lou home?" I said, before she had even got out of the car. "It looks like he's about had it." She looked at me doubtfully through the car window.

"What about you?"

"The night's not quite over yet. Things to do, people to see."

"I could try to take him back, but I'm not sure he'll go for it."

"Sure, he will. Look at him." I poked him gently and he raised his head and looked at me bleary-eyed. "Go home with Campbell," I said, gesturing toward the car. "I'll be fine.

Lou climbed wearily to his feet and headed off toward her Land Cruiser, stumbling a couple of times. He was used up. A couple of quick assurances to Campbell that things were under control, a brief explanation of our next stop, and she drove away without much protest. I was on my own again, and hopefully I would take better care of myself this time.

Victor and I made our way back to his car, and ten minutes later we were in front of Ramsey's place, a huge Victorian on Sutter Street broken up into apartments, the way a lot of those old buildings are. Ramsey's apartment was number 4, but only three apartments were visible. A walkway leads around to the back, though, where a rear door reveals another apartment that you wouldn't know was there unless you'd visited before. The door was warded of course, since a practitioner lived there.

"Do we knock?" I asked in a low voice. Victor shook his head without hesitation.

"We go right in. If he's the shape-shifter, we'll need the surprise. If he's not—" He shrugged. "We'll just apologize. He won't give a damn when he sees it's us."

He was right. Ramsey would be so thrilled by the thought of being in on something exciting that he wouldn't care that we'd just waltzed in uninvited, even though that's unforgivable by practitioner etiquette.

Victor looked up and down the door, examining the warding. You can't actually see warding unless you're another practitioner, and even then you don't exactly see it. You feel it and sense it, in a way ordinaries can't. It's an overlay, and for someone like Victor, or even myself, it's as obvious as a new paint job on an old rusted car.

The warding was not only over the door but the entire

side of the building. Quite ambitious, but pitiful even for someone as unskilled as Ramsey. Worse, he hadn't kept up with it—warding doesn't last forever; it needs to be maintained. I'd neglected that myself a couple of years ago, much to my sorrow. I'm a lot more conscientious these days.

"Give me a hand with this," said Victor, pointing to a spot right over the door.

The warding there had completely degraded to the point where it was nonexistent. He reached out with his talent, I did the same, and together we peeled the rest of the warding off like loose skin off an onion. Victor reached under his jacket and brought out the Glock. He motioned toward the door with it.

"Kick the door. Hit it right next to the lock, and hit it hard."

"Are you sure we shouldn't just knock?" I said. He looked at me in exasperation.

So I was to be the muscle. I don't mind being the B player in the movie, but Victor is the one with martial arts skills. He doesn't often use those skills; he prefers simple weapons like guns, things that won't mess up his hair. But he's got those skills in reserve if he needs them, and even though he's not a very big guy, I'm sure he would have done a better job at door crashing than me. But he had the gun and wanted to stand back, ready in case anything came flying out. Or maybe he thought it would be good for my self-esteem to feel useful. More likely he just wanted me in front if things went sour—sometimes I think he feels that in the grand scheme of things I wouldn't be that much of a loss.

I was still wearing my heavy boots, though. I gathered myself, got my balance, and unleashed a side kick, striking the door just above the lock right next to the doorjamb. I could feel the shock all the way up my leg. The door remained stubbornly fast, and I bounced off and lost my balance, falling to the ground.

Victor smirked at me and stepped forward. He spun

around with one of his tricky martial arts moves and hit the door, which of course obligingly flew open. It was like the pickle jar, I was sure. I'd softened it up, almost breaking my foot in the process, and then he stepped in. It would have flown open if he'd simply breathed on it. One good thing—he was now the first through the door.

I scrambled to my feet and followed him inside. We didn't have to secure the room—it was tiny, consisting of a kitchenette with a ratty table and plastic chairs, plus an additional living area no more than six feet square. It made my in-law space seem like a mansion. Stairs led to an upstairs room that clearly couldn't be any larger than the downstairs.

There was that familiar taint of corruption in the air, along with the musky odor of a bear's den, but I wasn't sure it came from any creature's lair. Bags of overflowing garbage were piled up in the kitchenette, leaving almost no floor space. The burners of the electric stove were crusted over with a year's worth of spilled soup and ramen noodles. In one corner near the stove was a shriveled piece of bacon, so old even Lou wouldn't have touched it. It looked like it could have been there since the earthquake of '89, if not the big one a century earlier. Maybe it was a lair, but more the one of a total slob than of a monster.

Victor was up the stairs in two seconds, not waiting for me, and back down in less than a minute.

"Not here," he said.

So the trip was a bust, a big anticlimax. I wasn't that displeased; I was tired and sore and the last thing I wanted was another deadly confrontation. Maybe I'm getting old, but I prefer a good night's rest before battling monsters.

But it wasn't over yet. As we stood crowded together in the tiny apartment, the sound of steps echoing on concrete reached our ears. They stopped outside the door, and then it slowly swung inward. Ramsey was home.

EIGHTEEN

USUALLY IT'S UNWISE TO BREAK INTO THE HOUSE of a fellow practitioner. There's a universally accepted convention that anyone who does deserves whatever they get. And every practitioner, no matter their level of talent, is stronger on their home turf. Partly it's psychological—the small dog syndrome where a little dog will drive off a larger dog who dares to enter its yard. But it's more than that—strength is absorbed from home base in a very real way, and even a very ordinary practitioner can be dangerous on his home territory.

There were two of us, though, and even on his home ground there wasn't much Ramsey could have done to either of us. I'd expected him at least to ask indignantly what we were doing there, but he surprised me. His eyes darted back and forth between us, and when he finally spoke it was a total non sequitur.

"I don't know where she is, honest," he said.

So he immediately assumed we were looking for Ruby. Interesting.

"Bullshit," Victor said. "Spill it."

I looked over at Victor and mouthed, "Spill it?" in mock amazement. He must have been watching too many late-night movies on TV. Ramsey didn't seem to notice.

"Really, I don't. I haven't even seen her for days."

Of course he hadn't. Ruby was dead. But why would he assume we'd broken into his place to look for her? Or was he the shape-shifter after all, stalling for time? Then I had that intuitive flash, the one that's almost always right.

"You knew," I said. "She wasn't using you—you knew all along what she was."

He tried on several expressions—bewilderment, fear, defiance—before settling on the truth.

"No, not at first. I swear it. I ran into her one day, and she seemed to like me. Then I started doing little things for her, just to hang around, you know? I mean, she was out of my league, really.

"I just thought—I don't know what I thought. I didn't think much about it, really. I was afraid to, if you know what I mean. And then she . . . Well, the sex was incredible."

There was an image I could have done without. Victor looked puzzled.

"But Ruby was gay."

"Maybe *Ruby* was," Ramsey said. "But the shape-shifter wasn't, at least, not completely. She was addicted to sex—couldn't go long without it and didn't care who it was or what gender they were. Something in her makeup, I think." He paused, and a faint smile came over his face, showing even through his fear. "She could become anything, or anyone. You have no idea."

So he'd been screwing her all along, knowing she was a monster, but not caring. Now, Ramsey was bound to have been hard up for sex, but this was beyond belief. I try not to be judgmental, but the very thought was enough to make me feel sick. I could barely wrap my mind around it.

"But you knew what she was," Victor said. "How long did it take you to figure it out?"

"A while. By the time I figured it out, I was in a bind. I

was afraid to leave; I was afraid to tell anybody. She would have killed me." He shuddered. "And eaten me."

"So you helped her out? Helped her find her victims, helped her avoid detection?"

"Never," he said. "Not the victims. Swear to God."

I didn't believe that. But I did believe it was the real Ramsey we were talking to. If it was a shape-shifter, it was more than a fine actor. Then again, if it had killed and eaten Ramsey, it would in essence *be* him. So how could we tell the difference? Even Lou couldn't tell, if it had consumed someone's essence. Victor was thinking along the same lines, I was sure. Earlier, he might have tied Ramsey up and taken him off to Bertram for some special questioning, but after the debacle with me, he wasn't quite so eager to go that route. Ramsey looked back and forth at Victor, then me, twitching like a lizard.

"You'll protect me, won't you? If she comes back . . ."

"She's not coming back," Victor said. "We killed her." Ramsey looked blankly at him, then a slow expression of immense relief spread over his face.

"Oh, thank God," he said.

It couldn't be an act. But Victor wanted to make sure.

"But she wasn't the only one. There's another shape-shifter, and it could be anyone. Even you."

"Don't," Ramsey said. "That's not funny."

"It wasn't meant to be."

"That's crazy." Ramsey turned to me and held out an imploring hand. "Tell him, Mason. You know me. That's crazy."

"Sorry," I said. Victor glanced over at me and then leveled the Glock at Ramsey's head.

"I'm sorry, too," he said. "But there's no way to tell if you're really Ramsey or not. We just can't take the chance."

He cocked the hammer back, which made a little snicking sound. There's no need to cock the hammer on a double-action automatic; in fact, it's overkill. Cocking the hammer to make it single-action is dangerous. It takes only the lightest imaginable pressure to fire, and the slightest flinch can be enough to accidentally discharge the gun. But the sound itself is enough to make one go weak in the knees, especially when the muzzle of the gun is pointed directly at your head.

So Victor was running a bluff. Even he wasn't harsh enough to coldly execute a fellow practitioner, or anyone else, based on mere suspicion. Then again, maybe it wasn't a bluff at all. Ramsey had assisted Ruby, or at least kept quiet about her, even knowing what she was and what she was doing. Maybe Victor didn't care whether Ramsey was the shape-shifter or the real thing—in Victor's eyes he was equally guilty, and I'm not sure I disagreed. Still, I could never execute someone in cold blood. That's why Victor is a chief enforcer and I'm a jazz musician.

In any case, the sound of the hammer being cocked would be the test. If Ramsey was really the shape-shifter, it wouldn't stand there meekly, accepting death without a struggle. It would launch itself forward and go down fighting, if it went down at all. I took a step back and gathered energy.

But it wasn't the shape-shifter after all. Ramsey collapsed on the floor, his legs no longer able to hold him upright.

"No, please. No. Don't kill me. Dear God, please."

He was speaking halfway between a whisper and a cry. I couldn't really feel that sorry for him; he was culpable in the deaths of more than one person. But he was so pitiful I got no pleasure from seeing him grovel. It was sad and pathetic, and it made me feel slimy and nauseated.

Victor waited a few long moments, giving him a chance to launch an attack if that was what he had in mind. But it was no act. Ramsey bowed his head, stared at the floor, and sobbed uncontrollably. Victor eased the hammer back down and put the gun away under his jacket.

"I'm not done with you yet," he said. "I'll be back when this is over. I may kill you yet."

He jerked his head at me and started out the door. Even in a situation like this, Victor had to be the drama queen with an exit line.

"Wait a minute," I said. "You spent a lot of time with Ruby. You knew what she was and you didn't care. Here's your chance to make some amends. There has to be something about these shape-shifters, some way they're different, some little tell we can use that gives them away."

Ramsey was now sitting up, back against the wall. He looked eager to please now. He was more afraid of Victor than he was of any shape-shifter. He paused almost imperceptibly, then shook his head regretfully.

"You hesitated," I said. "You know something." Victor stopped in the doorway and reached back under his jacket.

"No, no," Ramsey said, panicking. "There was one thing I noticed, but it wouldn't be any use to you. That's why I didn't say anything." Victor and I waited, but he didn't go on.

"Well?" I prompted.

"It's about the sex. You know, we had a lot of sex." He seemed half ashamed, half proud. "Well, it was pretty normal, nothing weird or kinky or anything." Not unless you considered having sex with a homicidal shape-shifting monster kinky. "Anyway, she always got off." Ramsey actually smirked as he said that. "And when she . . . ah, came, she made this funny noise. I guess it was the shape-shifter in her coming out."

"What noise?" Victor asked. I didn't say anything. My throat had suddenly closed up.

"A weird kind of trill. Almost like a hummingbird."

NINETEEN

I WALKED OUT OF RAMSEY'S WITHOUT ANOTHER look at him. He had told me all I needed to know. A trill, he'd said. A goddamned trill. I was as creeped out as I'd ever been in my life. I might never have sex again.

This explained why I hadn't heard from Morgan. How foolish of me to have worried about her. She wasn't at her parents' house; she wasn't out of state. She was holed up over at her lair in Bernal Heights, figuring out new and better ways to eliminate dangers to her existence like Victor and myself. And snacking on unfortunate acquaintances.

That thought hit me full force. Morgan was dead, of course, probably killed at the same time as her beloved dog. When I'd shown up there, the shape-shifter had taken the form of Beulah. When I drove it off, it had circled back and reappeared at the front door as Morgan. The real Morgan, or parts of her, had probably been down in the basement all along.

Victor followed me outside, but I didn't stop walking until he grabbed me by the arm.

"You got something," he said. I nodded. "And?"

"Morgan. She's the shape-shifter."

"How do you know that?" he asked, then stopped and cocked his head to one side, thinking. I could see his quick mind turning it over. Ramsey's comment. My reaction. The night I'd called him when Morgan had spent the night. "Oh," he said. Then the further implications struck him. "*Oh,*" he said again. "Well, you certainly can pick them."

"Let's get out of here," I said.

When we got back to Victor's, everyone was still up. Timothy and Sherwood were talking quietly in a corner of the study, and they were relieved to see us safe and sound. Eli had made it back from Berkeley and had to be filled in on the night's doings.

"So it imitated me," he said. "Fascinating."

"Frightening is more like it," said Sherwood.

"And you couldn't tell?" Eli asked.

"It wasn't perfect," Victor said. "But in the heat of the moment, it could pass."

"There's worse," I said. "It took over Morgan's persona, and that one *was* perfect. Which means Morgan's dead, and has been for a while."

I sat down heavily on a small chair by the stone fireplace. The weariness I'd been keeping at bay washed over me. One thing was all too clear—I had royally screwed things up. Again. I sat there feeling sorry for myself, then realized how petty that was. It was Morgan who had paid the price, not me. Not only was I a screwup; I was an ass.

Maggie walked over and jumped into my lap. I was so astonished I almost fell off the chair. She'd never done such a thing before. She didn't even like me much. Comfort and pity from an Ifrit with attitude. How low could I sink?

I hadn't known Morgan that well, but I'd certainly liked her. And due to me, she was dead. If she'd never met me, if I hadn't pulled her into this, she'd be blissfully going about her life, unaware and unafraid. If I hadn't flirted with her and invited her to hear me play, if I hadn't thought it would be neat to date a nonpractitioner for once, she and her beloved Beulah would still be alive.

I'm a practitioner; I deal with demons and monsters all the time, and even though I'm not that good at it, I can take care of myself. But she couldn't, and I'd had no right to drag her into my world.

Sherwood came over from her spot in the corner and put an arm around me.

"You couldn't have known what would happen, Mason. It's not your fault."

"No? How is it not my fault?"

"It's not, son," Eli said. "You can't foresee everything."

I looked over at Victor. He understood, and unlike Sherwood and Eli, wasn't about to comfort and excuse me. He looked back at me for a long time, and finally gave a slight nod.

"Welcome to the world of grown-ups, Mason."

"One thing I don't understand," I said. "Morgan, the shape-shifter Morgan, was with me all night after I brought her home. Why didn't she just kill me while I slept?"

"Well, that might have been tricky for it," said Eli. "It takes a while for it to change, does it not? It can't just revert back to form instantly?"

"Apparently not."

"And where was Lou?"

"On the end of the bed."

"He would have given warning at the first sign, don't you think? And you were on your own territory, where you're strongest. And one of the few advantages we have is that it's vulnerable itself. It's strong and powerful, but without the element of surprise, it can be killed. As we've seen."

"It's simpler than that," Victor put in. "You called me, remember? So I knew she was there with you. If anything had happened to you, we would have known just where to look. I imagine it thought the Morgan persona, with its connection to all of us, was too useful to abandon. So that call may have inadvertently saved your life."

"Gee, thanks," I said. "I guess that makes up for your trying to kill me tonight. But why didn't she stay, hang out with me, wait for a better opportunity?"

"I can't say for sure," Eli said, "but I think it must be quite a strain to keep up the deception, even if it's almost perfect. The longer she hung around with you, the more chance there was of you catching on. The longest Ruby was ever around any of us was a few hours that day you fought the other one at Morgan's house, and she looked exhausted by the time she left."

Eli was right; I remembered how tired she'd looked that same day when I'd run into her coming out of Victor's.

"So what now?" asked Sherwood. "Do we go after it?"

Victor gave it his usual careful consideration.

"No, I don't think so, not right now at least. There's no big rush this time; it hasn't the slightest idea we're onto it. I think the best way is to set up a trap for it." He turned to me. "Can you call Morgan, have her meet you?"

"I could if I wasn't supposed to think she's out of town. Or if she were answering her cell."

"Hmm, too bad. I'll have to think on this awhile."

I was glad to hear him say that. I needed a night's sleep more than anything. And I definitely wanted Lou healthy and ready to go. I didn't feel comfortable without him.

I got up slowly, giving a Maggie a chance to jump down unhurriedly. Unlike Lou, she wasn't a forgiving creature and if I'd rudely spilled her off my lap, she wouldn't forget it.

I drove home in a dazed stupor and stumbled around when I got home, waking up Campbell and Lou. Lou sank back into sleep immediately. Campbell sat up in bed and turned on the bedside lamp.

"Everything okay?" she asked.

"Peachy. Go back to sleep." For a moment it looked like she was going to pursue it, but instead she just gave me a long enough look so that I could change my mind if I wanted to talk, and then turned the light off again.

As soon as my head hit the pillow I was out, but I wouldn't really call it sleep. I had one of those nights where I woke up every half hour or so, thinking morning had come, and then dropped off again in relief when I realized I still had plenty of night to go. It wasn't very restful.

In the morning, Lou was bright-eyed and bushy-tailed, ready for breakfast, with no indication anything had ever been wrong with him. Campbell made pancakes, which was a tradition of sorts with us, and Lou was in hog heaven. Or dog heaven.

I discussed the night's events with Campbell over coffee and pancakes. She ate slowly and carefully, listening all the while. Lou of course had finished his and was looking up hopefully for more.

"This is quite a mess, isn't it?" she finally said.

"You could say that." She poured herself another cup of coffee.

"I feel I should stay and help out."

"No need," I said. "Hopefully it will all be straightened out before long."

I knew she didn't really want to get involved with any of this. She was a healer, and killing things, even bad things, was not her karmic mission in life. Mine, on the other hand, seemed to be just that, which was another reason why we hadn't lasted. Even standing on the sidelines acting as a medic made her a participant, at least in her eyes. Of course, if anyone did get hurt and we needed her, she'd be there in a second.

"You sure?" she asked.

"Go on home," I said. "We'll be fine, honest. This time we're the ones who have the element of surprise. The shapeshifter has no real power, no talent. It's nothing more than a dangerous beast, when you come right down to it. And if we need you, you know we'll call. It wouldn't be the first time."

Campbell looked at me doubtfully, but she didn't take much convincing. We had a quick breakfast, and she'd barely left when Victor rang again.

"It's time," he said. "And bring the shotgun."

When I got to Victor's house, everyone was there—

Victor, Eli, Sherwood, and Timothy. Timothy wasn't going with us, of course, but he often came up with solid ideas, and acted as a reality check when we overlooked the obvious. I was hoping Victor had come up with a clever plan, but no. His idea was simply to go over to Morgan's house and confront the thing.

"That's it?" I said. "We go knock on her door? Brilliant. What if she's not there, or won't answer?"

"Simple is often best," Eli said. "These shape-shifters seem to like operating out of a home base. They're comfortable in their own lair. She knows we think she's gone; she has no idea we're onto her, so what better place to hunker down in safety? If she finds you on her doorstep alone and unsuspecting, I'm guessing she'll see it as another opportunity."

Victor outlined the simple plan. I was to go up and knock on the door, while the rest of them hung back out of sight. If she answered, I would hold the door while everyone else rushed up to confront her.

"What if there's no answer?" I said.

"We go in and search the house. It's a simple tactical operation. We're hunting a clever and dangerous creature, but it's not like we're dealing with another practitioner."

A half hour later, everyone was in position. I handed off the shotgun to Eli—if I showed up at the front door carrying a large weapon, it would rouse suspicion in even the dullest of minds. And the shape-shifter was not dull— far from it.

I strolled casually up to the front door, Lou acting nonchalant as usual. Except, with him, it's not an act. I rang the bell, waited, rang again, then finally knocked. No response. I listened for any sounds inside, but it was quiet as the grave, probably literally. The real Morgan was somewhere inside, I was sure.

After a while, I turned and walked back to where the others were waiting and shook my head.

"Okay," said Victor. "Mason, you and Lou go around to the back in case it bolts. Take the shotgun, but wait here a moment until I take the wards down. The rest of us will go through the front door."

I wondered how Victor would handle the wards. He was the one who'd put them up, but even so it would take a while to remove them completely. A small opening to squeeze through wasn't going to do the job. I should have known.

He took a large chunk of clear quartz out of his carrying bag and set it down at the base of the house. He looked carefully at the wall in front, as if looking for something. Finally he gave a little grunt of satisfaction, raised a hand, and spoke one word. The wards collapsed in on themselves and drained into the quartz, like water swirling down a drain. The piece of quartz now glowed a deep and vibrant red, and the house was unprotected.

I know Victor's good, but this was outstanding, even for him. Eli saw the expression on my face.

"Back door," he said.

I thought for a moment he was telling me to go to the back of the house, but then realized it was an explanation. Just like programmers will sometimes leave a back door in a program they write, Victor had inserted a back door in the wards so that he could circumvent them at any time. There was no reason for him to do that, but it was just habit, I guess. I had done something similar myself last year, but not nearly as elegant.

Lou and I went round the back and waited. After five minutes, Victor appeared at the back door, Glock in hand, and motioned me inside. The place was trashed, in the familiar fashion, fast food wrappers and garbage strewn over the floor. But Morgan was no slob; I'd been here before. Any doubts I might have had were rapidly disappearing. Whatever had been living here, it wasn't Morgan.

"Nothing on the ground floor," he said. "Downstairs next."

Downstairs was mostly all empty garage, with a small room off to the side that was bare and obviously empty. We climbed back up to the main floor.

"Upstairs," Victor said.

Only two rooms, the bedroom and the other, were at the top of those stairs. We went in the spare room first, Victor turning left and me turning right. Lou checked under the bed—he's useful that way. For Victor or me to check, we'd have to get down on our hands and knees and put our heads right next to the floor. Not a great position to be in when you're looking for something with sharp claws. A quick check of the closet turned up nothing. All clear.

The bedroom was next, and we repeated the drill. Again nothing. I was convinced by now that the shape-shifter wasn't in the house, but we had to check everything to be sure. Lou checked under the bed again, but this time after looking under it, he turned slowly toward the closet on the back wall. Victor nodded, positioned himself on one side of the closet door, and waved me back as I positioned myself on the other. Of course, if something came bursting out of that closet, it would be between us by the time we reacted. We'd be shooting directly at each other.

I circled back until I was at the end of the bed, directly in front of the closet door, but ten feet away. Not a good position to be in if there was a man with a gun behind the closet door, but not bad at all for intercepting something armed with only teeth and claws. I leveled the shotgun, making sure the safety was off.

Victor held up his right hand and showed three fingers, then clenched his fist. With his left hand, he reached out and grasped the closed door handle. He pumped his right hand three times, shooting out a finger each time, and on the count of three jerked the door open and jumped back.

It was an anticlimax when nothing jumped out. The closet wasn't that deep, and coats and shirts and blouses on hangers took up every square foot. There wasn't enough space left to hide a ravenous six-foot-tall monster.

I relaxed and lowered the shotgun, and that was when it burst out of the closet and straight toward me. It was on me before I could raise the gun again, but it wasn't the Morgan creature. It was the fake Ifrit.

It had been crouched down low, small enough to hide at the base of the closet underneath the hanging clothes. It moved so fast it seemed to be flying through the air as it launched itself toward my unprotected stomach. It didn't have the huge bearlike claws of the shape-shifter we were hunting, but it was easily capable of disemboweling me on the spot.

As it leapt off the floor, I heard four flat cracking sounds, and it jerked, seemingly pausing in midair. It gave me just enough time to interpose the shotgun between it and me, like a protective staff. It crashed at my feet and, snarling, tried to rise again, but Victor took three quick steps over to where I stood and carefully put four more shots into it as it lay there. It jerked again, gave one last burbling snarl, and finally lay still.

Eli burst into the room seconds later, Sherwood a step behind. He saw the fake Ifrit lying dead on the floor and stopped in surprise.

"Not what we expected," I said.

Victor walked over and prodded it with the toe of his shoe.

"Good riddance, though."

"Yeah. Nice shooting. But did you happen to notice I was directly in the line of fire? A slight miss and I'd have been lying on the floor alongside it."

"I don't miss," Victor said. The smallest hint of a smile flitted across his face. "At least, not often."

I supposed he was right. The other option would have been for him to wait for an opening, and after that for me to pick up my entrails and try to stuff them back in my stomach.

"Is that the fake Ifrit?" Sherwood asked. Unlike the rest of us, she hadn't seen it before. I nodded, but couldn't answer her next question. "But what was it doing here?"

Eli looked thoughtful. "I'm not sure, but I think it found the shape-shifter and attached itself to her—in much the same way a true Ifrit might find a practitioner and do the same. Then it stayed here to guard the house, another base of operations for her, as a faithful ally. That might also be why we haven't seen it for a while—it went to ground here. The real question is, where is the shapeshifter now?"

"Not here, obviously," Victor said.

"So what next?" I asked, but he just shook his head.

We looked around the house, hoping to find a lead, but apart from the garbage strewn about, there was nothing. I'd assumed we'd find the remains of Morgan's body somewhere in the house, but there was no sign of her, either. We finally gave up and left the house. We drove back to Victor's, but by the time we reached his house, we had our lead. Lounging casually against the side of my van, waiting for us, was the Wendigo.

TWENTY

"WELL, GREETINGS, FELLOW TRAVELERS," HE SAID. "Fancy running into you here." He noticed Lou, who was looking at him with some distaste. "I see you found Lou," he said to me. "Nice work."

"What are you doing here?" I asked.

"Is that any way to talk to a friend? No thank-you for my troubles?"

"Thanks," I said grudgingly. He had helped, but the memory of his pushing me into the energy pool was not a pleasant one. "I do appreciate that."

"*De nada.*" He waited for me to say something more, then pouted when I remained silent. Finally he shrugged. "You were out looking for the other shape-shifter, weren't you? Any luck?"

"What's that to you?" Victor said.

"Nothing, really. I just thought I might be of some help."

"And why would you want to help us?"

Eli, who usually smooths over such confrontations, watched and said nothing.

"Well, I don't, actually. Not you, specifically. But Mason's not so bad. Almost a kindred spirit. And I've decided I like it here." He pushed himself away from the van. "I was getting bored; now I'm not. But I do want to blend in, and the less trouble, the better. Trouble has a way of expanding outward, and pulling innocent bystanders—like myself—into its orbit."

"Terrific," said Victor. He wasn't impressed by this explanation, but I made a small "cool it" gesture with my hand. I saw no point in antagonizing the Wendigo. He surely had his own agenda, but he could also be a great help.

"Yeah," I said. "We were out looking for it, but it's gone to earth. I don't suppose there's any chance you know where it is?"

"Not right at this moment, no. But I can point you in the right direction."

"That would be helpful indeed," Eli said mildly, finally speaking up.

Victor shook his head in disgust and turned away. He wanted nothing to do with another uncanny creature. The Wendigo looked over at him.

"I get the feeling you don't much care for me," he said. "I'm hurt, deeply wounded."

"I'll bet," said Victor. The Wendigo smiled.

"Come on," he said to me. "Let's go somewhere we can talk."

I didn't trust him any more than did Victor. He wanted something, I was sure, but there was only one way to find out what that might be.

"Sure," I said.

I climbed into my van and the Wendigo got in beside me. Lou jumped in the back, not happy, but without protest.

"Watch him," I told Lou. The Wendigo started to say something, but I held up a hand. "I know, you're deeply hurt."

"Anywhere in particular?" I asked as I pulled out of the

driveway. He held up a hand for silence, as if he were listening for something.

"Do you know where the Beach Chalet is?"

"Of course."

The Beach Chalet is a café across from Ocean Beach, just down from the Cliff House. They mostly serve food, but you can also get just a beer or a cup of coffee, and they have an outdoor patio around back, right next to one of the Golden Gate Park trails. It's perfect for Lou—he can wander from table to table, begging snacks from soft-hearted diners.

On the way over, the Wendigo seemed content to sit quietly for once, although he kept up a constant drumming with his fingers. It would have been annoying on a longer drive, but I have to admit he kept good time.

We got a table in the back and ordered coffee and bagels with cream cheese at twice the price of an ordinary café. The Wendigo had no money, naturally, so I had to pick up the check. Lou darted off into the bushes on the other side of the nearby trail as soon as we got there. He hadn't gone far, I was sure. He was watching us from a secure and undisclosed location under a bush. For once he had taken my instruction seriously; otherwise he would have been making the rounds at the other tables, begging for scraps.

"So what's up?" I finally said, after we'd chatted for a while about music and ordinary things, just as if we were normal people. "I don't have any more of those stones, you know. Really."

The Wendigo crumbled up a corner of bagel and threw the crumbs on the ground, where a horde of small Brewer's blackbirds were hopping around scavenging.

"I believe you. But I think I've found another way to remain here. Something's happened to me since I crossed over—I've become more human, in some fashion I don't quite understand. And I've lost some of my powers—not all of them, not by any means, but some. That's why I wanted to get away from Victor. If he knew I was weakened, he might decide to do something about me, just in case."

That was not an entirely irrational fear. Victor was big on preemptive action. And what the Wendigo was saying wasn't that difficult to accept. Rolf and his friends had once been practitioners, as human as I was. Over the years they'd morphed into something not quite human. Some of them weren't even remotely human, not anymore. I saw no reason it couldn't work the other way around.

"Anyway," he continued, "one of the things I seem to have acquired is a conscience of sorts. Things that once amused me no longer seem quite as funny. Like people dying."

If he'd acquired a conscience, it would have been in the last couple of days, which seemed rather convenient.

"Well, that's good to hear," I said, smiling insincerely. Hopefully he hadn't yet developed enough humanity to be able to read subtleties.

"So, I do want to help. And as I said, I haven't lost all my powers. I can still find people, and shape-shifters, even if I can't call them anymore. I know where the shape-shifter is, and who she's adopted as an aspect."

"Who would that be?" I asked, although I already knew the answer.

"You're not going to like it."

"I don't expect to."

"It's your friend Morgan, the woman who helped to find me in the first place."

"I don't believe it," I said, although of course I already did.

An expression of concern appeared on his face. It didn't look exactly phony, but there was something not quite right about it, either. Maybe he felt nothing and was just aping human emotions. Maybe he hadn't got the human thing down quite yet. True sociopaths will do exactly the same thing, but they have it down perfectly and it's almost impossible to distinguish their manufactured emotion from the real thing. And sociopaths are still human, after all. In a way.

"I imagine it's a hard thing to accept, that a friend could have been taken like that," he said. "But believe me, it's true."

He pointed to the path that paralleled the back of the café. I followed the direction of his finger, and there, walking quickly with her head down, was Morgan. I sat very still, hoping she wouldn't glance over and notice us. This was no place for a confrontation, and with the shotgun sitting uselessly in my van, it probably wouldn't turn out well for me anyway. I couldn't let her just stroll away, though.

She had already passed by when a small black-and-tan head poked its way out from the corner of a bush and looked at me inquiringly. I hesitated. Lou could follow her easily enough and he wouldn't let himself be spotted, but chances were she was just headed for her car. It wouldn't do any good for him to lead me to an empty parking spot on a curb.

The Wendigo saw my indecision and laughed.

"Don't worry," he said. "I can find her again. I just wanted to show you I'm not full of bullshit." He laughed again. "Not about this, anyway."

Lou, meanwhile, was getting antsy. I shook my head, and he stared at me to make sure what I was saying, then disappeared back into the bushes.

The Wendigo sat quietly for a time, no longer fidgeting, again listening. After a while he nodded.

"I think she's going back to her lair," he said. "Or close by it. Shall we?"

It was all very convenient—him knowing exactly where she was and where she was going. Could he be in league with her for some reason? That didn't make much sense, either, though.

"Why not," I said.

We walked back to where the van was parked, Lou appearing behind us halfway there. He was taking his guard responsibilities very seriously for once, which was a good thing. But it also meant he sensed things were not quite right as well, and that wasn't so good.

Once back in the van, the Wendigo went through his listening routine again before giving a satisfied grunt.

"Upper Haight," he said. "Not that far."

We drove down Fulton to Stanyan, then turned up Haight Street. We hadn't gone more than a couple of blocks when the Wendigo told me to pull over. Easier said than done. Parking on Haight is as hard as anywhere in the city, harder than most. I pulled off on a side street and finally located a space.

"She's a couple of blocks away, I think," he said. She's staying somewhere near here—I can sense the approximate area, but I can't pinpoint it exactly. So we'll have to follow her."

That presented two problems. First, Morgan might recognize me. Second, the shotgun wasn't going to do me any good. The Haight sees its share of violence, but I still couldn't get away with blasting a shotgun at someone in broad daylight. Even if I disguised it, there was no way to disguise its effects.

The first issue was easy to deal with, though. I didn't need to establish a full-scale illusion. All I needed was a slight alteration—make my hair a shade longer and lighter, change my nose, and put a few lines in my face. If you're not expecting to see someone, or if you see them out of context, sometimes it takes a moment to recognize them, even if you know them well. A slight veneer of illusion is all you need to throw them off totally.

Lou presented more of a problem. Anyone walking down the street with a small dog by their side would instantly arouse her suspicions, no matter what we looked like. He'd just have to stay well back and out of sight.

I hadn't been in the Haight for a while. It's a place that still holds on to the sixties in many ways; the same head shops and coffeehouses, the same kids sitting on the sidewalk harassing passersby for spare change. But if you look at them more closely, they're not the same at all. Their eyes are sly and knowing instead of open and friendly, cynical and jaded instead of naïve. Their faces are hard and wary. Fourteen-year-olds look twenty, twenty-year-olds look thirty, and their drugs of choice are crystal and smack instead of trippy psychedelics.

"Well, good luck," said the Wendigo. "This is where I get off."

"I thought you wanted to help," I said.

"I have helped. But that thing is dangerous, and it's your problem, not mine."

He turned and walked back the other way with a cheery wave of his hand. This was looking more like a setup with every passing moment. But if he expected me to challenge the shape-shifter on my own, he was mistaken. I'd track it to its lair and come back later with the rest of the crew. Revenge is a dish best eaten cold, they say. They don't mention how difficult it is to eat anything if you're dead.

Lou and I continued up Haight Street, weaving our way through the people crowding the sidewalk. I didn't see Morgan until I was almost on top of her and had to back off quickly. She was walking slowly, looking from side to side and occasionally glancing over her shoulder, obviously wary.

She stopped inside a small corner grocery and Lou and I waited half a block away where we had a good view of the entrance. A short while later, she came out holding a paper bag and continued up the street. As she passed by storefronts, she occasionally stopped and gazed in the display windows, just like an ordinary person out for a day of window-shopping. I moved up closer, trying to get a feel for what she was up to. Scoping out the area for potential victims? Picking up a Sara Lee cheesecake to tide her over until brain-eating time?

Farther down the street, she stopped in front of a pet store that featured a box of puppies in the window. I couldn't tell what breed they were, but puppies are puppies, after all. The tumbled around, falling down randomly and launching mock attacks on one another. One of them, a black-and-white toughie, got hold of a littermate's back leg and wouldn't let go, even though he was dragged all over the place.

Morgan stood transfixed, and I took the chance and moved up closer. She was smiling as she watched them, with what I would call a sad, nostalgic air. Then, even though I was still a ways off, I could have sworn I saw tears running down her face. A moment later, she wiped her cheek with the back of her hand.

I drifted back, farther away. What was going on here? There was no one watching, as far as the shape-shifter knew. Was it like method acting, where she never slipped out of character? When she took over an identity, did she experience the same emotions, feel the same griefs? Was she becoming more human, like the Wendigo?

The scene nagged at me, instilling a seed of doubt. Maybe this wasn't the shape-shifter after all. Maybe this was really Morgan, and I'd got it wrong again. It wouldn't be the first time. But if this was really Morgan, what was she doing wandering around the Haight? What about the fake Ifrit at her home? How had the Wendigo tracked her down, and why was he so sure she was the shape-shifter? And most damning of all, why hadn't she called me to let me know she was still in town?

She started walking again, so I kept on her tail. Whatever was going on, I was going to follow her until I came up with an answer. She was moving faster now, more purposefully, and before long we arrived at the corner of Haight and Ashbury, that infamous intersection. She hesitated a moment, then turned up Ashbury Street and followed it up the hill until it reached a residential section full of curving streets. Now that we were off the main drag, there were fewer people to blend in with, so I stayed even farther back, a block at least. Lou could always find her again if she unexpectedly turned a corner or entered a house or apartment, now that he had her in his sights.

She finally reached her destination, a lavender house at the tip of a cul-de-sac, set up high on a hillside. Below, a terraced area spread out, an urban garden filled with squash and tomatoes and herbs. A long stretch of rickety wooden stairs wound up the slope, and she climbed them and disappeared into the house at the top.

Decision time. Did I go back to Victor's? Did I go up there and deal with her myself? The obvious choice was to play it safe and get help. But the whole business bothered me. It didn't add up, and I wanted answers. Victor makes a great backup, but he's also prone to shoot first and ask questions later. Then again, if I wandered up to the house alone to politely ask questions, I might just as easily end up as tonight's dinner menu.

What I needed was an edge. The shape-shifter had shown a resistance to attacks using talent, so relying on my talent wasn't going to cut it. But what if it wasn't precisely an attack? That gunk-on-the-face trick up by Coit Tower had worked pretty well. Some kind of holding spell? I began to get the germ of an idea.

Something that wasn't designed to attack or overpower. Instead, maybe something that would interfere with the shape-shifter's ability to change—sand in the gears of the mechanism. If it was unable to change, it wouldn't pose much of a threat—the Morgan persona had puny human teeth and delicate nails instead of long sharp canines and rending claws. As long as it had to remain Morgan, it wouldn't matter whether I could use talent or not.

I moved up to the edge of one of the terraces. The soil there was moist, fed by a makeshift drip irrigation system. I scooped up a good-sized handful of dirt and worked it into a ball.

The next thing I needed was some DNA. However the shape-shifter managed its transformations, it had to involve DNA on some level. Even if the transformation were accomplished by purely magical means, DNA still had to be the basis of the change. And if I could interrupt the DNA process, it would stay frozen in whatever form it had already taken.

The best source for the DNA I needed would be blood— not only did it contain the necessary DNA but blood also makes a spell more potent. Black practitioners use blood the most often, naturally; they can hardly cast a spell to make water wet without some. Personally, I don't care to use it myself. Whenever I do it always seems like I'm tiptoeing along the line close to the dark side. But I have used it.

Using my own blood and DNA wasn't the best option, though. The same principles that make self-healing so difficult also come into play whenever you try to use your own blood. It works for some things—in fact, it's vital for certain types of spells, but this wasn't one of those. I could use it and it would work, but it wasn't ideal.

I took out the Buck knife I still was carrying and looked over at Lou. He stared at me with suspicion and took two quick steps backward.

"Come on," I said. "I just need a drop. You won't even feel it." He retreated two more steps, putting more distance between us.

So it was my own blood or none at all. I pricked my forearm with the tip of the blade and got a respectable bead, then smeared it off into dirt and worked it in thoroughly until it was a neat ball the size of an orange. I sealed it with a pulse of energy, set it down on the ground, let some talent flow into the knife blade, and carefully sliced the ball of dirt in half. I took one of the halves, added another drop of blood, and repeated the process. A good-sized portion of earth still remained, and that quarter now had a history. It had been cut, then cut again. It was divided, interrupted, and incomplete. If I now smeared it on the shape-shifter, it would interfere with the other DNA and block any transformation. It wouldn't be able to effect a change until the dirt was cleaned off.

A useful trick, but to use it you have to know who the shape-shifter is ahead of time and then get close enough to apply it. That can be a tricky proposition, but this time it wouldn't be a problem.

I climbed the stairs to the door up above. No wards, but that was no surprise. It was a shape-shifter, not a practitioner. The door was slightly ajar, so Morgan hadn't quite latched it when she came in. Or maybe she had realized she was being followed and was making it too easy for me. When you're hunting monsters, there's a fine line between being careful and giving in to rampant paranoia.

I pushed the door gently and it swung silently inward. Lou eased in ahead of me, alert but apparently not too worried. The inside was one long room, a straight shot from the door through a front section and into a kitchen area.

Morgan was sitting on a stool at a counter that divided the room part of the kitchen from the stove and fridge and sink. Her back was toward me and she was eating whatever she'd bought at the grocery.

I squeezed the earth in my hand, taking comfort in my weapon. It was my ace in the hole—if it worked, that was. There was no reason it shouldn't; I'd thought it out clearly and constructed it well, but you never really know for sure if something will do the job until you try it out in real life.

"Hello, Morgan," I said.

She jumped and knocked over whatever she'd been eating onto the floor. It looked like yogurt. She spun around on the stool and I got a clear view of her face. Surprise, almost shock, and some fear as well. Interesting.

We all like to think we can read faces, that we can tell when someone's being evasive, or is angry, or fearful. But in truth, we can't. Sure, some people are an open book, but most of us become quite adept at masking our emotions.

But if you startle someone, you can sometimes get a true reading. There's still a problem, though—how to interpret what you see. Was Morgan the shape-shifter afraid because she knew I'd come for her? Or was it the real Morgan, afraid because she feared I was the shape-shifter myself?

"I thought you were out of town," I said, keeping alert for the slightest hint of a change in her appearance.

"I couldn't do it," she said. "I was all set to go, and then I thought what if that thing followed me, tracked me down, and killed my parents, too? I couldn't do that to them." I nodded and looked around the room.

"Nice place," I said. She glanced around abstractedly.

"It's my friend Missy's. She's out of town." She focused on me again. "How did you find me?"

I shrugged. I was more concerned with finding out for sure who she was than making small talk.

"Why didn't you tell me?" I asked. "Why didn't you answer your cell?"

She didn't say anything. She didn't have to; it was obvious. She hadn't trusted me. Fair enough—I wasn't in a trusting mood myself.

I looked closely at her, hoping irrationally for some clue. My gut told me she was really Morgan, but the gut can be mistaken. If it couldn't, there wouldn't be so many failed love affairs. But my head also weighed in. I'd seen those tears by the pet store, when she thought no one was watching. They could have been faked, but for what reason? She'd thought she was alone.

But the Wendigo had fingered her. That should be proof enough right there—what possible reason would he have to lie about such a thing? Unless . . . More thoughts raced through my head. What if he weren't the Wendigo at all? Shape-shifters weren't restricted to human form, as I'd seen. Could the shape-shifter have killed him?

Maybe not—the Wendigo was quite capable of taking care of himself. But she wouldn't have needed to. A perfect imitation wasn't necessary—the Wendigo was so odd that I wouldn't be able to tell what was normal for him and what wasn't anyway. And Lou wouldn't necessarily have caught on, either—since both the Wendigo and the shape-shifter weren't quite of our world.

But what was the point in putting me on Morgan's trail? If the shape-shifter wanted her dead, it would have been simple for it to kill her. A moment's thought and I had it. If the shape-shifter killed her, I'd still be after it, more determined than ever. And if the shape-shifter somehow managed to kill me, Victor and Eli would never rest until they got it. After what had happened to the first shape-shifter, it had to be wary of us.

But if it convinced me that Morgan was the shape-shifter, and I killed Morgan, it would be home free. No more shape-shifter; problem solved. As long as it kept a low profile, we wouldn't even know it was still out there. It could even leave, relocate to another city, and we'd never suspect. And as far as it knew, there was no reason I'd ever see the Wendigo again.

I sat down across from Morgan, keeping some space between us, and keeping the moist earth ready in my hand, just in case. I was 99 percent sure I had it right, but that 1 percent is what usually kills you.

"You should have left town," I said. "It's not too late. If you don't want to go to your parents' house, find a motel somewhere, anywhere, just so long as it's away from here. I'll have this taken care of in a day or two." I hoped. "And answer your cell if I call—I'll let you know when it's over." She nodded, resigned.

"Okay."

Lou ran up to her, put his paws on her knee, and wagged his tail in an exaggerated manner. It was his way of reassuring her, and it worked. He can be a thoughtful guy. She didn't smile, but the muscles around her eyes relaxed. I got up and walked to the door.

"Don't worry," I said. "It will all be over soon." It wasn't until I'd left that I realized that statement could be taken more than one way.

TWENTY-ONE

I THOUGHT THE SUPPOSED WENDIGO MIGHT BE waiting for me by my van, but no. At least that gave me breathing space. There was some more information I wanted to get before tackling him, and I knew just where to get it.

Twenty minutes later I was back at Ramsey's apartment. The little creep had suckered us. He'd even made me feel a little sorry for him. But the one thing that had put me on Morgan's trail, the thing that was too weird for coincidence and made me so quick to accept what the Wendigo said, was that little story of his about Ruby and sex and the odd trill. Why wouldn't I have believed it? How else could he have come up with such a thing unless it was true? Unless he'd heard Morgan that night she spent at my house. Like if he'd been crouched outside my bedroom window, leaving only traces in the dirt to mark where he'd been.

He hadn't just been in league with just the Ruby shapeshifter—he was in tight with the other shape-shifter as well. So, time for a visit.

I strolled around back of the Victorian to his door and politely knocked. No answer, but when I knocked again, louder, I heard movement from inside. Ramsey answered the door, bleary-eyed from sleep. Either he'd been up all night the night before or he routinely slept into the late afternoon every chance he got, or both.

"Mason," he said. His tone was wary, but not fearful. Not yet.

"Ramsey. Invite me in, why don't you?" He didn't want to, but he was afraid not to.

"Sure," he said, stepping aside. "Come on in." Lou slipped in ahead and Ramsey peered around me, trying to see if I was alone.

"Victor's not with me this time," I said.

"Thank God for small favors," he muttered, then looked nervously over at me as if he might have gone too far. I stared him down until he started getting ill at ease.

"To what do I owe this pleasure?" he said, false hearty, trying to make a joke out of it. He wasn't very good at that sort of thing. I ignored him and walked the few steps it took to reach the kitchen area. I glanced down and saw that same piece of bacon from our last visit still curled up on a corner of the floor.

Ramsey had edged back and now was standing between me and the door, as if guarding against my retreat. Alarm bells went off. He should have wanted me out of his apartment, not in it. Which meant, quite possibly, that he wasn't alone. Lou's warning growl almost covered up the sound of footsteps coming down the stairs. When I looked up I saw who it was.

For a moment I stood paralyzed. It was one of those situations so unexpected, so wrong, that your entire world turns upside down. The universe suddenly makes no sense. It couldn't be. The room hummed as blood rushed into my head. Gliding down the stairs, smiling sweetly and relishing my surprise, was Morgan. Or maybe it was the smile of a gourmet about to embark on a particularly tasty meal.

I almost let her get right up next to me, stunned as I was. Which was the point of her little deception, and it almost worked.

The hackles on Lou's back raised up, and the sight of that cleared my head. How stupid of me. This time it wasn't Morgan at all. This time it was a shape-shifter, clothing herself in Morgan's persona. Maybe Ramsey hadn't been exactly sleeping after all. She reached toward me, but I had a surprise for her as well. I reached into my pocket and balled up the change-inhibiting ball of earth I carried. Matching her smile, I walked right up to her, and for a moment she hesitated, unsure of herself. Then I flung my hand out, quick as a snake. She jerked her head back, but not in time. The glob of dirt plastered itself over her neck and shoulder, dripping down and staining her tee shirt. She couldn't transform herself now until she cleaned it all off, and that would take her a while.

It was still two against one, but Ramsey hardly counted and the Morgan persona had no real strength or defense. And I wasn't just one, anyway—I had Lou. He's too small to have much use in a physical fight, but he has strong jaws and sharp teeth, and could keep someone like Ramsey at bay until I had time to deal with him. My talent could easily overcome Ramsey, and although the Morgan shape-shifter wouldn't be affected much by it, I had one more thing as well. I had my knife.

I took it out and snapped open the blade. Morgan had spread her fingers wide and seemed to be straining. Her smile faded as she realized nothing was happening, and an expression of frustration appeared on her face. Then the beginning of panic. I allowed myself a moment of sweet satisfaction.

Lou spun around and gave two quick warning barks. Ramsey was up to something. I'd dismissed him as a threat, but that's never a good idea, no matter who it is. He was on home turf, and desperate, and anyone can be dangerous if you give them the chance.

I turned quickly, leaving the fake Morgan on her own

for the moment. Ramsey hadn't moved from the door, but he wasn't quite Ramsey anymore. His face had narrowed considerably, his hands had sprouted fresh new claws, and he'd grown a bit in height.

The Wendigo had originally warned me that they traveled in pairs. Always. I'd neglected to ask what happened if one of them died. Since we hadn't been able to close the energy pool, an open conduit remained between their world and ours, and apparently a bench player had been brought in to help out. Maybe these shape-shifters had a psychic connection between each other, or maybe the Morgan imitator had just been thoroughly briefed. Either way, there were now two of them to deal with and I was in trouble.

My knife, which a moment before had seemed a weapon of deadly purpose, now seemed weak and ineffective. A four-inch blade is a dangerous thing. It can slice through flesh and sever arteries. If you're strong, you can even plunge it straight into a heart, even if you don't know what you're doing. I'd never before used a knife for anything more violent that cutting rope or slicing salami, and against a tiger or a bear or a brain-eating shape-shifter it seemed a very long shot indeed. But a long shot is better than no shot at all, and at the moment of truth you either do what you must or you die. It doesn't get any simpler than that.

Lou poked his nose into the back of my knee once, then again, sharper. That's his signal for when he's about to do something he thinks is clever. Sometimes it is, and sometimes it isn't. I hoped this was one of his cleverer thoughts.

He charged the shape-shifter, snarling in his most ferocious manner, but before he reached it he uttered a strangled yelp, stiffened, and keeled over. Immediately he started twitching, then jerking, then howling with a tone that set my teeth on edge. His legs flailed around and shook with tremors, foam came out of his mouth, and he snapped his jaws over and over, so strongly I thought he was going to break some teeth. He was in the midst of a typical grand mal seizure.

It was impossible to ignore. I had a hard time looking away, and I knew it was all an act. The shape-shifter was momentarily transfixed—it was something totally unexpected, outside its experience. Its head was turned away from me, and for just an instant it forgot I was even there.

I would have bolted past it through the door, but it was blocking the exit. I had one chance, and I took it. I was across the tiny room in half a second, knife held low, and by the time it reacted and turned its head toward me it was too late. I was right up on it, and I plunged the knife into its throat and immediately yanked it out toward the blade side. I sliced partly through the tough trachea, and more important, tore through the carotid artery. Blood spurted out, pulsing with every strong beat of its heart.

It could still have killed me then with one swipe of its powerful claws, but it instinctively reached up in a vain attempt to staunch the gushing blood streaming from its throat. I jumped back as Lou scrambled to his feet, miraculously healed.

The thing was tough. It could have taken a bullet and still have fought on. But when blood is draining from a main artery, it doesn't take long to sap the strength. And there's a psychological element as well. A wound like that, a wound you instantly realize must be mortal, produces a paralyzing fear and robs the will. It gave a bloody cough, took two hesitant steps, and sank down with its back against the door. I was no longer even in its thoughts.

I turned to face the Morgan one. She was frantically scraping off the dirt I'd smeared on her, and had managed to get rid of most of it. There was still enough left on her body to inhibit her ability to transform, but not enough left to stop it completely. She was stuck in the middle, a weird hybrid of attractive young woman and voracious shape-shifter, still recognizable as Morgan, but with those trademark claws and a horribly distorted jaw and mouth. She was larger than she'd been, not a full-sized monster, but not a slim girl anymore.

I thought she might run when she saw her partner dying on the floor, but the thought never entered her mind. She bounded over to the fallen shape-shifter, looked down briefly at it, and then sprang at me, claws outstretched.

I wasn't going to get lucky twice, and she wasn't going to be taken by surprise. Without thinking, I spun and headed up the stairs to the level above.

Now I had the high ground, and I'd have at least some advantage when she came after me up those narrow stairs. It wasn't much, but every bit counts. Lou was behind me when I made my break toward the stairs, but he made it to the top before I did.

The room upstairs was windowless and even tinier than the room below. A bureau was pushed up against one wall, and almost the entire rest of the space was taken up by a mattress on the floor, reeking of the creature's lair and covered with tangled sheets and blankets. And blood. Now it was my turn to be distracted.

Ramsey, the true Ramsey, lay crumpled on a corner of the mattress, chest opened in a familiar fashion, skull shattered and empty and smeared with viscous gray matter. He couldn't have been dead more than a few hours. Karma. Ramsey might have been weak and morally repugnant, but he'd paid for his sins.

I wrestled the bureau to the front of the room and jammed it between the narrow walls of the stairway. It wouldn't slow down the shape-shifter for long, but every second was precious. The sight of Ramsey's body had given me an idea. Not a nice one, but beggars can't be choosers.

When I was young, before Eli straightened me out, I'd had a brief fling with the dark arts. I never got into it seriously; it just wasn't me. But I'd learned a few things that I'd just as soon have forgotten, except you don't forget things like that. And one of those things, not surprisingly, had to do with fresh corpses and blood. There's a reason they call it the dark arts.

It was no time to be squeamish, though. Moral and ethical considerations tend to vanish when you're faced with a deadly shape-shifter and nowhere to hide.

I was still covered in the blood that had spurted out from the Ramsey shape-shifter's carotid artery. I focused all my energy and reached out toward Lou, siphoning a bit of his life force. My own wouldn't work nearly as well—it's that whole closed-loop feedback thing again.

Lou felt it, and his knees buckled. He whipped his head around and looked at me with disgust. He knew what I was up to, and he didn't like it.

"Sorry," I muttered. "Would you rather we both die?"

I wove the life force through the shape-shifter's blood that was still dripping off my arms. I knew about this spell, but I'd never done it. How could I have? It requires a blood sacrifice. But this time, when I'd cut the shape-shifter's throat, for all magical intents and purposes, that was exactly what I'd done.

I bound up the blood and the life force and let it flow into Ramsey's corpse, using every bit of magical energy I possessed. It would leave me helpless on the magical plane, but so what? Talent wasn't going to affect that shape-shifter anyway. As usual that much effort left me feeling weak and dizzy, but this time I also felt nauseous. I was trembling, and the edges of a panic attack were nibbling at me. Necromancy is more than just dark arts; it's profoundly disturbing. I suppose after a while you get used to it, but I don't see how.

But it worked. Ramsey's corpse stirred and sat up, not slowly, but with a sudden jerk as if its strings had been pulled by a giant puppeteer. It had one good eye left, so apparently it could see. No heart or liver, but that didn't seem to bother it any. Its head swiveled around with a jerky motion like an animatronic robot. Lou sank down so low he was almost like a black-and-tan puddle on the floor. I stood motionless against the wall, pretending I was a floor lamp.

So far, so good. But the most important part of the spell, and the most difficult, was control. And that was something I'd never learned and never wanted to, thank God. Animating a corpse is one thing; making it do what you want it to is quite another. If I'd had one of those green rune stones, I might have managed it, but they were all gone.

It all depended on timing, and the shape-shifter downstairs did its part perfectly. By this time it had managed to scrape most of the earth off of it, and had transformed itself nearly back to its original form. A loud noise came from the stairs, and the bureau blocking the stairway suddenly splintered, pieces flying off it as the shape-shifter tore it apart like a rotting log.

Apparently Ramsey could still hear, as well. He bounced to his feet, surprisingly spry for someone who was dead, and lurched past Lou and me to confront the threat. When the shape-shifter came through the door, the first thing it saw was a creature as frightening as itself. It stopped dead and made a high keening sound of surprise. I'm not sure what it would have done, but Ramsey left it no choice. He threw himself at the shape-shifter and wrapped himself around it, groping for its throat.

When I'd made the golem out of wood and nails, it was frightening but totally ineffective. The Ramsey corpse was a different matter. He might not have been very strong in life, but he was strong now. And being dead, he didn't get tired. An all-out attack takes up so much energy that if it doesn't succeed very quickly, it fails. Arms grow tired, breath becomes labored, and before long you can barely stand upright.

But in the best zombie tradition, Ramsey was tireless. And, of course, immune to injury and pain. The shape-shifter recovered in a second, whipped her long muzzle around, and took a good-sized chunk out of his shoulder. Ramsey ignored it and managed to get his hands around the shape-shifter's throat. It tried to shake him off, but he was glued to it like the death he was. The shape-shifter brought up its powerful claws and ripped his stomach open. Some fluid gushed forth and long ropy intestines dangled out, but again it made no difference. Ramsey's hands continued to squeeze the shape-shifter's throat, cutting off its air. And unlike Ramsey, the shape-shifter was getting tired, especially with no oxygen fueling its high metabolism. Worse, as far as the shape-shifter was concerned, blood flow to the brain was being cut off, and if it couldn't free itself quickly, it would pass out and never wake up.

It was like a scene in a George Romero film, except the blood and gore was real and the combination of feral stink and reek of blood and meat was overwhelming. I'd thought I could slip past them to freedom while they were occupied with each other, but naturally I'd overlooked something again. The two of them were blocking the stairs, the only exit, and there was no way past them.

The shape-shifter was losing the fight. It finally realized its best defense would be to chew off one of Ramsey's arms, making it impossible for him to maintain a grip. But it had realized that too late. It was losing focus as its blood-deprived brain began to shut down. Its arms started to flail, and it was biting and snapping at random now, with no clear purpose. They both lost balance, the shape-shifter because it was passing out, Ramsey because there wasn't that much left of his physical body. As they toppled over, Lou took a running start and leapt over them, doing his hurdler imitation again, landing on the stairs below. I took my cue and tried to do the same, but when my trailing leg knocked against Ramsey, he let go of the shape-shifter's throat and reached up automatically, grabbing my ankle as I passed. I knew his magically enhanced grip would be powerful, but I'd had no idea. A little more pressure and bone would crumble under his fingers. No wonder the shape-shifter had collapsed.

I had to do something quickly. If Ramsey lost focus on the shape-shifter and concentrated on me instead, not only would that be bad in itself but the shape-shifter might recover as well. Monster and zombie together would be a bit too much to deal with. Already, with the choking pressure removed, the shape-shifter was struggling upward with renewed purpose.

But even though I had no idea how to control Ramsey,

I was the one who had animated him. That gave me some magical standing. And blood was the key. I threw my jacket down the stairs, stripped off my blood-covered shirt, and dropped it over Ramsey's head. That blood had been a vital factor in the animation, and so much of it touching him temporarily overloaded the circuits in whatever now passed for a brain. Ramsey's hand slackened and he lay motionless, like a falcon that had just been hooded.

I pulled my leg free, scrambled over the two bodies on the floor, and then as I made it to the stairs I reached back and plucked the shirt from Ramsey's head. Instantly his hand snapped back to the shape-shifter's throat as he resumed his relentless pressure.

I was tempted to run out the door and get the hell out of there, but I couldn't just yet. I had to make sure the shape-shifter didn't survive, and equally important, I had to deactivate Ramsey—if he finished the job, his next step might be to shamble around the neighborhood. There are a lot of strange things that people will shrug off because they couldn't possibly be true, but a ravaged corpse stalking the streets is not one of them. Even if he didn't manage to kill anyone, it would open a can of worms that would shake the practitioner community to its core.

So I stood quietly in Ramsey's pitiful little kitchen, listening to the sounds of thumping and scrabbling coming from up above. Eventually, all sounds stopped, followed by a brief but ominous silence. Then the sound of heavy footsteps stumbling down the stairs.

I was ready. I turned on the water in the kitchen sink, squirted in a good-sized glob from an untouched bottle of dishwashing liquid, and frantically started scrubbing the blood out of my shirt. The water ran pink as it swirled down the drain, and the footsteps from the stairs became slow and hesitant. I used a roll of paper towels to clean off any of it that had spattered on my leather jacket, until both the jacket and the shirt were as clean as I could get them in such a short time. The animating force had been funneled through the blood, and if there was not enough blood left, the force would weaken. When it dropped below a certain threshold it would cease to operate.

The steps from up above faltered, and finally, with a heavy thud, Ramsey's body collapsed and tumbled down, ending up sprawled out at the bottom of the stairs. Between the original dismemberment and the large chunks ripped off during the last struggle, what was left was barely recognizable as a human being.

I stood in the small kitchen, staring at dismembered bodies and pools of blood, and felt nothing. No horror, no relief, certainly no satisfaction.

I was burned out, blank and empty. Lou looked up at me, worried. Or maybe he just wanted to go home. Our work here was done, after all.

"Come on," I said, and walked out the door.

TWENTY-TWO

THE CLEANUP OF RAMSEY'S APARTMENT MUST have been a nightmare. Victor handled it, along with the team he uses for such things. "Welcome to the world of grown-ups," he'd said to me earlier. But I couldn't begin to deal with that sort of thing; I just wanted to walk away and forget it ever happened. Someone had to do it, though, and as usual, that someone was Victor. For the first time, I got some real insight into our relationship, and why he never really took me seriously. To him, I wasn't a grown-up, and never would be. And he might just be right about that.

Morgan was happy to find out that things were back to normal, though they'd never really be normal for her again. Collateral damage. I called her a couple of times, mostly out of a sense of obligation, but she made it clear she wanted nothing more to do with me or my world.

I never saw the Wendigo again. Well, that's not exactly true. I was over at Emily Janover's house one night, talking about a project she had in mind. Emily is a keyboard player and singer, a Diana Krall type. She's good, but she could have been really good if she'd only applied herself. Of course, I'm hardly one to talk. We shared dinner and stayed up late, talking about who else she wanted for her CD and what songs to do.

She turned on the TV and switched over to a late-night talk show.

"There's a band from the Bay Area on tonight I want to see," she said. "The Death Turtles. Supposedly they're the next big thing."

We listened to them, and they weren't bad, though not to my taste. But in the back, sitting behind a massive set of drums and grinning from ear to ear, was a curly-headed fellow I knew all too well. Emily was less than impressed by the band.

"Same old thing." She sighed. "If you want to hit the big time, three chords and a loud voice is what you need."

"That song had five chords," I pointed out.

"Same difference. They sucked. Except for the drummer. I have to admit it—he's out of this world."

"You have no idea," I said.

ABOUT THE AUTHOR

John Levitt grew up in New York City. After a stint at the University of Chicago, he traveled around the country and ended up running light shows for bands in San Francisco. Eventually, he moved to the Wasatch Mountains and worked at a ski lodge in Alta, Utah. After a number of years as a ski bum, he joined the Salt Lake City Police Department, where for eight years he worked as a patrol officer and later as an investigator. His experiences on the job formed the background for two mystery novels, *Carnivores* and *Ten of Swords*. For the last few years, he has split his time between Alta, where he manages the Alta Lodge, and San Francisco. When he's not working or writing, he plays guitar with the SF rock band The Procrastinistas and also plays the occasional jazz gig. He owns no dogs, although his girlfriend now has four.

He is currently at work on the fourth book in the Dog Days series. You can visit him on the Web at www.jlevitt.com.